OH, CANADA!

Longarm laughed and said, "You'd best start at the beginning. I've never heard tell of any gunslick called the Calgary Kid. But you say he fought three-to-one and came out ahead?"

Vail shrugged and declared, "If I knew all the details I'd have no call to send you up yonder to fetch him, would I? All I have, so far, is three strange riders striding into a local saloon and getting into a fuss with a vaguely sinister regular drinker with no visible means of support. His given name is Percival Harcourt. He prefers you call him the Calgary Kid... On the face of it, the Calgary Kid just whipped out his .442 Webly Bulldog and shot all three at point-blank range with their guns in their holsters."

Longarm whistled softly and said, "He sounds like a gent I'd be disinclined to drink with. You have to really catch a man by surprise if his gun's holstered after you've shot two of his pals in front of him!"

DON'T MISS THESE
ALL-ACTION WESTERN SERIES
FROM THE BERKLEY PUBLISHING GROUP

THE GUNSMITH by J. R. Roberts
Clint Adams was a legend among lawmen, outlaws, and ladies. They called him . . . the Gunsmith.

LONGARM by Tabor Evans
The popular long-running series about U.S. Deputy Marshal Long—his life, his loves, his fight for justice.

SLOCUM by Jake Logan
Today's longest-running action Western. John Slocum rides a deadly trail of hot blood and cold steel.

BUSHWHACKERS by B. J. Lanagan
An action-packed series by the creators of Longarm! The rousing adventures of the most brutal gang of cutthroats ever assembled—Quantrill's Raiders.

TABOR EVANS

LONGARM

AND THE CALGARY KID

JOVE BOOKS, NEW YORK

LONGARM AND THE CALGARY KID

A Jove Book / published by arrangement with
the author

PRINTING HISTORY
Jove edition / May 1998

All rights reserved.
Copyright © 1998 by Jove Publications, Inc.
This book may not be reproduced in whole
or in part, by mimeograph or any other means,
without permission. For information address:
The Berkley Publishing Group, a member of Penguin Putnam Inc.,
200 Madison Avenue, New York, New York 10016.

The Penguin Putnam Inc. World Wide Web site address is
http://www.penguinputnam.com

ISBN: 0-515-12276-9

A JOVE BOOK®
Jove Books are published by The Berkley Publishing Group,
a member of Penguin Putnam Inc.,
200 Madison Avenue, New York, New York 10016.
JOVE and the "J" design are trademarks
belonging to Jove Publications, Inc.

PRINTED IN THE UNITED STATES OF AMERICA

10 9 8 7 6 5 4 3 2 1

Chapter 1

One raw, wet April morning the Burlington night flier tore into Denver an hour overdue with its throttle wide open, its whistle wailing, and its bell tolling fit to bust. Though none of the passengers or crew had been roughed up enough to need more than a stitch or two, the train robbers had left the mail car in an awful mess. Their take was estimated at close to thirty grand in the form of cash, stamps, and postal money orders.

The combined federal, state, and railroad posse they sent out to cut sign that very morning was bossed by U.S. Deputy Marshal Custis Long of the Denver District Court. This was partly because robbing the U.S. mails was a federal offense and partly because Longarm, as he was better known to friend and foe alike, was considered the best tracker riding for the U.S. government since they buried Kit Carson down at Fort Lyon.

The gang had materialized out of the rain in the wee small hours when the night train had stopped to jerk water at a remote windmill-fed tank an hour by rail from anywhere. It would have taken a full day on horseback to get there, so the posse loaded their two dozen mounts aboard a boxcar and had a Baldwin 4-4-0 run them out to the scene of the crime.

The rain had let up and the sun was winking on and off through scudding clouds by the time they arrived. Some of the greener posse riders were a bit surprised when Longarm had them all driven further up the track to detrain a good mile north of the lonely windmill and its waist-high tank of corrugated iron. Had any been dumb enough to ask, he'd have been told a schoolmarm knew chalk marks were easier to spot where the blackboard was cleanest. A hundred-odd passengers and crew had been marched up and down around that water tank. But nobody from that night train would have strayed this far out, over fresh-sprouting greenup. So Longarm meant to commence with a wide sweep around the windmill, scouting for any sign that any number of riders might have left across mighty soft sod.

As they were hauling their balking ponies down the steep ramp, the brakeman in command of the special approached Longarm to say he had to clear the main line they were on as soon as possible.

Longarm nodded and suggested, "Why don't you all steam up to the next handy siding, allow us three hours, and come back for us? If we've cut sign by then, you won't see all that much of us. If we ain't cut sign by that time, we'll be ready to load up and head back to town. No sense scouting where there ain't no sign."

The brakeman nodded, but said, "There *has* to be sign. I read that report myself. There was six or eight of 'em in the gang, dressed up like graveyard ghouls in feed-sack hoods and rain slickers. You can see they ain't in sight out this way now. So they must have gone somewheres else, on horse, on foot, or slithering through the wet grass on their bellies like Lulu the Crocodile Gal who works for Mr. P. T. Barnum!"

Longarm said that was about the size of it, though he doubted the gang had anyone as odd as Miss Lulu the Crocodile Gal tagging along.

The brakeman strode up the tracks to consult with the engine crew as Longarm mounted the cordovan barb he'd borrowed off his pals at the Diamond K south of Cherry Creek. He left his rain slicker lashed to the skirts of his McClellan saddle for now as he forked himself up to sit taller than most riders in his tobacco tweeds and dark pancaked Stetson. The lawmen he was leading knew who he was. So he left his German-silver federal badge where it usually rode, pinned inside his wallet.

You could see better than three miles from horseback on

2

such open range. So he had no call to tote his Winchester outside its saddle boot. Both his .44-40 Colt and double derringer were within easy drawing distance in the unlikely event they flushed a train robber out of a prairie-dog hole. Wherever the sons of bitches had gone with all that loot, they already had a better than four-hour lead on the law. So which damn way had they run?

Longarm had his fellow lawmen fan out so they could cut a fairly wide swath as they circled the crime scene abreast a good mile or more out. The light was tricky, but the sod was soft. It took them an hour to trot the six-mile circle, and then they were staring at the deep hoofprints they'd left themselves. So they spiraled in, cutting against the sunlight as much as they could, until they were close to the water tank and the sod was all torn and trampled by confounding shoe prints. Longarm reined in to shout, "So much for horse sign. Now we scout for signs of loitering. Spent matches, snuffed smokes, the ashes of any night fires. We have to consider what six or eight men would do to while away the hours as they waited out here in the middle of nowhere for that night train rolling in from Chicago. The folks on board her say it was raining fire and salt when they stopped here at around four in the morning. I just can't picture the outlaws waiting for them here without so much as a stick to whittle or a toothpick to chew!"

Nobody else could either. So they dismounted and fanned out afoot to stare down at the trampled mud and scuffed-up grass. It was a Colorado deputy who found the pile of wet newspapers between that windmill and the corrugated iron wall of the tank it pumped water into.

As Longarm and some of the others joined him, he was marveling aloud. "These all appear the same edition of last Sunday's *Chicago Tribune*. I don't see what use a good two dozen copies of the same newspaper would be. Do you?"

Longarm nodded soberly and said, "Porters are likely to remember a passenger getting on with light baggage and off with heavy. They must have had those disguises in the same bags with all that heavy newsprint. It's commencing to fall together, boys. I ran across what you might call a variation on the same notion over Utah way a spell back. I sure wish the newspapers wouldn't print so much about slick train-robbing tricks."

Longarm consulted his pocket watch, saw he'd given himself a bit too much time, and hoped like hell it wouldn't rain again before their ride came back for them.

He said as much after he'd lit a three-for-a-nickel cheroot and suggested they water their ponies and get them back from the tracks a ways to graze on the greenup as they waited for that Baldwin.

One of the railroad detectives complained, "I'm missing something here. Are you saying you know which way those train robbers rode with all that loot even though we've cut no trail?"

Longarm nodded, exhaled, and explained. "They left here the same as everyone else did, aboard that Burlington night flier."

The railroad detective wasn't the only one who let fly with a dubious snort, so Longarm enjoyed another drag, let it drift off across the prairie, and said, "I'd best start at the beginning. That would be Chicago, where six or eight well-dressed gents board the night flier to Denver separately, with heavy baggage, to take their seats or, hell, Pullman berths like their more innocent fellow passengers."

The railroad detective protested. "But the gang was waiting *here,* at this lonely water tank, when the train stopped in the wee small hours."

"Where they dropped off unseen from the platforms of dark sleeping cars, ran around the far side of this tank, dumped their ballast, put on their disguises, and popped out of nowhere with their guns to menace the shit out of everyone!" Longarm explained.

Some of the older riders nodded thoughtfully. Others looked a bit dubious. Longarm insisted, "It's the only way that works. A man or beast who leaves no sign across soft greenup ain't crossed it. Yet we've all those statements agreeing that part of the gang made everyone get off the train and mill about in the rain, whilst others broke into the mail car and almost surely stuffed the loot in the innocent-looking baggage. Then they simply shoved the baggage back in place, seeing they had the whole empty train to themselves. The conductor told us they ordered him not to let anyone back aboard until they'd had the time to ride off through the rain. He naturally got everyone aboard and steaming on for Denver as soon as he figured they'd left. But they *hadn't* left. They'd just shucked those masks and rain slickers to mill about with their fellow victims

4

till that conductor figured it was safe for everyone to be on their way. Like I said, it's been done before.''

The railroad detective said, ''You mean they rode on into Denver aboard a train they'd robbed, with our very own porters likely packing the loot through the depot for the sons of bitches?''

Longarm smiled thinly. ''They likely found it more amusing. I wasn't at the depot this morning during the first excitement. So I can't say if anyone questioned each and every passenger before they went their separate ways. Seeing there were over a hundred trying to be on their way at once, I doubt anyone who was there could describe a particular passenger carrying distinctive baggage. I wish they'd get back here with that boxcar. There ain't a damned thing we can do out here, whether it rains some more or not.''

The rider who'd found the newpaper ballast looked mad as a rained-on hen as he marveled, ''Hornswoggled by train robbers who might not know which end of a horse the shit falls outten! We could be looking for city boys, or even city *girls,* considering how nobody never got a clear look at 'em, and they've scattered to the four winds by now!''

The railroad detective shot a wistful glance up at the telegraph wires strung on the far side of the track as he said, ''Old Mr. Allan Pinkerton ain't going to like this at all, but I fear I'm going to have to go along with your notion when I wire headquarters this afternoon. Frank and Jesse have caused us trouble enough, and this time we don't even have one general description to put on the wire!''

The Colorado deputy opined, ''These sissy rascals work a whole lot sneakier than country boys gone wrong. They've got away clean, and I can't wait to read how much the *Rocky Mountain News* admires us for letting 'em get away clean!''

Longarm spied coal smoke on the horizon as he said, ''Let's not get our bowels in an uproar, boys. New tricks are only new the first few times, and like I said, I've run across this particular dodge at least once before. The next time they try her, they may find it tougher to fool us. You did say there'll be Pinkerton as well as federal wires out on the rascals and their fandango, didn't you?''

The railroad detective sighed and said, ''We also keep warning passengers not to play cards for high stakes with total

5

strangers. Our only hope is for the slippery rascals to make some really stupid mistake!''

"They've made it,'' Longarm said as he spotted move locomotive smoke in the distance. He explained, ''They've chosen to ride the owlhoot trail and risk their freedom when the price of beef keeps rising and a dumb but honest rider can start at a dollar a day. Two can keep a secret if one of them is dead, and there were at least half a dozen out this way this morning. So time and the contrary nature of the crooked mind are on our side. We'd best just pack it in for now and give them time to brag to some whore, fight over the spoils, or try to cash one of those purloined money orders.''

So that was what they did, and for the better part of the week it appeared the gang had gone to ground or to Mexico for the foreseeable future.

Then, on a Saturday morning when Longarm only meant to put in half a day at the Federal Building, intending later to drive a new gal in town out to Cherry Hill to watch the sun go down behind the Front Range, Henry, the young squirt who played the typewriter out front, told him the boss wanted to see him right away in the back office.

So Longarm ambled on back, lighting a cheroot along the way in self-defense. For while Marshal William Vail's private office had glazed windows, and the oak-paneled walls had been scrubbed down at least once in living memory, the effect was something like the interior of some Cheyenne medicine lodge. Billy Vail was one of the few pure whites Longarm had ever met who could stare so dry-eyed through that much awful-smelling smoke. Longarm knew Billy Vail paid more for those pungent cigars than *he* would have. Yet they still reminded him of smoldering stable bedding. He tried not to weep as he sat down across the cluttered desk from his older, shorter, and far fatter superior.

Vail glanced at the banjo clock on his wall, and decided not to fuss at Longarm about the time, seeing he'd often reported in even later. Rolling his evil-smelling stogie to one corner of his moist lips, Vail said, ''We got lucky on that train robbery. Three down and a live suspect on ice up to Fort Morgan, on the Burlington right-of-way. They're holding the cadavers and the man who killed them for us. The next train you can catch will be a way freight leaving the yards here in Denver around

6

three this afternoon and getting you there an hour or so after sundown.''

Longarm sighed and said, "That's an awkward time to pester lawmen expected home for supper. To tell the truth, I'd made other plans for the coming sunset, Boss.''

Vail chuckled dryly and replied, "I've seen that gal who works at the chocolate shop and take my word, she'll be fat by the time she's thirty at the rate she's going.''

To which Longarm could only reply with a sheepish smile, "Wasn't planning on waiting till she was thirty to take her for a buggy ride. I could catch that night train leaving later, and be up in Morgan County with the early birds, right?''

Vail shook his bullet head. "Wrong. I've already wired the sheriff's office you'd be there around eight this evening. I had to make sure the Calgary Kid would still be there. It's tough to hold a man without bail after he's killed three suspected train robbers. We suspect the bunch he had it out with robbed that Burlington night flier because one of 'em had some stolen postal money orders on him. Are you paying any attention at all, or are you still lusting for the chocolate-fed charms of that new gal in town?''

Longarm laughed and said, "You'd best start at the beginning. I've never heard tell of any gunslick called the Calgary Kid. But you say he fought three-to-one and came out ahead?''

Vail shrugged and declared, "If I knew all the details, I'd have no call to send you up yonder to fetch him, would I? All I have so far is three strange riders striding into a local saloon and getting into a fuss with a vaguely sinister regular drinker with no visible means of support. His given name is Percival Harcourt. He prefers you call him the Calgary Kid.''

Longarm nodded soberly and said, "I follow his drift. The only Calgary I know of would be that Canadian Mountie post at the junction of the Bow and Elbow Rivers. It ain't been there long enough for anyone to have been born and reared there, though.''

Vail shrugged and said, "Maybe one time the Mounties up there arrested him. Getting back to the shootout at Fort Morgan, nobody was paying that much attention to the three strangers. Regulars at that particular saloon were more inclined to keep a wary eye on a gent they knew with an ominous rep. The Calgary Kid had never killed anybody in Fort Morgan before. But it was said he'd left Canada in a hurry and hadn't gotten on too well up Wyoming way last year.''

Longarm nodded soberly. ''In sum, no witness has come forward to say for certain who drew first.''

Vail shrugged and said, ''On the face of it, the Calgary Kid just whipped out his .442 Webley Bulldog and shot all three at point-blank range with their guns in their holsters.''

Longarm whistled softly and said, ''He sounds like a gent I'd be disinclined to drink with. You have to really catch a man by surprise if his gun's still holstered after you've shot two of his pals in front of him!''

Vail said, ''The town law arrested him for cold-blooded murder as he was taking a leak out back. Then, with him in jail and nobody on earth showing a lick of interest in those bodies, their riding stock, or other personal belongings, interest sort of shifted.''

Vail rummaged through the papers on his cluttered desk as he went on. ''Got a copy of the wire they sent out somewhere in here. Maybe Henry's already filed it, the infernal priss. Anyhow, like I told you before, one of them riders had a whole sheaf of postal money orders from that robbery in a saddlebag. But before anyone could let the Calgary Kid out of jail and hold a parade in his honor, they had sense enough to send me a Western Union night letter, and I've told them you'll be transporting this Calgary Kid down here for a closer look. It *appears* he wasn't on closer terms with 'em before the party got rough. On the other hand, thieves have fallen out in the past, and all four of 'em might have worn feed sacks and slickers when they robbed that train.''

Vail glanced at his wall clock again and added, ''I'll let you leave here early so's you can take that gal to noon dinner and swear you'll come back to her by moonlight though Hell should bar the way. Just make sure you catch that way freight this afternoon and bring me pictures of all three dead men, along with the mean drunk who gunned them.''

Longarm said he would, rose, and ducked outside to marvel at how fresh the air between Henry's musty files could smell after that much time in Billy Vail's smokehouse.

Henry had already typed up Longarm's travel orders, a summons to be served on one Percival Harcourt of Morgan County, and so on. Longarm stuffed them in a side pocket of his tobacco-tweed frock coat and lit out before anyone could call him back.

Thanks to Billy Vail's unusually generous attitude about new gals in town, it was way too early to amble over to that chocolate shop. As a man who planned ahead, Longarm had already had a tub bath and changed his shirt, underdrawers, and socks that morning. He didn't need a shave or a haircut. So he headed for the nearby Parthenon Saloon, a favorite haunt of the more sensible gents who worked around the Federal Building. No whores or professional gamblers were served at the Parthenon. But they served a fine free lunch with their affordable drinks, and a regular willing to bring his own gals could be discreetly served in one of the small side rooms, screened from vulgar stares by genuine frosted glass all the way from New York City.

Thus it came to pass that, as Longarm lounged at one end of the main bar, consuming needled beer and pickled pigs feet, they told him a lady was waiting for him in one of those side rooms, and he assumed it was someone he knew.

Longarm laughed in a self-mocking way as he checked the time and saw how little he had to work with. He'd never been able to figure out how the unfair sex managed to do it, but like many another man before him, he'd noticed they had an uncanny ability to gang up like this.

He washed down the morsel he'd been chewing, picked up his beer stein, and ambled back to face up to the gal who'd sent for him for whatever reason.

"We got to meet that other gal when she gets off at noon," he told himself. "No matter who this might be or what she might want!"

For he'd long suspected that this female tendency to present a poor boy with either nothing at all or more than he could handle was a diabolical plot by that Professor Darwin meant to keep fools from getting any at all.

He still had to grin every time he recalled that poor simp he'd known in Dodge. The one who'd sent East for his wife, even though they were short of money, because he just hadn't been able to get any west of the Big Muddy no matter how he begged and pleaded.

So naturally, with his old woman aboard a westbound and due to arrive any minute, two different Dodge City gals had gotten into a hair-pulling fight over him. He'd just made up his mind which one he wanted to kiss when his old woman

9

barged in, and after he recovered, he never wound up with *any* of them.

Longarm hoped nobody he really admired had found out about him and that chocolate-shop gal as he opened the sliding door to enter the small side chamber.

He didn't know either of the two painted dolls who were seated on either side of the marble-topped table between the cushioned benches along opposing walls. He could see they were both built swell under their summerweight pongee frocks, and either could have been pretty, once you scraped some of that pink powder and theatrical makeup away. He was sure they both wore wigs because it would make real hair fall out if you bleached it that shade of blond when your natural eye coloring was so dark. It would have been rude to ask right out which opera company or circus they might be with. He doubted they were whores. Neither Emma Gould nor Madame Ruth Jacobs would allow such clownish-looking faces on the premises, lest they scare paying customers away.

He could see they'd ordered a pitcher of rum punch, as if they thought it was July instead of April on the High Plains. There were three tumblers to go with the pitcher. One was still empty, on the far side of the gal to his right. She rose to indicate where they wanted him to sit, nearer the private exit to the side street the frosted windows faced.

He was willing, and he said so as he slid in across from the other, allowing that they had the advantage on him.

As the one who'd stood up slid down beside him close, the one across the table poured him a glass of punch as she told him he could call them Ginger and Candy. His beer stein was still a third full. But he reached for the tumbler to be polite as he asked them to get to the point, explaining, "I ain't usually this abrupt to ladies, but I have a train to catch and a noon appointment before I do that."

The clownishly made-up gal across the table smiled, a sort of frightening sight, and demurely replied, "We were told what a busy day you'd planned, Deputy Long. Drink up and we'll get right down to business."

As Longarm soberly put the glass back on the table untasted, she asked, "What's wrong? Don't you like rum punch?"

To which he could only reply, "Not when it's spiked that strong, ma'am. Didn't your momma ever tell you chloral hydrate smells sort of distinctive to the educated nose?"

10

The one called Ginger, across from him, sighed and confessed the sedative had been chosen more with his weight in mind. She explained, "We figured it might take a lot because you're such a big man. It was only meant to capture you without a fuss."

Longarm smiled thinly and replied, "We'd best talk about it over to the Federal Building. I'm fixing to reach for my handcuffs now, and I'd be obliged if you both sit still till I render the two of you a tad less lethal."

Then something cold and solid was jammed against that mastoid bone behind Longarm's left ear as Candy, the one seated on his side of the table, purred, "I've a better idea, handsome. You're going to drink that dose we measured out for you or Momma's just going to have to blow your fucking brains out!"

Longarm was still considering those options as Ginger, across the way, slid out of sight below the table rim as if someone had pulled her seat out from under her.

But he could only conclude someone had scouted him good for the painted pair as he found himself being relieved of his own pocket derringer as well as his gunbelt by clever unseen hands while he, perforce, sat there like a big-ass bird with his own hands atop the cold marble table.

Ginger popped back into sight across the way, grinning, with her wig just a little awry as she braced Longarm's own .44-40 over the far edge at him and cocked it, saying, "This is fun. Now drink that nice punch we ordered for you and nobody outside in the saloon will hear a thing!"

Longarm considered that option carefully. The both of them could gun him and be out that side exit before he stopped twitching. That heavy theatrical makeup they'd disguised themselves with would wipe off fast and leave them looking like two different gals entirely before a description of his possible killers could be spread across town. So calling their bluff didn't seem to offer him any edges. But on the other hand, they'd just confessed that that infernal punch had been spiked with a heavy dose of chloral hydrate!

As if she'd been listening in on Longarm's thoughts, the one with the gun against his skull prodded harder and hissed, "We're taking you with us, dead or alive. It's up to you. I'm counting to three!"

As she started, the one aiming his own six-gun at him almost

11

pleaded, "Would we resort to knockout drops if we never meant to give you a chance?"

So seeing that Candy had counted to two by then, Longarm heaved a vast sigh and picked up the innocent-looking tumbler, muttering, "If this kills me I'll never speak to either of you ladies again!"

The drink would have seemed sickly sweet if they'd made it from rum, sugar, and lime juice alone. He was sure he'd puke easily if only they gave him the chance to bust loose and shove a finger down his throat before the sedative got to his brain.

But even as he tensed his palms against the marble table, Candy hissed, "Don't even think about it. I never wanted to risk this sissy approach to begin with. They sell hats and ready-made suits like yours at the Denver Dry Goods cheap!"

The softer-talking one with the bigger gun purred, "Candy, dear, you're talking too much. I can hold him safer from this range with this gun. Why don't you go tell Hamish to fetch the carriage around to this side while we wait for my love potion to cast its spell."

So Candy slid away and away and away, through all those cobwebs the little room had filled with, as Longarm stared owlishly at the two guns the two Gingers were covering him with while he tried to get his boot heels under his own center of balance, if only he could figure out where that might be at the moment.

"Who Hamish?" Longarm numbly asked as his tongue seemed to feel swollen and numb. But neither of the Gingers across the way answered as he tried to decide which of his own guns to make a grab for. He heard that sliding door shut and knew it was now or never if he meant to do *something* he'd been thinking about doing.

But somehow, it didn't seem important as Longarm laid his weary head down against that soft warm marble to catch just forty winks or so before he drove out to Cherry Hill with the Calgary Kid to watch the evening sun go down.

Chapter 2

The next thing Longarm knew he was puking over the side of a four-poster bed like a seasick cabin boy in a howling gale. He heard a dry sardonic voice warning him, "If you taste hair, you'd better swallow hard. It's likely to be your own asshole."

Then he realized it had been his own voice, from some distance, and pulled his scattered brain together, despite the throbbing headache, to try another dry heave, cuss like a mule skinner who'd just backlashed his fool self, and try to sit up for a look-see around in the gloom.

It wasn't easy. They'd stripped him bare-ass and put him to bed with his gun hand fastened to one bedpost by what seemed to be his very own handcuffs. The key to them would be in the fob pocket of his own tweed pants, had a stitch of his duds been in sight.

Longarm reached with his free left hand for the sheet he'd thrown off in his first struggles, and draped it across his lap with his bare feet on what seemed a damp cement floor. The four-poster he sat on was the only item of furniture, unless one counted the chamber pot he'd missed with his puking beside the bed. The bed was jammed against a wall behind him. All four walls were that chocolate-brown sandstone Denver builders used for more substantial structures. He could be in anything from the cellar of some fashionable home to the basement of some warehouse. He figured there would have been

13

windows if they'd stored him on a higher floor.

Such light as there was came from what seemed like a rail-road lantern hanging from the middle of the low-beamed ceiling. The rough beams hinted at some less fashionable address in the industrial bottomlands of Denver. That would account for the damp floor and mildewed aroma after those recent spring rains. Private homes with quarried stone foundations tended to stand on the higher and drier ground at a safer distance from the flood plain of the South Platte than the business district and railroad yards. That one flight of stone steps to his left as he sat edgewise looked rain-streaked. That was likely the way out to the street or alleyway, bare-ass or not, if only he could slip that damned cuff! He couldn't get as good a look at the doorway in line with the head of the bed. He tried sliding his naked rump further to the left, but it remained no more than a break in the sandstone masonry until, suddenly, a clownishly made-up gal in a bathrobe and slippers popped into view to stare down at him with her hands on her hips. "You naughty boy!" she chided. "Why didn't you throw up in the chamber pot we left in plain sight for you?"

Longarm soberly replied, "I was sick. I'd be proud to mop up for you if you'd unchain me from this bed, Miss Ginger."

She giggled and said, "I'm Candy. But I'm glad you find it hard to tell us apart. I'll bet you'd never in a million years be able to recognize either one of us if we were made up more sedately—say, in church."

Longarm sighed and said, "That's the simple truth. It was already tough to tell you apart in that well-lit side room at the Parthenon. By this dim lantern light I'd be unwilling to bet a month's pay on how old, how young, or no offense, how ugly or pretty either one of you might look in her Sunday-Go-to-Meeting outfit!"

She didn't seem to be listening. Longarm stared after her as she turned and left him alone again, wondering what he'd said to piss her off. But then she was back, still smiling, with a mop and bucket. "Move your feet up out of the way while I slosh some suds over that mess you made," she said. "We knew you were likely to puke up the nice drink we served you. So there's plenty of pine oil and naptha soap in this *other* potion we prepared ahead of time."

He believed her as the pungent fumes of soap and disinfectant rose around him. She mopped up the mess and wrung it

14

out in the bucket with a galvanized cruncher. She was bent over, with her bathrobe hanging open.

He pretended not to notice as he made a mental note that at least one of his kidnappers was a natural brunette. The one nipple he could see went with a dark complexion as well as a great tit. He couldn't say if her eyes were almond, or just painted to look that way. Her accent seemed plain English, a little on the country side. But even a fancy gal with hired help could sound like a farm gal from anywhere north of Saint Louis.

After whoever she was took the mop and bucket somewhere else, he was chagrined as well as surprised to note he had a raging hard-on under the sheet across his bare thighs.

"Asshole!" he growled at himself. "The crazy bitch has dosed you with knockout drops and chained you up in her cellar! So what difference does it make that she's built like a brick shithouse and doesn't seem to care who notices? We got to escape from her, not peek at her pussy hair, so behave your fool self, old organ-grinder!"

Then Candy was back, robe more or less closed down the front, as she carried a big tray of coffee and cake over to him with a friendly smile on her garishly painted lips. "You'd better eat some of this sponge cake before you swallow any coffee, dear heart," she said. "We'll serve you something more solid for supper, of course. But for now we'd better stick with light yummies."

Longarm nodded his thanks—he'd been raised to be polite to women, even when they acted loco—and reached for a slice of cake with the only hand he had to work with. He resisted the impulse to ask her how much experience she'd had nursing other victims back from puking. For some reason he just didn't trust her answers, and he didn't want her to know how well his brain was starting to tick again. The cake went down easy and seemed content to stay put. He tried some of her coffee. It was too weak, and she'd messed it up worse with sugar and cream. But it did a lot for his dried-out mouth, and he said so. He tried asking for black coffee and some smokes, just to see what she'd say, and to his mild surprise she declared her only aim was to please him.

Then she proved it by whirling about to dash off somewhere while he washed down more sponge cake with more sweet coffee. He'd no sooner finished than Candy was back, smelling stronger of lilac water, with her nose powdered even more, to sit down beside him, leaning back against his outstretched cuffed arm, as she handed over his own three-for-a-nickel cheroots and waterproof Mex matches, then poured him another cup of blacker coffee from the pot she'd fetched as well.

He dryly asked, "Didn't Hamish fancy my tobacco as well as my duds and identification?"

She sat up straighter and primly replied, "We're not going to be such good friends if you try to ask me trick questions. Your only chance of getting out of this alive is for us to know you don't know enough to matter."

Longarm shrugged and stuck a cheroot between his teeth. As he was lighting it one-handed, Candy snuggled closer along his naked arm and demanded with familiar female logic, "How much have you been able to figure out so far, dear heart?"

Longarm had to laugh. He shook out the wax match, enjoyed a long thoughtful drag on the cheroot, and said, "I've been abducted by a couple of gals I doubt I'd recognize again, and mayhaps one Hamish I've yet to lay eyes on. The three of you got me out of the Parthenon and over here to this cellar by closed carriage in broad daylight, meaning not a soul noticed or I'd have been saved by now. Your turn, Miss Candy."

She coyly asked, "What was that you said about Hamish putting on your clothes and pretending to be you, dear heart?"

"Is that what I said?" Longarm answered carefully. He knew any number could play at getting answers out of a reluctant witness. He was good at it. He suspected she was too. His best bet was to flood her with more jaw juice than she could remember. He'd found in his own questioning of witnesses that the strong silent type tended to give a lot more away in their few reluctant words than a windbag might let slip as he gabbed about this, that, and the other.

Candy pressed on. "Why do you think someone would want to show your badge and identification to anyone, handsome?"

Longarm took another drag, shrugged, and replied, "Beats me. Ain't anyone here in Denver you could fool by saying you was me. I hate to brag, but they know me on sight from Larimer Street to Capitol Hill. I've been riding for Marshal Vail out of the Denver Federal Building six or eight years now."

He could feel how tense she was as she thought about that.

So he tried to sound worried as he exclaimed, "Jesus H. Christ! You wasn't fixing to cash checks or order things on credit out on the outskirts of town, were you?"

It worked. He could feel her spine relax as she took him for the fool he was pretending to be. He told her firmly, "I ain't about to stand credit for anything somebody else signed for in my place!"

She told him not to worry about that, and asked if there was anything else she could do for him before suppertime. He laughed wickedly and said, "I doubt your pals would approve of what I'd *really* cotton to, Miss Candy. But I'll settle for something to read, and you were right about that sponge cake and weak coffee. I could swear it was almost suppertime already! What time is it anyways?"

She said her watch was upstairs as she rose to leave with the tray. He finished his smoke, waited a spell, and lit another. It surely did seem he hadn't eaten in quite a spell. Throwing up his breakfast and the free lunch from the Parthenon had likely made him hungry earlier than usual.

But when Candy came back, in what seemed less than an hour, she'd brought a tray of grub along with a copy of the *Police Gazette*. As she sat down beside him again, she set the paper to one side and told him she'd have to feed him his supper like her naughty baby boy, lest he get his hands on anything sharp enough to whittle away a bedpost.

She'd brought him steak and potatoes with buttered string beans, bless her treacherous heart, and he probably could have wrested the knife and fork from her with his free left hand as she daintily cut and served a bite at a time for him. But even if he knocked her cold and got right to work on that hard-maple post with a table knife, it would be a bitch to explain when they came down to ask what might be keeping her in, say, an hour or so.

There was no way to ask if the two of them were alone in the house, or wherever they were. It would only alert her to the fact he was that interested. There was no way to be sure of any answer.

Meanwhile, the steak was rare and the spuds were done just right. He was able to sip the stronger black coffee she'd brought him with his free left hand. He made a desperately casual point of sipping all the black coffee he could. For this

17

was surely not a night made for deep sleep while at least three of his captors made further plans.

He'd already decided it made more sense to escape and then figure out what they were up to than it did to play guessing games while he was at their mercy. He wasn't ready to buy goldbricks from any woman painted like a clown in a fake hair wig, but there was some sense to what she'd said about them feeling safer if he stayed confused. Why they'd risk leaving a federal lawman alive after doing him this dirty was a mystery that might be best solved later, once he got out of this alive. He sensed that nobody in the bunch was out to do him any favors. They hadn't killed him when they'd had the chance because they were out to sell him a red herring. So this was hardly the time to display too much sales resistance.

Candy fed him the last of his main course, poured him some more coffee, and scampered out to fetch him some dessert.

This turned out to be apple pie à la mode, with two scoops of ice cream, and she'd brought a dish of it along for herself so she could feed the two of them with the same spoon.

Longarm made a mental note that the vanilla ice cream tasted store-bought, meaning they were fairly close to the center of town. Then he told her, sincerely, that she'd sure gone out of her way to make a kidnap victim feel at home.

She demurely replied, "It was never our intention to make you feel uncomfortable, dear heart. Just think of yourself as our guest for a little while."

He sighed and asked, "Could you mayhaps cuff me by this *other* wrist for a spell, seeing you'd like me to feel comfortable?"

She shook her bewigged head and replied, "I'm afraid I don't have the key, dear heart. You weren't planning to overpower me as I released your two big strong arms, were you?"

He grimaced and said, "Perish the thought. No offense, but ain't you snuggled sort of close for a gal who's worried about being overpowered, Miss Candy?"

To which she demurely replied, "I'm not too worried about who gets on top, as long as you can't get loose from this bed, naughty boy!"

So Longarm set the tray on the cement at their feet and fell back across the bed with her, his free hand reaching for what seemed to be ailing her. But even as they French-kissed, with his fingers parting the darker thatch down yonder, Candy

18

twisted free to gasp, "Not yet! I really don't want to kill you if I don't have to."

So he just watched as she skipped out to the center of the room to trim the hanging lantern, plunging them into total darkness as she confessed with a dirty giggle, "I want to pee first anyhow."

That made two of them, Longarm realized as he lay across the mattress in his birthday suit, listening to the soft hiss of a gal relieving her bladder in the darkness.

He said so as she rejoined him on the bed, her bathrobe cast off, and she shoved the chamber pot against his bare ankle with her own toe, saying, "Go ahead, then wipe it nice and clean on this top sheet for me, dear heart."

So he took a leak, seated on the edge of the bed, wishing he could stand and do it right. She giggled and said she could smell the mingled results. Then they were all over one another in the musky darkness, with him wishing he could get *both* palms under her squirming bare buttocks as she pleaded for him to shove the pillow under her.

He did, and they could get him deeper inside her that way, as she hammered his bounding behind with her bare heels and begged him for more. It would have been rude as well as possibly unwise to ask if her pal Ginger was the one getting the most attention from that mysterious Hamish. He could tell *she* sure needed more than she'd been getting of late.

He consoled himself that he was giving it to her in the line of duty, as he pounded her to glory and found he still wanted more. For while she was built better than half the gals in the *Police Gazette,* and tight as a schoolmarm in heat, he was able to examine her by feel a little more dispassionately.

She had a triangle of tiny moles nestled in the hollow between her pubic hair and right hipbone. It might have made her suspicious if he'd run his free hand over her face as she rolled it from side to side in pure passion. So he explored her eyelids and such with his lips and tongue, even as she giggled and said she'd have to put her face back together in another room. He'd already noticed that her wig had fallen off in the dark as they'd thrashed about. He was able to tell, with the tip of his passionately questing tongue, that her real hair, whatever its color, was straight, though finer than most Indian or breed gals' hair. So her natural looks were likely darker-than-usual white. Like one of those waitress gals at Romero's Italian Gar-

19

dens. Only this wasn't one of them, unless he'd lost his knack for undressing pretty young gals with his eyes.

Warning himself not to draw himself too clear a picture of Candy as she might really look, Longarm thought about lighting a casual smoke, recalled the mess that gal in the Greek legend had gotten into by lighting a lantern when one of those Greek gods had warned her not to, and settled for just running a friendly hand all over Candy as they lay there fighting for their second winds, with her real hair spread across his cuffed arm and right shoulder.

Now that she'd had her wicked way with him, she seemed to feel he ought to be ashamed of himself. A lot of gals were like that. He said he'd still respect her in the morning, if ever he figured out what she looked like, and that cheered her up a lot.

She giggled lewdly in the darkness and purred, "That's right. This night of sweet abandon will be mine and mine alone to remember. I'll be able to savor every handsome inch of your famous face and body for as long as I live. But to you, I'll always be just a mysterious form in pitch blackness who may or may not be named Candy."

He rolled a nipple gently between thumb and forefinger as he sighed and said, "I told you when first we met that you ladies had the advantage on me. I'll bet that other gal ain't really named Ginger either."

She laughed and said, "This is turning out even better than I hoped, and I'd heard around town you were hung like a horse. You won't ever be able to gossip about this, will you? You've no idea how we women worry about men bragging when we show a little bit of weakness."

He said he hardly ever bragged about gals, even when he was in any position to point them out on the street. So the next thing he knew she was on her knees, between his, to try what she called a naughty notion she'd always been curious about.

He didn't think it would be wise to ask her how she'd gotten so good at blowing the French horn if she'd never tried it before. He just put a friendly free hand down to stroke her real hair as her head bobbed fast, with her pursed lips sliding wetly up and down a whole lot of renewed interest.

He wondered idly whether it was really black hair, or maybe streaked with more experience than she wanted to own up to.

20

He didn't have her down as a whore. She liked it too much to be a pure professional. But she'd been around the mulberry bush in her day, maybe as a married-up gal who hadn't been getting all she wanted at home. He warned her he was as inspired as she likely wanted him to be, and she proved that had been her aim by kissing his renewed erection fondly and moving up to impale herself on it, gasping, "Good heavens, I seem to have created a monster! Have you ever put anyone in the hospital with this thing, dear heart?"

He thrust up playfully and replied, "It sure beats all how you gals will stretch a mile before you tear an inch down yonder. I could tell you tales of shy young maids who swore they'd never even *seen* such an organ-grinder, but I'd sound as if I was bragging when I told you how things turned out."

She sobbed, "Bastard! Who told you I was no shy young maid?"

To which he could only reply, with a gallant thrust, "Nobody. You could look sixteen to sixty with that lantern lit, for all I can *see*. But to tell the truth, we ain't neither of us been screwing like a pair of schoolkids playing hooky down by the creek."

So she laughed, in a dirty but mollified way, and screwed herself into a shuddering mass of limp curves on top of him as he tried in vain to discharge his own weapon in her from that position.

He'd rolled her over and mounted her from behind with his one arm at an awkward angle indeed when, suddenly, the room was flooded with light and the one called Ginger was saying, "What's going on down here? Good God, have you gone crazy, you slut?"

The one he'd been enjoying dog-style wailed, "Douse that light!" as she groped for the loose sheet to cover her head and thrust her rump up, demanding he take it out.

So he did, rolling to one side with his unsatisfied erection at half-mast as he smiled sheepishly up at the fully dressed Ginger with a globe lantern and said, "Evening, ma'am. I would sound more sincere if I felt it was myself who ought to say they were sorry. You sure did pick an awkward time to break this party up!"

The garishly painted Ginger smiled coldly down at his waving dick as she dryly observed, "So I see. Do you think he saw your face just now, Candy?"

The one he'd been screwing was moving for the door, stark naked from the waist down, as she held her wig in one hand and the sheet over her head as though she'd just joined the Ku Klux Klan. She wailed something spiteful at her amused partner as she left. Ginger bent to pick up the other gal's discarded bathrobe and slippers as she told Longarm, "Let's hope that was a *no* just now. How did you manage to seduce the poor thing like that, and what good did you think it would do you? Neither of us has the key to those handcuffs. Candy had no way of letting you go if she'd wanted to. So you see, all those flattering words and false promises were for naught!"

Longarm shrugged and softly replied, "Oh, I dunno, ma'am. For one thing, it sure helped me pass some time away. How late might it be outside now?"

Ginger coldly replied, "The less we tell you, the less you'll know. I have to go talk to Candy. Pray to God you didn't get more than an easy lay out of her!"

She moved for the door with her awkward load of light and clothing. Longarm asked her to light the railroad lantern again, explaining, "I ain't tired enough to sleep and I got a *Police Gazette* here I ain't read yet."

Ginger said, "That's too bad. Jerk off with your free hand if you haven't had enough."

Then she was gone, leaving him alone in the dark to make some mighty rude remarks about her spoilsport attitude.

He got up and stood near the head of the bed to lower his right wrist a little as he pissed in the half-filled chamber pot some more. He knew he'd have more to dump in it before morning. It wasn't his fault one or the other of them would have to empty it for him. He'd never invited himself to this fool charade.

He shifted his weight back and forth on his bare heels, wishing he could pace up and down at least, until his legs got tired enough for him to sit and smoke some more while he wondered what time it was and why on earth he'd ever swallowed all that coffee.

Somewhere in the night he heard a switch engine banging a string of boxcars to make up a train. He'd been right about this place being down on the flood plain of the Platte. He figured he was at least a quarter mile from the rail yards, though, thanks to sounds carrying better after dark.

He inhaled deeply, letting the ruddy tip of his cheroot cast

22

a faint ruby glow on his own naked knees as he wondered what good it would do him if he could place this fool cellar on a city map.

"I'll know where I was as soon as I bust out!" he muttered to himself grimly. Of the three suspects, the only one he'd have a prayer of describing was a medium-sized gal in her late twenties or early fifties with three moles on her gut and straight hair, likely black.

He had to chuckle as he pictured himself and a posse stopping all the brunette ladies on the streets of Denver to say, "Howdy, ma'am. Would you mind us searching under your skirts for moles?"

Smoking wasn't as much fun in the dark, for some reason. So he bent over to snuff the cheroot on the cement for later. Then he got back to his bare feet and quietly experimented with taking the bedstead apart. It seemed evident they'd never carried this big old four-poster through either narrow entrance in one piece.

But as he heaved and tried not to grunt aloud, he discovered that while it might be possible to slip the side rails free of the headboard, the damned posts, including the one he was cuffed to, were as one with the massive mahogany cross-piece.

He tried sliding the cuff up the post as he stood atop the soft bedding. He found he could reach the square framework connecting the upper ends of all four posts, in case one wanted to hang mosquito nets or fancy brocades all around you while you snored.

Straining some, he got his free hand up over that one corner to learn, with considerable cussing, that the son-of-a-bitching crossbars were fastened to the end of the damned post with steel nuts twisted as tight as a miser's purse. Getting a grip on a nut with one bare hand was no problem. *Turning* the son of a bitch without at least a pair of pliers was the problem. It felt as if it was welded to the bolt as a solid mass. More likely, that Hamish rascal had only used the assembly wrench that came with such furniture. There was no way in Hell Longarm was ever going to *disassemble* this bedstead with just his bare hands!

The effort seemed to have tired him more than it should have. He got back down to sit and ponder. He needed just a little better grip and a little more leverage, and then what?

He was still bare-ass naked and unarmed. They'd likely

23

locked the two possible exits, and if he did bust on through to Lord only knows where, there were at least two of them somewhere up above, with Lord only knows what weaponry.

He lay back with one arm up and a foot on the floor, wondering why he felt so tired after a little slap and tickle and all that black coffee.

"It was likely in that apple pie à la mode," he decided, knowing he'd have surely smelled more knockout drops in warm coffee. But for some reason it didn't seem important *how* they kept drugging him as *why* they kept drugging him.

He'd almost dozed off again when he heard the soft rustle of cloth and a shy whisper from the darkness, warning, "Don't make a sound. I don't want her to know I came back."

So Longarm didn't say anything as she groped her way over to the bedstead to grasp him unerringly by his virile member and softly gasp, "Good heavens, it's so soft compared to the last time I saw it proudly waving!"

Longarm felt a tingle down yonder, even as he wondered if he'd be able to knock her cold with a wild swing in total darkness. As he considered how much good that might do him, she was suddenly on her knees on the floor to fondle and lick his dawning interest as if it was a peppermint cane and she might be practicing a sword-swallowing act for Mr. P. T. Barnum.

So seeing as old Candy still seemed to like him, and might be the weak link in this mighty convoluted chain, he reached down to fondle her bobbing head and dryly suggest, "We could do this better over at the Tremont House with nobody fixing to bust in on us with her own globe lantern again, honey."

It didn't seem to be working. She removed her saucy lips from his wet erection to giggle. "I only came down here to be naughty, not to betray my own side, you silly!"

Then she demurely rose to roll across him aboard the rumpled sheets as she husked, "What are you waiting for? Didn't Mamma kiss it and make it all better?"

He chuckled and allowed she surely had as he forked a leg over between her welcoming thighs. His one arm, stretched awkwardly right over her right tit, made it tougher than it might have been to enter her. He said so. But she just reached down to take the problem in hand, move her own hips toward

24

the headboard, and guide him in, gasping, "Ooh! I really like it this deep!"

That made two of them, even though he was sore at her and groggy as hell from that shit she'd been feeding him—with ice cream, for Gawd's sake.

He knew she was only enjoying her ownself with a kidnap victim they could be plotting most anything against. The way a mind and body could each make its own play was a caution. He was humping her hard and kissing her sincerely, even as he was trying to figure some way to get the upper hand on her.

He felt himself coming in her shuddering warmth. She begged him not to stop, and he managed to boot her over the edge with the last of his passion, muttering, "You shouldn't ought to feed a man sleeping potions if you want him to screw you all night, Miss Candy."

She sighed and said, "Don't take it out just yet. It feels so nice where I'm cuddling it. Kiss me again, handsome."

So he did, running his free hand over her passion-warmed curves as he tried not to really like a gal who was that treacherous.

It took him more than one languid pass with his damp palm before he noticed those three moles seemed to be missing down yonder. That accounted for a lot of other minor differences. He'd just been going at it friendly as all hell with the meaner one, Ginger!

Were the both of them some sort of sex maniacs? Was this whole wild adventure no more than the mad desire to get laid by a pair of weird old maids? He sure wished he didn't feel so groggy just now. Had he felt up to any more conversation, he'd have asked her.

Chapter 3

Somewhere in the distance a train whistle was moaning the tune of a dirty schoolboy song. Longarm stared up through the gloom at the rough ceiling beams as he tried to recall the way it went.

> Two old maids from Canada
> Were drinking cherry wine.
> The song that they were singing went,
> Your hole's no bigger than mine!

Then he noticed that that distant train whistle was really signaling it was pulling out of the yards, and that he could *see* those ceiling beams! So he sat up and swung his bare feet to the cement floor to see what else he could make out.

The light was dim, gray, and diffuse. But as best he could tell, it was coming through the doorway those two old maids from Canada had been using to get at him. It appeared to be daylight. He didn't know why. But it didn't really matter whether either gal hailed from Canada. Neither one had seemed to have Canadian accents or, come to study on it, such big holes. He'd probably been dreaming about that Calgary Kid earlier. The alienists who studied the way brains worked had all sorts of notions about how and why folks dreamed.

Longarm had long since decided *he* dreamed to keep from waking up.

He tore a narrow strip down one seam of the bottom sheet. It wasn't easy, holding a corner with his cuffed hand as he ripped carefully with the other. But at least his brain seemed to be working again after all that sleep it had never volunteered for.

He wadded the seam-enforced strip up and dunked it in the chamber pot. By now the mingled piss was commencing to smell pungent. But as any country boy could tell you, shit and piss were valuable industrial chemicals to cottage industries.

He'd allowed himself to get citified enough to grimace as he wrung the pungent textile strip out with his bare hands and twisted it into a sort of damp noose before he rose to climb back atop the mattress with it, sliding his cuffed wrist up the bedpost as well.

Working more by feel despite the better view he now had of all that framework near the ceiling, Longarm got some wet cloth over that retaining nut and twisted as hard as he could to grip the stubborn son of a bitch.

He kept twisting, and then, as if with no effort at all, the bolt popped loose. Then it was simple to just unscrew it, pop the corner of the top frame off the carriage bolt, and slip the other loop of the cuffs free!

That only meant he was free from the four-poster, of course. So for lack of any other weapon, Longarm picked up the half-filled chamber pot and eased toward the light. He wasn't expecting to kill anyone with half a gallon of stale piss, but catching it full in the face by surprise might throw anyone's aim off a bit.

As he made it to the doorway, he saw that another flight of stone steps led upward to the ground floor. The door at the top stood open, and he could see the daylight was bouncing off a pressed-tin ceiling that could have used a fresh coat of ivory paint. He eased silently up on bare feet to find himself in a long corridor with a grimy window at the far end and doorways leading off to either side. So it felt sort of spooky as he slid along one wall, taking a deep breath and cocking his pot of piss each time he risked a peek around a doorjamb.

But all the rooms were empty, save for dust and cobwebs, until he came at last to the only one with a lick of anything in it.

He almost let the pot of piss fly before he realized he was staring at his own duds, draped over a bentwood chair, with his Stetson perched mockingly atop the buttoned collar and his stovepipe boots lined up in front. Then, better yet, he saw his own gun rig folded to rest in what would have been his lap, had he been wearing the outfit.

He soon was. First things coming first, he got to his .44-40 on the double to check and make sure it still held five in the wheel before he put down the chamber pot, barred the one door behind him, and shook out his duds to make sure nobody had laced them with, say, black widow spiders.

The brown tweed smelled of dry cleaning, and both his shirt and underdrawers had been laundered cleaner than when he'd first put them on! He suspected his damned hat had been cleaned and blocked overnight as well. But why?

He hurriedly dressed, finding his clean socks in his boots and not a nickel missing from his pocket change, as far as he could tell. He found his watch, chain, and derringer in his vest pockets. The key to the infernal handcuffs was in its usual fob pocket. As he got them off and examined his wallet he found his badge, U.S. deputy marshal's warrant, and fourteen dollars in silver certificates were still with him. It sure seemed a peculiar way to kidnap a gent.

Hat and gunbelt in place and .44-40 in hand, Longarm unbolted the door to go looking for some answers.

He didn't find any. He'd been left alone and unguarded in what he suspected to be an empty warehouse with showrooms toward the front. His pocket watch and the angle of the sunlight through the grimed-up windows agreed they'd held him here at least twenty-four hours. Had they meant to do him dirtier than that, they'd had plenty of chances.

He found his way out to a cobblestone street. He could make out the hazy peaks of the Front Range down at one end. So he turned the other way, knowing he had to be somewhere east of Downtown Denver. As he picked up the pace and put his side arm away, he tried to put the charges together, muttering, "It was those two ladies, I reckon, Your Honor, who abducted me out of a saloon to screw me silly when they weren't having my suit dry-cleaned or insisting on feeding me pie à la mode. It's true I ain't out a nickel, but they surely must have done something unconstitutional to this child and I want 'em put away for treating me so mean!"

He heard a switch engine picking up some empty boxcars, and had his bearings now. He was just west of the railroad yards in a run-down stretch of abandoned supply houses for the dying buffalo-hide and Indian-trading industries. He'd worry later how those crazy gals had known they'd be safe with him in that particular empty shell. For if he hurried he could still make that same train, twenty-four hours after the fact, of course. But anything beat having to explain all this shit about pie à la mode to Billy Vail before he carried out his damned orders!

Cutting through an alley to the bobwire strung along the western reaches of the rail yards, Longarm hopscotched across the tangle of sunbaked rails and dusty ballast as he made sure he still had those travel orders Henry had typed up for him. Nothing seemed to be out of place. He still had the writ signed by Judge Dickerson, citing one Percival Harcourt alias the Calgary Kid as a federal witness. So there went a grim notion indeed. He'd likely been thinking of old maids from Canada with a needlessly worried mind.

He made his way across the yards to the red brick mass of the Union Station. He didn't have time for a shave, but as long as he was there he sent a wire to Morgan County, allowing he was sorry he'd been detained but meant to arrive by 7:45 that evening. He was coming out of the Western Union when he heard his name hailed and turned to see Sergeant Nolan of the Denver police bearing down on him with a puzzled expression.

The blue-uniformed and gilt-badged Denver lawman demanded, "Are you all right? We were tipped you were being held prisoner over in Glover's Warehouse off Twenty-second Street. Only, nobody was there and here you are. What's going on, Longarm?"

It was a good question. Longarm compared notes with the sergeant as they moved back through the station so he could catch that way freight bound for Fort Morgan.

Nolan agreed he'd never heard of outlaws kidnapping a grown man to screw him silly, although he'd heard of it happening to *ladies* on more than one occasion. He explained how a wire from the nearby mining town of Golden had been sent less than an hour back to tell them about Longarm's predicament. They hadn't known what to make of the chamber pot or busted-up bedstead in an otherwise empty building.

Nolan said, "Nobody in that neck of the woods was able

29

to tell us anything because there's nobody there. That whole tract has been bought up by a company with a view to tearing down and rebuilding. The Glover outfit that used to own that warehouse you were held in went out of business when the Arapaho were moved out of these parts. Old Man Glover used to trade with White Antelope, Left Hand, and other tame Arapaho years ago. Lost the property when he failed to keep up his mortgage and tax payments. We're still working on where that heavy four-poster might have come from. I don't see how they ever moved it into an abandoned warehouse without anyone at all noticing.''

Longarm shrugged and said, ''I have a boss who just loves to track through dusty records. He may or may not feel like tracing property deeds, furniture delivery bills, and so on once we decide whether all that horseshit constituted a felony.''

Nolan blinked and said, ''I thought you just said they kidnapped you and held you prisoner a good twenty-four hours!''

To which Longarm could only reply with a sigh, ''We've both heard of fraternity initiations that caused more distress. I wasn't robbed. I wasn't even roughed up enough to leave bruises. If I could identify either of those mischief-making gals, just what would I charge them with, seeing I was willing to go along with so much of their scandalous game?''

Nolan agreed he'd feel silly taking the witness stand against a gal he'd screwed willingly as Longarm moved up the platform to see the dispatcher about that way freight.

It only took a three-for-a-nickel cheroot and a few minutes of friendly jawing to wrangle Longarm a ride up to Fort Morgan aboard the brakemen's caboose. The train pulled out within the hour, and he knew most of the crew from earlier runs up and down the Burlington line. Longarm and his extra gun were always welcome in such an uncertain world, although it was seldom a way freight got robbed.

Such trains got their name from the way they operated, as a local freight train dropping off and picking up individual boxcars along the way. Outlaws were seldom attracted to the heavy bulk freight such plodding workhorse trains might be carrying. Only an outsider who'd been reading the Burlington timetables carefully might have sought a ride on such a poky stop-and-go freight. But as he and old Henry had agreed the day before, the afternoon way freight had the evening highball beat if you'd missed the noon northbound and only needed to ride as far as Morgan County. They'd agreed it would feel like a mighty long trip, but he'd still be getting off at Fort Morgan before the faster evening highball was halfway there.

Of course, long before sundown, Longarm was sincerely sorry he'd listened to old Henry and hadn't waited for that later but faster train. For even though there was plenty of coffee on the stove in the caboose, and a man was free to smoke all he wanted out on the back deck, it sure got tedious after they'd stopped and started a few dozen times.

Following this same line aboard a regular train, you hardly noticed the small flag stops consisting of little more than a siding and an open loading platform every few miles. But local settlers sure shipped a lot of petty produce, and ordered everything from pianos to windmill kits by rail.

The afternoon breezes blew pleasantly across the greened-up rolling prairie, and a train-weary traveler who knew the deceptions of the High Plains less might have been tempted to drop off at one of the spreads they passed to borrow a damn horse and get a move on.

But Longarm never did. He knew that even though they *seemed* to crawl toward the northeast slower than an ambitious hobo could stride the cross-ties, the train ran close to twenty miles an hour between its stops, to average better time than a cavalry column, or even the old Pony Express, could have sustained over the course of the afternoon.

So after supping in the caboose with the friendly train crew, he stared back along the tracks to watch a whole herd of whooping cranes flying north against the sunset. Not long after that, they let him off at Fort Morgan, where the tracks rejoined the wide and shallow South Platte as it wound its way northeast from Denver.

Like a lot of Western towns with a fort in front of their names, Fort Morgan had grown into a river crossing, rail stop, and county seat near the site of an outpost meant to guard against Mister Lo, the Poor Indian. These days you saw more cowboys than Indians around Morgan County. Arriving after dark, as he had, Longarm didn't see much of anything but a few dim street lamps and a mess of lit-up windows leading from the railroad platform toward the river crossing. But the wire he'd sent from Denver had alerted the local law to his arrival, and a quartet of badge-toting gents were waiting on the sun-silvered platform for him with puzzled smiles in lieu of any brass band.

Longarm had pinned his own federal badge to the lapel of his dark frock coat, hoping to save a certain amount of sniffing in a town he hadn't visited that often. So he wasn't surprised when one of the town lawmen came right over to ask if he was the one claiming to be U.S. Deputy Marshal Custis Long from the Denver District Court.

When Longarm modestly allowed that he was, the bewhiskered older gent, who said he was Deputy Sheriff Goodman, demanded in a puzzled tone, "Then who was that getting off at this same time last night, with the same name, same identification, and same court order asking us for the Calgary Kid?"

Longarm felt a fuzzy gray cat stand up and turn around inside his gut, with its brushy tail swishing as he numbly replied, "I can't say. I wasn't here. What did this other Deputy Long look like?"

Goodman stared harder at the slightly taller federal man before he said, "A lot like you, if I was pressed to describe either one of you. Tall galoot with a mustache and gray eyes, dark hat crushed Colorado-style, and a .44-40 riding cross-draw under a tweed frock coat, just like the *Rocky Mountain News* described you in that recent article about the robbing of the Burlington night flier. We still have those three likely train robbers on rock salt and ice, by the way."

Longarm got out his wallet and the writ signed by Judge Dickerson as he demanded, "Never mind about *them* just now. Are you still holding Percival Harcourt alias the Calgary Kid for us?"

Deputy Goodman replied with a puzzled tone and a clear conscience, "Why should we? Didn't you just now hear me say you or somebody a lot like you arrived last night, when we were *told* you would, with papers demanding we hand over the cuss as a possible federal witness?"

Longarm groaned, "Oh, shit, I thought those gals just *liked* me! I see it all now. But how could I be packing the federal writ from the Denver District Court if someone else was waving it at you last night? You *would* have *kept* such papers for your own files, right?"

Goodman nodded and took the writ from Longarm as he replied, "We would have and we did. Let me move over by that hanging lantern with this, ah, Deputy Long. It *looks* about the same as the judge's orders that other Longarm swapped us for the Calgary Kid.''

Then he held the paper up to the light and declared, ''This one seems a tad fancier. His didn't have this here engraved letterhead and the paper wasn't as thick. It was just typed up on good-quality lawyer's bond. But it looked all right and . . . Are you saying we've been screwed out of a gunfighting federal want by some flimflam artist?''

To which Longarm felt obliged to reply, ''It might be fairer to say *I* have! Which way did they go after this brazen son of a bitch walked out of your jail with my prisoner trying not to laugh out loud?''

Goodman said, ''They caught that night train to Denver when it passed through in the wee small hours. Before that they spent some time holed up in the Buckhorn Hotel, that two-story edifice you can just make out from here on the west corner. If they were in cahoots, they didn't act it. The tall dark gent who came for the Calgary Kid led him off in handcuffs and they had a late supper sent up to their room. This other Longarm surely *acted* as if he was guarding Harcourt serious enough!''

Longarm sighed and said, ''You might have gotten suspicious had he told you they were both putting on an act before they caught a train out of town. Somebody else hopped a shortline ride up to Golden to flimflam the Denver police with a telegram today. Lord only knows where the bunch of them might be right now, laughing at me fit to bust!''

Goodman suggested they'd all converse more comfortably over at the county jail, sitting down with some liquid refreshments. So that was where they all headed as Longarm filled Deputy Goodman in on his wild adventure in the Glover Warehouse, leaving out how much he'd enjoyed some of it.

The older lawman then pointed at a lamp-lit frosted glass doorway down the plank walk a ways and said, ''Yonder's our spread. Office up front and lockup in the back. I believe you're the real Longarm and I know you've a rep for telling the plain truth. But there's something about your odd tale that rubs me the wrong way, no offense.''

Longarm nodded and said, ''It beats the shit out of me too. I just can't say why a gang of desperados who aimed to free a pal by switching places with a lawman sent to fetch him would leave said lawman alive and well to bear witness against them when, not if, we catch up with the peculiar bunch.''

One of Goodman's junior deputies moved ahead to open the heavy glass door for them as Goodman opined, "Oh, I dunno. They do seem to have a good head start on us, having gotten the Calgary Kid out of jail as slick as a whistle!''

As they all trooped inside, Longarm explained, "Percival Harcourt alias the Calgary Kid is the loose cannon on their deck. I'd be hard-pressed to describe either of those painted hussies, and I'll take your word on the man who looks a lot like me, until he changes his duds and maybe removes his mustache, that is. But the wild-shooting Calgary Kid is a hell of a lot less mysterious! We know exactly what he looks like, and you did say he hailed from around here, didn't you?''

Goodman waved Longarm to one of the chairs around the desk nobody was seated at as he scouted up a bottle of bourbon filed under B.

One of his junior deputies rustled up some hotel tumblers as the hospitable older lawman said, "Yes and no. Like we wired your boss when we were trying to figure out whether to charge him with murder or hold a parade in his honor, Harcourt drifted into town by rail just a few months back. Nobody can say for certain just when that was. It was cold and everyone was bundled up in public—this side of, say, last Thanksgiving. As far as we've been able to determine, he spent most of his time at that Buckhorn Hotel near the tracks or one of the three local houses of ill repute that provided all-night accommodations. His local rep was that of a solitary drinker it was best not to pester if you didn't like to be called a nosy cocksucker. But while there were rumors about his being involved in shootings all over the West, that gunfight the other night was the only serious trouble he ever caused here in Fort Morgan.''

As he poured a round, one of the other hands quietly declared, "It ain't dead certain he was in the wrong. The strangers he gunned sure seem to be connected to that train robbery and the Burlington line has a standing reward on such pests as he shot.''

As Longarm accepted his own share with a nod, Goodman grimaced and said, "Some who were there said Harcourt butchered them like lambs, no matter who they were. But it does seem odd he'd go to all that trouble to escape if all he had on his conscience was the execution of three wanted criminals. You reckon he could be wanted himself, and didn't feel like appearing at a public hearing that would doubtless make the *Denver Post* and *Rocky Mountain News* combined?''

Longarm sipped his drink. It was smooth, and he said so before he pointed out, ''Whatever his real name, we've dozens of witnesses who can pick him out of a crowd, and we'll soon know whether he's really wanted in other parts or just a nasty drunk.''

Goodman said, ''You want to talk to Gimpy Joe. Go back and fetch him for us, will you, Spuds?''

The junior deputy he'd addressed headed back to the cell block with his bourbon as Goodman explained, ''Gimpy Joe is serving thirty days because he couldn't raise the thirty dollars. We're getting sick of him pissing on the street in front of women when he's in his cups. He makes more sense when he's sober, and the Calgary Kid spent at least a few sober hours with him out back whilst we were trying to decide what to do with him.''

Another local lawman volunteered, ''The Calgary Kid talks prissy English, like them Thompson Brothers you don't want to mess with neither.''

Longarm frowned and asked if they were talking about the notorious Ben and Billy Thompson, who'd made folks from Ellsworth to Dodge sort of proddy in recent memory.

When the junior deputy allowed he was, Longarm frowned thoughtfully and declared, ''The Thompson Brothers got to Texas by way of Old England. They don't like to be teased about their accents either. Are you saying this unfortunately named Percival Harcourt is saddled with a high-toned English manner of speech as well?''

Goodman shrugged and said he hadn't met that many lime-juicers. A foreigner sounded foreign to him.

The junior deputy he'd sent back to the cell block returned with a gray old codger with a swollen red nose and a pronounced limp. Deputy Goodman nodded and introduced Gimpy Joe to Longarm, ordering the old jailbird to recall all he could about his recent cell mate.

Gimpy Joe asked if he could have just a little sip of that snake medicine. Goodman told him he'd have to sing for it. So the poor old wretch pleaded, ''What do you want me to say? He like to bit my head off when they first brought him

35

in. I'd already learned not to talk to him from over to the Wagon Wheel Tavern. Later on, after he'd sobered a mite, he said he was sorry he'd called me a dirty old queer, and allowed someone from the British consulate would soon be along to bail him out.''

Longarm and Goodman exchanged glances. Longarm said, "There is a British trade mission back in Denver. I ain't sure it qualifies as a consulate. But I sure mean to ask!"

Turning to the old drunk, Longarm demanded, "Did this odd cuss with English ways and a Canadian nickname say he had some sort of diplomatic immunity, for Pete's sake?''

Gimpy Joe stubbornly replied, "I need a drink. I don't know what the Calgary Kid thought he had. They throwed him in with me drunk as a skunk and cussing awful after he'd just shot down three other men. So to tell you the truth, I was up on the top bunk shaking some while he paced like a caged cougar and swore he'd eat cucumbers and do other wonders as soon as some pals with that there British consulate set him free!"

Goodman poured a tiny sip of bourbon for Gimpy Joe as the lawman said to the room in general, "That was a Royal Issue .442 Webley Bulldog he shot those boys with, come to study on it. But saying he *could* have had some standing with Queen Victoria . . .''

"Exactly," Longarm declared, downing the last of his bourbon. "Nobody acting for Her Majesty would shilly-shally with imposters and forged federal writs. If there *is* a British consulate in these parts, and they wanted Percival Harcourt out of jail, they'd have just sent somebody over to talk to *us* about it. Morgan County ain't charged Harcourt with any local felony, and we only wanted him as a possible link to that mail car robbery. My boss and Judge Dickerson can be discreet as hell when they're asked politely. So all that bullshit with painted ladies and pie à la mode just don't add up to a British diplomatic mission!"

Longarm never would have sent a hopeless drunk back to a lonely jail cell after serving him just a few teasing drops of booze. But he wasn't running the town law.

He asked Goodman if he could have a look at the Calgary Kid's mysterious victims, at least.

Goodman cheerfully complied, seeing he was on duty until twelve and the undertaker's was just down the way. A friendly enough old cuss who smelled as if he'd been embalming himself met them in the front parlor and led them down to the chilly cellar, lighting a wall fixture as he cheerfully announced, "I expect we may get to embalm and ship at least one of those poor boys after all. I just got a wire from Montana asking if by any chance the light-haired lad might have a mermaid tattoo on his left shoulder and an old scar on his right thigh."

He slid open an oak drawer, lined with sheet zinc, to reveal a pale nude cadaver reposing on a bed of crushed ice. Longarm could make out the tattoo and scar at a glance. He said, "I see you drained him to help him keep better whilst you waited. Could I see that wire you got on him?"

The undertaker said he'd been expecting someone to ask, and handed over a hand-printed copy of the Western Union day letter they'd just delivered that evening. When he said he had the original on file if anyone doubted his penmanship, Longarm assured him the copy would do the federal law just fine. As he put it away in his frock coat he told them all, "Either this Montana gent who says he might know this dead boy is acting in good faith, or he won't be there at all when we wire Montana to see if he'd like to make a more total statement. Should the more decent kin of only one of the rascals come forward, we'll be on our way to naming the whole bunch! Could I see the other two now?"

The undertaker allowed he surely could, adding that nobody else had shown much interest in them as he exposed their chilled remains to the harsh lamplight. All Longarm could make out was that, like the one who *could* be a wayward Montana lad called Lem Collier, none of them had made it all that far past their twenty-first birthdays.

Staring soberly down, Longarm thought back to a West-by-God-Virginia boy who'd left home early under the impression he was immortal.

He grimaced and softly said, "At least I had a war as an excuse to swap shots with other kids. None of these boys look like they were driven by starvation to train robbing. They look soft and lazy for their age, and they sure as shit didn't know how to handle themselves in a saloon fight with a seriously mean drunk! You say they had stuff in their pockets that seemed to tie 'em into that train robbery?"

Goodman said, "Over to the courthouse, impounded as evidence under lock and key. None of 'em had any identification papers. But they all packed enough cash to avoid any vagrancy charges as long as they were behaving themselves. The one who might be Lem Collier was packing a Schofield .45. These other two were armed with Remingtons, a .44 and a .38. You were right about none of them knowing how to use any gun against the real thing. Witnesses say the youngest one just wailed like a gal and waited his turn as the Calgary Kid blew his pals down like stationary targets.''

He poured himself another drink as he said, "What I still can't get over is why the Calgary Kid didn't want to just brag and put in for the bounty on these dead outlaws.''

Longarm suggested, "They might have been friends earlier.''

But Goodman shook his head and insisted, "Harcourt wasn't riding with them the night of that robbery. He was misbehaving in other ways, right here in town, at Madame Camille's. We already checked his two alibis. They answer to Slitherhips Sally and Frenching Fran. A pair of painted dolls who've never lied to us about anything that serious. According to Slitherhips Sally and Frenching Franny, the Calgary Kid was in no position to rob trains, or even stand up by himself, the night this one boy wound up with all them postal money orders. You can ask the sassy gals if you like.''

Longarm nodded thoughtfully and said, "I would. Percival Harcourt alias the Calgary Kid seems to get along swell with sassy painted dolls, and I can identify at least one of the bunch in the dark, in the manner of Mr. Louis Braille, speaking of French notions!''

Chapter 4

But Longarm felt neither the call nor desire to feel anybody up when Deputy Goodman led him down to the whorehouse to make a sanitary inspection. Madame Camille showed them to a discreet back room and sent a towel gal to fetch some refreshments and the two painted dolls who'd been bedded down with the Calgary Kid on the night of that train robbery closer to Denver.

Slitherhips Sally was too skinny, while Frenching Fran was far too big-assed to pass for either of the painted dolls who'd kidnapped him to screw him silly the night before. Madame Camille was just too plain obese. Her notion of refreshments ran to lager beer and soft pretzels instead of rum punch and pie à la mode.

Longarm got out his notebook and assured all the soiled doves he was sure they'd had no hand in that federal offense against the U.S. mails. Then he took notes as he got them to assure him that the Calgary Kid had been committing crimes against nature right upstairs the night of the robbery.

"He's a fish queer," Slitherhips Sally demurely explained when Longarm asked how it had been possible for one man to spend a whole night with two such attractive playmates.

Longarm knew what she meant, but the bawd explained with no hint of embarrassment, "He likes to eat pussy and sip gin and tonic, by the hour, when he's too tired, or too drunk, to do a gal in a more manly way. He has this game he calls ring-around-the-rosy, where everybody in the bed is sniffing and slurping like a hound dog at someone else's tail.''

''We charge extra for such services,'' Madame Camille said with a disapproving sniff. ''None of my girls are queer-natured. I tell them when they come to work for me that I expect them to shut their eyes, grit their teeth, and give the customers anything that doesn't leave cuts or bruises.''

Frenching Fran nodded primly and declared, ''I can't say I *like* to go down on anyone, even when it's a nice-looking young gent. But so many other gals refuse to, you might say I've found a specialty that pays well and doesn't take near as much out of a girl as being humped by a brute with his boots on in bed.''

Longarm nodded gravely and said, ''I'm just putting down that he has exotic tastes and the wherewithal to pay extra. You say he likes gin and tonic with his slap and tickle?''

Madame Camille nodded and said, ''We had to send out for the quinine water. They stock it over at the drugstore near Town Hall, but nobody else we serve here seems to drink such bitter stuff for pleasure!''

Deputy Goodman suggested, ''The crazy cuss could have caught the ague at some time and place before he got here. Lots of old boys who came down with the ague during the Mexican War are dosing themselves with quinine tonic to this very day!''

Longarm put a question mark in his notebook and said, ''I'll ask when I catch up with him. I have heard that high-toned lime-juicers order gin and tonic just to sound like other empire builders who've been all over Queen Victoria's dominion of palm and pine. I've got more on his bedroom habits than I likely need. I've yet to see a photograph of the peculiar cuss, and no offense, you ladies are in a better position than most to fill us in on any distinguishing marks we might not have on file.''

So the three of them got to work at describing the Calgary Kid. It always jarred Longarm a mite to hear how frankly folks in the sex trade discussed each other's dimensions and bodily functions. But he was a good questioner who didn't let his own judgments show as he took down more about the missing mystery man than his own family doctor might have been able to detail.

A doc might have described him as a taller than average cuss with a pale and flabby-looking torso. But both whores agreed Harcourt was inclined to be brutal right from the start with a gal, and stronger than he looked. That tied in with what others said about his speed with a gun, drunk or sober. The description was that of a self-indulgent cuss with natural athletic abilities he was too lazy to cultivate.

Frenching Fran declared with no sense of shame that the sensuous rascal was possessed of an average-sized dong that was good for two or three shots, in as many gals, before he settled down to a longer session of languid eating and drinking. They described his face as almost nice-looking, save for yellow rat teeth and a constant pout.

Deputy Goodman tossed in, "Light brown or dirty-blond hair, a mite greasy, like he combs it with pomade, and oh, yeah, he has pale blue eyes. Only, one of 'em has a brown patch. The left eye, I think."

Longarm made a note of that. He asked the whores if either recalled whether their well-heeled customer had been vaccinated or not.

They stared at one another blankly.

Longarm nodded and said, "That's one of those details nobody seems to notice because they just don't look for it. I'd best leave that an open question."

Goodman asked, "Ain't most lime-juicers vaccinated, Longarm? Seems to me it was this English sawbones who first come up with the notion of vaccinating kids against the pox."

Longarm nodded. "His name was Dr. William Jenner, and he's saved more folks than Napoleon and every great general since managed to kill. But great generals still rate the statues in town squares for some reason. I like to keep track of vaccination marks because sometimes gents you'd expect to be vaccinated ain't, and vice versa. I exposed a fake Indian medicine man at a glance a spell back. Not even the Indian agent he was making all that trouble for had thought to question why a self-proclaimed Quill Indian had been vaccinated U.S.-Army style."

He made a brief notation and added, "I'll ask about such matters when I talk to the folks at that British trade mission down Denver way. Might any of you ladies have heard Harcourt spouting off about some connection with the British Government?"

Frenching Fran said the Calgary Kid had punched her hard the one time she'd presumed to ask what he did for a living.

But Madame Camille allowed that the pouty young cuss had paid up like a sport, in advance, for the games he played there.

Longarm wanted to know what they thought of the spoiled brat at other such establishments. So Deputy Goodman showed him the way, and they made it over to Aunt Rhoda's just as that passenger train leaving Denver after his way freight hissed to a distant clanging stop to drop off the mail and anyone getting off at Fort Morgan. Longarm smiled to himself as he considered he was a bourbon, a beer, a soft pretzel, and even a few answers ahead of when he would have arrived from a ride that would have felt quicker.

The only things they could tell him at Aunt Rhoda's was that the Calgary Kid liked to play three-in-a-bed no matter what their names might be, never dickered about the prices of such pleasures, and hit gals who asked questions about his finances.

They got much the same rundown at Madame Fishmonger's really seedy sod-walled bordello. Adding up the nights spent at such addresses, it seemed he'd been laboring four to six nights in a row, and resting at the Buckhorn Hotel near the railroad stop to lay slugabed in the daytime.

By this time Longarm was seriously hungry, and Goodman explained that they called the Wagon Wheel a tavern instead of a saloon because a man could eat seriously there while sitting down.

The streets of the small town weren't nearly as crowded now as they headed for the Wagon Wheel and a late supper. As they strode along the darker walk Longarm muttered, half to himself, "It costs money to eat, sleep, and screw whores. What do you reckon the Calgary Kid did for *dinero*—when he wasn't raising Ned, I mean."

Deputy Goodman replied, "He didn't have any job. He was a whole lot more interested in drinking and whoring than card-playing. After we arrested him, my boss, the sheriff, had us ask all around. Harcourt neither kept nor hired no pony at the town livery. Nobody at any of the spreads beyond the outskirts of town recalled any dealing with him. We added up what it must have cost to eat, drink, and be as merry, and it tallied up to a top cowhand's monthly wages blown every week. A merchant who'd cashed a money order for him said it had been made out for twenty-odd dollars.''

Longarm frowned and asked, "*Postal* money order?"

But Goodman replied, "Western Union. We already talked to them. He cashed most of the money orders wired his way at the telegraph office. But sometimes they were short and asked him to come back later. So he cussed 'em and cashed in somewheres else. Western Union was coy about who sent him all them funds by wire. But we got 'em to admit the return address was a Denver furniture outlet. You reckon the Calgary Kid might be a clandestine furniture drummer?''

Longarm allowed the local law was in a better position to judge how many four-poster beds the missing mystery man might have peddled up this way. He muttered, "I thought that one bed had been assembled new. The mattress and bedding smelled fresh and clean to start with. But have you ever had the feeling you had too many pieces to fit into any sensible pattern?''

Deputy Goodman said he wasn't sure he followed Longarm's drift, but that he still could go for something to eat.

So they crossed over to the Wagon Wheel, took a corner table, and ordered a pitcher of suds with corned beef and cabbage.

The waiter who took their order said it would only take a jiffy, and asked Deputy Goodman if he'd met up with that newspaper reporter yet.

The local lawman looked puzzled and asked what reporter they might be talking about. The waiter said, "He said his name was Crawford and that he worked for the *Denver Post*. Said he'd caught that night train up from Denver to do a piece on that shootout we had in here just the other night. Said he was staying at the Buckhorn, and asked directions to the undertaker's so's he could have a look-see at them three dead boys.''

The two lawmen exchanged glances. Longarm nodded and said he knew Reporter Crawford from the *Denver Post*. Smiling up at the waiter, he said, "Beefy gent who favors a checkered suit and five-cent cigars, right?"

The waiter shook his head and replied, "Skinny runt in a black frock coat and matching Stetson. Hook nose and brows as meet in the middle. He wasn't smoking nothing when I

43

spoke with him just a few minutes ago. You gents ready for that corned beef now?"

They said they were, and the waiter left them to thrash it out. It made as much sense one way as it did another. Meaning there seemed no sensible reason for a cuss who didn't look a thing like Crawford of the *Denver Post* to identify himself as the man.

Deputy Goodman growled, "This is getting to be a habit in this neck of the woods. Last night a bare-faced liar showed up, claiming to be you. Tonight we have some hook-nosed midget pretending to be a bigger gent you say you know personal!"

Longarm said, "This latest imposter must not have expected anyone here in Fort Morgan who drinks with Denver newspapermen as often as me. I vote we play our cards close to our vests and just let the cuss hang his fool self with his own fibs. He's bound to come looking for you, seeing he's been asking where you might be."

Deputy Goodman nodded thoughtfully and said, "I follow your drift. What do you reckon he's really up to? Bounty hunter?"

Longarm shrugged and said, "That would explain why he asked his way to those three dead outlaws. But I fail to see how anyone but the Calgary Kid could claim any blood money posted on them."

The waiter returned with their hearty repast. The corned beef and cabbage tasted as good as it smelled, and the chilled beer washed it down with a clean aftertaste that made a man want to swallow more.

Both of them being country-bred, Longarm and Deputy Goodman ate and drank without much conversation. But as they leaned back and lit up, Goodman belched delicately and said, "That mysterious dark dwarf couldn't be after the personal property of those three naked cadavers. Their guns and stuff are all locked away in the vault of the county courthouse. You reckon he could be a real reporter, albeit working for a rival paper and out to sweep your pal Crawford?"

Longarm smiled thinly and said, "Newspapermen call it a *scoop* when they get the story out first. Anything's possible, but like I said, it'll be easy enough to just ask him when and if he comes back."

But as they smoked and sipped suds, with Goodman calling

some of the regulars over to fill Longarm in on the details of the Calgary Kid's fight the other night over by the bar, the runty stranger in black failed to show.

After a time, Longarm snubbed out the last of his smoked-down cheroot and declared, "They say that when the mountain won't come to Mohammed, Mohammed had best go looking for the mountain."

As he rose, Deputy Goodman shifted in his own chair. But Longarm told him, "One of us had best stay here in case he comes by. I'll ask at the hotel, and I was going by the Western Union in any case. I'll be back within the hour, with or without the peculiar cuss."

Suiting actions to his words, Longarm strode first toward the hotel, noting as he did so that the lamps along the railroad platform had gone out, or been blown out, to plunge that end of the street into blackness. He found his way to the Buckhorn Hotel by the soft lamp light flowing from its lobby entrance.

Inside the small trackside hotel, he found an old geezer seated under a paper palm tree instead of behind the mock marble desk. He didn't know for certain he was talking to the night clerk until he asked for him.

The old geezer set his copy of *Frank Leslie's Illustrated* aside and asked what he could do for Longarm.

The tall deputy flashed his badge before he declared, "For openers, I reckon I'd better book me a room for later. I see they've started to roll up the sidewalks and blow out the lights outside."

The ancient night clerk rose from his leather armchair to totter over to the desk as he agreed Fort Morgan was a quiet town on the night of a working day. He added, "Room will run you seventy-five cents and no guests, male or female, after midnight. We run a respectable hotel here."

Longarm said he could see that as he paid up, signed the register, and pocketed the key. Then he said, "I was told a Reporter Crawford from the *Denver Post* might be staying here too."

The clerk nodded. "Room 204, right down from your own. He ain't in now, though. Went out to do a story about that shooting at the Wagon Wheel the other night. The gunslick who put those three strangers away was staying here at this hotel too. He ain't now, of course. Like I told that reporter, a federal lawman came up from Denver to fetch him last night."

45

Longarm allowed he'd heard as much, and excused himself to leg it over to the nearby Western Union office, which was open all night if that lamplit black and yellow sign meant anything.

The lone telegraph clerk on duty was a bit younger but just about as sleepy-looking as the hotel clerk had been until Longarm showed him his badge and offered him a cheroot.

They had the usual dumb argument about company policy before the Western Union man said, "I can tell you one thing without betraying the confidences of a paying customer. It wouldn't do you any good if I could give you the return addresses of those money orders sent here from Denver to your Percival Harcourt. They were faked."

Longarm got both their smokes going as he mildly asked how his newfound pal knew that.

The clerk explained, "A twenty-one-dollar money order was sent to him about an hour after he'd been arrested for his part in that shootout at the Wagon Wheel. Naturally, we couldn't deliver it. So we sent it back to our Denver office. They couldn't return the money to the sender because there was no such place as they'd put down as the return address. You see, when you send money by wire . . ."

"I know how it works," Longarm told him in a weary tone. "Your outfit would have no call to check any return address until and unless a wire was returned as undeliverable. If I take your word on fake return addresses, can you offer me an educated guess on just how much Harcourt was averaging by wire?"

The clerk decided he was betraying no paying customers by telling the law they'd been sending him twenty-one dollars every Monday and another twenty-one every Friday.

Longarm whistled softly and said, "I wish I had a fairy godmother sending me six damned dollars a day! I reckon they spaced it out to keep him from blowing it all over the weekend!"

The Western Union man agreed that it had been more drinking money than he'd have ever sent a mean drunk.

Longarm said, "I have one more question and I want you to tell me true. I need to know whether a short cuss in black with a big nose and mayhaps a fake press pass has been by to ask these same questions about the Calgary Kid."

The Western Union man sounded truthful as he said nobody

46

else had been asking about the Calgary Kid that evening. So Longarm thanked him and headed back to the Wagon Wheel, where he found Deputy Goodman at the same table, holding court with a fresh pitcher of beer, although the crowd had thinned considerably by this time.

Goodman nodded up at Longarm and declared, "He never showed up. I've sent some of my boys out to scout for the skunk around town. They came up empty. Our sly fox has gone to ground. Or maybe he just went to visit someone he knows here in town. At a private house, I mean."

Longarm said that worked for him. Some of the others, who hadn't even seen the small dark stranger, offered other, odder notions. None of them worked any better, though.

Deputy Goodman yawned and said, "If he rides out of town, they'll be able to tell us about it at the livery down by the crossing. In the meantime, it's getting late and my old woman is going to send the kids out looking for *me* if I don't get it on home. Do you have a place to bunk, Longarm?"

The younger and somewhat more wide-awake lawman nodded and thanked the gent for the implied offer as he said he'd hired a room at the hotel. So they shared the last of the beer, exchanged some more bullshit about mystery men in black, and agreed to call it a night.

Longarm was feeling that beer a bit as he made his way toward the hotel along a deserted street that now seemed dark indeed. He froze and went for his .44-40 when something hissed and skittered across his path in a really dark stretch. He had to laugh when he saw it was a cat as big as a terrier chasing a rat as big as a prairie dog.

He put his revolver away, but still feeling lonesome amid the surrounding black shadows, he got out his double derringer, unclipped it from his watch chain, and carried it palmed down at his side lest somebody take him for a proddy galoot who'd been at it too long.

A man who packed a badge had to draw fine lines with his guns. A man made enemies riding for the law. So he had to stay on his toes lest somebody shoot him in the back. But at the same time, he had to avoid drifting past mighty careful into crazy-mean. Poor old James Butler Hickok had gotten wild enough to deserve that silly handle of Wild Bill by the time he'd shot his own pal, Mike Williams, in the tricky light of a wild night in Abilene.

On the other hand, the lesser known but more professional Deputy Marshal Tom Smith had been shot down like a dog by a trash white he'd dismissed as harmless. You just had to keep your damned wits about you and hope you'd spot Mr. Death's grin in time.

Back at the hotel, derringer still palmed in the dim light of the musty lobby, Longarm asked the old geezer whether that Reporter Crawford had come home yet.

The old geezer nodded, but said, "Came in and went out some more. It's a funny thing you just asked about him. He was asking about *you* just now."

Longarm's mouth went a mite dry as he cautiously replied, "Do tell? He didn't say what he wanted with me, did he?"

He wasn't surprised when the geezer said the small dark cuss had only scuttled off into the night. Longarm almost missed it when the night clerk volunteered, "He might look you up in the morning. I told him when he asked that you'd booked a room for the night."

Longarm went on upstairs. That had to make more sense than a late-night stalk along the dark streets of a strange town for a cuss he didn't know on sight.

As he locked himself in, stripped, and slid between the rough but clean cotton sheets, he reflected wryly that even if he caught up with the man impersonating Reporter Crawford, no federal statute was involved. He could ask the obvious imposter what his real game was, and then the son of a bitch would have the same constitutional right to tell him it was none of his damned business. You had to have a warrant, a writ, or probable cause to arrest anybody. The real Reporter Crawford might be able to file a civil suit against another man using his name, unless he'd given another reporter permission to act for him.

Longarm muttered, "Screw it. We'll ask Reporter Crawford the next time we see him. If his namesake busts any civic or county statutes here in Fort Morgan, there's plenty of local lawmen to settle his hash."

Then he was asleep, after a long day that had started out confusing enough. But after not more than a few hours of pure dreamless slumber, he was suddenly wide awake, stomach growling, sure there were more important things to be wondering about than where a man might be able to order a decent bowl of chili at this hour.

Somewhere in the night a train whistle moaned a warning at a grade crossing, and Longarm realized it had to be that Burlington night flyer from Chicago, likely fixing to stop across the way just to swap some mail sacks before it rumbled on to Denver one hell of a lot faster than that way freight had rolled.

"I could breakfast on fried eggs over chili con carne at that all-nighter near Union Station!" Longarm chortled as he threw off the covers and swung his feet to the rug.

It crossed his mind as he dressed that he might be leaving more than one loose end up here in Fort Morgan. But the world was filled with loose ends he didn't have any warrants on, and both the Calgary Kid and that other imposter who'd gotten him out of jail had doubtless hopped that same night train out of this glorified trail stop.

The Burlington night flier was making damned good time. It pulled into Fort Morgan while Longarm was still hauling on his boots and arguing with himself whether to get while the getting was good or poke about some more and catch a slower local closer to noon.

He jumped up and ran for it, cinching his gun rig as he tore down the stairs. He tossed the key in the general direction of the old room clerk as he ran through the lobby and out the door. For across the way, the train had finished its predawn chores in Fort Morgan and was already moving on!

Running like hell, with his mind made up for him as he thought of being stuck there another six or eight hours, Longarm caught up with the brass railing of the observation car's rear platform, just as it was starting to recede too fast, and somehow swung himself up and aboard. He clung to the rail doubled over, panting, until he had his breath under control again. Then he straightened up and slid the rear door open to saunter into the dimly lit interior.

The rear half of the car was filled with armchairs and small side tables, all empty at this hour. A couple of other sleepless gents stood at the bar, near the forward end, jawing with the barkeep over smokes and suds. As Longarm approached, one of them smiled at him and observed, "You sure must have wanted to go to Denver at the last possible minute, pilgrim."

Longarm allowed he'd have a needled beer while he waited for the conductor right there. The barkeep asked if he'd mind paying as he was served.

But things thawed some when the short stubby conductor came back a few minutes later to greet Longarm by name and tell him not to be silly about tickets.

Longarm nodded soberly and said, "We're still working on that last robbery, Gus. I take it you've read our fliers and that you don't have any others on board as suspicious-looking as me."

Gus smiled dryly and replied, "Our porters are watching for bags that feel like they're loaded with heavy newsprint. But you and that other gent who got on at Fort Morgan are the only ones I haven't had my eye on all night."

Longarm cocked a brow. "You say someone else got on back yonder? Might we be talking about a short cuss with a big nose, a black frock coat, and a hat to match?"

The conductor nodded. "Wears his Merwin-Hubert six-gun side-draw and tied down. But I've seen him on this line a lot of times. He must be some sort of business gent who packs enough money along to worry him some. He's never given us any trouble."

Longarm put down half his schooner of needled beer as he quietly replied, "You mean, not as far as you know, Gus. Where's this cuss you're so sure of riding right now?"

Gus stared owl-eyed up at Longarm. "All the way forward, in the smoking car before the diner."

"That diner would be closed at this hour, right?" Longarm asked as he stepped away from the bar.

Gus said that was about the size of it, and then, as one of the other late-nighters started to follow, the conductor softly warned, "Don't. He's a federal lawman and he hardly goes after any sissies!"

When one other apparent passenger insisted, "I'm with Pinkerton and they pay me to go after anybody who needs going after!" Longarm paused in the swaying aisle to half turn and growl, "I'll be proud to write you up for an assist later. But right now I want you to stay out of it, Pinky."

So the railroad detective stayed out of it as Longarm moved on to the next car, then the next, past travelers dozing in coach car seats and others snoring, or giggling, behind the green canvas drapes of the Pullman cars until, farther on, he eased open the rear door of a smoke-filled and dimly lit coach car where most of the few late-night passengers sat smoking or dozing with their backs to him as they faced forward.

But up at the far end a lonely figure in black had shoved one of the reversible backrests against the forward bulkhead to ride with his back facing forward. So he naturally saw Longarm at the same time, and crabbed sideways off his seat to drop into a gunfighter's semi-crouch, his butt against the locked dining car and the tail of his sooty black coat brushed clear of the Merwin-Hubert .45 he packed side-draw in a low-slung *buscadero* holster.

Tied to his right thigh.

As other passengers moved closer to the windows on either side, the far taller lawman moved on along the swaying aisle, calling ahead in a conversational tone, "I've heard it said a side-draw has the edge on a cross-draw in a face-to-face contest on foot. But before we get to acting silly, *amigo mio,* I don't have a warrant on you because I don't know who in blue blazes you are. So why don't we calm down and talk it over like sensible gents?"

The gnomish stranger snarled, "Somebody's ratted on me! Who told you I was headed up this way? How did you know I was fixing to catch the first train out once I knew you were stalking me?"

Then, without waiting for an answer, he went for his gun.

He was good. Damned good. Whoever he was. He had his revolver out of its tied-down holster, and managed to peg one shot into the floorboards between them as Longarm slammed two rounds into him at point-blank range and slammed him back against the sliding door to stare in numb, dying wonder at the tiny derringer smoking in Longarm's big right fist.

As the short, dark gunslick slid slowly down the door, blood streaks following him from the two bullet holes in the hardwood, the lawman who'd just won observed, not unkindly, "I know I never had a chance of beating you cross-draw. But I warned you not to test me, didn't I?"

The mysterious stranger tried to say something, blew some bloody bubbles instead, and collapsed at Longarm's feet like a bundle of black rags with a hat and gun left over.

Behind Longarm, that Pinkerton man called out, "I thought he had you, pard! Who the hell was he anyways?"

It was a good question.

Longarm still had no idea.

Chapter 5

The dead man had been packing close to a hundred dollars and far more identification than he'd have ever wanted to show anyone at one time. It seemed somehow doubtful he was a Mormon elder, a dealer in ladies' notions, or a cattle buyer from Omaha—with as many different surnames. But things started looking up once they had him tidied up for public view at the Denver morgue.

Thanks to a dozen eyewitnesses, including that professional working for the Pinkerton Detective Agency, nobody said anything silly about the shootout aboard the Burlington night flier as they removed the remains from the train when they got into town. The local coroner's office allowed a carbon copy of Longarm's federal report on the cuss would do them just fine.

It was a copper badge working for the Denver Police Department who first suggested the possible identity of the big-nosed runt with a hasty trigger finger. Once they commenced comparing federal yellow sheets with recent police reports, it seemed highly likely Longarm had shot a recent graduate of Leavenworth known along the owlhoot trail as Big Frenchy Moreau, a habitual criminal of some forty summers who'd spent most of his adult life behind bars assuring all the younger cons who'd listen that he was even better than that Mister Fagin in *Oliver Twist* when it came to teaching all the tricks of the crooked careers.

It might have been easier to dismiss Big Frenchy as a cell-block blowhard if he hadn't been packing all that cash along with a serious shooting iron at the time of his demise. Someone dug out another local police report, filed by a Denver detective who cultivated petty lowlifes along Larimer Street. His informer had tipped him off about strange hardcases in town, led by a shrimp with a big nose, who'd been asking around town for a fence willing to pay two bits on the dollar for hot paper.

It got better when someone recalled the late Big Frenchy hadn't been a real Frenchman from France. Longarm sent a wire from downtown before he reported in at the Federal Building to face the music with Billy Vail.

Fortunately for Longarm, Vail had already heard from two of his own street informers, a shoeshine boy and a more dapper pimp who'd been operating in the vicinity of the Parthenon, that one of his own senior deputies had been seen getting into a Berlin coach, with lots of help, in the company of two garishly painted dolls the pimp simply didn't know and a taller tan gent who had been built a lot like the drooling deputy he'd been loading aboard that Berlin.

When Longarm explained he'd been in too great a hurry to report in as soon as he'd escaped, Vail flatly stated, "Don't never do that to this child again. You had us going loco till we heard about you and that dead rascal rolling into town together this morning. The wires we got from Fort Morgan in answer to our simple questions were mighty confusing. So for openers, who do you reckon stole the Calgary Kid from you, that taller cuss with the two whores or the shorter one you shot it out with this morning?"

Longarm sat down uninvited and fished out a cheroot without asking permission as he quietly replied, "Don't put the cart before a bunch of horses and let's eat this apple a bite at a time."

He lit his cheroot, leaned back in the leather chair, and tersely but sensibly filled Vail in on all the confusing events since last they'd been sitting there.

Once he finished, he told Vail, "I never got a sober look at the gent those gals called Hamish. But Big Frenchy Moreau just won't work as the imposter who passed himself off as me, in my duds, with my identification, to sneak that Calgary Kid out of jail up yonder."

He blew a thoughtful smoke ring and explained. "To begin with, the local lawmen who reported Big Frenchy was in town, after I was there, had seen that taller imposter as well. So I suspect Big Frenchy, like myself, was up yonder sniffing around. Say he was a member, or even the leader, of that train-robbing bunch. He'd have naturally been sort of interested in how at least three of them wound up dead on the floor in the Wagon Wheel Tavern. He didn't ask where the Calgary Kid had been getting his own pocket jingle. That might have been because he knew way less than us, or way more. Somebody here in Denver had been wiring a mighty handsome forty-two dollars a week to the apparently idle young cuss. Someone who'd been doing that would hardly see fit to ask a heap of questions about a mean drunk's finances, would he?"

Vail exhaled a thoughtful cloud of his smellier cigar smoke and said, "I follow your drift. A falling-out among thieves might be a sensible reason for the drunk to surprise a trio of his usual drinking pals with a nasty fusillade. A mastermind who'd sent all four of them up the Burlington line to cool off, or get set up for something, would naturally be curious as hell when he heard the four of them had shot it out, allowing the law to recover some of the postal money orders from that recent robbery. But where did this Big Frenchy get off with slapping leather on you, old son?"

Longarm shrugged modestly and said, "Guilty conscience on his part combined with my arrest record, I reckon. Like I was trying to assure him when he drew on me, I didn't have anything on him. I didn't know who he was or what he might have been doing up yonder. But Big Frenchy knew who he was and what he'd been up to. When he heard I was in town he hopped the first train out. When I hopped the same train, meaning him no harm, he added two and two to come up with a dozen and did exactly what I warned him not to do."

Vail rolled the wet stub of his cigar to one corner of his mouth, a habit his wife had been trying to break him of, and growled, "*Bueno.* By pure shithouse luck you seem to have accounted for their leader. For whatever surly reasons of his own, Percival Harcourt alias the Calgary Kid seems to have shot down three more. How many robbers did we agree on the other morning? Betwixt six and a dozen?"

"At least six," Longarm replied, counting off on his fingers with the cheroot gripped in his teeth. "Three on ice up in Fort

Morgan, plus Big Frenchy down at the morgue to make four.''

Vail nodded. ''The Calgary Kid and this mysterious Hamish makes it an even six on this child's slate! Them gals was just gals. Outlaws screw, the same as the rest of us. What'll you bet the Calgary Kid and the pal who saved him are screwing your Ginger and Candy even as we speak?''

Longarm replied, ''One bite at a time, and let's stick with brass tacks we know to be facts. I've been working my way up to Big Frenchy hailing from Montreal. Calgary is up Canada way as well. After that, we have a tentative identification on at least one of the robbers gunned down in the Wagon Wheel Tavern. If he was really Lem Collier, known as a Montana rider . . .''

''I admire a man who can tally bits and pieces!'' Billy Vail said with a fatherly smile. ''Montana is just this side of the Canadian line, and who's to say which side of it a suspected crook might have been born on? Ain't that Canadian rebel, Louis Riel, hiding out in Montana right now?''

''Teaching school. He's a well-educated cuss,'' Longarm replied. ''Old Premier MacDonald wants to hang him for starting that big fuss about his followers' rights in the Red River Valley back in '69. Lucky for Louis, neither President Grant nor President Hayes admired MacDonald's Yankee-baiting political machine in Ottawa enough to send the poor cuss back to face the Queen's justice. But I doubt the late Big Frenchy Moreau had anything to do with Riel's bunch, save for the same French-Canadian grand-folks way back. Riel and his Métis, or Red River Breeds, were left over from the breakup of the Hudson Bay Company holdings in '69–'70. They were the mixed bloods of the Hudson Bay hunters and trappers and their Indian women. Old Louis Riel in the flesh is part Plains Cree. When government survey teams came west to start mapping and platting the banks of the Red River, paying no mind to the six or seven thousand Métis who were already on the ground, the Métis got excited. But despite all the pushing and shoving around Fort Garry, Riel ended up in Montana, where they needed a teacher who could speak English, French, and Cree. I met him a spell back and he struck me as a nice, sensible gent, save on the subject of the North West Territories and who might have been there first.''

Vail groaned. ''Jesus H. Christ. I swear if I asked you to tell me the time, you'd instruct me in watch repair. What has all this recent Canadian history have to do with the robbery of the Burlington night flier the other morning, damn it?''

Longarm exhaled lazily and replied, ''Likely nothing. Canadians from the eastern provinces tend to look down their noses at folks who ain't as purely white. You were the one who brought up Louis Riel and his Red River Breeds, remember?''

Vail moaned, ''I do, and can you ever forgive me?''

Longarm chuckled and said, ''I've already sent a wire to old Crown Sergeant Foster at Fort MacLeod. We've had our differences, but he's not as stuffy about working with Uncle Sam as his current government seems to be. I wired him a night letter so I could put more words in for the same price. He'll likely wire back the same way. But we ought to know by this weekend whether the Mounties have any warrants on either Big Frenchy Moreau or Percival Harcourt alias the Calgary Kid.''

Vail grumbled, ''I'd forgot about that friendly rivalry you enjoy with Sergeant Foster. I've already wired Ottawa, day rates, and Lord only knows whether they've leveled with us or not on Harcourt. Old Sir John MacDonald acts as if he's still sore about the War of 1812. But for what it was worth, they wired back they'd never heard of a Yankee outlaw called Percival Harcourt and that Calgary is little more than a stockaded outpost under canvas. I reckon they missed what I wired them about folks saying he was one of their own.''

Longarm said, ''Old Foster will know why Harcourt's named for a smaller Mountie post, if he has anything on him at all. I met an old boy called Shiloh, riding for the Jingle Bob one time. When I asked him a few questions about Shiloh, it turned out he'd never been near the place. There's no accounting for the names some folks give themselves as they wander through this vale of tears. When do you want me to go up to Montana Territory about the late Lem Collier?''

Vail snapped, ''I don't. I see no reason to expend six cents a mile of the taxpayers' money when Western Union charges no more'n a nickel a word. I've already wired my opposite number in Helena, to see if he'd send a deputy over to interview that possible uncle of the possible Lem Collier at a handy stock spread up the Prickly Pear Valley. We ought to know more about that before we get anything from your Mountie pal at Fort MacLeod.''

Vail hesitated, sighed, and said, "I know I'm likely to regret the asking, but just what does a crown sergeant add up to in our army?"

Longarm took a drag on his cheroot, flicked some ash on the rug for the carpet mites, seeing that Vail was too tight to provide a damned ashtray on his side of the desk, and explained. "The North West Mounted Police are a constabulary force, not a branch of Her Majesty's military. They operate in ones or twos, like us or the Texas Rangers. Those Currier and Ives prints showing columns of red-coated Mounties out on patrol like the U.S. Cav are poetic license. What we'd call a deputy or a ranger holds the Mountie rank of constable. Then they have sergeants the way the Denver police has sergeants. Crown sergeant is lime-juicer slang for the official rank of sergeant major. Foster wears this little royal crown, the same as a British major wears on his shoulders, above his three gold stripes. As the ranking NCO in his district, Foster can eat cucumbers and do wonders neither a common constable nor a prim-and-proper police inspector, supervisor, or whatever could get away with. He'll level with me about the Calgary Kid. We've sort of agreed not to play pranks on one another anymore."

But while Billy Vail seemed convinced, Miss Morgana Floyd of the Arvada Orphan Asylum raised an interesting point as he was stuffing her with bratwurst and potato dumplings at Krieger's Rathskeller that evening.

He hadn't been telling the perky pigeon-breasted brunette about the case because he thought she gave a damn. He'd had to explain where he'd been the past few nights, and she'd cocked a mighty suspicious eyebrow when he'd said Fort Morgan without considering her unusual first name. So he'd gone into more detail than usual, leaving out a few bawdy parts, and the trained nurse and orphan wrangler said she couldn't fathom why he'd come out of that deserted warehouse alive.

The Rathskeller band was playing "Marching through Georgia" in a manner Herr Otto von Bismarck surely would have approved of, and Longarm knew old Morgana expected some dancing and a carriage ride before he took her home to abuse her, as she was inclined to accuse him of doing. But they still had some grub to finish. So he said it seemed to him the gang had simply used common sense.

Washing down some rib-stick, he explained. "They only

wanted the loan of my identity to get the Calgary Kid out of jail, which they did slick as a whistle. The mysterious Hamish was back, likely with young Harcourt in tow, long before I could bust out of there. They'd planned on my being locked in that cellar longer. But even though I got out before they could wire the Denver police to free me . . ."

"Why?" insisted the suspicious brunette, possibly alerted to the devious nature of wicked young gals by some of the pranks her orphans pulled, or tried to, when Morgana was on duty as head matron.

Longarm shrugged and asked, "Why not? Murder is a hanging offense, whilst locking even a federal agent in a cellar overnight could well be sold as some sort of initiation prank to a judge and jury, when or if you were ever caught."

Morgana stared soberly across the table at him, reached for one of his hands, and almost sobbed, "But Custis, they *were* murderers! Some of them, at any rate. That dreadful Calgary Kid sent three other boys to eternity for no reason anyone's been able to come up with! And you just told me more than I'd read in the *Post* about that crazy-mean Big Frenchy Moreau trying to kill you aboard that late-night train! Do either of those murderous fiends sound like they'd have an unconscious lawman in their clutches, and then cater to his creature comforts and even have his suit dry-cleaned for him whilst he lay safely snugabed at their mercy?"

Longarm had to allow the pattern she laid out was sort of crazy-quilt. But he said, "Mayhaps, like some have already suggested, I was dealing with a bunch that had fallen out over methods as well as other things. Say Percival Harcourt and his side, old Hamish and the two sneaky gals, disapproved of the murderous ways of the late Big Frenchy."

"Darling," she said with that sweet voice of reason only the unfair sex could manage, "the Calgary Kid cut down three men without warning, at point-blank range. Are you suggesting he and his own chums sound less murderous than that poor dwarf who panicked when you surprised him aboard that night train this morning?"

Longarm covered his mouth as he yawned and replied, "Lord have mercy, was it only this morning? It feels as if I've been up and on the go for at least a week. What time is it getting to be anyhow?"

"Not *my* bedtime, if that's what you're getting at!" she

demurely replied, as the band switched to a polka and she added that she sure felt like dancing.

So they got up and danced. Then they danced some more. A lot of women were like that.

Longarm knew he had to be a good sport about it. Hence, by the time he finally got the well-danced brunette to the private quarters she kept in town for her off-duty nights, being sort of delicate about her rep, Longarm was sincerely tired.

She naturally made him work some more at loving her up and out of her dancing duds, even though he hadn't slept since three or four in the morning. So when he finally did herd the two of them into her feather bed, tickle her fancy a spell, and finally roll into her welcoming love saddle, she detected a certain weariness in his organ-grinding and naturally suspected the worst.

"You told me you'd talked to a bunch of whores up in Fort Morgan," she exclaimed, even as she hugged him to her with shapely bare legs. "It seems you did more than talk!"

Longarm tried to show more enthusiasm—it wasn't all that impossible with a gal built so fine—and assured her, "You have my word I never messed with any of them Fort Morgan gals. I haven't been doing anything like this since last week, when you said you liked it standing yonder at your dressing table."

She told him to just keep doing her the same way as they both warmed up to the chore. But of course, once they'd climaxed, shared a smoke, and gotten their second winds, she hauled him out of bed by his love handle so they could repeat a stunt she'd read in some book with a plain cover. Matrons at orphan asylums got to read a lot at night once they had all the little bastards bedded down.

Morgana faced her dressing table mirror to bend over and grasp the stool she usually sat on combing her hair and such. Only, now her long dark hair hung down between her bare shoulders as she thrust her naked rump out and up behind her. So Longarm took a marshmallow-soft buttock in each hand, spread them apart, and slid his love-slicked erection up inside her dog-style, while he grinned at them both in the mirror.

He had a mighty interesting view of the lamplit proceedings as they went at it in what she declared a "shockingly brazen manner!" Gals who read books with plain covers tended to talk like that. But they were more fun than the ones who read romantic novels by the Brontë sisters. He found it easy enough to act shockingly brazen with a horny young thing, but moaning sensitively across moors was a hard row to hoe.

Morgana gasped, "Ooh, faster! I can see my naked nipples swinging in time with your thrusts and . . . Do you like it when I move my hips like this, darling?"

He allowed that he'd always wanted to watch a hula dance without all that grass in the way. But then she wanted to lie sideways atop her dressing table so he could move down to one end and do her that way, still standing up but facing her. So he did, and she stared goggle-eyed into the mirror at her side and marveled, "Ooh, it looks like I'm lined up with my twin whilst we both get humped by brutes, and I can see you going in and out of us down there, you horny thing!"

He gallantly allowed her to think all the wild positions stemmed from his own imagination. So a good time was had by all, with Morgana insisting she couldn't see where he got all these mad Gypsy notions as they went at it everywhere but on her ceiling.

He knew better than to ask her if she'd ever tried that. For by midnight he was really tired, and sensed she was pushing it past pure passion into showing off.

She didn't complain when they finally stopped, cuddled together with him still inside her. They must have both fallen asleep that way. For the next Longarm knew, it was sunrise and the fool bed table lamp had burned dry. So he had to light a cheroot with a match as Morgana snored softly with her head on his shoulder, her dark hair spread out across his chest, and the rumpled bedding in wild disarray.

It was a swell way to greet the day, although it was a workday, damn it to Hell. For unlike the beauty sleeping late beside him, Longarm didn't get to shift between day and night duty, or take time off on regular workdays.

He decided to smoke the cheroot down and work up a wideawake call to breakfast before he eased out without disturbing her. But as if she'd sensed his smoking in her sleep, Morgana commenced to nuzzle his neck with her nose as she reached for his wilted virility with unerring aim.

So he snubbed out the cheroot, and by the time they'd come they were both wide awake and she was offering to rustle up some ham and eggs if only he'd stay until noon at least.

Longarm sighed and said, "I'd *never* get out of this bed if it was up to me alone, pretty lady. But Billy Vail does so much damage to the furniture when I show up more than an hour late."

So they settled on just one more quick one after she'd served him a hearty breakfast in bed, and Longarm arrived at the Federal Building no later than quarter to ten. When he reached the second story Billy Vail was waiting for him in the corridor, a sheaf of typed-up onionskins in one hand being waved like a medicine man's rattle as Vail sort of war-danced on his stubby legs and chanted, "Where in God's name have you been? What do you think we're running here, a retirement home for crippled veterans? You should have been here hours ago and the sons of bitches already have a good lead on us!"

Longarm said, "I'm here now. Don't get your bowels in an uproar about the dead past, and tell me what's got you so excited, Boss."

Vail thrust the papers at him and grabbed him by one elbow to spin him around, thundering, "I'll fill you in along the way. You have to get home to your furnished digs, pick up your saddle and Winchester, then hop the noon northbound for Montana Territory!"

As the two of them tore down the stairs, almost head over heels, Longarm mildly protested that he'd thought Vail wanted that Helena District Court to ride out and interview those possible kin of the late Lem Collier.

Hauling Longarm out into the morning sunlight, Vail answered, "I did. They sent a rider out to that kinsman's spread and wired me the results this morning, when you should have already been on the job."

As Longarm raised a hand to flag down a passing hansom cab, Marshal Vail said, "I had Henry type up a copy of their wire for you. But you can read it aboard the train. Suffice it to say, it was awful. Collier's kin—his uncle, the uncle's wife, and two small children—lay dead on the dirt floor of their soddy. Covered with bluebottle flies!"

Longarm asked where all the dead folks were now.

Vail said, "In the Helena morgue, I reckon. They were still tying up some loose ends when they wired the important part. Pay attention and don't horn in on your elders. The stockman, his wife, and likely both kids were gunned down by a weapon

61

firing .442 lime-juicer lead! You have my permit to comment now.''

Longarm whistled softly and said, ''I thought they took that Webley Bulldog off the Calgary Kid after he'd used it to such deadly effect up in Fort Morgan. But sure, a persuasive law-man transporting him to our jurisdiction as a federal witness would naturally be handed the prisoner's personal property. But that Hamish cuss had me at his mercy the other night and never saw fit to finish *me*. So why on earth would he aid and abet his murderous pal in gunning down women and children?''

Vail suggested, ''Maybe he never did. Maybe the imposter who got that Calgary Kid out of jail split up with him after. As to why the kid would go all the way to Montana to gun the kin of a man he'd already gunned in Colorado, that's one of the things I'm sending you north to find out.''

Longarm nodded soberly. ''It sure is commencing to look as if that shootout in the Wagon Wheel Tavern couldn't have been the casual brawl everyone took it for. Say the Calgary Kid demanded something, or some information, he thought Lem Collier had. Say he failed to get it there in Fort Morgan, so he went up to Montana, confronted Collier's kin, and got overexcited again. But what could he be after?''

Vail growled, ''If I knew that I'd never send you all that way at six cents a mile both ways to find out. Henry typed in all the names you want to look up as soon as you get to He-lena. My opposite number tells me they've scouted high and low for anyone who might have laid eyes on a rat-toothed cuss with a brown-spotted blue eye talking with a fancy foreign accent. Meanwhile, since Canada can't or won't tell us any-thing about the cuss, I've sent a cable to Scotland Yard over in London Town. Sir Bobby Peel sure organized his Metro-politan Police in a businesslike as well as fancy manner. They keep thorough records on all their serious felons, and you have to admit a son of a bitch who goes around shooting men, women, and children with a Webley Bulldog is a serious felon!''

They rumbled across the Larimer Street Bridge to the more affordable southwest flats as Longarm mentioned his own night letter to Crown Sergeant Foster, adding, ''You can have old Henry wire me Foster's reply, condensed, if the Mounties don't have anything on him. Meanwhile, Helena is only a few days' ride from the Canadian line, and seeing I'll be up that way with a horse and saddle . . ."

"Don't you dare. That's an order," Vail stated flatly. "In the first place, it's a good week's ride up the Front Range. And after you get there, things are delicate as Humpty Dumpty's ass! Those Red River Breeds are threatening another uprising, Sitting Bull's holdouts are hunkered on the Canadian prairie fussing with the Canadian Cree and Blackfoot as General Terry tries to get them back, the Mounties keep bitching about Montana whiskey runners smuggling firewater across the line to all the Indians in general, and Sir John MacDonald has never cottoned to these United States to begin with!"

Longarm grumbled that that was all the more reason to suspect a killer named for a Canadian outpost might be headed for home.

Then they were overtaken by another hired hack, with both its driver and passenger yelling at them to pull over. As their own driver reined in by a weed-grown vacant lot, they saw it was young Henry from their office. Henry jumped out to join them, panting, "We just got another message from the Helena District Court. It happened just this morning and they're sore as heck about it! A U.S. Deputy Marshal Braxton had been posted at the railroad depot because they figured nobody could be getting around the country that sudden on horseback."

Vail asked for the yellow telegram in Henry's hand. So Henry gave it to him, but still went on. "Nobody knows exactly what Braxton saw or said. Whatever happened, he wound up dead on the platform with two .442 slugs in his back. A train was rolling out as others responded to the sounds of the gunshots."

Longarm and Vail exchanged glances. Vail asked quietly whether they were talking about a southbound or a northbound train.

When Henry answered, "Northbound," Vail told Longarm, "Forget what I just said about Humpty Dumpty's delicate ass. The rat-toothed son of a bitch has killed one of our own and I want you to cut his trail, follow it wherever it might lead, and bring him back dead or alive!"

Chapter 6

Helena was one hell of a place to get to from Denver. But good old Henry had worked out a series of connections, broad-gauge and narrow, that would carry a man more or less in line with the east slope of the Rockies to Prickly Pear Valley and the rough and ready capital of Montana Territory.

Hence a quarter hour before his first train north was due, Longarm was waiting on the platform with his awkward load. The uncertain conditions of the high country to the north at greenup time dictated more possibles than usual, lashed with his Winchester '73 to his McClellan saddle. Henry had warned him some of the transfers might call for sudden movements. So there was no way to check his baggage through to Helena and let others worry about it.

He'd set his baggage at his feet and lit a smoke when Miss Morgana Floyd hove into view, her hair pinned up and all her buttons sedately buttoned, but looking flushed and out of breath as she strode over to him. He kissed her pretty face, as most men would have, but asked her in a puzzled tone how she'd managed to catch up with him, seeing he'd only just found out he'd be here at the depot.

She said, "Your friend Detective James told me you had to go up to the Montana gold fields, and I wanted to tell you I was sorry for ever doubting you, darling!"

Longarm really sounded puzzled as he asked who in blue

blazes Detective James might be and what she'd been doubting him about.

Morgana shyly confessed, "I thought it sounded a little glib to tell a girl named Morgana you'd been sent to Morgan County when you knew she was expecting you to come by."

Longarm heaved an inward sigh of relief, realizing that the mysterious Detective James hadn't mentioned that other gal from the chocolate shop. But that still left a man he didn't know knowing about him and this *other* pretty secret.

Longarm liked to keep his personal life personal, seeing that some gals could be so possessive. He remembered the night he'd spied Morgana seated in the orchestra section at the opera house while he'd been seated in a private box with a wealthy widow gal who never went to places like Krieger's Rathskeller.

He asked her, "What did this cuss who knows so much about where I've been and where I'm going look like, honey?"

Morgana smiled up innocently and replied, "Tall, lean, well-dressed, and clean-shaven, like you'd expect a lawman to look. He said he was a friend of yours. Surely James can't be a hard name to remember!"

He dryly answered, "I recall the reward posters well enough. What else did he tell you about me?"

She shrugged and said, "Very little. He seemed to know all about you, and wanted to know more about . . . well . . . us?"

Longarm blew a smoke ring past her pretty head as he digested that, then cautiously asked, "You mean he was asking personal questions, as to who might be doing what to whom on our own damned time?"

She fluttered her lashes and protested, "Heavens, I'd have never answered *those* kind of questions. He came knocking on my door about an hour ago to ask if you'd left for Helena yet. He said the two of you had been working on the same case and he wanted to speak with you before you left town. I naturally made him tell me what the two of you had been up to, and that's when he confirmed your tale about Morgan County, you poor innocent thing."

Longarm blew smoke out both nostrils and firmly stated, "I haven't been working on anything with any lawman, public or private, by the name of James. He could have gotten your name and address from anyone who knew us from Krieger's, the Paris Cafe, or any of the other places we've been seen together. If he'd guessed I'd be headed for Helena at this very moment, he knew blamed well I wasn't still at your place. So he wanted to pump you, and what did you tell him?''

She stared up big-eyed, and replied, "There wasn't much I *could* tell him, darling! I don't know anything about those train-robbing rascals that hasn't been in the papers. He seemed awfully interested in *me*, now that I think back on it. I mean, just who I was and how I fit into your comings and goings.''

Longarm pressed her for more details. She managed to recall that the so-called Detective James had pressed her about any connection her unusual first name might have with Morgan County. Then, once they'd agreed that that was just a coincidence, he'd pressed her harder about her background as an orphan wrangler in a public institution. She said, "He seemed to feel I ought to have had training as a psychopathic nurse.''

"He must have meant psychiatric. A nurse who was psychopathic would be loco herself.''

Morgana shrugged. "Whatever. He seemed to find it hard to believe we didn't have any crazy kids at the Arvada Orphan Asylum. I told him we sent orphans like that to another home. But he asked how the head matron would know an orphan was touched in the head unless she'd had some training as an alienist. I told him anyone with a lick of sense could tell a really nutty kid from one who was only naughty. Then I gave him the name of the doctor we call in to examine such cases. Do you think I might have made a mistake, Custis?''

Longarm answered simply, "I can't say. I don't know who this other nosy cuss is or what he's really up to. On the face of it, he found out I was sparking a public health worker, added that up with other stuff, and wanted some more answers.''

She asked, "Can I ride as far as Fort Collins with you, seeing I don't have to be back at the orphanage until tomorrow morning?''

It was tempting. But Longarm told her, "I have to run for a narrow-gauge the minute my ride gets there. So all you'd get out of a long sooty train ride would be another long sooty train ride back. I don't think you or anyone else connected with your orphanage could be in any danger no matter who that nosy cuss was. But I'm going to give you a note to a pal with the Denver police, and if that Detective James comes around again, he'll have some questions from old Sergeant Nolan to answer."

He spied the rising coal smoke of the train he had to catch as he scribbled a hasty message in his notebook and ripped out the page to hand her. "Just give this to the roundsman patrolling your neighborhood and he'll get it to my pal at Police Headquarters. I've asked them to keep an eye on your place and question anyone pestering you. So you'd best behave yourself till I get back to pester you some more!"

Then there was just time to kiss her again before he had to get on board with his heavy baggage. She wanted to come after him and hold hands until the train moved on. He talked her out of it, and ducked on inside with his bulky McClellan braced on his right hip. He was glad he had when he spied the ash-blonde in the straw boater and seersucker travel duster, seated down at the far end alone.

He chose an empty seat across the aisle from her and heaved his McClellan up on the overhead rack, lashing it to the brass rails by its saddle strings before he sat down, cheroot gripped between his grinning teeth, to wave through the grimy glass at the brunette down yonder on the platform. Morgana was blowing him kisses and mouthing sweet things at him as the train started up with a jerk. There was no way either gal could have noticed the other. It sure beat all how they always accused a man of straying where he'd never strayed at all. Morgana was sure he'd been fooling with his elderly landlady, and she'd been sure, even while kissing him the night before, he'd just made up that mission to Morgan County. Yet she'd never glanced his way that night at the opera, or asked one thing about those swell chocolates he'd shown up with, after they'd told him at the chocolate shop about the other gent a plumper gal had just left with.

The composed blonde across the way had nothing to suspect him about, of course. He might have seen her around town before. But if he had, he couldn't recall just where. He leaned back in his plush seat and snubbed out his cheroot, lest she find it offensive with all the windows shut. He had plenty of time. It didn't really matter if they ever got past this stage. For he'd be getting off at Fort Collins, and this mutual awareness was enough to take both their minds off the long tedious miles of rolling prairie ahead.

More than one married-up pal had confided to him, over the

67

years, that it wasn't the actual prize of a strange pussy that a tied-down man really missed. It was the festering feeling that even if you met up with strange pussy, you couldn't try for it. You couldn't even *hope* for it. You'd just never *know* if that stenographer gal who worked down the hall was willing to go out on the town with you or not.

Such considerations, along with some lawmen's funerals he'd been to, kept Longarm free to pursue such dreams. And what the hell, if less than half of them panned out, it sure beat hankering without a chance of finding out. He wasn't worried about that gal at the chocolate shop this afternoon. He'd started up with her, it hadn't worked out, and he was still ahead of some poor cuss passing by her shop one night after the other, never daring to more than smile in at her, lest his old lady fetch him a good lick with her rolling pin.

A somewhat older and more travel-worn gal came along the aisle in the wake of a pretty little brat of, say, four, dressed up in a Scotch-plaid outfit with a beribboned Glengarry bonnet. When she spotted the Stetson Longarm was wearing, the little gal stopped, put her hand on her hips, and asked him if he was a real cowboy.

He soberly ticked the brim of his dark hat to her and assured her, "Top hand of the Diamond K, ma'am. They call me West Virginia and I'm off to Montana to dance the hoolihan."

She said Virginia was a silly name for a cowboy and asked what a hoolihan was as her mother pleaded, "Nancy, don't be fresh!"

Longarm smiled up at the harassed young matron to assure her he could handle it. Then he told little Nancy, "Hoolihan is cowboy talk for busting fresh cows or unruly ponies with a tight noose thrown sudden and jerked hard. When you dance the hoolihan with livestock, you gather them all together in a hurry and move 'em out. When you dance the hoolihan with ladies, it means something else. But like you said, I'm a pure cowboy. So we'll say no more about it."

Her mother must not have wanted him to. Blushing like a rose, she herded her Nancy past him out of sight, as the ash-blonde across the way tried not to smile. He admired gals who could keep their thoughts to themselves, like Miss Mona Lisa.

He hadn't meant to embarrass anyone. He'd had no call to add the double meaning of hoolihan. The cute little gal had just caught him off guard with her childish questions. He figured she and her poor young mother had to be from back East. Colorado folks were more used to seeing men wearing riding boots and Stetsons with regular suits on. No Denver kid ever asked him if he was a cowboy.

He stared idly out at the northern reaches of the Denver sprawl as he regretted the opportunity he'd missed to ask little Nancy if she was really Scotch. He knew Queen Victoria and her German Prince Consort had made hitherto forbidden Highland notions fashionable as all get-out, once they'd built that big fake castle in Scotland and had all those royal children running around in kilts and argyle socks. He'd laughed when he'd seen that young crown prince of Prussia in the *Police Gazette,* gussied up like some Highland chief on a visit to his grandmother up at Balmoral. He'd wondered how anyone kept a straight face while royal grandchildren played at being Scotch with German, Russian, even Greek accents. Real Scotchmen talked odd enough, choking on half their words as if they had sore throats and calling each other odd names, such as Ian for John, Tavish for Thomas, and . . . "Son of a bitch!"

"I beg your pardon?" said the handsome gal across the aisle.

Longarm blurted out, "*Hamish* is the Scotch way of saying *James*! How come it took me all this while to notice that?"

The blonde across the aisle smiled uncertainly and asked if he'd been talking to her.

Longarm smiled sheepishly and confessed, "Worse than that. I've been talking to myself and I'm not half as pretty. I wasn't so forward, ma'am. I just surprised myself and let it pop. Have you ever been staring right at something without seeing it, until it was all of a sudden there?"

She allowed that she sort of understood, and asked if he might be able to open her window a crack.

He rose and moved over to her side, but felt obliged to warn her she'd get her seersucker sooty with the glass cracked open to the west. "The prevailing winds blow out across the plains from yonder mountains, ma'am," he said.

She sighed. "It's still so stuffy in here with the sun starting to come through the glass on this side!"

He suggested, "Why don't we trade seats then? I can open the window a crack on that shadier downwind side and you ought to ride a tad more comfortable."

She hesitantly asked, "But what about you? Wouldn't it be

69

better for both of us if we sat together across the aisle?"

He said it sure sounded swell to him. So in no time at all they had her carpetbag up by his saddle with her seated by the slightly open window to the east.

By then she'd introduced herself as Miss Aura Taylor, bound for the Montana gold fields to look into some mining property she owned stock in. She said her late daddy had left her shares in a hitherto paying mine that had stopped sending dividends, even though it was still advertised on the Denver Stock Exchange as a fine investment.

He told her she'd do better hiring an assay outfit he could point her to in Helena, explaining, "No offense, but gents who manipulate mining shares can confuse professional prospectors with some of the tricks they've been known to pull. You don't want to go poking about in your daddy's hole in the ground. You want a licensed assay man to scout it for you, see?"

She did, and allowed she'd be ever so grateful if he'd introduce her to honest mining men who could set her straight.

He was glad they'd be getting off together in Helena. It sounded like a swell way to while away the otherwise mighty tedious trip, no matter how things turned out for them after they got there.

He had no call to lie about his own reasons for helping her get on up to Montana Territory, so he introduced himself to her as a lawman likely on a fool's errand.

They talked some more about her gold mining stock and the little one could do about a bottomed-out mine unless you could prove bad faith. He said she had a good point when she asked if it didn't sound mean to keep selling stock in a mine if it didn't seem to be paying dividends to its original investors.

She knew the old hymn "Farther Along." But they didn't sing it as he got her to agree that stewing about questions nobody could answer before they got there would only make the trip seem longer.

She asked what he was stewing about. He laughed and confessed he was trying not to, but added, "This Russian lady I met up with one time told me about this folk tale from her country. Russian farm folks hold that a human being can learn to talk to the ants, like they were little Russian folks, and get them to swap gold dust from deep in the earth for sugar, grains, and such, if only he can perform a really tough magic chore."

Aura allowed that she'd always wanted to be able to talk to

the ants. So Longarm chuckled and said, "All right. All you have to do is go out in the woods, sit on a stump, and not think about big white bears for a whole five minutes."

She stared blankly, caught on, and laughed in a way that made him think about anything but big white bears as she declared, "In other words, neither one of us are going to be able to put your case or my mining stock out of our minds for very long."

He shrugged and said, "I'm more comfortable fretting about salted gold mines than cold trails. My boss has more faith in me than I have. I don't see how he expects me to cut the sign of a man nobody saw, who left town on another train entirely long before I could board this one!"

She wanted to hear more. He had nothing better to worry about. So by the time their view to the east had given way to greened-up open range, he'd brought her up to date on the case so far.

She agreed it sounded mighty confusing, and allowed that if she'd been in his boots she'd have never left Denver. She declared, "That unknown and undescribed killer must be hours out of Helena by this time. You say some mysterious stranger has been pestering your sweetheart, pretending he was another lawman who knew you?"

Longarm thought back to his recent words, couldn't recall saying anything that certain about any gal back in Denver, and told this one, "The lady he was pumping about me was just a friend and I don't know how well the jasper knows me. But have you ever ridden through sandy country when the plover birds were nesting, Miss Aura?"

She said she couldn't recall such a ride, and asked what on earth it might have to do with the mysterious Detective James.

He explained, "When you're headed for a plover bird's nest mounted or afoot, the momma plover bird flutters into sight, dragging one wing like she's too crippled to fly as she flaps and twitters pitifully just out of easy grabbing range."

Aura nodded and said, "I've heard of mother birds doing that. They want you, or any other beast of prey, to chase after them, away from their eggs or nestlings, right?"

He nodded. "They do, and most times it works. Coyotes, cats, and small boys are inclined to chase old wing-dragging plover birds away from their nests. Experienced egg hunters

71

just let them flutter and start searching the tall grass for that nest.''

She nodded soberly and asked, "Then you think that stranger who pestered that girl in Denver was trying to draw you away from some more important target by behaving so suspiciously?''

Longarm nodded, but grumbled, "I'm still working on what that could be. It's *possible* but hardly certain that Detective James and a cuss called Hamish could be the same plover bird, fluttering up to Fort Morgan to get the Calgary Kid out of jail, then fluttering around Denver to hide the fact they split up, with the kid headed back to his old stomping grounds.''

She said that made a lot of sense.

But Longarm said, "Not when you study on it. If the Calgary Kid had any reason at all to go back to the Prickly Pear Valley and finish off the family of a man he'd killed in Fort Morgan, he'd be mighty stupid to stay there, and witnesses say he or some other killer left after gunning another man in the Helena depot.''

"Brrr!'' she said. "This Calgary Kid sounds like a homicidal maniac!''

To which Longarm could only reply, "I know. So why would his pals keep trying to distract me if he's not only loco but long gone?''

She suggested he could be dealing with a whole gang of lunatics.

He started to object, then declared, "It happens. There was that Bean family in Scotland and the more recent Benders of Kansas. In both cases lunatic parents raised litters of vicious brats and lay for innocent travelers. The Beans lived in a cave by the side of the King's Highway, and the Benders ran what they called a wayside inn on the Kansas prairie. But neither bunch did anything as clever as the pals of the Calgary Kid. They stayed put like spiders catching flies until somebody noticed. Nobody wore disguises or impersonated federal lawmen.''

He steered them back to her less complicated problems, which seemed to have one of two answers. Either the gents running that mining operation were on the up-and-up, or they were crooked. He started to say he wished he could simply ride out to a fixed place on the map and demand a sample from an ore tram. Then he saw he was fixing to run himself in circles after plover birds some more, and wrote down the address of the government assay man she wanted to get together with in Helena.

They had time for sit-down coffee and cake in Fort Collins, but had to run across a rail yard in the foothills for a mountain combination drawn by a narrow-gauge Shay locomotive.

Things went on that way, with him packing her light baggage as well, till they lost count of how many times they'd changed trains to hairpin back and forth across the grain of the Rockies until, along about midnight, with Aura's sleepy head resting on his shoulder, the combination they were on hissed to a halt in the moonlight and their conductor came back to cheerfully announce a rock slide across the tracks ahead, without a prayer of moving on before morning, if then.

As other passengers cussed and grumbled, Longarm asked where they were. It didn't cheer him at all to learn they were just too far from the Wyoming settlement of Lander to walk on in.

As Aura rubbed at her sleep-gummed eyes and asked the conductor to be more specific, Longarm gently explained, "We're about halfway there, up in the mountains where it figures to get colder before sunrise."

He asked the conductor if there was anywhere on board to unroll the bedding from his saddle. The conductor pointed down at the grime-and-spit-spattered flooring between the hardwood seats and allowed it would be at least eight hours before they moved on.

Longarm asked if there might be a settlement or at least a stock spread within easy reach. The conductor grimaced and declared, "Surely you jest. We had to send a crewman up a trackside telegraph pole to get our message out to the world, and like I said, no repair train is about to hazard this section with the dad-blamed mountains spilling spring-thawed boulders at all hours."

He waved expansively at the jet-black window glass. "There's mountain meadow, spruce, and aspen all around out yonder. If I was spreading a bedroll on the slopes, I'd avoid them aspen like the plague, though."

Longarm allowed that he knew about aspen and tick bugs as he rose to unlash and take down his saddle and Aura's carpetbag. When she got to her own feet asking where they were going, he gently explained, "Anywhere less soot-grimed

73

and rock-hard, Miss Aura. If I spread a ground cloth across fresh-sprouted blue-eyed grass, it'll feel almost as soft as a Pullman bunk and you can stretch out under my blankets in your shimmy shirt if you like.''

She followed after him, seeing he had her baggage, but as soon as they were alone on the platform between cars she demanded, "Give me back my things! What kind of a girl do you take me for, good sir?''

He smiled thinly and assured her, "I always take a lady for a lady until she acts different, ma'am. But no offense, you're the one who seems to have the dirty mind here. I never said nothing about getting forward with a lady in a shimmy shirt, or even under the blankets with her, did I?''

She allowed that she was sorry, but asked, "Where *were* you planning to bed down, in that case?''

He shrugged and said, "It don't look like rain. So I'll sleep warm enough in these duds if I just wrap my fool self in the waterproof top tarp.''

So she didn't put up a fight as he helped her down in the dark from the stalled narrow-gauge and led her by one hand up the gentle slope to the southeast. It seemed obvious that the steeper slopes to the northwest were the ones spilling boulders.

Longarm led the way toward a patch of inky spruce he could just make out in the moonlight, knowing nothing serious was inclined to roll out of tall timber at you. As they moved to higher ground, Aura sniffed and asked, "What's that I smell? *Onions*?''

He said, "Blue-eyed grass," making a mental note she couldn't be a native of Colorado, despite her natural way of talking, as he went on to explain. "Blue-eyed grass ain't exactly grass and it ain't exactly wild onions, Miss Aura. We have serious wild onions growing up here in these mountains, big as those scallions they serve in fancy restaurants. Beef critters thrive on blue-eyed grass, albeit dairy farmers try to keep 'em off it. Makes their milk smell odd.''

He put down their baggage and removed the bedroll from behind his saddle's cantle. He unrolled it across the pungent sod, removing only the top tarp and setting the spare duds and such to one side as he told her, "There you go. Would you like me to open you a can of pork and beans, or tomato preserves, before you turn in?''

Aura laughed weakly and declared she hadn't known she was this tired until she'd been offered this heavenly opportunity to just lie down and die. So he told her to go ahead, and moved up the slope out of sight in case she wanted to take some of her duds off.

Since he couldn't see whether she was undressing or not, he had no way of knowing. He spread the one tarp he had on the grass, and sat cross-legged on it to remove his guns and empty his pockets of hard lumps. He put everything but his gun rig in his overturned Stetson. He folded his gunbelt so the grips of his .44-40 rose handy as a snake's head from its coils near his hat. Then he smoked a cheroot, staring absently down at the dimly lamplit windows of their passenger-freight combination as he wished they'd get cracking on those horseless carriages they kept predicting in the *Scientific American.* For he had too much ground to cover on horseback, and these infernal rails didn't run half the ways a man might want to go!

That son of a bitch who'd gunned his fellow deputy was gaining one hell of a lead on him, while all he could do was blow smoke out his nose like a bull mired in quicksand.

He warned himself to stop snorting like a critter and consider the disgusting situation like a trained lawman. Dumb critters such as bloodhounds trailed by sniffing for footfalls. A good human tracker thought ahead. He didn't search for a dotted line to follow. Few outlaws or even clever deer were inclined to leave that much sign. You had to guess where the man or beast you were after might be *headed,* and then get there first.

Longarm took a thoughtful drag on his cheroot and muttered to himself, "Two can play at sending telegrams, and by now our momma plovers down in Denver will have wired the son of a bitch, wherever he went, that I'm this far behind him. That sneaky Detective James or Hamish *told* Morgana I'd be catching that train out earlier!"

He snubbed out his smoke, wrapped himself in the tarp, and tried to count sheep instead. He wound up counting back to decide exactly how many gals he'd laid so far. He kept losing track and having to go back for one-night stands after he'd gotten past the first few dozen, but that worked as well as sheep to take a man's mind off his real worries. So after a while, someone was clanging a brass bell in the middle of his swell dream, and Longarm sat bolt upright in the early dawn light and groaned, "Time to rise and shine, I reckon."

He hastily refilled his pockets, strapped on his .44-40, and put on his hat to stride down the slope, folding the dew-dampened tarp as he did so.

Tossing the tarp aside near his saddle, Longarm knelt to gently shake the sleeping Aura's exposed bare shoulder.

She whimpered, "Please don't spoil it, Custis!"

So he never did. He just woke her all the way up and told her they'd best get back aboard their train. Then he moved off to let her dress under the blankets. When she called out she was ready, he returned to help her to her feet.

She said, "I'm sorry I fussed at you like that. But in my sleepy state I fear I missed your gentlemanly intent."

He assured her he'd remember she was a lady, and he managed to do so all that long tedious day along the twisty rails through the high country. For whether they ever got closer or not, thinking about it, as her body odors got ever more pungent, sure beat counting telegraph poles.

Chapter 7

They got into Helena along about mid-afternoon, aboard yet another broad-gauge, over twenty-four hours after leaving Denver. They were both soot-stained and as smelly as lost sheep by that time. So Longarm took her to the Big Belt Hotel across from the depot and registered them in separate rooms with baths. As he carried her carpetbag into her hired room for her, he suggested they meet downstairs at supper time to compare notes. He said he was sorry, but he was just too busy at the moment to go after gold-stock swindlers with her.

She allowed that his note to the assay man would do fine, told him he was a dear, and stood up on her tiptoes to kiss his unshaven, soot-grimed cheek in a sisterly way.

Later, he told his pecker not to be silly when it rose like that, slicked with soap, as he washed more soot out of his hide in a warm tub than he ought to have picked up shoveling coal all the way.

After running a fresh tub of rinse water and getting out with it only light gray, Longarm dried off and put on a fresh work shirt with clean jeans and a denim jacket. He knew the boys back at his Denver office might say he'd been foolish to travel by steam in his only good suit. On the other hand, he now had a swell excuse to dress comfortably on duty while he had his filthy tweed dry-cleaned. A man had to think ahead when he rode for a reform Administration that served lemonade to grown men visiting the White House, for Pete's sake!

Longarm knew the same sniffy regulations required him to make a courtesy call on Billy Vail's opposite number up this way before he poked about. But he just pinned his badge to the wilted lapel of his denim jacket, lest someone take him for a saddle tramp packing a .44-40 in plain view, and carried his travel-stained suit downstairs to scout up a tailor who'd clean and press it.

He headed next to the nearby Western Union, where sure enough, the wire Crown Sergeant Foster had sent to Denver had been relayed up this way by good old Henry.

Reading the Mountie's laconic reply to his own questions, Longarm saw they didn't have anyone on their wanted lists who answered to the Calgary Kid or Percival Harcourt. Foster assured him nobody by any name had deserted their smaller outpost at Calgary. The Mountie added that there was nobody else but Indians camped within miles, and asked how anyone could have been born and raised in a place barely five years old to begin with.

Longarm borrowed a pencil stub and telegram blank to suggest you didn't have to be born and raised in a place to be named after it. He asked some questions he hadn't thought of the last time, and told Foster not to be so impolite to a fellow lawman if he knew what was good for him and his sissy outfit.

The part of Foster's wire inspiring Longarm's ire looked as if it had been tacked on as an afterthought, or maybe by someone's order. It read:

BE ADVISED MONTANA BORDER HAS BEEN CLOSED TO EVERYONE PRO TEM BECAUSE OF VERY UNSETTLED CONDITIONS INVOLVING HALF BREEDS COMMA THREE FULL BLOOD NATIONS AND DELETED BY WESTERN UNION YANKEE GUN AND LIQUOR RUNNERS STOP IF YOU ARE DETECTED NORTH OF BORDER WE SHALL BE FORCED TO ARREST YOU STOP FOSTER SERGEANT MAJOR NWMP FORT MACLEOD

After he got off his impolite reply to that, Longarm still needed two days' worth of shaving. So he found his way to a barbershop and let the barber and other waiting customers ask all they wanted about his badge, gun, and reasons for visiting their fair city.

Everyone who'd been anywhere in town the day before had naturally heard all about the shooting at the nearby depot. Longarm heard more versions than he really needed to, once it was agreed that nobody had seen who shot Deputy Braxton.

Still waiting his turn, Longarm tried switching the conversation to the troubles he'd heard they were having up along the border, and hit pay dirt. He barely had to prod anyone as he enjoyed a hot towel shave and a lot of small-town gossip.

One local rider opined, "Serves that stiff-necked Sir John right. Them Red River Breeds have offered to take out homestead claims and such since they moved northwest to the forks of the Saskatchewan. But he keeps pretending they ain't there, all *six thousand* of 'em. So now Louis Riel's closed that school up around Saint Peter's Mission, whilst some say he's slipped back to Canada to organize a second uprising. Whether it was Riel or one of his lieutenants, they say them Métis have stirred up their Plains Cree relations with promises about plenty of firewater and white pussy come that great-getting-up-morning when the bunch of them take over!"

Another Montana rider chimed in. "The Plains Cree may not be the half of it. Sitting Bull and his unreconstructed Sioux are still squatting up around Legare's trading post near Wood Mountain. So far, the Sioux ain't joined up with the Cree, and can't get along with the Canadian Blackfoot at all, but there's close to five thousand of them Sioux, fifteen hundred of 'em fighting men just spoiling for trouble with most anyone!"

A sport who wore a derby and high-button shoes protested that he'd heard the Blackfoot had *ridden* with the Sioux at Little Big Horn.

Longarm had a hot towel over his face. So he let another old Indian fighter explain, "Them was Blackfoot Sioux, or Sihasapa, regular old Sioux who wear black moccasins. The real Blackfeet or Siksika don't join up with *nobody*. They don't *like* nobody!"

Another Montana rider volunteered, "Mean Injuns, them Blackfoot. I hear the Mounties have been trying to keep them from buying firewater and repeating rifles to go with their dispositions. That's likely why they've closed the border from the Divide to the Red River. Sure is shaping up to be an interesting summer up yonder."

Longarm didn't join in the laughter. He knew folks he was

fond of on all the sides mentioned, and it sure seemed somebody was fixing to get hurt!

The recent history of the Canadian West had been far less dramatic than the American West's. There wasn't nearly as much of it, and when Ottawa clamped down at all it clamped *hard*. They didn't change their Indian policy with every election, and there was none of that bullshit about feeding them in the winter and fighting them in the summer.

Up to ten years or so back, the vast spaces between the Great Lakes and Rockies had been the private property of the Hudson Bay Company, a chartered trading monopoly with an Indian policy that had been easy for anyone, red or white, to grasp. If you wanted to swap hides and furs for sugar, salt, gunpowder, and mighty nice blankets, you were welcome to do so at any of their scattered trading posts. If you tried to *raid* those trading posts; the Hudson Bay boys would track you all the way home and blow holes in you. Some Jesuit Black Robes were allowed to set up missions, mostly for the second-generation breeds of the company's white trappers and their squaws, or *eskwas* as the western Algonquin speakers said it.

But as the sprawling North West Territories commenced to fill up with more folks, the Canadian Government back East had bought out the governing powers of the Hudson Bay Charter and organized three or four hundred North West Mounted Police to uphold the Queen's justice.

Longarm had worked with the Mounties. They did a fair but firm job, especially next to the U.S. Bureau of Indian Affairs. They left the Indians alone as long as they were behaving themselves. When a Canadian Indian took it into his head to count coup by lifting a horse or some hair, the Mounties charged *him,* not his nation, with being a horse thief or a murderer, and dealt with him accordingly, after as fair a trial as any other Canadian was entitled to. He'd heard tell that poor old Tatanka Yatanka, or Sitting Bull, had been mighty confused when he'd led his Lakota survivors north and petitioned the Canadian Government for new status as Canadian Indians. A Mounty had ridden in alone to sternly explain that there were no such folks as Canadian Indians. Just plain Indians were allowed to camp and hunt where they didn't seem to be in anybody else's way. If the Lakota wanted to trade hides and robes for supplies at the nearest trading post, the Grandmother Victoria wouldn't mind. But she wasn't going to *give* them *shit,* and she'd be cross as an old she-bear if they caused any trouble to any of her other children.

By the time the barber had finished with him, Longarm had put the tense conditions to the north aside. Old Foster had told him not to head up that way, and so far, he had no evidence the man he was after had headed back to Calgary.

Feeling far more presentable, Longarm dropped by a beanery to stoke up on some fried hash and black coffee. He knew what would be coming next, and dry heaves were uncomfortable as hell.

When he finally reported in to the Helena District Court, Billy Vail's somewhat younger but no more indulgent counterpart said it was about time he showed up. Then he sent Longarm over to the morgue with a junior deputy while he scouted up the hand who'd found the bodies.

All four bodies in the cool cellar had been stripped naked for the usual Y-shaped autopsy incisions. Sewed back together with butcher's twine, the four of them wore little embarrassed smiles, as if they knew live gents were peeking at them.

Old Jingles Jim Collier and his handsome but careworn wife had little blue holes in their naked chests. The morgue attendant explained the two kids had been shot in their backs, likely as they'd run for it, and asked if Longarm wanted them turned over.

Longarm shook his head gently as he stared down at the boy of about nine and the just-budding gal of maybe thirteen. Her little perky breasts and the light brown peach fuzz between her skinny legs hinted at wonders the world would just never know now. He said he'd take the coroner's word they'd been shot from behind, and asked if anyone had kept the bullets.

They had. All four of the Colliers had been shot with an English-made .442, a tad heavier than Longarm's side arm, but lighter than the .45 U.S. Army issue. The morgue attendant volunteered, "Armenian George picked up some .442-short brass when he was out at the Collier place. It's over at the courthouse, though."

Longarm was just fixing to ask who Armenian George might be when a dark, husky cuss came down to the cellar to stick out a hamlike fist and declare he was U.S. Deputy Marshal George Mandalian, the lawman who'd found those dead folks for the Helena District Court.

Longarm shook, but asked, "How come? Do you ride door to door in these parts to make sure everyone's all right?"

Mandalian shook his oversized head and explained, "Folks riding in from Prickly Pear Valley told us something about the Collier spread looked odd. The ponies in the corral were acting frantic for water, with their trough bone-dry. The hogs out back had busted loose. You can't keep hogs in *any* sort of pen if you don't slop 'em regular."

Longarm allowed he followed the local lawman's drift. So Mandalian asked if he'd like to ride out to the scene of the crime, seeing they could likely make it yonder and back by sundown.

None of the dead folks in this cellar had told him much. So he said Mandalian's offer suited him fine.

Armenian George led him around the back of the courthouse to their remuda, and loaned Longarm one of their stock saddles to save him going back to his hotel. Longarm mounted the cordovan mare they'd chosen for him with a certain wariness. But they were good old boys who hadn't set out to green a hand from another jurisdiction with a bronco.

The Prickly Pear Valley you rode up from Helena was drained by a tributary of the Missouri and looked it, the water running muddy as coffee and cream before it was even out of the high country.

There was far more bunchgrass and sagebrush than cactus growing to either side of the dusty trail. Early settlers had likely found the widely scattered *opuntia* or *tuna* more exciting than sagebrush, although if the truth were told, the species grew mighty puny up this way, where the winters were bitter instead of dry. Most greenhorns who got stuck with cactus thorns in the Rockies did so squatting bare-ass in the grass to take a crap. The dwarfish one-or-two-pad *mountain* cactus made up for its short stature with long spines.

As they rode along, Armenian George pointed out some black Cherokee beef stock and said, "Them's Collier stock. Free-ranging. Lord knows who owns them now. We haven't been able to locate any next of kin."

Longarm nodded and said, "It was Jingles Jim Collier who contacted us about possible kin in the Fort Morgan morgue. What can you tell me about the late Lem Collier?"

Armenian George grimaced and replied, "Lazy, ungrateful pup. Word has it the boy had gotten in trouble in other parts.

82

So Jingles Jim took him under his wing as a yard hand and occasional rider. Like the other smallholders in this valley, Jingles Jim only raised fresh beef, pork, and produce for the local miners and their families. So despite some fretting about being handed a shovel, young Lem only got to drive stock into town on horseback now and again. What are the two of us reining in for?''

Longarm twisted in the borrowed saddle to peer back along the trail they'd been following. The sun was low in the west and the shadows had gotten longer. But he decided, ''Just proddy, I reckon. I don't see any company back yonder. But have you ever had this feeling somebody unfriendly was staring at the back of your neck?''

Armenian George said, ''Nope. But my granddaddy had the gift in our old country. Got the family out just as the Turks were fixing to start killing Christians again. The Turks are prone to do that every now and then. Lord knows why.''

Then he peered ahead in the tricky light, cussed, and spurred his mount forward at a gallop. Longarm perforce loped after him, and as they rode through stirrup-deep sage toward a cluster of sod and lodgepole-pin structures situated between the shallow river and the dusty road, Longarm saw a mule-drawn dray in the dooryard, with an old lady and two raggedy young gals loading house furnishings into it.

As the two lawmen reined in, Armenian George yelled, ''Don't you go trying to tell us you can't read, Mother Graham. When the county impounded that property they sealed the durned door with a notice posted across the crack. Couldn't you wait until the Colliers were in the ground to rob them, you ghoulish old gal?''

The elderly white-trash woman took the corncob pipe from her toothless jaws and innocently replied, ''Me and the girls only came by to see if there was anything we could use that nobody would care about. We haven't found any money or real silverware, dad blast it.''

Mandalian heaved a vast sigh and said, ''We ain't got time to run the bunch of you petty thieves in. So I'll tell you what we're going to do out this way. Are you listening to me, Mother Graham?''

She said she was. One of her daughters or granddaughters coyly raised flour-sack shift to show them what she had under it. Mandalian said, ''Cut that out, Willie Mae. When we get back to town I aim to report all this to the county clerk. He'll likely send a sheriff's deputy out here. If you've put everything back exactly as you found it, you might not go to jail. If you don't, you're *sure* to. Have I made myself clear?''

He must have. Mother Graham told Willie Mae to cover her fresh snatch and start moving stuff back inside.

It made it a bit awkward for the two lawmen to poke around for sign in the stripped-down soddy. But Mandalian assured Longarm he'd gathered up such evidence as there'd been to gather.

He said, ''The bullets were in the bodies and all the empty brass was just inside the door, where the killer reloaded. It would have been a big help if he'd carved his initials in the door, but he never did. You can see how tough it is to read footprints in that tamped clay floor. You want to look around out back? The hogs and free-ranging chickens were long gone. I turned loose the ponies to fend for themselves down by the river. The cesspit under the outhouse was dry. Nobody had shit for a couple of days as far as I could tell. The coroner says it's tough to say how long a body's been cooling in this high dry air at this time of the year. But we know the killer was still in town to gun Deputy Braxton two evenings ago!''

''Assuming we're talking about the same killer, you mean,'' Longarm pointed out as they returned to their tethered mounts out front.

Armenian George swung his beefy bulk into his saddle before he grunted, ''What are you talking about? Four folks get gunned down by a killer with a .442. We fan out to look for strangers in town with side arms of that description and poor Deputy Braxton gets lucky. He was shot with the same unusual ammunition. Add it up.''

Longarm did as they headed back to town in the soft light of the high country gloaming, the sage casting long purple shadows where it wasn't glowing like old gold in the slanting rays of the sunset.

He said, ''Tell me more about the late Lem Collier when he worked here for his aunt and uncle. This would be the very road he drove the beef to town along, right?''

Mandalian shrugged and said, ''I reckon. Him, the Dillon brothers, and that Lime Juice Kid he hung around with. The four of 'em together were barely enough for one cowhand. But Jingles Jim was generous and knew they could use the work.''

Longarm nodded soberly, and pointed back at the women putting things back together at the Collier spread as he said, "It's ever thus around mining camps. Wages are higher than usual, if you manage to get a job. But prices are higher than usual whether you have any job or not. You're sure this other one was called the Lime Juice Kid, not the Calgary Kid?"

Mandalian shrugged and replied, "I never paid that much mind to him. Now that you mention it, I reckon that English boy *did* want them to call him California, Calgary, or mayhaps Cauliflower. No grown men paid that much mind to him. The only grown women who called him anything were the whores down by the freight yards, who called him sucker. He was a caution when it came to playing three-in-a-bed. We thought for a time he might be an owlhoot rider enjoying his ill-gotten gains. But it turned out he was getting money orders from somebody down Colorado way. We figured he was only tagging along with young Collier and the Dillon brothers because he liked to play cowboy. He couldn't rope for shit, but anyone who can set a pony can herd a few head along a damned road."

Longarm nodded soberly and declared, "The worthless wretch you've described has to be the same mean drunk. When was he putting in all this apprentice time with Lem Collier and these Dillon boys?"

Mandalian thought. "Summer before last, I reckon. The four of 'em had some sort of falling-out. The Lime Juice Kid was the first to leave, sudden, after pegging a backshot at Lem Collier and *missing*. That's how come we know the stuff we do about the ornery kid. We were expecting to find him dead in some ditch, with both Lem and his uncle after him along with both the Dillon brothers!"

Longarm asked if anyone could say what the surly young whoremaster and his occasional playmates had quarreled over.

Mandalian nodded soberly. "Yep. Edith Alma Collier, the daughter of the family."

Longarm blinked in dismay. "That poor little skinny girl-child in the morgue? She couldn't have been twelve a good two years ago. The Calgary Kid has to be at least twenty-five. He'd have been way too old for her!"

Mandalian said, "I reckon that's what Lem Collier told him. Her dad went after him too once he'd pegged that wild shot at Lem. A spell later, when Lem and them brothers left town of a sudden, a mess of folks said they could be going after the Lime Juice Kid for leaving Edith Alma in a family way.''

The heavyset deputy spat as if disgusted with small-town gossip, and added, ''She wasn't. Died a virgin, according to the doc at the morgue. I reckon Lem Collier being killed with all them postal money orders on him shows what they were *really* after. Like you just said yourself, prices are high out our way when you don't want to work at no steady job.''

Longarm pursed his lips thoughtfully and allowed, ''We might well have read that shootout in Fort Morgan ass-backwards. Tell me more about those Dillon brothers.''

Mandalian shrugged and said, ''I told you. Assholes. Came west to get rich quick but couldn't hold steady jobs. Before they had their falling-out, all four of them liked to get gussied up like top hands on payday. Silk bandannas, woolly chaps, and such. The Dillon boys had no kin in these parts and looked mighty ordinary, when they weren't playing cowboy.''

As lights commenced to wink on in the town ahead, with the valley almost dark now, Longarm asked if there was a photography studio a man could find open after sundown.

Mandalian said, ''Sure. Near the stockyards. Lots of cowhands with a little silver to rub together like to send their pictures to their Eastern kin. You'd be surprised how many old boys out this way began as farm boys east of the Big Muddy.''

Longarm said, ''No, I wouldn't. I'm one of 'em. Hardly any of the white folks *born* out this way have had time to grow up yet. So let's hope those even younger Western riders had their pictures took, and then let's hope your local photographer keeps his glass negatives!''

As it turned out, the tall cadaverous gent who'd make you a set of sepia-tones for seventy-five cents was able to help them, once he got over the sorrow of two whole riders coming in after sundown with no desire to be photographed in front of a painted landscape.

He recalled Percival Harcourt by name, seeing he'd been the one who'd treated himself and his three pals to heroic portraits with the studio supplying buffalo guns and a stuffed buffalo.

Better yet, he had kept the negatives. Sports like the Lime Juice Kid were inclined to come back for extra prints.

As he ducked into his darkroom to run some off for them,

Mandalian sighed. "They told us you were good. You must think we were stupid as hell not to have thought of this, right?"

Longarm shook his head and said, "I've been at this a spell. I ain't sure we get smarter as we get older. But we do gain experience, and this ain't the first time I've asked for help from a small-town photographer. I disremember who the older lawman was who told me lots of owlhoot riders like to have their pictures took. But *somebody* must have, and now you know the secret too."

He'd asked, and offered to pay, for three full sets. One for himself, one for the Helena District Court, and one to send south to his home office. That added up in the end to quite a profit for the now mighty friendly photographer. For he developed prints showing the four former pals together and individual close-ups of the undistinguished idlers.

When the photographer spread the still-damp sepia-tone prints on his glass countertop, Longarm needed little help with identification.

Pointing at one close-up, he declared, "That's Lem Collier. His uncle was right. That was him on ice down to Fort Morgan. This one and this one were keeping him company in the same morgue. All three had been shot with a .442 Webley Bulldog. So this last one ought to be the one who gunned them, right?"

Mandalian nodded and said, "This one's Dave and that one's Steve Dillon. They called this other bastard the Lime Juice Kid."

"Or the Calgary Kid," Longarm pointed out, noting you couldn't see what sort of teeth the plain-looking rascal had, or any discoloration in either eye in monochrome. But at least he now had a real face to go with his mental picture.

As he paid the photographer Longarm mused to Mandalian, "Ain't it a bitch how, try as we might to avoid it, we form our own picture of a man we're tracking? I could have passed this murderous son of a bitch on the street without a second glance up to now. Thanks to his liking to pose with stuffed buffalos, I'll be able to spot him in a crowded saloon!"

As they were leaving, he handed Mandalian one set for the local law.

He put the others in a jacket pocket. Then they rode over to the corral behind the courthouse to see the ponies were well tended to. Mandalian asked if there was anywhere else Longarm needed to be led to. Longarm said he knew the way to the Western Union and his nearby hotel. He added he was packing it in for the night once he'd wired home what he'd learned so far. So they shook on it and parted friendly.

At the telegraph office, as Longarm was composing a night letter, the Western Union clerk on duty told him they were holding a message for him from the North West Mounted Police.

Longarm accepted it and offered the night man a cheroot. After the two of them had lit up, he read good old Foster's answer to the last wire he'd sent to Fort MacLeod.

It read:

NWMP STILL ISSUED WEBLEY REVOLVERS AND MARTINI DASH HENRY CARBINES STOP WHY DO YOU ASK QUESTION MARK FOSTER SERGEANT MAJOR NWMP FORT MACLEOD

Longarm nodded thoughtfully, got back to work on his report to old Billy Vail, and thought about Foster's wire some more as he strode on back to the Big Belt Hotel in the gathering darkness.

Percival Harcourt had left little impression up Canada way, whether he'd bought, borrowed, or stolen that Canadian-issue .442, and had made not much more of an impression here in Helena, before he'd started acting uglier. His drinking and whoring in Fort Morgan, together with a well-deserved rep as a mean drunk to be avoided, had resulted in his being called what he'd always wanted to be called, the Calgary Kid. Had the would-be Western bad man only read somewhere about that wild and woolly outpost at Calgary? Deadwood Dick had been a dime-novel range detective to begin with. But Longarm had met at least two flamboyant barflies who'd assured him they were the dangerous Deadwood Dick.

He'd almost forgotten Miss Aura Taylor. But when he got to their hotel he found her pacing the lobby having changed her dress and looking mad as a wet hen.

The pretty ash-blonde managed a relieved smile as she caught sight of him, though. "Custis, where have you been? I've so much to tell you, and I'm famished besides!"

He sheepishly told her she should have supped without him,

explaining he'd uncovered more on the Calgary Kid than he'd hoped for.

She said, "You can tell me about it over supper. I didn't care for the dining room next door at all. I simply don't see why anyone would care to sup with dead elk, deer, bighorn sheep, and even buffalo looking down from the walls all around."

He said, "Well, there's a fair hash house over by the depot, if you don't mind simple fare."

She dimpled up at him. "I've already spoken to the kitchen help here at out hotel. They said they often serve guests upstairs in their own rooms. Oh, Custis, wait till you see the view!"

He didn't argue, and she stepped over to the desk to give the order to the old female night clerk, who laughed in a dirty sort of way, but allowed she'd see that the waiter knocked before entering with the table on wheels.

So Aura was set for the stairs. But Longarm stepped over to the counter to ask if they sold stamps. When the clerk allowed they sure did, he helped himself to some hotel stationery on her counter, used her sign-in pen to compose a brief note, and put it in a hotel envelope with a set of those prints he'd just paid for. He addressed it to Billy Vail and asked where the nearest letter drop might be.

The friendly old gal said she'd see his letter left early in the morning with the rest of their mail. So he thanked her and followed Aura up the stairwell.

She naturally asked what all that had been about as she showed him into her room. There was just enough space for a supper table on wheels by the open window. He tried not to stare at the bedstead taking up a third of the space.

Aura shut the door without striking a light, and led him over to her window as he told her he'd just found some pictures of that wild and woolly Calgary Kid.

She pointed out to the east, saying, "Look! Have you ever seen a more heavenly sight?"

She was pointing at the Big Belt range to the east of the Montana gold fields. He could see why she was. In Denver the sun went down *behind* the Front Range, making for pretty sunsets with the jagged peaks black as a whore's future. But up here, with snow still lingering on the higher crags and the last red glow from the west rendering them pink against the deep purple sky to the east, the Big Belts did look mighty fine.

She said, "It's so soft and romantic, and I've so much to tell you! I've had ever such encouraging help from that assay man you told me to see. I don't know how I'm ever going to be able to thank you, you dear shaggy brute."

He smiled uncertainly and asked, "How come I seem shaggy, Miss Aura? I just had a professional shave, after a good hot bath, and there's not a tuft of shag sprouting out of these clean denims."

She dimpled up at him sweetly. "You're still like a big shaggy dog that tends to grow on a girl after she's sure it's not as growly as it looks. You've been ever so kind and helpful ever since we met, and I'm not nearly as nervous around you as I was earlier."

Then she rose on tiptoe to kiss him, and he, being a natural man, kissed back. But before he could ease her over to the bedstead, their damned supper arrived on wheels, so it was over an hour and a half before he ever managed to get Aura Taylor in that fool bed with a pillow under her sweet ass.

Chapter 8

"That was lovely, darling," Aura was saying as he lit a cheroot in bed to share with her. He had no call to argue with her. She was a warm-natured gal who just moved naturally under a man and didn't seem to need any acrobatics to inspire her. It had felt as if he'd gone to bed with an old pal, like that rich young widow on Capitol Hill who screwed more fondly than passionately, taking her time to climax and not too worried about getting there. A lot of gals who'd been married up with a man they liked were like that in bed. Aura wore no ring. He figured she'd tell him about her past if she wanted to. It was starting to look as if she might have one.

As they passed the cheroot back and forth, she filled him in on more of the details of her own mission to Helena. She'd been assured at the assay office that the mining men operating the shaft she held stock in were respected in the gold fields as men of their words. She'd had it explained to her that while many a stockholder had been left with a lot of excuses and a hole in the ground, real mines producing real pay dirt had to ease off on the drilling and blasting now and again to lay track and install more pit props, drainpipes, and such. They'd told her they'd send a man out for a look come morning, but they were sure she was only confused about the rules of the game. When you owned shares in any business, you had to share the red ink as well as black. Nobody but a crooked faro dealer could hope for continuous profit.

Longarm assured her that made sense to him. She snuggled closer to butterfly-kiss his bare shoulder with her lashes and confide, "I'm tempted to leave it to them and catch the morning train south. There won't be another one all day, and they told me it would only take until ten or eleven to clear the whole matter up at that mine. What if we both caught that same train, darling? That way, if there were any more layovers in the mountains . . ."

He patted her bare rump, inspiring her to throw a shapely naked thigh across him, as he wistfully replied, "Like to. Can't. I ain't done here, and such sign as I've cut seems to lead the other way, to the north, not the south."

She repressed a naked shudder and said, "Surely you don't think that awful Calgary Kid could be here in Helena, darling."

He answered, "Not now, I hope. But up until today I fear I've been reading things all wrong. So there's just no saying how this is all fixing to turn out."

She snuggled her pubic thatch up against his naked hip, but seemed really interested, so he gripped the cheroot in his teeth to compose his own thoughts as well as bring her up to date. "It's commencing to look as if we're dealing with what the high-toned English call a remittance man."

She asked, "A *what,* dear?"

He explained. "We'd be more apt to call 'em black sheep. When you have a seat in the House of Lords and a black sheep younger son or kid brother who could disgrace the hell out of you, you can have him killed or send him off somewhere to just disgrace his fool self. Most such worthless aristocrats I've heard of are sent to live in India, some tropical isle, or other British outpost."

"Such as Canada?" she asked, as if she really gave a hang.

He nodded. "As far away from proper folks as possible. You call such outcasts remittance men because they naturally have to get a regular remittance, or money from home, to keep 'em where you sent 'em. The Calgary Kid has boasted more than once that he has pull with some British consul. I just wired Marshal Vail to look into that for us. If some belted earl or duke sent Percival Harcourt off to Canada because of his self-indulgence and bad temper, he may have asked some British consulate to handle the transfer of funds. Harcourt seems to have some such lower-ranking lime-juicer overindulging him a heap! He ain't been staying put, like a regular remittance man. He's been drifting all over, acting like some sort of bad man, while getter badder as he goes.''

He could tell from the way she was idly grinding her pelvis against him that he was losing her interest when it came to other wickedness. So he snuffed out the smoke, took her in his arms some more, and treated her wrong for a too short spell that they both tried to hold onto forever.

After he'd made her come again, almost against her will, Aura sighed and said, ''Please come back to Denver with me. You've just told me the Calgary Kid could be most anywhere right now. Why couldn't he be in Denver? Hasn't he seemed to be working his way south from that Calgary town in Canada?''

They got into a more comfortable cuddle, and Longarm said, ''Yes and no. As I've put things together just now, Harcourt was likely sent to the wilds of Canada on a remittance too generous to be spent up yonder. Bribing his keepers on this side of the main ocean, he drifted down here to the Montana gold fields, where there was more action. He fell in with some local hell-raisers, assuring them he was the one and original Calgary Kid, a bad man from up Canada way. They called him the Lime Juice Kid to his face, but allowed him to stand treat in town at the photography studio, saloons, and worse. They let him tag along until he met the budding Edith Alma out at the Collier spread, and then things got ugly. Harcourt had neither brains nor self-restraint when it came to females of all ages. Lem Collier, to his only natural credit, had no desire to see his little cousin messed up with a mean womanizing drunk.''

Aura coyly reached for Longarm's limp shaft as she asked what was wrong with men who liked women.

He said, ''The girl was only eleven or twelve at the time. After her kin warned Harcourt off, likely with firm instructions to keep away from all concerned, the black sheep got liquored up and, being a mean drunk, pegged a backshot at the little gal's defender. He aimed drunk as well as mean, and the rest we know, I hope.''

This time Aura got on top. As he lay there playing with her firm generous breasts, he wished the bed lamp was lit. She was moving in a way that seemed barely enough to keep it hard for him, in the dark.

He groaned. "Let me move more, if you don't want to. No offense, but you are teasing the pure Ned out of me with that languid hula dance you're putting on!"

She purred, "We'll both be moving faster soon. I've found you shaggy dogs last longer for a girl when she paces your outbursts of passion!"

He had to chuckle, and asked if she'd been taught to screw in some fancy finishing school.

"I suppose you've guessed I'm not exactly a virgin," she replied.

He said the thought had crossed his mind. That inspired her to let fly with some family secrets he hadn't asked, although it sure explained why her dear old dad might have wanted to leave her all that mining stock.

As she got to another older man who'd put her up in her own Denver brownstone, Longarm grimaced and said, "I don't like having other folks in bed with us, honey. That's the Calgary Kid's pleasure."

That reminded her that they'd only gotten the morose young remittance man as far as Fort Morgan. So she asked what he'd been doing there.

Longarm said, "Enjoying his fool self. He was getting his money from home by wire and spending most of it on hard liquor and soft flesh. He wanted it known he was a big bad hombre called the Calgary Kid, and the Fort Morgan boys were willing to ride wide of him, a surly drunk packing a short-barreled six-gun made for fast drawing."

He snuggled her closer and continued. "He hadn't been holding up trains or anything else. He didn't need to, and it's been established he's moody but lazy as sin. Meanwhile his erstwhile pals, Lem Collier and the Dillon brothers, had been recruited by an older Fagin called Big Frenchy Moreau to rob the Burlington night flier. It don't matter whether Moreau was French Canuck or not. They pulled it off without a lick of help from the Calgary Kid. Then they scattered by rail up and down the same Burlington line to let things cool down. The three pals who picked Fort Morgan had no idea their erstwhile pal, their Lime Juicer Kid, would be there. But when he saw the three of them coming his way in the Wagon Wheel Tavern, he thought they were still after him and it was pure *panic,* not

94

homicidal lunacy, that inspired him to slap leather on three apparent strangers, see?"

She said she did, and added, ''Poor thing's just a weakling with a drinking problem. Why can't you let him be and come back to Denver with me, seeing those other boys were wanted outlaws after all.''

Longarm was too polite to say other gals had shown the same lack of logic when it came to simple justice. He just said, ''Harcourt would have been commended and turned loose, in the end, had he let it go with cutting down three wanted train robbers. But we were holding him as a material witness when he busted out illegally, and I want that so and so who impersonated me as well!''

She butterflied his shoulder some more and said, ''I can see how a thing like that might upset my shaggy dog. Who do you think that other rascal was, darling?''

He said, ''A rascal for certain. He answers to James or Hamish, and I'm pretty sure he headed back to Denver after he set his black sheep free. Somebody tall and natural acting as me was seen in Denver just before you and me left aboard that train.''

He shook his head wearily and said, ''They must have split up right away, with Hamish headed south and Harcourt headed north. The meaner one must have ridden out to the Collier spread and killed everyone as soon as he got there. Another deputy who seems to know his onions has the timing figured that way. We haven't found anyone in Helena who's seen the once-familiar Lime Juice Kid. But he must have hung around a day or so. The Colliers had gone stiff and been found by the time he shot that Deputy Braxton by the depot and lit out, we reckon, on that northbound night train.''

She asked why he said ''reckon.''

He explained. ''Nobody *saw* him board that northbound train. That's why I have to stick around Helena a spell. The town ain't all that big, and now that I have a photograph of the rascal, I ought to be able to pick him out of the crowd he's inclined to hang out with. You were right about him not being wanted for the deaths of Lem Collier or the Dillon boys. But Montana wants him for the Collier family, and Uncle Sam wants him for United States Deputy Marshal Braxton. We'll figure out who gets to hang him after I catch him.''

She said that in that case she might as well stay in town

long enough to take the later train with her paid-for report on her gold shares.

He sighed and warned her he'd be out most of the day, and might be hopping a northbound that left sooner than her south-bound. So they had one last friendly encounter and tried to get some sleep.

He knew they'd succeeded when they were awakened by the sunrise streaking in through the open window and one hell of a lot of noise from downstairs. Aura sat up naked in bed—she looked grand in the golden light—to ask what was going on.

He yawned, said he didn't know, but allowed he'd soon find out. He told Aura to hold his place between the sheets as he swiftly washed up and dressed in the small next-door bath.

He went downstairs in just his jeans and shirt, though with his gun rig and badge in place, to join the cluster of noisy gents in the lobby. As he elbowed his way through the buzzing crowd toward the hotel desk, he asked anyone he could what was going on.

A local with a copper badge pinned to his own shirtfront sort of sobbed, "Murder most foul! Some son of a bitch slit the throat of old Aunt Nelly ear to ear!"

That big fuzzy cat swished its tail in Longarm's gut as he craned over the countertop for a better look at their female room clerk, sprawled in buckets of blood on the floor, while one of the men Longarm had met the day before at the morgue hunkered over her with a thermometer.

Someone in the crowd protested, "Aw, come on, that ain't no way to treat no woman!"

But the man from the coroner's office draped the old woman's skirt hem over a naked hip and shoved the thermom-eter up her rectum just the same, as Longarm explained to the growling onlookers, "He's only out to set the time of death, boys."

Then he was rolling himself over the counter as the man with the thermometer up the dead woman's ass told him he wasn't supposed to do that.

Longarm said, "I have to look for a letter I left with her last night. If it's missing, I may have your motive before you have that thermometer out of her!"

But when he found the mail sack under the counter, the envelope he'd addressed to Billy Vail was still there. Mean-while, the coroner's man had decided, "Betwixt three and four in the morning. She was likely half asleep behind this counter and never spied her killer until too late to even holler!''

Someone in the crowd volunteered that old Aunt Nelly had been known to sip snake medicine when things were slow.

Longarm asked about bullet wounds. The coroner's deputy said he hadn't found any so far, and asked, ''Wouldn't someone in town have noticed gunshots betwixt three and four in the morning?''

Longarm searched through the drawers on the inside of the counter until he found the locked sheet-metal till. He opened it with a blade of his pocket knife that might have gotten lesser lights arrested.

There was close to forty dollars on hand. It sure left out robbery as a motive.

He told the man from the morgue, ''The killer wasn't after the mail or money. How do you feel about a crime of passion?''

The deputy coroner grimaced and said, ''I don't think she's been raped, if that's what you meant. Maybe somebody just didn't *like* old Aunt Nelly!''

Longarm had to allow such things happened. Nobody had a monopoly on small-town grudges, and there was nothing about this one pointing to the Calgary Kid or anyone else with a gun.

He went back upstairs to tell Aura what had happened. When he got to the probable time, she gasped and declared, ''Oh, Lord, I might have heard them! I think it was about that time in the morning I had to get up to go in there and . . . you know. As I was squatting there half-awake I thought I heard someone out in the hall trying doorknobs, or maybe just groping along the hallway in the dark. I asked you if you'd heard it after I got back in bed. You said something about old maids from Canada, don't you remember?''

He sighed and said, ''It's likely just as well we forget most of our dreams when we wake up. It ain't likely dreams predict things to come. I figure they're tricks our sleeping brain plays on itself to keep from waking up. You dream about being in a snowstorm to keep from waking up to put more blankets over you. You dream dirty songs about old maids from Canada because you have a piss hard-on and don't really want to study too hard on Canada, see?''

She said she'd be happy to do something about his erection,

seeing it was early and she hadn't even thought of dressing yet.

He laughed, hung his gun rig over a bedpost, and took her up on her kind offer. He'd been right about how swell her tits might look in the daylight. She said his experiment with the looking glass across the room made her blush. So he told her not to look, and of course she did, and blushed all over as they were climaxing together without a thing to hide.

Then they bathed together, got dressed, and had time for a hearty breakfast before he carried her and her carpetbag over to the depot and put her on the morning southbound.

He promised he'd look her up when he got back to Denver and tell her all about the way things turned out. The address she had him put in his notebook was on Logan Street, a tad closer than he liked to another fashionable address on Capitol Hill. But that was what a man got for admiring fashionable women. They tended to herd in the fashionable parts of this limited world.

By noon Longarm was regretting he hadn't left with her. A man could cope with musical beds on Capitol Hill better than walking in circles, and in a town the size of Helena, you could question more folks than you needed to in a half a day.

He told the hotel help cleaning up after poor Aunt Nelly that he'd be proud to leave by noon, seeing he'd likely be taking the next train out. *They* had no idea who'd cut her throat, or why, either.

Longarm carried his heavily laden saddle to the nearby federal courthouse, and asked if he could leave it in their tack room out back. They were a lot nicer about storing a man's possibles free.

Then he strode streets broad and narrow in search of anyone who remembered the Lime Juice or Calgary Kid, alias Percival Harcourt.

He found plenty of saloon regulars and even more whores who'd known the young cuss when he'd been raising hell with Lem Collier and the Dillon brothers a spell back.

The man's odd eye had made more of an impression than his teeth because he hadn't smiled a whole lot. Barkeeps recalled being told to do dreadful things to their mothers after refusing to serve a rubber-legged and glassy-eyed gent with a gun on his hip. But as far as anyone could recall, he hadn't really drawn on anyone before he tried to shoot Lem Collier in the back that time.

Longarm asked a Helena copper badge to tour their sin district with him. The ramshackle structures on the downwind side of the tracks didn't officially exist. But Longarm had noticed in the past that whores were more inclined to talk around lawmen they'd been paying off.

He hit pay dirt with some of the soiled doves of Helena. More than one recalled that goatlike lust for perfumed flesh.

They said Harcourt would drop out of sight for a spell, then show up with a wad of money to shoot his wad in two or three gals at a pop, taking them and a bottle of liquor to bed with him.

The town lawman told Longarm, "We'd heard about a horny young cuss with no visible means of support getting expensively disgusting with these gals. So we asked around, and it seems he was having money wired to him regular, like he was some sort of spoiled rich kid playing bad man out our way."

Longarm had already covered that sign. Billy Vail, or more likely Henry, would be poking around any British consulate within a day's ride of Denver.

He explained that to the younger town lawman as they were headed for a boardinghouse where one of the whores said Harcourt might have been resting up between his labors. Like a lot of folks, the Helena lawman had a consulate mixed up with an embassy, and couldn't fathom why old Queen Victoria would send an ambassador to the state of Colorado.

Longarm said, "The British embassy is in Washington Town, so Her Majesty's personal *segundos* can sip lemonade at the White House with President Hayes and Miss Lucy when they ain't throwing shindigs for all the other fancy folks of diplomatic circles. *A consulate* is a whole other kettle of fish. Governments set up consulates all over other lands for their own citizens to call on should they get in trouble."

The Helena lawman showed he'd been listening by saying, "I reckon I follow your drift. If I was Miss Lemonade Lucy Hayes and wanted to trade dress patterns with Queen Victoria, I'd get in touch with that British embassy across town. But if I was an Englishman picked up in a whorehouse raid, I'd want somebody to tell the nearest British consul, right?"

Longarm said, "That's about the size of it. They have consulates, sub-consulates, or trade missions scattered all across the world because Napoleon was right when he described them as a nation of shopkeepers. A British subject in trouble, or just doing business and needing good advice, can call on their British consul for help.''

It appeared Percival Harcourt *had,* once they got to the boardinghouse he'd been staying at in Helena. For the landlady, a tough-looking crone with her hair or wig dyed cherry red, served them coffee and cake in her kitchen and recalled the time her slugabed boarder hadn't been able to pay up in advance, as any sensible landlady required in a transient mining town.

She said he'd begged and pleaded and promised her he could get an extra advance from some consolidated or mayhaps constipated British pals. She said she'd given him one extra night under her roof to make good on his promise and that, to her surprise, he had.

After thanking her and leaving for the nearest saloon to refresh themselves more substantially, Longarm and his newfound sidekick had to agree that the Calgary Kid's trail had grown cold in those parts. They hadn't found a soul who could say where he'd stayed, or with whom, during his last short savage visit.

Sipping some suds, the kid copper badge stated flatly, "He must have gone out of his head from all that fast living. I follow your drift about that shootout in Fort Morgan. But what would possess a sane man who'd just been busted out of jail to streak up here and gun down the rest of the Collier family?"

Longarm shrugged. "Who's saying he's sane? He might have enjoyed playing cowboy with Lem Collier and the Dillon boys. He likely blamed poor little Edith Alma Collier and her folks for putting him in a bad light with his pals."

The copper badge objected. "Hold on. It wasn't that young gal's fault that a man too old for her got fresh!"

Longarm nodded soberly, but said, "The jails of this wicked world wouldn't be near as full if your average sinner was willing to own up to his or her own sins. When your average owlhoot rider ain't pistol-whipping his victims, he's prone to whimper and whine about the way cruel fate turned an honest young cowhand into a wanted man with no place to rest his weary head."

The local lawman, who sometimes arrested Helena's drunks,

made a wry face and muttered, "I've heard about cruel bar-keeps tempting poor boys with needled beer. There's less mystery about Harcourt gunning a lawman by the depot. He saw poor Deputy Braxton first and grabbed for his gun without thinking, like down Fort Morgan way, right?"

Longarm said, "That's the way it looks from here. Farther along, as the old song goes, we may know more about it. I sure thank you for your help. But no offense, I don't see what in blue blazes I'm doing here in Helena when that jasper with the Webley Bulldog could be anywhere by this late in the game!"

They shook and parted friendly, so Longarm could go enjoy a sit-down noon dinner without having to issue any invitation. His expense account allowed him six cents a travel mile and seventy-five cents a day to eat on, Lord willing and he didn't return empty-handed to have the expenses of this whole mission disallowed by the paymaster.

He was eating at that same hash house near the depot, their special being venison, mashed potatoes, and asparagus, when Armenian George Mandalian caught up with him.

The beefy federal man swung a bentwood chair around to straddle it across the table from Longarm and tell the plump waitress gal he'd settle for coffee.

Mandalian then told Longarm, "I've been looking all over for you. Lucky for us somebody we both know spotted you headed this way."

Longarm washed down some grub with his own coffee, and asked what made them both so lucky.

Mandalian replied, "I figured you'd have been by the courthouse if you'd heard. Looks like our Calgary Kid has struck again!"

Longarm stared thunderstruck. "Here in Helena? I've been out on the streets most of the morning. You can hear the distant rumble when they're blasting down in the mines. So how can anyone miss gunfire in a town this size?"

Mandalian explained, "Nobody did. We just got word from Fort Peck, where the Milk meets the Missouri out on the open prairie."

"I know where Fort Peck is. *Both* of them. Are we talking about that army outpost or the trading post a few miles off?"

"Trading post. The military's all moved west to Fort Assiniboine or east to Fort Buford. General Terry's at Buford, trying to get Canada's permit to go Indian hunting further north. Old Sitting Bull has Terry fit to be tied, camped just north of the damned border.''

Longarm said, ''I wouldn't bet a month's pay on where old Tatanka Yatanka might show up next. He surely gets around for a *Sitting* Bull. But you say the Calgary Kid's done something else up around Fort Peck?''

Mandalian nodded. ''Gunned an Indian trader. Or a sort of mysterious French Canuck who claimed to be an Indian trader. His name was Debrun. Claimed to be pure white. Might have been one of those Métis. His wife, who rode to the Poplar Agency downstream to report the dustup, was pure Crow for certain. She said she had a time following the whole argument, seeing she's better at Crow or French Canuck than English. But as far as we've been able to put things together, Harcourt rode in on a jaded pony, started out friendly enough by swapping a fair pony for a fresher one, then paid cash for a whole lot of trail supplies.''

Longarm half closed his eyes as he tried to picture a mental map of the range they were talking about. He figured the ride north from Fort Peck would have you crossing the border late at night, on another jaded pony, if you were a hard rider who didn't mind a little blood on your spurs.

He asked Mandalian what the fight had been about if the trader had been willing to supply Harcourt with a fresh mount and grub.

Mandalian said, ''Grub ain't all he bought. The squaw recalls him picking up two boxes of .442-shorts, the right load for a Webley Bulldog, which is why we ain't waiting on any autopsy report this time!''

Longarm whistled softly and asked, ''Did the victim's woman recall a spotty blue eye or ratty teeth?''

Mandalian shrugged. ''Why not just ask her once we get there? My own boss is sending me up to Fort Peck with you, since he owes us for Deputy Braxton too. The squaw thinks her man had that falling-out with the stranger when he asked to tag along with a mule train old Debrun was fixing to send out across the buffalo grass. His widow won't admit it now, but everyone knows about the profits to be made running guns and firewater across the border. The squaw said her man had just yelled something sarcastic about strangers packing Mountie-issue side arms when their mysterious visitor got ugly and allowed he'd show Debrun how you *fired* a Webley.''

Mandalian swallowed some coffee and added, ''We can figure it all out once we get there. If we catch the night train up to the junction and pick up some trail stock . . .''

''You go on up to Fort Peck if that's your fancy,'' Longarm said, cutting another bit of venison. ''If the thin-spread Mounties catch him for us, they'll catch him for us. If he's made the border by now and they ain't, they won't.''

He washed down the morsel and told the other lawman, not unkindly but flatly, ''I'm tired of chasing him. I aim to head him off. If he's riding the way I suspect, I ought to. If he ain't, I won't. I'd offer to let you tag along, but what I have in mind could get you in a whole lot of trouble if I mess up. So I don't aim to take you along, or tell you where I'm going, no offense.''

Chapter 9

Forty-odd hours later Longarm reined his hired livery pony in by the gate of a country churchyard near the Blackfoot Agency snuggled against both the foothills of the Rockies and the Canadian border.

Longarm dismounted and tethered his mount to a gatepost before he trod the sod softly over to Roping Sally's rustic grave marker.

Roping Sally had been one of the best riders and ropers of either sex that he'd ever met up with, and a swell kisser besides.

As he stood there, hat in hand, a second shadow joined his own across the grass their old pal lay under. Without turning, Longarm quietly asked, *"How ne tucka?"*

So Sergeant Rain Crow of the Indian Police replied, *"Neet ahksaey. Ochinnuyah.* I knew I would find you here when they told me you got off the train to hire that fat *kekstaki* to ride. We will find you a real *ponoka meta* out at the agency. This is not a happy place to talk. She was too young to die when she helped us fight that very evil spirit called the Wendigo. It was not a good fight. Too many died, on our side, before you caught up with that evil spirit and the land thieves of your own nation who were causing us so much trouble."

Longarm nodded soberly down at the marker. "She was sure a fine lady, and one hell of a roper too!"

As he turned to face his old Indian pal, Longarm managed not to laugh out loud. But it wasn't easy. The Indian police officer's blue tunic was clean and neatly buttoned. But there were coup feathers in the band of the government-issue hat set square on his broad skull, and doubtless owing to the warm afternoon they were enjoying, the tawny lawman wasn't wearing anything below his tunic. His brawny legs were a mite bowed as well as exposed to the elements and public gaze.

Oblivious to his own appearance, Rain Crow assured the denim-clad Longarm, "You should not say she *was*. Her hair was yellow and her eyes were the color of cornflowers. But she died fighting for my Siksika Nation, and so her four ghosts must still live on as the ghosts of a real person."

The Indian pointed his brown chin at a clump of cottonwood saplings to the west, with the afternoon sun flashing scattered light through fluttering leaves. Rain Crow softly declared, "I think one of her ghosts smiles at us through that dappled sunlight. *Mahto mahksim,* she will never grow old and there is no need for the ghost who stays by her bones to turn ugly. Nobody ever comes by here to dig people up and send them back east to lie in glass cases. It is not our custom. But sometimes, when I come by in cornflower time, I leave some of their blue eyes here for that part of her."

The Indian gravely pointed north to state, with no doubt in his mind, "Her second ghost dwells in the lodge of *Ki-pe-tah-ki,* singing and telling stories under the Northern Lights. But I like to think of Roping Sally's third ghost, riding with warm winds in her long hair on a pony that never tires, across the always green grass on the other side of the sky."

Longarm said that might have strumming harps beat, and asked where Rain Crow figured that *fourth* ghost of Roping Sally was right now.

The Indian stared at him. "Don't you pay any attention to real medicine at all? Her fourth ghost is naturally seeking revenge on those land thieves and their hired evil spirit!"

Longarm frowned and pointed out, "But that fake Wendigo and the crooked land agent who ordered him to murder Roping Sally are as dead as she is, Rain Crow!"

The Indian sniffed and said, "I'll never understand how you people keep winning, winning. Of *course* the evildoers who caused all that trouble and murdered Roping Sally are dead. Could her ghost pursue their ghosts, except in dreams, if they

105

had no ghosts running loose for her ghost to go after?''

Longarm shook his head as if to clear it and said, "I just dropped by here to pay my respects. I'm up this way in pursuit of a real live outlaw. Wanted for killing a federal deputy as well as others.''

The Indian nodded and said, "*Hah,* you will tell me how we can help you as we ride out to my place. If what you want of us is possible, we will do it for you.''

So Longarm brought the canny Rain Crow up to date as they rode a fair piece to what the BIA had down as their Blackfoot Agency. The Indians so described called themselves Siksika, and most of their feet were in fact encased in *blue* beaded moccasins. Like the so-called Sioux and perfectly normal Flatheads, the Siksika had been named to whites by enemies on better terms with the early trappers and traders. The Crow word for blue and black were the same. They considered blue a pale shade of black. Hence the hazy blue ridges of the Black Hills and the confusion of the Siksika and Blackfoot Sioux, who really did wear black moccasins.

Since Rain Crow was an experienced lawman in his own right, and seeing the two of them were grown men, Longarm left nothing out as he told his old pal all he'd been through since first he'd ever heard of the son-of-a-bitching Calgary Kid.

By the time he finished, they could see the limp stars and stripes of the agency ahead. Rain Crow suggested they swing wide and ride in behind the screen of some outhouses unless Longarm wanted coffee and cake with the white BIA agent and his sort of silly young wife.

Rain Crow explained, "He means well, but he keeps talking baby talk to us, and seems to think a *pera* is a *papoose* and calls an *ogh tum* a *tom-tom.*''

Longarm explained, "Someone must have told him you Siksika speak an Algonquin dialect. I reckon it would be like trying to talk French to a Spaniard because you'd heard they were related languages. At least the poor simp seems to be trying.''

Rain Crow grunted, "I just said that. His wife wanted me to arrest some young people she caught fucking in a wooded draw when she went out riding. I asked her why she rode through such good cover if she didn't like what people did there. She yelled as me and said her Cristecoom would not invite me to his lodge when I died. I asked if she expected to be there. When she said all the people like her would be there, I told her I would rather haunt a shithouse. We have not spoken since.''

They got to Rain Crow's unpainted frame cabin, and dismounted on the far side. Some grinning Siksika boys ran over to take the reins and see to the riding stock.

As they slipped around to the front door, two pretty young gals met them there giggling like hell. Rain Crow wasn't allowed to have more than one wife under BIA regulations. On the other hand, they expected him to wear pants too.

The three Indians dragged Longarm inside. He knew better than to comment on the haze of blue smoke, or ask them to crack open one damned window. All the Plains nations admired the smell of smoke, and when it made their eyes run, they said it proved they were emotional.

As the gals rustled up some grub, Rain Crow asked, ''What does our brother Ochinnuyah want of this person? The killer he is after has not ridden this way.''

Longarm got out a sepia-tone of the Calgary Kid to show the Indian police officer as he explained, ''If he lingers around Fort Peck or tries to double back, another federal deputy and the local lawmen ought to nail him. He might have managed to join up with other whiskey or gunrunners. He might try it on his own, seeing he's crossed that same border before. Am I safe in suspecting he'd want to slip north betwixt the Mounties stationed at East End fort and the Wood Mountain fort, close to a hundred miles apart?''

Rain Crow shrugged, gazing absently down at the wanted man's photograph, and said, ''You are asking the wrong person. I know nothing, nothing about the Grandmother Victoria's blanket that far east.''

He told one of his wives to do something else, too fast for a white man to even try to follow. As she nodded smiling and lit out, Rain Crow explained, ''I have sent for Mumeyasain. You would say Red Fish. Red Fish used to live on the Grandmother Victoria's blanket. But hear me, her blanket is a big one. One rider crossing the prairies between the Red River and the Shining Mountains would look smaller than a flea on a ten-beaver blanket! But that is the easy part. Things are *pah kapa* north of the border right now. The Grandmother Victoria must feel as if she has a beehive under her skirts. The Cree and their Métis half brothers are massing for war on the Saskatchewan. The Nadowessi you people call Sioux have moved north to hunting grounds they had never camped on in the Shining Times. I have to say this, because it is true. Our own Siksika cousins north of the border are ready to put on paint and fight to save what is left of their *eneuh.*''

Longarm had to think back before it came to him they were talking about buffalo, called *pte* or *tatanka* by the Lakota. He asked, ''Hasn't Her Majesty been feeding those fugitive Lakota enough to keep 'em off the hunting grounds of her own Indians?''

Rain Crow shrugged. ''I don't think she invited them to her blanket to begin with. Why should she give them anything? Maybe she was hoping they'd go home to the Dakota Territory when they got hungry enough. But the Sioux know Star Chief Terry and the blue sleeves are waiting for them there. Some of them have chosen to hunt further west, on *Siksika* hunting grounds!''

Longarm could only whistle soberly. He had no call to lecture a paid-up Blackfoot on the history of his own nation. But he knew gents who paid no attention to history could wind up reliving it, and the Siksika bands along a strip of foothills and rolling prairie between the headwaters of the Missouri and Saskatchewan made for some mighty grim reading indeed. The so-called Blackfoot had been considered the most truculent nation of the northern plains. More inclined than even the Cheyenne or Lakota to simply shoot you, scalp you, and worry later about what you might have been doing on their holy hunting grounds.

Siksika had been less inclined to wander than other Horse Indians. They held that they'd been granted their vast but finite patch of the world by White Buffalo Woman, and in fairness to their well-deserved reputation for cruelty, they'd been far less inclined to seek visions or plunder in *other* parts.

In their Shining Times, the Mountain Salish of Flatheads, along with the Plains Absaroka or Crow, had raided them from time to time, and had such favors returned with interest and glee. But once white mountain men had learned how to approach them—very, very delicately—neither the Canadian nor U.S. Governments had had as much trouble with them as expected. Neither government had ever made a serious attempt to *move* the Siksika, and unlike more nomadic nations, they understood and accepted the notion of fixed boundaries.

They expected no less from others, and the Lakota were notorious gadabouts, despite their bullshit about sacred lands they'd just grabbed from other Indians.

Taking the photograph back, Longarm said, "I don't think the Calgary Kid could be on any of the sides you just mentioned. I think he's a dangerous lone wolf, taking advantage of the confusion to the north. I don't know where he's headed up Canada way, but I do know anyone with an eye to escape would want to beeline north through the troubled prairie along the border before he heads anywhere else. He'll be working his way north of the Saskatchewan before he swings seriously east or west. I figure that would take him close to three weeks if he set a cavalry pace and managed thirty miles a day whilst dodging Mounties and Lord knows who else."

"I don't think he could do it," Rain Crow stated flatly.

Longarm nodded and said, "I know. But *I* might, riding up through Siksika range with your Canadian cousins helping me instead of forcing me to scout every draw ahead with a puckered ass. Given fresh mounts along the way, I could beat him easy to that big trading post settlement at Edmonton. Then I could sort of play spider in the middle of a web. For once you're north of all the current troubles and resulting Mountie patrols, all trails lead through Edmonton as if it was some sort of prairie Rome. I figure Harcourt will want to try for the Yellowhead Pass west of Edmonton. But should he aim for the lower east-west trails controlled by that Mountie post at Calgary, he'll still want to make a run through Edmonton, see?"

Rain Crow said, "Red Fish knows more about the Grandmother Victoria's blanket than me. Why aren't you eating? Don't you like *a meetah*?"

Longarm hoped he was wrong about what *a meetah* meant as he dug in. It tasted good, despite a disturbing doggy smell to the sauce. Rain Crow said something to his young wife before she could put white flour in Longarm's coffee.

As they dined, Rain Crow asked, "What if this crazy man you are after heads somewhere other than British Columbia and the great salt water? I told you the Grandmother's blanket was very big, very."

Longarm nodded. "More crowded as you head east, though. The Canadian authorities have been told to expect him. He dare not head for the Atlantic ports or even Hudson's Bay. If he heads up into the serious north country, he'll wind up with a frozen ass if he tries to winter alone, whilst the Déné and Eskimo are both inclined to gossip to the Mounties about mysterious strangers. His best bet, like I said, would be a run down to one of those many fishing ports along that Inland Passage of British Columbia. That would put him home free in any big West Coast city from Vancouver to Tijuana and beyond!"

Rain Crow objected, "You said he might be crazy. Would a crazy man be smart enough to do as you just said?"

Longarm shrugged, ate some more whatever, and replied, "If he's not, somebody *else* will catch him. It happens that way. It can't be helped. The point is that you generally wind up caught once you get to killing others."

The wife who'd been sent to fetch Red Fish returned with a pouty-faced young Siksika gal in her late teens or early twenties. As Rain Crow introduced her to the mighty Ochinnuyah, who'd slain the Wendigo and saved their land, Red Fish didn't seem impressed. She fiddled with a braid hanging down the front of her beaded calico smock and muttered something in her own language.

Rain Crow snapped, "Speak American. You may think it didn't matter to your own people north of the border, but the Wendigo took more than agency land from people. He took their *lives*. When the Wendigo killed you he did not settle for your scalp. He took your whole head. All of us were frightened, frightened, and the government told us we were a bunch of children, making up ghost stories, until our brother with the good heart and long arms proved there *was* a Wendigo and *killed* it!"

Red Fish raised her sullen gaze to stare thoughtfully at Longarm, not looking too convinced. She shrugged and said, "If my uncle thinks we owe him a favor, I am listening."

Rain Crow said, "He wants to ride north along the foothills so the red sleeves will not see him. Should some of our own people see him riding across their range without any presents for them, they may kill him. He does not speak our tongue well enough to explain himself in the time strangers are usually given. You must ride with him to show him the way and to act as his *mai'oi Siksika* and speak for him. If you do this we shall be even, Mumeyasain."

The bilingual Siksika gal stamped a blue moccasin and replied, "I don't want to ride anywhere with this hairy stranger!

There is going to be a new moon *pascat* in just *kaypi* days, and I have told a certain young man I might dance with him then if he stops teasing me.''

Rain Crow frowned slightly and said, ''I do not think my cousin's willful child could have been listening. I said we would be even if you did this thing I ask for my brother Ochinnuyah. What I mean was that you owe us all a favor for telling the BIA you were not at this agency when the Grandmother Victoria's red sleeves wanted to know where you had gone after slashing that other girl's face at another *pascat* not so long ago!''

Red Fish gulped and tried a weak smile instead of a queenly scowl as she protested, ''That is why I don't want to go north with anybody at all right now. I am not afraid of the red sleeves. They are as easy to avoid as blind children. But that other Siksika girl's scars have not healed yet, and our friends all say that we should fight some more and finish it the right way this time.''

Rain Crow grimaced and said, ''Such advice is never given by true friends. Did not your uncle, my cousin, give presents to the family of the girl you slashed?''

''Yes. But she is still angry, angry,'' Red Fish replied.

Rain Crow shrugged and said, ''Don't lead our brother here by your own camp. He does not expect to find the man he is after hiding among Siksika. Guide him as far as the Brazeau trading post north of Calgary, then come back alone another way, and we'll see about getting you an American allotment number so that you can draw your own rations from the BIA.''

Longarm knew he wasn't supposed to be listening in on such plotting against the U.S. taxpaying public. He swallowed the last of his black coffee and said, ''My brother Rain Crow said something about fixing me up with some real riding stock. How far west do Miss Red Fish and me have to ride before we swing north for the border?''

Red Fish stamped her foot again and sobbed, ''I don't want to ride with you! I want to go dancing, dancing, with Otokan Mastoa. He is very pretty and knows many nose-flute tunes, many!''

But of course, she and Longarm were headed west along a wooded draw by mid-afternoon, with her still bitching softly in her own mother tongue. She'd changed to a more practical Mother Hubbard of maroon calico, cinched at the waist with a beadwork belt. She rode astride a buckskin pony, seated in a store-bought stock saddle, with her own Yellowboy Winchester's stock sticking up between her bedroll and her pert rump. The afternoon had gotten unseasonably warm, and Longarm had lashed his denim jacket to the swells of his McClellan. He trailed after Red Fish, leading their one pack pony through the dappled shade of the east-west draw.

An hour's ride west of the agency, Longarm called a trail break to rest their riding stock. Since all three ponies were Siksika-raised, they didn't need to be told the surrounding fresh green leaves were as digestible as grass. Red Fish dismounted to scoot out of sight in the scrub for a spell. Longarm took his time, lit a cheroot, and strolled up the opposite slope to water some red birch.

When he got back to the tethered ponies, Red Fish was hunkered with her spine to a sapling, complaining about missing her infernal new-moon dance. Longarm knew it was doubtless all that talk of spooks at the churchyard earlier, but he seemed to see Roping Sally, over in that patch of sun-shimmer, setting a transparent dappled pony and laughing at him. So he blew smoke out both nostrils like a pissed-off bull, and told Red Fish to go on back to the agency and dance all she wanted for all he cared.

The Siksika gal looked up surprised and asked, "Do you really mean that?"

Longarm nodded grimly. "I don't say things I don't mean unless I have to. There are some things to be said for civilization. My kind is inclined to give mean brats a good spanking. I know your kind holds with spoiling kids rotten and hoping they might grow out of it. Anyone can see you never did, and life is too short to spend more time than you have to in the company of a spoiled bitchy brat!"

She rose slowly to stand in her beaded blue moccasins, asking him in a less surly tone how he expected to find his way to a safe place to cross the border, or to talk to her truculent Canadian kinfolk without her help.

Longarm shrugged and said, "I've scouted Shoshoni in high country. I reckon I can avoid white boys patroling in white helmets and scarlet tunics if I have to. As for unfriendly Indians, the only Indian acting mean to me right now is Miss Mumeyasain. So why don't you just get the hell out of my hair. That would be my *otokan*, right?"

She laughed despite herself and said, "Close enough. When my kinsmen scalp you they will hold an *otokan epascat* with your hair!"

Then she was up in her saddle and lashing her buckskin as she let out a wild triumphant whoop and rode it out of sight, back the way they'd just come.

Longarm forced himself to finish his smoke before he changed his McClellan from the paint to the roan, letting the pony that had carried him that far pack the lighter trail supplies for a spell. Seeing they were headed for the foothills of the northern Rockies in springtime, they were able to save a hell of a lot of weight in the form of water. There was a trickle of water down the very draw they were following, and he knew that, if anything, he'd be fording more whitewater streams in flood than he liked to think about before he made it to the damned Canadian border!

Like the wooded draw Red Fish had led him to, most all the drainage off the mountains to the west ran more or less east and west. He was way out of sight, in the open, from any border patrol a good twenty miles to the north. But the Indians on *his* side had told him that the Mounties had Indians on *their* side, paid well to inform the NWMP about any white strangers riding up through Indian country from the south. Rain Crow had warned him that such informers could be listed officially as American or Canadian Blackfeet. The Blackfeet were a nation that had never invited outsiders to draw lines across their traditional hunting grounds.

Longarm made sure the smoked-down cheroot was out before he mounted the roan, jerked the lead line, and declared, "Well, let's see what I got us into with my big mouth."

Things went about the same at first. The wooded draw did grow a bit less wide and deep with every mile as they forged on toward the mountains. That was the way erosion worked. He knew that somewhere out ahead, on higher ground, this draw would be starting east as a whole mess of shallow grass-lined swales. At the rate they were traveling, he had reason to hope it would be dark by then. He might be able to feel his way along the slopes without tripping over any border posts. He knew it would be risky to follow any pony tracks or game trails he came upon. He'd just have to do the best he could, without that mean little kid, and hope for the best, damn her sassy ass!

113

He reined in more than once to suddenly twist in the saddle for a gander through the dappled shade behind him. He saw nothing, and when he thought about it, he hadn't heard anything. He muttered, "All right, Roping Sally. It's been nice seeing you again, but you'd best ride on back to the churchyard now. I got enough on my plate without worrying about one bitty gal sprouting four whole haunts!"

Trying not to think of Roping Sally and the way she'd died not so far off was like trying not to think about bears in the Russian woods. That murderous fake spook, working for a crooked land agent, had done poor Roping Sally in near that railroad line a bit to the south. He tried to recall how far west that branch line ran. There'd be a stop and some sort of settlement where the tracks met up with the more serious grade ahead. He wondered what difference that could possibly make. Then he considered how whiskey or gunrunners would get bulk cargo close enough to the border for a moonlit mule train dash, and murmured, "Thanks, Sally. There ought to be some sort of foothill trail with a railroad stop at one end and an unguarded border crossing at the other. We don't want to stumble over any smugglers in the dark. So Red Fish was likely figuring on us following . . . right, a somewhat lower contour line. An established mule trace will already be hugging the highest practical contour line. There ought to be more cover from the aspen and sticker bush you see downslope from most mountain trails as well."

The shadows were getting longer as the wooded draw grew smaller by late afternoon. Longarm reined in by a sweetwater pool, where the rill ran over a natural dam of fallen timber. He unsaddled both ponies and let them drink their fill before he broke out two nose bags to feed them some of the cracked corn he'd brought along.

They seemed pleasantly surprised. He told them as he fastened the nose bags and tethered them in some crack willow, where there'd be fewer bugs, "I know you Indian ponies are used to rougher fodder. That's how come the Pony Express and cavalry has outrun your kind so often. We may have to dodge some Mounties, and they feed *their* ponies grain too."

Then, having seen to his riding stock, Longarm unrolled his bedding under another willow, mostly to get at the canned goods rolled up in the tarp. Sitting cross-legged on the flannel blankets, Longarm opened a can of pork and beans, ate the unwarmed contents from the can as if it had been thick soup, and then opened a can of tomato preserves to serve as dessert and cut the greasy taste. Such popular trail-herding fare would do him well enough for supper. He didn't have the right cover to brew coffee.

It wasn't true, as you read in dime novels, that old hands in Indian country built fires by day and avoided them at night. It was easy enough to hide a night fire in a deep draw or handy rock cleft. It was the *smoke* from any campfire, rising against a cloudless sky, that could be spotted from many a mile away.

He scuffed a hole in the soft soil with a boot heel, buried the two crushed cans to rust away just under the moldering leaf duff, and lit another cheroot to do him for coffee.

As he got rid of his waterproof match stem the same way, he spotted movement to the east, but never let on as Red Fish dismounted on the downstream side of the log dam to quietly lead her buckskin pony up his way.

Longarm just went on smoking as the Siksika gal tethered her own mount next to his and came over to him, sinking to the blankets at his side as if nothing had happened.

Longarm reached for another can, groping for the proper Siksika phrase as he opened a can and handed it to her, saying, *"Cho hetta ke tesistico?"*

She took the can, but said, "I am *hungry,* not *tired.* Why do you try to speak Siksika badly, badly, when you know I speak your own tongue?"

He said, "Trying to be polite. It's a notion too complicated for the likes of you. So don't worry your spoiled head about it, brat."

Red Fish ate some pork and beans, belched delicately, and quietly said, "I have been beaten many times by hairy people like you. My people sent me with some other Siksika children to a mission school named after the mother of Cristecoom. When we giggled in class, they beat us on our wrists with rulers. When we got the words on the blackboard wrong, they made us wear paper hats and sit in a corner. When we told them what we thought of that, they beat us, beat us with birch branches on our bare asses. I am sorry now I only ran away from that mission school as soon as I grew big enough. I should have cut one of those black-robed baby-beaters instead of another Siksika girl who only called me a brother-fucker."

Red Fish sighed and confessed, "Maybe she was right. The

115

boy I took away from her did belong to the Mastoa clan, the same as me. I have a very hasty heart. Sometimes I do things I feel sorry about, almost as soon as I do them. While I was riding back alone just now, I thought maybe all this shit was not your fault.''

''Apology accepted,'' Longarm said with a chuckle, graciously adding, ''I may have spoken more out of heat than common sense myself. Ever since you rode off I've been trying to figure out how in blue blazes I'll ever make it across the border and north through Siksika country to the easier sailing north of all this current tension.''

She asked if she could take a drag on his smoke. After she had, she said, ''Nobody will bother you north of the Bow River. I think I can get you there. But you must let me do the talking for you and do as I tell you!''

He cocked a brow and said mockingly, ''Just don't smack my wrist with that ruler and I'll be good, Teacher.''

She said, ''It wasn't funny at the time. None of us had ever been struck by an adult before and we were terrified, terrified. It was a long time before I could look at one of you people without fearing I was about to wet myself. I am not ashamed to say I have always enjoyed kissing men a lot. But I have never kissed a man like you with hair on his face!''

From the owl-eyed way she was staring at him closely, he tended to doubt her words were meant as discouragement. So he took her in his arms and kissed her.

She kissed back with enthusiasm. But just as he was getting his free hand under the hem of her maroon Mother Hubbard, she pulled free with a laugh and said they'd wasted enough time there and it was time to ride on.

So they did. For he'd just promised to do as she told him, cuss her changeable nature.

Chapter 10

Longarm was ready to forgive the Siksika gal more than her prick-teasing ways after they crossed that mule trace he'd been expecting to come upon. They were still under cover. The trail from the railroad stop to the south, leading north to a stretch of border entrusted to hard-drinking Canadian Siksika, was littered a bit where it passed through their wooden draw. There were no campfire ashes. The smugglers knew about rising smoke too. But you could read how a lot of men and mules had rested, eaten, and crapped there more than once. Longarm was glad he'd resisted that impulse to take Red Fish swimming in that pool downstream.

She said, "There was no train this morning. That is how I knew it was safe to ride in without scouting this campsite. The red sleeves to the north know this too. They will not be as alert as they are when a mule train of medicine water or guns could be moving along the trails out of here."

He stood in his stirrups, peering north across the open rolling sea of emerald buffalo grass as he asked her, "How soon do you reckon we'll be safe breaking cover?"

She sniffed and said, "We don't want to go that way. I said the red sleeves will be less alert. I never said they would be sleeping in their dens like bears. They are more worried, very worried, about the guns some of our young men have been buying from the border jumpers. I think we should circle high,

117

very high, through the always green timber. Little game will be grazing that high this early. We will get these three good *ponoka meta Siksika* to carry us where steel-shod mules would not dare to go. We shall ride a little further through this cover. Then we shall stop and let it get darker before we cross the open slopes of the foothills. By moonlight we shall follow the war trail my people call 'Going to the Sun.' They used to follow it to raid the Salish on the far side of the everlasting snowfields. By morning, if all goes well, we shall be alone above the clouds with nobody but the eagle and the bighorn to ask what we are doing there!''

And that was about the way it worked out, although it took the better part of the whole night to work themselves up among the junipers and spruce just below the timberline.

At midnight they built a small fire in a hollow to brew coffee, and the strong black coffee just about got them through to dawn in the thin dry air that made a body pant like it was working even sitting down. How the Indian ponies managed was a mystery. All three were gasping like whipped husky dogs pulling a sled through mud, even when Longarm and Red Fish got off to lead on foot from time to time. He could follow her drift about a white party's mule team. There was something to be said for the Indians' way of breaking riding stock at times like these. Despite all the blather about Mister Lo, the Poor Indian and his noble companion, the wild western mustang, Indians were inclined to *eat* ponies that couldn't cut the mustard, and they were rough as all get-out on the ponies that could.

All three of their "elk-dogs" had been chosen for them by Rain Crow with hard riding and packing in mind. So not one of them had died by the time Red Fish called a halt by the dawn's misty light.

It was misty because they were up in the cloud forest on the eastern slope of the Continental Divide. The prevailing west winds dumped most of their moisture on the far slope, feeding glaciers left over from the Ice Age, but managed to hold onto enough in springtime to form banner clouds to drizzle down the eastern slopes as far as the aspen groves of the foothills.

Red Fish didn't have to tell Longarm why they wanted to avoid the easier going above the timberline. The alpine meadows up yonder made for as easy riding as the open prairies

118

off to the east. But anyone with a good pair of field glasses would be able to spot them against the open slopes from ten or more miles away.

As they made camp in a natural ring of elephant-gray granite outcrops with tall timber all around, they could see way the hell off to the east through the tall bare trunks that weren't really packed that tight as soon as you studied on them. There was really far more open grass than timber in the apparently heavy cover below the timberline. But most of it was just shade, cast by the evergreen crowns higher up.

Once they'd seen to the riding stock and spread their two bedrolls in the hollow, they ate a cold breakfast of pemmican and corn pone from *her* supplies, and agreed to take turns on watch until later that afternoon. For she pointed out, and he agreed, that once the sun was low in the west, they'd be safe to move along the shaded slope, with the sun shining smack in the lenses of any red-sleeved snoop with a fancy pair of field glasses.

He offered to stand first watch. She said she knew this country better and wanted to make sure they were alone up there before she risked some sleep. So he let her. It was easy to fall asleep in the thin mountain air, even with the sunrise shining through that thin maroon calico as Red Fish stood atop a big tit of granite, her Yellowboy cradled across her own, with her shapely legs spread for balance.

Longarm had already noticed she was built nice. He was soon fast asleep in the Denver Public Library, asking a naked white lady with a pencil stuck in her hair bun if they had any copies of *Burke's Peerage*.

The naked librarian demurely asked him what a man with a raging erection wanted with a listing of all the noble British families. He was trying to get it in her, but for some reason he couldn't find her front entrance as he explained, "Harcourt sounds noble, and I just now thought I might be able to trace a remittance man's weekly remittance back to the source. How come you don't seem to have no pussy, ma'am?"

The librarian took the matter in hand and began to gently stroke it as she said, "You're pretty fresh, Cowboy. Are you saying you might be able to tell where the Calgary Kid is going if you could find out where his allowance is coming from?"

He started to take her wrist and make it move faster. Then he was pulling on braided hair and Red Fish was whispering,

"Wake up, but do not speak! There is someone or something stalking us. I haven't been able to spot it. But it is there. Moving through the trees like . . . like that *thing* that killed the woman called Roping Sally!"

Longarm threw off his light bedding, glad he'd been wearing his pants over that hard-on, and picked up his own Winchester, whispering, "Stay back and cover me!" as he eased hatless toward the surrounding ring of granite.

He found a cleft a man could wriggle through on his gut instead of rolling over to expose himself against the sky to anyone downslope. He wanted to be downslope himself as he circled to see who'd been circling them. He froze when he heard a frantic oinking. It sounded like a piglet stuck in a fence. But there were no fences up this way, and you hardly ever met stray pigs at this altitude.

He crawfished back to the outcrop to brace his back against solid granite as, sure enough, he made out a large ominous shadow ghosting through the mist between the tree trucks, just inside carbine range.

He heard Red Fish hissing, "What is it, Ochinnuyah?"

He hissed back, "*Keahyu!* Don't say another word!"

So she never did, even as the old sow grizzly down the slope rose on her hind legs to stare their way, swaying, as it tried to make out what it had just heard.

Then all concerned heard its cub oink again, further down the mountain, and the worried momma bear dropped back down to present her massive rump to them as it ambled slowly out of sight through the trees.

Red Fish let out a long shuddering sigh and said, "I feel silly. When it wasn't moving through the trees the way animals usually move, I thought it might be a ghost!"

Longarm rose to his feet to rejoin her inside the outcropping, observing, "She was acting natural, for a sow bear searching for a stray cub. But that wasn't the way a grazing elk or even a hunting bear would have acted. So it naturally startled you some."

She said, "No elk are grazing this high this early. That *keahyu* should have denned further down the slope to bear her winter cub as well."

He nodded and said, "There you go. It's like when folks hear creaks at midnight when they could swear they were alone in the house. Nobody spooks at sights and sounds they can easily explain. But that old sow bear's well on her way now. So that's the end of the ghost story. Do you want to see if you can sleep now? I'm wide awake, for some fool reason.''

She said she was too, and asked why he hadn't shot the grizzly, seeing he'd had it in his power to do so, and seeing few men ever got a chance to kill the secretive *keahyu* with so little risk.

He set his Winchester aside near his bedding as he grimaced and asked her, ''What would we do with three hundred pounds of bear meat and an orphan cub at this altitude?''

She laughed at the picture, but put her own gun aside and sat in the grass nearby as she quietly declared, ''I just don't understand you hairy people. You beat children, but spare the lives of animals when a real person would shoot them. Killing a real *keahyu* makes for a great brag. Its claws are powerful medicine and you could trade them for good things, even if you do not believe in our medicine!''

Longarm fished out a cheroot and struck a light to give himself time to choose his words. He decided the straight truth would do him as well, and said, ''You worry about your medicine and let me worry about my medicine. Some of my folks judge all of your folks by only one or two they've had any experience with. It's too bad you were mistreated at that mission school. Down Denver way years ago, a young mother and her two little girls were raped, killed, and scalped by Cheyenne. Their name was Hungate. Nobody made the whole thing up. They were really treated awful by Indians and the Indians were really Cheyenne. So the Third Colorado rode out of Camp Weld to avenge them, and they avenged the hell out of them at a place called Sand Creek. The only trouble was, they'd attacked the wrong Cheyenne. The ones they wanted to slaughter, with justice, were the followers of a mean cuss called Roman Nose. Butchering the hitherto friendly band under Black Kettle just made Black Kettle's band mean and ugly too. Custer had to finish Black Kettle off one winter's day on the Washita. There's just no telling where hurting little gals, red or white, can lead you when you're careless who you blame.''

She took a drag on the cheroot and handed it back before she told him, ''I don't think you would strike a child for forgetting she was not supposed to giggle in class. I think I would like to try kissing your hairy face some more.''

Longarm hesitated, then asked, "Who's going to keep watch if both of us lie down here?"

She asked him simply, "Were you expecting either one of us to go to sleep?"

So he took her in his arms again and, this time, she didn't break free as they fell back across the bedding, half on and half off the blue-eyed grass all around.

The swell thing about her big loose Mother Hubbard was the way she could cock one tawny leg across him as she unbuttoned his jeans to make that dream about naked librarians come true. She impaled her small firm form on his erection with him still almost dressed, hissing with delighted surprise as she got it all inside her. Then she was too busy to say anything else as she got her heels under her hips to bounce with the skill of a gal broken in under smoky hides and tipi poles.

It wasn't Longarm's first introduction to Plains Indian romance, bless their practical positions. So he knew why gals used to sleeping on the ground liked to get on top. She was pounding his tailbone into the sod pretty good, with his legs down straight and the cheeks of his own ass softening the blows.

By the time she'd made him come in her, and kept pounding until she caught up, he'd unfastened her beadwork belt and worked the loose-fitting Mother Hubbard off over her braided head. Her nut-brown body looked so pretty in the warmer light they were enjoying now that he wanted more, and told her so.

She rolled off, panting for breath as she lay on her side to watch him undress in turn. As he did so, her eyes widened and she gasped, "Cristecoom, you are so hairy, hairy, and did you really have all that in me just now?"

He crawled over to hug her naked breasts to his bare chest. She hugged him back, but protested, "*Sah!* I don't think I can bear a man as big as you on top. You are too *sacoay* and ... *Hah!* Keep doing what you are doing down there with your *okitchis,* I mean fingers, and we can *try* it your way."

So they did, and she was pleasantly surprised to discover how nice it worked with her spine arched across his McClellan saddle, with him keeping most of his weight on his hands and knees, while she wriggled her firm little bottom in ways it had never been able to wriggle up until that very morning.

So the rest of the morning went well, followed by a swell

afternoon and even a few hours sleep, in turn, before they were moving on along the unmarked path through the timber she'd chosen.

They rode by day where the timber was dense, and by moonlight where they had to cross wide burns. They grazed their ponies in moonlit fields of flowers, and went swimming in mountain tarns so cold he had a time getting it up for her when she suggested the quickest way to get rid of their goose-flesh. She said she liked to feel it growing, growing between her lips when she took it that way, clean as snowmelt and almost as cold.

As they worked their haphazard way north along the spine of the continent, Longarm sensed his appointed guide was in no great hurry to get him anywhere but under her Mother Hubbard. She'd assured him after a few days along the Divide that they were north of the Canadian line, but advised against dropping down to the foothills lest they meet up with some of her own nation.

He let it go the first few times she put him off that way. But a day later, as they were having a cold breakfast and he could *see* the distant haze of a prairie encampment, Longarm insisted, "Rain Crow told me you would be my Siksika mouth up this way. I want to talk to some of your folks, honey. I want to ask if anyone else has seen hide or hair of that killer I've been trailing."

She swallowed some of the tomato preserves she'd come to admire, along with his mustache and tobacco, before she shook her head to answer, "*Sah,* we are not far enough from the border. Some of my people tell things to the red sleeves for presents. Even when the things they say can get a *Siksika* in trouble with the Grandmother Victoria, they *still* tell the red sleeves. Such people would fuck dogs or even strike children, but you are right about there being good and bad in all the nations. If the other hairy one you are after has been through any Siksika village down below, the red sleeves will have been told by now."

He insisted, "I don't want the Calgary Kid caught by the Mounties. I'm out to serve him with a murder warrant in the name of the U.S. of A.! But think how dumb I'll look if I stay up in the clouds like this, out of touch with anyone but you, no offense, whilst down below the whole case is being argued by your government and mine!"

She shrugged and answered, "I don't accept either government as *mine*! Maybe I should tell you the truth. I have reasons to keep you up here with me—aside from how well you kiss with all that hair on your face, I mean. But can I trust you not to tell the red sleeves?"

He patted her thigh, held onto it, and said, "Honey, I've been busting a gut trying to *avoid* the damned Mounties! They're fixing to arrest me and deport me the minute they hear I'm up this way. What else have we been keeping from them, for Pete's sake?"

She moved his hand further along her thigh as she confided, "My people have been beating the *soop ogh tum* and dancing the *sooppascat*. A great Siksika *nah tosey,* you say medicine man, has told our people what they must do about those sister-fucking Sioux the red sleeves will do nothing, nothing about!"

Longarm whistled softly and quietly said, "Those refugee Lakota the U.S. Cav chased up this way have been giving the Canadian Indians a hard time?"

She nodded and asked, "Why did you think everyone has always fought them? We Siksika always fought the Crow. And yet even the Crow, who speak the same tongue as the Sioux, hate them, hate them, want to fight with them. Sioux are liars. Sioux are thieves. That bunch who came up this way under Sitting Bull promised they would not bother anyone. They said they were beaten and afraid and only wanted to live in peace on the Grandmother Victoria's blanket. But now they have started to hunt *eneuh* on Siksika hunting grounds, and steal out Siksika *ponoka meta* anywhere they find them!"

Longarm soberly asked, "Have you told the red sleeves about those refugee Lakota helping themselves to buffalo and ponies claimed by you Siksika?"

She nodded and grimly replied, "Of course we have. The Grandmother Victoria keeps smiling, smiling, like a captive woman smiles at the men lined up to rape her. What can she do? Those Sioux are the least of her worries, even though there are at least fifteen hundred fighting Sioux with their women and children for three hundred red sleeves to deal with."

She let that sink in, and added, "They say Louis Riel is back, and the Red River Métis and Plains Cree together can muster at least five thousand riflemen. The man we are listening to, the Painted One, thinks we should wait until the red sleeves are busy with the Métis. Then, while the Métis and

124

Cree are killing the red sleeves, we can kill all those thieving Sioux."

Longarm shook his head and said, "I've had much this same dumb conversation with some Métis pals in the past. Rightly or wrongly, it just ain't possible for any six or eight thousand rebels to overthrow a Canadian Government backed by the British Empire."

She asked simply, "Why? There are only three hundred red sleeves west of the Great Waters. Your eagle chief, Custer, had more men than that with him when he lost the war with the Sioux at Little Big Horn, right?"

Longarm shook his head and said, "Wrong. Custer lost a *battle*. The Lakota Confederacy lost the *war*. Once the U.S. Army saw the situation was serious, they put their backs into it and had every hostile on a reservation or hiding out up this way within eighteen months or less. General Terry and the U.S. Army stand ready and willing to ride up here and finish the job the minute the Queen or Ottawa invites them to!"

He lit a smoke for them to let that sink in before he hauled his other hand out of her lap and said, "Pay attention. You folks have to stop this suicidal dreaming, honey. Like it or not, the Shining Times are over! Like I told Louis Riel to his face, Queen Victoria ain't trying to police all this territory with three hundred riders because she's weak. She's just cheap! Should push come to shove, she'll just say she ain't amused and there'll be more British troops than you could shake a stick at, with bagpipes and Gatling guns to go with her field artillery. The Widow of Windsor ain't as delicate with what she calls native uprisings as she is with a teacup. When those Sepoys rose on her a few years back, the British Army lashed the leaders' arms along the muzzles of twelve-pounders and fired double-charge blanks to scatter their remains considerably."

Red Fish pulled his hand back into her lap as she insisted, "My people are not going to fight the red sleeves of the Grandmother. I just told you they are going to wait until the Cree and Métis fight the red sleeves so that *they* can fight the *Sioux*. Painted One will soon have all the guns we need. Good guns, with cranks on the stocks to make them fire boom-boom-boom like Gatling guns."

Longarm left his hand in her warm crotch, being only human, but told her with a wry chuckle that there were no such guns as she described.

When she insisted her tribal leaders were not fools who would pay for guns that didn't exist, Longarm shook his head and said, "Spencer made a seven-shot repeater with a coffee mill built into its stock a few years back. They hoped it might recapture some of the cowboy trade Winchester was taking away from them. The model never caught on. Trail herders don't grind their own coffee along the way. Captain Goodnight invented the chuck wagon with such chores in mind."

Red Fish slid the hem of her Mother Hubbard up out of the way of his hand. He sighed in mock dismay and asked, "Don't you ever get your fill of slap and tickle, girl?"

She lay back and spread her thighs, purring, "No. I would rather let you get on top than talk-talk-talk about things that don't concern anyone but my people!"

Getting rid of the cheroot and his Stetson, Longarm reclined beside her, strumming on her old banjo at first. But once he had her really hot he paused and, allowing his hand to rest in place as she thrust eagerly upward with her pelvis, said soberly, "My heart hangs heavy, knowing you and my old friend Rain Crow have lied to me and led me up here among the clouds to hunt the winds among these trees."

She gasped, "Don't stop! I am still your friend! So is Rain Crow! You wanted us to help you catch that spot-eye who killed another lawman south of the border. We have been helping you. I have led you a good part of the way and . . . *Please* get on top now, Ochinnuyah!"

He moved his love-slicked fingers just a bit as he insisted he was waiting for the whole story, all of it.

She said, "Later! Put it in me and I will tell you all I know!"

But he knew better. So he tickled her just enough to keep her hot as he got the whole simple notion out of her.

There was no more than divided loyalty to it. The Mounties counted on the Indian Police to patrol the border where it passed through the Blackfoot Reserve. Rain Crow hadn't wanted a fellow lawman with no jurisdiction mixed up in what he considered his own nation's business. So he'd told Red Fish not to mix Longarm up in it. Knowing full well where the gunrunners had been all this time, Red Fish had simply steered Longarm another way. She promised that if he treated her right

126

that morning, she'd carry him down to that big village of Painted One so he could ask if the gunrunners had allowed that spot-eyed Calgary Kid to tag along.

After he'd stripped and skewered her, she said she was getting used to being on the bottom now. As they sunbathed with another cheroot, she told him that they had to wait until sundown.

When he scowled, she grabbed him by the dong and hastily explained. "Hear me. Painted One and our war chiefs would be angry, angry if those gunrunners saw a well-known lawman in our village and ran away without delivering those rapid-fire guns!"

He blew a thoughtful smoke ring at one of her nipples and soberly asked what the Indians were using for money down below.

She said, "Gold and silver money, of course. My people do not sell furs, hides, or horses for sea shells. Each of those new boom-boom-boom guns with a crank costs *natchip pee*. I think they are worth it if they shoot that fast!"

Longarm grimaced and said, "I'd pay twenty dollars for such a gun my ownself. But I don't see how those gunrunners will deliver any. Nobody *makes* such guns yet as far as I know."

She suggested maybe they were a new invention.

Longarm shook his head and explained, "No offense, but when you're marketing a seriously improved firearm you don't offer first refusal to a medicine man! You show up at the front door in Washington, Paris, or London Town, and any ordnance officer will be proud to let you show him what you got!"

She asked if she could get on top.

He laughed, but said, "Damn it, honey. This is serious. I have to make sure the Calgary Kid didn't manage to join up with a bunch of border jumpers as he was trying to do over by Fort Peck."

As she tossed her Mother Hubbard to the winds to straddle him in all her glory in the morning sunlight, he added, "Besides, your own folks could be getting flimflammed. I'd like a good look at the guns they're paying all that money for."

She shook her head, brushing his bare chest with her braids as she told him, "You can't. They won't let you. Nobody is supposed to know they have them until they use them on the

127

Sioux. But hear me, Painted One is not a fool. He will make them boom-boom-boom before he parts with one silver dollar. Shove it up inside me again and I will take you down there later after those other hairy ones leave!"

He couldn't keep from shoving upward into such a welcome. But as he did so he groaned, "How will you know when it's time?"

She began to grind her hips atop him as she demurely replied, "Boom-boom-boom. Painted One will test the new guns. When I hear them up here, I will know it is time to start down from where we are having so much fun waiting. Those others will be gone by the time we get there. You can ask my people if one of them had a spot in one eye. My people stare closely at strange visitors."

He started to object that he wanted to *catch* the Calgary Kid, not give him another lead. But as he studied on it, enjoying the position he was in at the time, he decided it would be dumb for even the Calgary Kid to head right back to Montana with those gunrunners. So the sneaky cuss could well be off in another direction, or better yet, dallying with some Siksika gals when they got there!

So they lazed, smoked, ate, and fornicated the better part of a whole day away up in the tall timber. But before sundown, Longarm insisted they get dressed and start down the long slopes. He pointed out that it could take them until after sundown to reach that distant prairie haze. So Red Fish agreed, provided he agreed to wait until they heard those guns being tested before they rode all the way in.

That was about the way things seemed to be turning out. They took their own sweet time, zigzagging down through more hogbacks than a body might expect such a steep-looking range to have around its shinbones. So the purple shadows were long and the crack willows were old gold in the wooded draw they paused in, waiting for darkness to fall. It barely did. There were only a few stars in the purple sky when they heard a distant fusillade of small-arms fire.

Red Fish laughed and said, "We can ride on now. If we walk our mounts we should get there as those others are leaving. They have not been invited to stay. The red sleeves get cross when you lie to them, and it is better to be able to tell them nobody they are looking for has been staying with you, see?"

He mounted up to follow, muttering, "I wish I had an honest Indian doing my expense accounts for me."

They rode on and on, further than he'd expected, until through the tree branches ahead they could make out a dull orange glow. Red Fish said, "They have lit fires for dancing. I hope the red sleeves don't wonder why and ride over to see!"

As they moved in, Longarm thoughtfully drew the Winchester from its saddle boot, saying, "Stay here and let me scout ahead. That's too much light for any bonfire. I smell burning hide too. Somebody's sure as hell set a tipi or more ablaze over yonder!"

He dropped the pack pony's lead and heeled the roan he was riding forward through the trees and scrub to where, sure enough, he could make out sullen columns of smoke, and then, as he rode up out of the draw, the flickering flames of crashed piles of poles and the cones of tipis still standing but on fire!

He searched for signs of other movement as he reined in a rifle shot out and dismounted to scout on afoot. Then Red Fish overtook him, riding her own paint at full gallop as she called out to her kith and kin in a bewildered wail.

Longarm yelled, "Red Fish! *Saha!* Don't ride no closer!"

But the pretty little Siksika stayed willful to the last, and paid him no mind as she reined in near a still form stretched on the ground near a burning tipi. Red Fish was screaming like a banshee as she must have recognized somebody important to her.

Then, as she dismounted gracefully to let her pony run free while she dropped to her knees by the downed villager, the rifle shot Longarm had been dreading rang out.

Red Fish jerked and flopped sideways toward him as he fired at the muzzle flash from the darkness beyond the burning ruins. He rolled away from his own muzzle flash to come up a few yards away just as Red Fish tried to rise up on one elbow, caught a second rifle round with her small frame, and fell back limply while, all along the line over to the southeast, gun muzzles winked his way like the eyes of a whole pack of wolves searching for him.

So all Longarm could do was hug the ground and sob, "I'm sorry, Red Fish! I should have listened and done this your way! But now that the bastards have dealt us this hand, I mean to play it *my* way!"

Chapter 11

Flickering flames cast tricky light and shifting shadows. So it wasn't strange that Longarm could see better as the widely scattered fires simmered down to white-hot embers.

By this time he'd rolled behind a knee-high fuel pile of buffalo chips and pinned his badge to the lapel of his jacket. He didn't have a lick of jurisdiction over outlaws up this way. But he didn't want a soul to suspect he was *with* them!

He sensed he'd made a wise move when another shot rang out behind him as a shrill voice yelled, *"Sah! Amo mahts pah kapa!"* He rolled over on one elbow to see a big fat gal in fringed deerskin had deflected the barrel of the Sharps .50 a skinny Siksika kid had been aiming his way!

The Indian woman called to him in English. "They have run away. If you want to go after them with our young men, I will give you an elk-dog. Your own two ran back toward the hills!"

Longarm rose gingerly to his feet, seeing others were doing the same all around in the ruby glow. He saw now that most of the confusion had been at this one end of a larger tipi town. At least two score barely visible ruby cones stretched away into the darkness as he strode over to where Red Fish and the earlier casualty lay.

The pretty little thing seemed to be staring up at him with a faint smile as he dropped to one knee beside her to feel for a pulse. Behind him, the fat gal said softly, "They are both dead. When our young men overtake the two-faced ones who killed them, they will not be satisfied with hair. They will build small fires on their chests and make them watch as they roast their tongues on sticks!"

Longarm grimaced and said, "Let me guess. Your Painted One had the money ready for them. But they didn't bring him those medicine guns?"

The Siksika woman said something to the kid with the rifle. As he ran off she said, "I was not invited into the council lodge. But we all heard Painted One yelling, very angry, something about a coffee mill, before the shooting started."

Longarm rose from the two sprawled bodies, nodding gravely as he said, "You can only fool some of the people some of the time. Those crooks must have intended to gun your leaders and take the money from the beginning. The question now is which way did they go?"

The fat woman pointed south into the darkness, saying, "That is the way back to Montana. They know what will happen to them if our young men catch them before they can get back across the border!"

Longarm shook his head. "Too far. They must know how many days they were on that foothill trail coming this way. They knew when they murdered and robbed your leaders just now, there were a whole lot of other Siksika camped all along that route."

Facing another way, he asked, "How far is Fort MacLeod to the east of here?"

She said, "A hard night's ride. They could be there a little after sunrise if they beat their elk-dogs half dead. But why would they ride that way? The red sleeves would hold them, even before we told the red sleeves what they did here."

She shook her fat arm at the surrounding darkness and cried aloud, "Hear me, two-faced ones! It won't hurt Painted One if we tell the red sleeves what was going on! You have taken all our money and given us no guns to fight the Sioux! We don't care now if the Grandmother Victoria knows this! We want her to help us catch you! She can hang the ones our young men fail to catch first!"

That kid with the buffalo rifle returned with three other kids. They'd caught Longarm's roan for him, and were leading a pair of barebacked Indian ponies, both paints.

131

The fat woman told him, "All of these elk-dogs are your own now. I think you will want to change your saddle and bridle to a fresher mount, though."

He allowed she was right, then asked, "Do those Mounties over to Fort MacLeod have east-west singing wires as well as a line running north and south?"

She asked one of the kids, who burbled at her in their own lingo until she shut him up and told Longarm, "*Ah.* Over the shining mountains through the pass where one can see far, very far."

He nodded, consulting his mental map, and said, half to himself, "Crowsnest Pass. The NWMP doesn't have jurisdiction over in British Columbia, but they'd naturally stay in touch with the BC Provincial Constabulary. So those outlaws will want to cut that line before they make a run for it over the Divide!"

He began to saddle one of the paint ponies as the fat woman jawed with the boys, then told him, "That does not seem a good direction for them to run. There is rough riding, much rough riding, through giant trees and mossy rocks in the hunting grounds of our Salish enemies."

Longarm cinched the McClellan, driving a knee up into the Indian pony's crafty gut as he did so, saying, "Anyone knowing enough about your nation to flimflam your leaders has to know your fighting men don't get over those mountains much. It would be pure suicide for them to try for Montana across all those miles of open prairie with both you and the Mounties dogging them and American lawmen alerted by wire to watch the border!"

He pointed north into the empty night and growled, "If they cut the wire over Crowsnest Pass before the Mounties alert the BCPC, they have a fair shot at getting all the way down to the seacoast with their ill-gotten cash before anyone over yonder gets to looking for them!"

He fought the bit and bridle in place, and swung aboard to drop the Winchester in its scabbard as he told the four Indians he was much obliged for the loan of a good elk-dog.

The fat woman called after him, "Wait! You have another elk-dog for us to catch for you! It was packing your supplies, *sah?*"

He was already moving out at a trot, not looking back. It would have cost precious moments to explain why a determined man with guns and matches hardly needed to pack supplies through the northern Rockies in the greenup time!

Hunting dogs tracked by following the spoor of the game they were after. Longarm was fairly sure he knew which way the outlaws were headed, and sniffing up behind a man in the dark was a good way to walk into a bullet.

As soon as he was sure he wasn't backlit from the Siksika village, he cut sharply to his left, assuring the confounded pony, "I ain't out to run you into no trees, and I'm counting on you not to run us over any cliffs by starlight. None of this matters for shit if I'm guessing wrong. But if I'm guessing right, those outlaws will head up along the foothills until they get to the east-west trail and that important telegraph line. They'll want to cut the wire before any Indians can report them to the Mounties at Fort MacLeod. They can't know for sure how much time they have. So they can't afford to shilly-shally!"

He sensed the change in his pony's balance as they moved diagonally along a gentle grassy grade. He patted the pony's neck and urged it on, muttering, "*We* don't have to beeline for that telegraph line. We want to intercept it higher up, where it won't matter whether they've cut it or not."

The pony answered by balking on the grassy slope. Longarm wasn't green enough to heel a mount forward in mountain country after dark. He dismounted and led it afoot slowly until he could make out the sudden gut-wrenching drop ahead.

He gulped hard, and told the pony, "That's one I owe you. But all these hogback outcrops come with two ends to 'em. So seeing we were headed north anyways, let's see if we can feel our way up to that end of this son of a bitch!"

They could. After they worked their way through the folded leaf of sandstone where it ducked underground for a ways, Longarm remounted, rode until they ran up on a hogback of shale, and repeated the process.

It got mighty tedious, but by midnight he seemed to be back aboard that gentler contour line Red Fish had been following through the tall timber up where the clouds held sway.

A mental map was only so accurate in strange country after dark. So the going was poky, and Longarm was sure those other riders would be over the Divide and long gone before he ever found his fool way to Crowsnest Pass.

But a million years later, as the eastern sky pearled pink

and he could make more sense of his surroundings, Longarm reined in along an open stretch to stare thoughtfully westward at the sort of eerie outline against the starry western sky. It looked as if some angel of the Lord, or Indian spirit, had etched a dotted line across the blackness with some magic glowing chalk. He realized it was the snowfields of the highest crests along the Divide, catching the first rays of the rising sun to his east. He stared soberly at the dark gap between two snow-covered massifs off to his northwest, and told his pony in a certain tone, "If that ain't Crowsnest Pass, it's *some* swell pass, and Crowsnest Pass is supposed to be the only one in these parts. So I vote we get on over there, Elk Dog."

They did. It wasn't easy, and as they moved up above the timberline at an angle, Longarm was sure any sharp-eyed son of a bitch with the sun behind him ought to notice them. For by this time the slanting rays were reaching way down the bare slopes, etching every rock and blade of grass in deep purple shadow and golden light. He could only hope, if they hadn't beaten him over the pass, they were somewhere down in the trees, unable to see just where they were headed at the moment.

He didn't try for the highest saddle between the peaks to the north and south. When he spotted distant telegraph poles cutting across the hairpin turns of the trail over the pass, he heeled his mount that way, but resisted the temptation to lope along the level grade. The human eye caught rapid distant movement before it might notice slow motion.

He reined in near a granite outcrop, where the trail swung around and the wires were strung over what looked like a herd of elephants holding a Roman orgy on the grassy slope. He led the Indian pony to the upgrade side and tethered it to a clump of wind-pruned dwarf juniper. Then he took off his hat and eased his head over the top for a serious stare down the eastern slopes of the Rocky Mountains.

It was easy to see why they'd named the pass behind him after the crow's nest of some ship. He could see fifty miles or more to the string-straight horizon below the sunrise. But he knew that in point of fact the distant prairie rolled like a vast sea of grass, and there was no saying what might lie closer, hidden by sun dazzle and the simple fact that things got smaller and smaller as they got further away from you.

Then he spied a faint vertical chalk line, rising from the

heavy belt of juniper and fir at that lower level, and grinned wolfishly to himself. The self-indulgent assholes were brewing breakfast coffee!

Longarm glanced up at the single strand of wire, softly humming in the wind. He knew they'd cut it further east. They'd figured on reaching it and cutting it before anyone could get word to the NWMP at Fort MacLeod. They'd planned this whole murderous game for a good while.

Sticking an unlit cheroot between his bared teeth and cupping both hands to light it in the vagrant but constant high-altitude winds, he figured he had time to show a little smoke on his own, but had to say aloud, "That other killer we're after can't be with 'em. The timing is all wrong. Harcourt was in other parts, killing other folks, whilst the bastards having coffee down yonder were setting up their confidence game with the pissed-off Siksika!"

He didn't care just now. He'd promised Red Fish he'd settle their account with this other bunch. The Calgary Kid was no damned good, but he could wait. Red Fish hadn't wanted to ride in that early, and the sons of bitches had already robbed her people before shooting her for no good reason!

Longarm smoked that first cheroot, forced himself to wait an hour, and smoked another as he watched that goddamned smoke still rising from those goddamned fool campfire all day?

That was a sobering thought. What if they were waiting for somebody, maybe some Indian turncoats working with them to steal tribal funds?

Or what if they weren't planning on heading over the pass to British Columbia after all? What if they just wanted to make everyone suspect as much, but camped near the cut wire to double back along the trail from Fort MacLeod and . . .

"What if the moon is made of blue cheese and there are really whores with hearts of gold?" he warned himself sternly. A man had to work with what he had to work with. Thinking of all the things that might be could lead a man from common sense to the mirror-maze of maybe so.

Poor old General McClellan, after designing a fair cavalry saddle, had snatched defeat from the jaws of victory by considering all the things General Lee *could* do instead of what he was *likely* to do with a way smaller army.

Up to now, those outlaws who'd robbed the Indians were

acting as expected, save for that late-morning fire down yonder.

He gazed all around as the light improved to where he could make out the pastel colors of the small alpine flowers mixed with the new sprung tussock grass. Then he slid down to ground level to untether the paint pony, telling it, "We seem to have more time than I feared. So let's see if we can't hide you out a tad safer."

Leading the brown and white paint at a slow walk, Longarm took it on to another granite outcrop that didn't seem that big until you got close. It lay in a meaningless gray jumble a quarter mile north of the telegraph line. Better yet, there was a puddle of standing water the natural drainage had run into on its upslope side.

Longarm watered the pony, took a swig from one of the canteens by his bedroll, and tethered the paint out of sight of the trail. Then he drew the Winchester from its boot, made sure he had fifteen in the tube and one in the chamber, with some spare rounds in one pocket, and walked slowly back to the first outcrop, hat back on but smokes out until further notice.

He didn't climb back atop the granite. He hunkered in its shadow to the northwest, keeping the telegraph line and winding trail from below just in sight, to the left of the rounded boulders.

Another million years went by. He was sure the whole bunch, along with the Calgary Kid, were laughing at him over on the west slope as they all slid downhill to freedom.

He told himself he was a fool for thinking Harcourt would want to work north of these troubles and maybe try for Yellowhead Pass. For why should a homicidal lunatic plan any escape route at all? The kid was likely just running without any destination. There was nothing sensible about anything he'd done since he *might* have felt just cause to shoot three old pals at Fort Morgan. He'd been acting just plain wild ever since.

Longarm found himself softly singing that same dumb ditty about the old maids from Canada. He wondered why, even as he crooned:

> The dirty old maid, she up and said,
> My hole's as big as the moon!

A man fell in last Fourth of July,
And didn't crawl out until June!

The song got dirtier after that. Longarm stopped singing it as he nodded to himself and declared, "Ginger and Candy, back in that cellar in Denver. Their holes weren't quite that big, but they surely were a couple of wild whores and here we are up in Canada! So what in the hell am I trying to *tell* myself? That all three of them, and that slicker they called Hamish, are homicidal lunatics?"

Then he spotted movement way the hell down the slope, and forgot about old maids from Canada as he made out a raggedy band of riders moving up the trail above the timberline!

"Here, pussy, pussy!" Longarm whispered as he made out nine of them in all. They were sharply backlit by the low morning sun. But there was no mistaking them for Indians, or Mounties. They could have passed for honest trail herders, had this been a cattle trail and they'd been out to move anything but their own asses and that Siksika silver over the Great Divide!

Behind them, that wood smoke still rose, to show they'd simply left their campfire burning as they'd ridden on.

Longarm wondered why that surprised him. Killers who'd leave an Indian village in flames after gunning men, women, and children were hardly likely to give a shit about burning down trees.

It took another million years for them to work their way up to his level. He could hear them joshing back and forth in the crisp thin air from half a mile off. Then they were closer, talking louder, as Longarm snicked the safety off with a round in the chamber. To see them for the first time, and hear them conversing lightly about some trail town they remembered fondly, a body could take them for a bunch of innocent cowhands, maybe Canadian cowhands, headed over Vancouver way on honest business.

That was a shitty consideration to contemplate at this eleventh hour! But it had to be considered. A man would never forgive himself if he learned, too late, he'd ambushed the wrong bunch.

Longarm rose slowly to his feet, telling himself not to be a total fool. There were nine of them to one of him, and they'd already shown no inclination to offer any sucker an even break!

But Longarm let them work their way up the trail until they were about even with him. Then he circled the big outcrop counterclockwise as they passed, to step out into sight down the slope from them before he took a deep breath, let half of it out so his voice wouldn't crack in the thin mountain air, and called out to the column headed the other way, "Hold her right there, gents! I got the drop on you and I'd be U.S. Deputy Marshal Custis Long of the Denver—"

Then all hell broke loose as some twisted in their saddles, guns in hand, while others spurred their mounts into dead runs in all directions across the wide-open approaches to Crowsnest Pass!

Longarm's Winchester reached accurately out to two hundred yards, but could only hit *most* of the time at four hundred, or a mite more than a city block. So he fired first at the farthest rider's pony to put him on his feet. Then he nailed two more, closer in, and by this time a red-bearded wonder on a crow-hopping bay just a few yards up the pass was pegging pistol shots his way with ass-puckering accuracy. So Longarm blew horse and rider down with his own shots aimed steadier.

Somebody took Longarm's hat off for him as he dropped to one knee to draw careful beads as all but one of the outlaws returned his fire at impossible pistol range with pistols. He hadn't taken them for deep thinkers. He nailed the one who was firing with a rifle from a moving pony, like an asshole. Then he crawfished out of his own big cloud of gunsmoke to dash around to the other side of his outcropping and put all but that cuss way up the slope out of business with a fusillade of rapid fire from the direction they'd never been braced for.

Longarm's Indian pony was far off as well as safe. He tried to grab a skittish pony with an empty saddle as he forged up the steep grade, cutting across the bends, after that distant figure on foot. The spooked pony shied the wrong way. Longarm cussed and kept going, chest hurting as he gasped for the air his wobbly legs kept demanding.

The air was as thin up ahead, and that first one he'd dismounted was staggering like a drunk, but holding on to his own Spencer .50 as Longarm called out, "Wait up! I'd like a word with you, old son!"

The outlaw dropped behind a wind-polished boulder and

pegged a shot back down the slope as Longarm gasped to within, say, three hundred yards. So Longarm dropped to one knee behind another outcrop, let the bastard pepper the other side with lead a spell, then sprang back to his feet and charged at an angle to drop behind another, further up the slope.

Longarm knew better than to gaze over the top at less than three hundred yards. He lay flat on the dusty scree to slither his head and shoulders, Winchester and all, at ground level where the uphill shade was bright-morning dark.

From his new vantage point Longarm could only make out one spurred boot, its toe dug in to brace the other man close to his own granite defenses. It would have to do for now. So Longarm drew a careful bead on the shiny buckle of the other man's spur as he let his breath out, held the thought, and squeezed off a round.

The sound of the single shot was still echoing as the outlaw up the slope wailed, "You son of a bitch! I paid good money for this boot and now you've shot the heel clean off!"

Longarm called back amiably enough, "I was aiming for your ankle bone. Must have misjudged the windage. I'll try to aim better next time."

The outlaw, now completely concealed, hesitated, then called down, "What was that about you being a U.S. deputy marshal? Don't you know we're in Canada now? Unincorporated North West Territory. Nobody has a lick of jurisdiction in these parts but them North West Mounted Police."

Longarm shrugged and replied, "Let's say this is on the house then. You boys killed a friend of mine last night. I promised her I'd take care of you lying sons of bitches."

Gazing back down the slope at the ponies grazing quietly now, a furlong downslope from those eight scattered forms, Longarm added in a dry tone, "Reckon I only owe her one more."

The rider he'd pinned down pleaded, "Give me a break! You got old Slick, the mastermind behind it all. You'll find the money we got off them Blackfoot in the saddlebags of that bay gelding you downed. In that patch of sulphur flowers up the slope from old Slick!"

Longarm fished out a cheroot and lit up one-handed before calling out, "I thank you for clearing that much up. I have another question to ask you. I'm really up this way in search of another dirty prick entirely. You might know him as the

Calgary Kid, the Lime Juice Kid, or even Percival Harcourt. Ain't that a bitch? Before he gunned a trader over by Fort Peck he allowed he was looking to travel north with some border jumpers. Your turn.''

The outlaw pinned down up the slope replied, ''He wasn't with us. Look here, it was Slick's notion to gun them Blackfoot last night. I thought he was only out to sell them some old trade rifles at a good profit.''

''Sure you did,'' sneered Longarm. ''Anyone can see a bunch of poor benighted Indians would hand over their wampum without a murmur to nine whole white men in the middle of their village. You murderous bastards had enough of an argument getting Painted One to show you he had the money before you showed him one damned gun. Then every one of you must have started shooting and kept shooting until you were out of range aboard the broncs you'd tethered separate from those mules. One of you hit a pretty little gal called Red Fish as you scampered off. That one could have been *you*. So you see how it is.''

The outlaw pleaded, ''I never shot no gals back there! It was all the fault of them damned Blackfoot anyways. We'd have only shot the ones in that tipi with us if the others hadn't acted so excited!''

Longarm took a deep drag on his cheroot without answering. He rolled on his back to blow smoke straight up. That other rascal's Spencer spanged, and something buzzed like a bee over Longarm's grim smile.

He spat the cheroot out. It landed a few feet away in the sunlight. As it smoldered quietly there, Longarm eased himself around to the back of his own boulder. The sun would get higher before it got lower, and that sliver of shade to the west of it had been meager to start with.

After a time the distant rifleman called out, ''Hey, Marshal?''

Longarm didn't answer. He just sat there with his back to the granite, gazing in satisfaction down the slope at those other dead bastards, until, sure enough, the survivor regarding his smoldering cheroot on the far side called out, ''Let's talk turkey, as one real American to another!''

Longarm didn't answer.

The other now sounded sincerely worried as he insisted, ''Aw, come on. I know I missed you. You got our leader and most of the other boys. You've recovered the money, to give back to the Indians or to keep for yourself. There's over six thousand dollars' worth of gold and silver specie in them saddlebags! So let me go! You know you don't have any jurisdiction up this way! Nobody but them Mounties can arrest me! They'll arrest *you* if they catch you flashing your own badge in these parts!''

Longarm had no call to answer. Everything the cuss said was true.

As he listened for something more important, the outlaw called to him, ''I reckon I'll be going now. I warn you that I mean to stand up and head backwards up the pass, with this rifle trained your way in case you do anything foolish, hear?''

Longarm didn't answer. The other must have risen some, because all at once big buffalo slugs were spanging off the granite Longarm had put between them. The outlaw aimed high, low, and to either side a greener lawman might have been peering around as, sure enough, he crabbed *down* the slope, a liar to last, to catch a ride out with all that loot!

Longarm judged his progress by the retreating muzzle blasts of his big repeating saddle gun. Longarm was counting the shots as well. So when he heard the seventh and last round of a Spencer magazine, he simply rolled up on his own knees, braced his elbows atop a steady rest, and growled, ''Adios, asshole!'' as he fired his own saddle gun from, say, seventy-five yards.

The exposed target, desperately trying to shove another tubular magazine up his Spencer's ass, squawked like a goose, landed on his back spread-eagle, and rolled down the steep slope a surprising ways before he just lay limp as a discarded rag doll.

Longarm rose, stepped over to where his cheroot still smoldered on the windswept scree, and picked it up to stick back between his bared teeth, murmuring, ''Waste not, want not, and Lord knows how far the next trading post may be!''

He reloaded as he strolled down the sloping battlefield. He got the saddlebags from the dead bay and draped the handsome weight over his left forearm. As he found his hat and put it on, he heard a weak groan.

The red-bearded cuss he'd shot earlier was still alive. Longarm went closer, kicked a six-gun further down the slope, and hunkered over the bearded wonder to say, "Howdy. Where did I hull you, Slick?"

The barely conscious rider croaked, "Spine, I reckon. I can't move my arms nor legs. Yet they hurt like fire. How come it hurts so bad to get shot this way?"

Longarm shrugged and said, "I ain't no doc. It's just as well. I doubt a doc could do shit for you if we *had* one up this way. I have another question for you. Do you recall a small Blackfoot gal bending over another Indian stretched out near that council lodge last night?"

The spine-shot killer mumbled, "Can't say as I do. You ain't going to let them Indians have this child, are you?"

Longarm rose to his feet again, smiling down at the ringleader, and said, "I have to get it on down the road now. It's only a question of time before *somebody* comes riding in response to all this recent gunplay."

Slick whimpered, "Don't leave me like this for them Indians! Hand me my damned pistol. Just leave one round in the wheel if you don't trust me! You can't let *Blackfoot* have another white man, damn it!"

Longarm asked not unkindly, "Why not? It was your own grand notion to mess with 'em. As for handing you a gun to let you take the easy way out, I don't see how you'd be able to *use* it, seeing how clever I shot you, I mean."

As he started to head up to his tethered paint, the helpless killer wailed, "No! Please don't leave me like this! Shoot me one more time before you go! Have mercy on me, for the love of God!"

Longarm didn't answer. The only cuss more disgusting than a cold-blooded killer was a cold-blooded crybaby.

Longarm got on up to his Indian pony, secured those saddlebags to the front swells, and rode off down the slope without a backward glance.

He was glad he hadn't taken the time to help himself to anything else when, a little over an hour later, he heard the distant jingle of harness metal as he'd just gotten back amid juniper and spruce.

He reined in and dismounted to lead his paint off the trail. Thanks to the recent spring rains, the forest duff between the trees was damp and springy. So he just aimed for denser cover without worrying about such slight sign as he might be leaving.

He stood by the paint in a tangle of second-growth sprouting from a windfallen spruce, and cupped a palm over the pony's muzzle to steady it while a million years went by.

Then he saw flashes of white and sunlit scarlet through the dark greens and browns of the forest. As the white-helmeted Mounties moved on up the pass, Longarm whispered to his pony, "Told you somebody else was sure to hear all that gunplay, didn't I? I hope that spine-shot son of a bitch has died by now. I can't see Mounties roasting his tongue on a stick for him, and I'd as soon they didn't hear about you and me!"

Chapter 12

Those saddlebags were the snag now. Longarm had many a reason not to go back to that Siksika village, starting with the simple fact that he wanted to ride the other way. But there was no lawful way a lawman could hang on to that much stolen property.

He thought of caching it somewhere and letting the Indians know about it when he had the time. But while he'd just been lucky as all get-out in one shootout, there was no way to make dead certain those Indians would get their money back unless he took it back to them.

So, cussing some and riding through all the cover he could manage, Longarm made his way back the many miles he'd ridden, and it was slower going by daylight with Lord only knows how many Mounties he had to duck.

He got back to the scene of the robbery, where Red Fish had died, in late afternoon. As he scouted from that same wooded draw, the first thing he noticed was that nobody was there.

Nobody living, at any rate. The Indians had struck all the undamaged lodges to leave an untidy campsite and, over on top of a nearby grassy swell, a grim grove of platform burials.

Longarm didn't want to. But he had to ride close enough to spook his pony, and sure enough, two small blue moccasins and the hem of a maroon Mother Hubbard showed at one end of an elkskin bundle laced with rawhide thongs. One braid of silky black hair hung out the other end. Longarm dismounted, tethered his edgy mount, and strode over to where they'd left the pretty little thing to the prairie winds.

He tucked the last of his cheroots through a thong across the dead gal's breast, reaching more than shoulder high to do so as he softly said, "This ain't the custom of my kind. But if your kind can put cornflowers on Roping Sally's grave, it's the least I can do."

Then he patted one of the lodgepole-pine posts holding her off the ground and added, "So long, friend. I could brag on getting the one who killed you, but it wouldn't do you a lick of good. So I'd best just move along now."

He did. The spooked Indian pony insisted on running until they were well clear of the desolate scene and the smell of death.

Where the Indians had gone was no mystery. They still hauled heavy goods by travois, the two dragging ends plowing deep in the soft sod of the greenup.

The reason was no mystery either. Considering their warlike ways, all the Horse Indians shared an almost childlike fear of dead folks. After busting a gut to kill you and cutting you up to cripple all four of your ghosts, a painted hero had to go through all sorts of purification rites before his own kin would eat or sleep with him. Dead *kin* could be even more worrisome. You couldn't mutilate them, and who knows *what* a ghost with hands and eyes might be up to? Quill Indians were horrified by the notion of churchyards full of dead folks smack in the middle of a settlement.

The sign he was following led eastward toward more open country. It was getting late enough in the season for them to risk leaving the shelter of the foothills, although he knew they'd still pitch their tipi rings in some well-drained wooded draw. For this was the time of the year the High Plains could kill you in your sleep with a flash flood or a dry midnight blast of polar air.

He figured they'd started to think about buffalo. It was a bit early for the spring hunt, but that was the way they were headed. He hoped the herds up this way were in better shape than, say, south of the cross-country rails through Wyoming Territory. The buffalo the Comanche and Kiowa had fought to save at Adobe Wells were as gone as the snows of yesteryear. The northern herds were melting away fast. Longarm wasn't as sure as some about the reasons.

The hunting pressure since the war had been a caution, with mighty nimrods blazing away from trains at buff they'd never skin or even get a close look at. But deer, crows, and coyotes were blasted away by the same jolly marksmen and kept bouncing back, even though you never saw as many deer, crows, or coyotes bunched together.

Old-timers had told him, and he'd studied on it some himself, that you never saw buffalo, passenger pigeons, or salmon in small bunches. You saw none at all, or more than you could shake a stick at. So maybe some critters could only reproduce like Ancient Romans in those wild public orgies. The early Christians had taught the Ancient Romans not to hold orgies, and then look what had happened to them!

"You miss one nesting pair of crows or one gravid coyote, and you've wasted a whole summer's shoot-off," Longarm explained to his trotting paint. But he doubted even an Indian pony cared, seeing that it ate grass instead of buffalo meat. Longarm knew that like the Ute to the south, the Siksika hunted elk and deer on the higher range they roamed. But nature grew much more meat, and above all *fat,* on a young cow buffalo. Indians hunted for tender cuts, not trophies.

A glorious Canadian sunset caught Longarm alone on the rolling green prairie. He knew he could probably ride on and locate the Indians' new camp after dark by its sky-glow. But riding within dog-bark of robbed and shot-up Siksika after dark could take years off a man's life.

So he camped in a shallow grassy draw, with no fire. He hobbled the pony to graze by a pool of standing water, and spread his bedding on a south-facing slope, wishing he had a smoke.

It made him feel just a bit better about leaving the last of his tobacco with Red Fish. A gift that didn't hurt a little to part with was only a brag.

He let himself wish Red Fish was still alive and under the bedding with him, smiling up at the Milky Way with him on top. He didn't mean this disrespectfully. When you got a pretty gal killed, you deserved to suffer the full loss of all she'd meant to you.

Roping Sally had been a great lay too, and now that made *two* swell gals who'd gotten themselves killed up this way in his company. It was enough to make a man consider celibacy.

But of course, he never did. He liked gals too much to do without any, and most of the time he could make them stay out of his other pursuits.

He lay there staring up at the big unwinking stars through the thin dry air, dying for a smoke, with a raging hard-on as he considered whether Red Fish or Roping Sally had been built tighter down yonder. He allowed himself to picture both of them in bed with him at once, not a bit jealous of one another, but refrained from jacking off to ease the torment, hoping that might atone just a bit for the both of them getting killed so young.

Then the sky above was pearling gray, and he figured he must have been asleep instead of killing that son-of-a-bitching Wendigo aboard that freight train some more. He sat up with a groan, washed his dry mouth out with canteen water, and opened a can of tomato preserves for a cold breakfast.

Then he had all the fun of catching a hobbled horse who'd had a whole cool night to regather its sass. But that was why hobbles had been invented, and after he'd proven a man on foot could run faster than a hobbled horse, he saddled up and rode on.

The Indians were further east than he'd expected. He spied no sign of buffalo as he headed up higher rises on purpose. But along about noon, as he was fixing to open a can of beans and try smoking a milkweed stem, he spotted a thin blue haze of smoke against the eastern horizon and headed for it a bit wide.

He circled until, as he'd hoped, he crossed the draw they'd camped in downstream a few furlongs. He dismounted and led his mount through the brushy crack willow and chokecherry to where he could make out the Siksika lodges among thinner and taller poplar and maples.

He tethered his paint to some aspen it might want to browse, and slipped through the trees along the shadier south slope. He knew they'd have their own ponies downwind, and well guarded. He didn't aim to pester their remuda. He only wanted a look at it.

Once he'd stared down at the whole layout for a time, from as high in the shade as he could manage, Longarm nodded in satisfaction and worked back to where he'd left his saddled mount.

He removed the saddlebags full of coins and draped them over his gun arm to show innocent intent. Then he led the pony with his left hand and simply strolled into the village by the bright light of noon until, sure enough, dogs were barking, kids were yelling, and better yet, that old fat gal in deerskins who spoke English led a welcoming committee of excited-looking Siksika out to greet him.

The fat woman sobbed, "We did not expect you back! There were too many of them for one man to track. You didn't cut their trail either."

It had been a statement rather than a question. But Longarm called back, "I caught up with them. In Crowsnest Pass. But I never came back to count coup. Who'd be in charge of your treasury now that Painted One is no more?"

She pointed at a bigger tipi painted with those dark blue diamonds and U-shapes Siksika considered *Natoya* or Medicine. She told him that was their council lodge. When she said all the important gents left were smoking in there, he asked if she'd have him announced.

She hesitated, then said, "Remember, this is what you said you wanted." She sent a boy in his teens ahead of Longarm to avoid any rude surprise on his part.

Longarm got the rude surprise when he ducked inside the dark, smoke-filled council lodge. A whole slew of Indians were obviously seated in council around a buffalo skin covered with medicine signs. The surprise was Crown Sergeant Foster of the NWMP, seated cross-legged to face the entrance in his immaculate scarlet tunic, pistol lanyard freshly whitened with pipe clay to match the tall police helmet atop his head. Nobody without a ramrod up his ass could have been sitting up as straight as the stuffy son of a bitch.

Foster wasn't alone. A younger Mountie seated to one side of the circle had a Martini-Henry carbine in his lap, trained casually but steadily in Longarm's direction.

Longarm smiled sheepishly and asked, "Where did you hide your own mounts, and ain't you supposed to have a desk job these days, Foster?"

The slightly older and far frostier Mountie replied without any emotion, "We had our hosts stable them in another tipi, assuming you'd be along. As for my being in the field at the moment, we're spread a little thin this spring."

He nodded at the younger Mountie. "Allow me to present

148

Constable Newton. He's just come out from Ottawa to give us a hand with a rather delicate problem.''

Pointing at Longarm, Foster smiled thinly and went on. "This would be Deputy Long, the chap we've been chatting about. You don't have to aim your carbine so dramatically, Newton. Longarm and I go back a good way, and he's a perishing pest, not a total idiot.''

Longarm sat down with his back to the door flap, hefted the saddlebags, and announced, ''I reckon this is most of the money those false-hearted gunrunners stole from Painted One the other night.''

Foster held out a hand and snapped, ''Toss it over to me. I'm impounding this band's funds during the present emergency.''

As Longarm perforce tossed the heavy saddlebags across the painted buffalo hide, an older Siksika in a full feather bonnet wailed, ''Hear me! That is not your money, Red Sleeves! It is *our* money! We came by it honestly, a prime hide or a fine elk-dog at a time!''

Foster sounded something like a schoolmarm with a hickory stick to back her brag as he firmly replied, ''We know how you lot intended to spend these combined funds. I just told you the NWMP would deal with those Yankee Sioux encroaching on your hunting grounds. Meanwhile, our Blackfoot brothers will be collecting interest on this specie as provided for under the British North American Acts of 1867. How much would you say you've recovered, Longarm?''

The American lawman shrugged and said, ''One of the outlaws bragged on six thousand. He may have been trying to sweeten the pot. I had the drop on him at the time.''

Foster soberly stated, ''We didn't hear that. No unauthorized U.S. lawman is about to go on report for getting the drop on anybody under our jurisdiction. I, ah, take it the whole Slick Cooper gang met up with some misfortune, allowing you to recover these saddlebags?''

Longarm nodded soberly and said, ''They fell off their horses a lot up by Crowsnest Pass.''

''All *nine* of them?'' marveled young Constable Newton, staring goggle-eyed at their lethal visitor from south of the border.

Foster snapped, ''You just heard us agree they perished

amid the wilds of the Rockies, Newton. I don't recall giving you permission to question this witness.''

The kid looked down at the painted hide red-faced.

Longarm said, ''I peeked inside the bags along the way, of course. I gave up trying to tally the dollar value of all that jingle-jangle. There's everything in there from British gold sovereigns to Mex double eagles. The silver runs from U.S. cartwheels to those dime-sized sixpence coins. Ain't one of your Canadian dollars worth about the same as our silver dollar and so on?''

Foster shrugged and said, ''We'll let the bank tellers work out the exact amount at the current rates of exchange.''

He nodded at the old Indian in the full bonnet and explained, ''I will have someone bring you a bank book with honest numbers written in it. Every moon your money in our bank will grow a little, as the trees grow taller when you do not cut them down. When all of this war talk has been forgotten, you may have better things to do with what is in these bags. When you think of something, send a delegation over to Fort MacLeod and if the superintendent approves, he may allow a withdrawal from your tribal account.''

The elder in the full bonnet bawled, ''*Sah!* That is our money and we are not children who cannot be allowed to play with sharp knives!''

Foster smiled thinly and replied, ''You weren't trying to buy knives. Had Slick Cooper been less treacherous, he could have made a profit on a Gatling gun the other night. But my heart hangs heavy because of the death of Painted One. So my Blackfoot Brothers will not be punished *this* time.''

Then he nodded at Longarm and young Newton, declaring, ''We'll be leaving now. I've finished here, and it's after noon.''

So they left. The Indians didn't like it much. But as they sobbed, pleaded, and shook their fists in his face, Crown Sergeant Foster just kept walking tall, and the crowd parted before him the way the Good Book said the Red Sea got out of the way of old Moses.

As long as they were about it, Longarm stretched his luck and got his saddle and self back aboard that now-well-rested roan. He figured trying for two might be rubbing it in, and old Foster and Newton already had their own matching bays out of that lodge by now.

As the three of them rode down the draw to the east, some younger Siksika trailed after them, whooping and lobbing arrows just wide enough so a man might look scared if he noticed them.

Longarm was more worried about being deported than arrowed. As the three of them left the taunting Indians behind, neither Mountie said a word about him giving up his guns. So Longarm just kept his mouth shut and his ears open as they rode abreast across the rolling sea of grass, with him in the middle and young Newton to his left. Longarm knew that in both American and British military circles, it was the custom for a junior to ride to the left of his senior. But he somehow doubted a paid-up constable of the NWMP felt he held less rank than an American who'd been told to stay the hell out of the North West Territory.

After they'd ridden a little over an hour, Foster raised a gauntlet and reined in atop a rise. After a desperately casual glance back to the west, the sergeant pointed down at a sluggish stream running along the sandy bottom of the draw beyond and said, "We'll water and rest our mounts down there. It will give us time for a serious talk, Longarm."

Foster waited until they'd watered the three mounts and unsaddled them to dry their hides as they grazed the juicy sedge and blue-eyed grass beside the stream. Then he offered Longarm a smoke before he said soberly, "You know better than most Yanks why we're spread so thin right now. I know you've scouted Sioux and know the universal sign language of the Plains tribes. I understand you're a bit cozy for comfort with Louis Riel and his troublesome Métis."

Longarm lit both their cigars, and took a grateful drag of a Turkish tobacco he'd have never bought himself before he quietly replied, "I ain't up here to round up Sitting Bull, and I've told more than one of those Red River Breeds they're going about it the wrong way if they ever expect to get legal title to an acre of prairie. I wired you before I headed up this way that I'm only after a U.S. federal want called Pecival Harcourt alias the Calgary Kid."

Foster braced one boot on a fallen box-elder bole as he nodded and replied, "Your superior, Marshal Vail, has been a bit of a pest about the same chap. No matter how many times we wire Denver that the bloody sod hasn't been reported anywhere in Canada, before or after all that Calgary Kid nonsense down your way, Vail keeps asking us to try again. As if we didn't have enough on our damned plate up this way!''

Pointing his own cigar at young Newton by the horses, Foster told Longarm, "I can't be everywhere and, as I told you, Constable Newton has just arrived. He's naturally an excellent rider, a crack shot, and all that rot. But he's unfamiliar with either Plains sign or the Indians who use it. How familiar might you be with a Sioux chief called Big Foot?''

Longarm shrugged and said, "His Lakota name, Hehaka Galeska, would translate more like Spotted Elk, unless it's really *Heyoka* Galeska, which would make him a spotted *Contrary*. I don't know why some have him down as Big Foot, which would be Sihatanka. You know what those contraries are like, right?''

Foster grimaced and said, "Only too well, and Big Foot, Spotted Elk, or whosoever he may be has been acting contrary indeed. Most of the Sioux your army chased up here have been behaving themselves around Wood Mountain and Willow Bunch, as well they should if they know what's good for them. Can I rely on you not to repeat a confidence I never shared with you, Yank?''

Longarm smiled thinly and allowed he could be deaf as a post if required.

Foster said, "Our government was caught off guard when all those Indians asked for asylum. I don't have to tell you how Premier MacDonald feels about your government in general and the Indian policy of the same. Our Inspector James Walsh, making the first contact with the refugees at Pinto Butte, sixty miles up the White Mud from the border, thought he was laying down the law, but may have exceeded his authority. When his own scouts spotted three stolen ponies he confronted the Indians, accepted a lame excuse, and recovered them. He told the Indians the Grandmother Victoria expected everybody to obey the same laws. If there was any more stealing on either side of the border, all bets were off and the whole lot would be marched back to the States forthwith. The Indians named Walsh Long Lance for his NWMP guidon, and nothing pleases Walsh more than to be known as the man who has Sitting Bull buffaloed.''

Longarm took a drag on the cigar and observed mildly, "Ain't certain old Tatanka Yatanka, or Sitting Bull, is up this way this summer. I know he's supposed to be. I still heard he's been seen with a band of hunters down along the Milk River recently.''

Foster wrinkled his nose and said, ''At least they had the sense to avoid other Canadian hunting grounds. We know the game has thinned out in these parts. Allowing at least five thousand extra hungry Indians up this way didn't help a bit. The Sioux have been trading robes over at the Legare trading post until recently. Now the herds have been thinned dangerously on the hunting grounds. Inspector Walsh allowed too damned many lodges. So some, as you suggest, have been hunting south of the border on the sneak, while others, under Big Foot or whoever, have been encroaching on those Blackfoot we just left. You saw how tense they were about it.''

Longarm whistled softly, and asked where the trespassers might be at the moment.

Foster pointed eastward with his cigar and said, ''Not far enough by half. Now we get to the even more awkward part. Inspector Walsh is about to be replaced by Inspector Crozier, a no-nonsense type who shares some of your General Sherman's views on dealing with Indians. Ottawa is about to appoint a new overall commissioner as well. The smart money is on an old army man and dour Scot, Lieutenant Colonel Acheson Irvine, who frankly scares the hell out of *us*!''

Longarm nodded gravely and said, ''In sum, any Lakota who doesn't toe the mark could quickly become a Good Indian sky-buried.''

Foster took a hesitant drag on his own cigar, chose his words, and said, ''Long Lance Jamie Walsh can be as big a pain in the ass as this U.S. deputy marshal I know. Walsh is too flamboyant for my taste, lacks the self-discipline to be a commissioned officer of the Crown, and saved my life one time.''

Longarm allowed he'd met pests like that.

Foster said, ''Remember that you're not supposed to be hearing most of this. But on or off the record, Inspector Walsh is still in charge of the Sioux situation, and rightly or wrongly, has more compassion for the unruly red rascals than most of us feel they deserve. Walsh wired Fort MacLeod about Big Foot's incursion into Blackfoot country with a view to peaceful negotiation. Knowing what my own superiors would almost certainly reply, I wired Walsh at Wood Mountain fort I'd see what *I* could do. I meant it at the time. But just as Newton

153

there and I were riding out, word came in about a killing at a trading post up near those new Métis encroachments along the Saskatchewan. Need I say which case is more politically explosive?''

Longarm shook his head and said, ''I see what you mean about being in two places at the same time. But tell me more about a killing at a trading post. That cuss I'm after killed a trader near Fort Peck on his way up here!''

Foster shook his head. ''How many times do I have to tell you you're on a wild-goose chase? Every scout as well as every constable has been on full alert, watching for any spark that can set this whole prairie on fire! We don't have any rat-toothed killer with a spotted eye on file. Even more *usual*-looking strangers are being reported as they ride over all this damned grass. We caught up with *you*, didn't we?''

Longarm smiled sheepishly and said, ''I told you I'd be coming. How come Harcourt calls his fool self the Calgary Kid if he's never been up here in Canada?''

Foster said, ''You just said he was a fool and our NWMP post up at Calgary is named for the home town of Inspector MacLeod, in Scotland.''

Longarm thought, shrugged, and said, ''Whatever. Folks down our way say he hails from Canada, and he was headed this way the last time he killed somebody. An Indian trader named Debrun near Fort Peck. Your turn.''

Foster shook his head stubbornly and insisted, ''Please don't confuse me with unrelated crimes by unrelated criminals. This possible murder far to the north is already confusing enough and I have to get up there as soon as possible.''

Foster called to young Constable Newton, then continued to Longarm. ''I'm sending Newton to talk to Big Foot or Spotted Whatever while I ride up to the Métis settlements alone. Lord knows when I'll ever make it that far, but I have to. The first reports are . . . Never mind. Suffice it to say, Constable Newton could use a translator and it was so good of you, as a saddle tramp of uncertain nationality, to volunteer your services.''

Longarm cocked a brow and said, ''I thought it was handsome as all hell of me my ownself. You're sending just me and this green kid to powwow possible contraries and certainly pissed-off Lakota into going hungry voluntarily? If Spotted

Elk won't listen to his own tribal elders, how do you expect us Wasichu to get anywhere?''

Young Newton, coming within earshot, smiled uncertainly and asked, "Wasichu?"

Longarm said, "That's us in Lakota, or Sioux. Sioux ain't a nice way to describe an Indian of that persuasion either."

Foster said, "See how much more you can teach the lad as the two of you ride on. Newton knows our orders to the Sioux, but you may have to fill in a bit for him."

"What do *I* get out of this simple chore?" asked Longarm quietly but firmly.

Foster smiled thinly and said, "Not a thing, old bean. I mean, if neither Constable Newton nor I are aware of your unlawful trespass on Canadian soil, we can hardly be expected to *offer* you anything, eh?"

"I follow your drift," Longarm said dryly, moving toward the three grazing mounts and their sunning saddles. "Say I get the kid and me in and out of that Lakota camp with all our hair still in place. Do I assume you won't see me when I push on to the north after the Calgary Kid?"

Foster shrugged and replied, "You're on your own if you step on anyone *else*'s toes. I may not be able to see as well as I used to, but I don't have the authority to speak for anyone who outranks me, and there's a lot of that going on around the NWMP since Ottawa's been taking things out this way more seriously."

Young Newton bent over to pick up his crown sergeant's saddle for him. Longarm picked up his own and commenced to saddle his roan as he said, "I'll cross that Rubicon when I catch up with the Calgary Kid."

Foster warned, "You have no authority to arrest anyone north of the Montana line, and I hope you understand that shooting people is a hanging offense under the British North American Acts?"

"Now, did I try to tell you how you were ever going to take Cotton Younger back to Canada that time we argued jurisdiction down by South Pass?"

Foster grinned despite himself and told Constable Newton, "You have to watch this rustic joker. He once let me steal a rather over-ripe corpse from him, suitably wrapped for delivery in high summer, of course."

He let the younger Mountie grimace at the picture, then

added in a weary tone, "It wasn't the body of the man we were both after. Make sure he takes you to the right Indians, and don't let him fix you up for the night with a pretty *winkte*."

The greenhorn in scarlet looked confused as Longarm grinned at Foster and muttered, "Spoilsport."

Foster swung himself tall in the saddle and replied, "I've farther to ride. So I'm off. Don't take too long with those Sioux and good luck with your hair."

He must have meant it. As they watched him spur his bay across the stream and up the far slope, Longarm declared, "He can make thirty or more miles a day in this weather with the grass still green. But how far might he have to ride?"

Newton said, "He'll make the upper South Saskatchewan by nightfall. After that it's one long river and those halfbreed squatters are at least a week's ride downstream to the northeast. What's a *winkte*?"

Longarm swung up into his McClellan and hauled his roan's muzzle out of the blue-eyed grass in a firm but gentle way as he explained. "I reckon we'd call 'em sissy boys, but there's more to it than that. Horse Indians set great store by dreams and visions, inspired by firewater, hunger, or both. Most Indian boys dream ferociously and grow up to act the same way. But now and again a boy has girlish dreams and grows up to act and dress like a woman."

"Good Lord, you mean there are actually queer Sioux?" gasped the baby-faced Mountie.

To which Longarm felt it fair to reply, "Not exactly. To begin with, the Indians don't consider it queer. A man is expected to follow his own *wakan* or medicine. The regular-fellow Indians, concerned as they are with stealing horses, lifting hair, and chasing women with a nose flute, seem to feel it would take mighty powerful medicine to turn any of *them* into *winktes*, so they treat 'em with more respect than we might. *Winktes* are supposed to be good at guessing the future and picking out lucky secret names. Indians have the names they were given by their folks, more honorable names they've been given my their fellow fighting men, and *secret* names only they and their guardian or vision spirits are supposed to know. *Winktes* only suggest such names. They never know for certain whether anyone took their advice."

Newton mounted up to trail after as he marveled aloud,

"Oh. When you said they were effeminate, I thought you meant they were sodomites."

Longarm said, "Most of 'em are. You wouldn't expect a self-respecting *woman* to sleep with a *winkte,* and young bucks have to have somebody to screw without getting their fool selves killed."

Then he said, "Let's ride. Don't worry your head about the *winkte* boys flirting with us. It's the *heyokas* or contraries you have to keep an eye on, old son."

Newton asked what Sioux contraries were apt to do to you.

Longarm said, "Nobody ever knows *what* a *heyoka* may be fixing to do. That's why you have to keep your eye on 'em."

Chapter 13

Riding side by side across the rolling prairie with Constable Newton, Longarm was inclined to let the kid talk more freely than your average crown sergeant. So it didn't take an experienced High Plains rider long to see the young Mountie was as green as the grass all around.

Longarm took advantage of their trail breaks to teach Newton a few basic hand signs. Newton kept asking dumb questions, such as which finger wiggle was the word for *wampum*.

Hunkered on a rise as they shared a can of Her Majesty's bully beef, Longarm took a deep breath and said, "*Wampum* is an Algonquin word. The folks we're headed for say *mazaska*. But forget about *words* when you're talking *sign*."

He thought, then said, "Think of nodding your head to mean yes in most any lingo. Don't matter if the gent you're nodding at would say *K'hoo, Ah, Nee koo la, How,* or *Unhuh* back home. He'd still know you meant *yes*, see?"

Newton gasped. "I say! Are the different Plains dialects as different as *that*?"

Longarm nodded agreeably. "That's how come the Kiowa invented sign talk. The Lakota we're headed for say *Ohan* for yes and what sounds a heap like *Yea* for no. But they nod or shake their heads the same as we do."

Longarm raised his hands in front of his chest with the left palm up and said, "This is the best sign to remember if you only manage to remember one. It means you've come in peace. If nobody pegs a shot at you, then you hold up these two fingers by your face to say you want to be friends.''

Newton said, ''Thank God Sergeant Foster and I fell in with you. I'd be helpless as a babe without a translator.''

He got out some tailor-made English cigarettes as if to prove he was good for something after all, and waited until they'd lit up before he soberly asked Longarm, ''Do you think those Sioux will do as we say, even if they understand us?''

It was a good question.

Longarm glanced at the sun and replied, ''We'd best mount up and get along. Old Foster says I ain't here official. So that only leaves you, and as I understand your mission, you're to order Spotted Elk's band back from these Siksika hunting grounds.''

Newton asked, ''What do I do if they tell me to go to Hell?''

Longarm rose, replying, ''I just said that. You can report to your superiors that you carried out your orders. After that, you're one man with one revolver and a single-shot carbine. What do they expect you to do if Spotted Elk won't do as he's told, arrest him?''

Newton sighed and said, ''Yes. The NWMP is barely seven years old. But some of its traditions have already been engraved in granite, and one of them reads that a Mountie always gets his man, or never comes back alive without him!''

Longarm mounted his Indian pony, muttering, ''I wish they wouldn't make up rules like that. It doesn't give me many bargaining chips when we lay down the law to those disgruntled buffalo hunters. Wouldn't it save a heap of hunting on the part of all Canadian Indians if your government issued 'em allotment money and rations, like we do down in the States?''

Newton mounted his own bay and settled into a walk at Longarm's side before he sighed and said, ''Ours not to reason why. But I suppose Ottawa feels that were we to put all those Sioux on the dole, they *would* be Canadian Indians forever more, and Sir John has expressed the not unreasonable opinion that Canada had quite enough Indians to begin with. We have been making treaties with the Blackfoot, Cree, and Déné, on more liberal if not generous terms than your Hayes Administration. You saw how those perishing Blackfoot were about to abuse the right to trade for money.''

Longarm stared ahead at the wavering horizon, observing,

"I sure don't see many Blackfoot *buffalo* in these parts. When you say Canada offers hunting and gathering bands more *liberty* than we do, is it safe to say you don't offer them much *more*?"

Newton shrugged and said, "As I understand it, Indians, Eskimos, and those Red River Breeds are free to live the way they say they want to live, as long as they don't break any laws or get in anybody's way."

Longarm finished his delicious but short-lived smoke, and made sure the butt was out before he got rid of it, saying, "I reckon it was a kindly French philosopher who pointed out that poor people enjoyed the same rights as rich people to sleep under the bridges of Paris Town. But fair is fair, and I reckon there's no way to let folks dwell in the Stone Age and on public charity at the same time. What happens if one of your Canadian Indians comes hat in hand to say he just can't make it out in the woods any more?"

Newton said, "He has the same right as any other British subject to apply for a steady job, or even alms, on the government's terms. We find it rather odd that you subsidize wild Indians and let them off with another stern lecture every time they go on the warpath. I understand your Apache are off the reservation this spring again."

Longarm smiled sheepishly and said, "Only Victorio, and they've got the Tenth Cav chasing him."

Newton was too polite to ask what Longarm's government meant to do with those Bronco Apaches once the gunsmoke cleared. Longarm could see some advantages to the Canadian Indian policy, but how in thunder was he supposed to explain it to Lakota who'd been playing another game entirely ever since Lincoln pardoned all those Santee Sioux charged with murder, rape, and worse?

He knew it would be as much a waste of time to try to sell the Lakota notions of manly dignity to a Mountie from back East. But the only way either he or Newton were going to leave that Lakota band alive and well called for them leaving Spotted Elk in the very same condition. No Lakota describing his fool self as *We chasa on ta peka,* or No-bullshit Chief, could ever let young Newton take him in alive if he didn't want little kids calling him a woman-heart.

Longarm said, "You'd best let me do the talking whether Spotted Elk savvies English or not. There's more than one way of saying much the same, as any lawyer can tell you.''

Newton shrugged and replied, ''I don't care how you explain it to him, as long as he agrees to return to the Wood Mountain range, where Ottawa ordered the Sioux to damned well stay.''

Longarm didn't answer. As the afternoon wore on, he began to hope the Lakota had already given up and headed back the way they'd come. For he and Newton came across sun-bleached bones from time to time, but nary a buffalo or even a scrawny pronghorn. Those Siksika had *said* they'd sold a lot of buffalo robes to collect that six thousand in specie.

The next time they took a dismounted break, Longarm asked Newton more about old Crown Sergeant Foster. He said, ''I know it's none of my beeswax. But I've been reading the fuzzy map of this country I have in my fool head.''

Newton lit another smoke for Longarm and replied, ''I told you where he was headed. Northeast, down the Saskatchewan.''

Longarm took a grateful drag and insisted, ''That's what I mean. A man with a desk job at Fort MacLeod riding clean on over to them Métis settlements alone way the hell outside his usual jurisdiction? When my boss sends me out that way, it usually means the case is sort of unusual.''

Newton nodded and said, ''Sergeant Foster has told me about some of the odd cases you've cracked for other federal districts down in the States. I suppose you might call Crown Sergeant Foster the Longarm of the NWMP. He seems to notice odd details and put them together the way nobody else might expect them to fit.''

Longarm smiled fondly and allowed, ''We did meet up, that first time, when the shoe was on the other foot and he was chasing a Canadian want down Wyoming way. What's so unusual about this killing at a trading post up in Métis country?''

Newton sniffed and said, ''It's not supposed to *be* Métis country. The buggers are squatting on land they hold no title to.''

''Folk have to set down *somewhere*,'' Longarm pointed out.

The Mountie shook his head and said, ''Those stubborn breeds are as bad as those flaming Sioux when it comes to behaving as the government tells them. I've *heard* Louis Riel's blather about a western republic under a red and white flag. He and his people would have been allowed to stay where

161

they were along the Red River when the government incorporated the Province of Manitoba in '70. French Canadian religious and cultural rights were guaranteed. It was law and order they rose up against!''

Longarm smiled fondly at the memory of a Métis maiden under the canvas hood of her Red River cart as he observed softly, ''I heard it was taxation without representation, Métis having the voting rights of Quill Indians. But that was then and this is now. You were saying somebody got killed unusually wherever?''

Newton shrugged and said, ''I don't know the details. You were right about the remote trading post being well outside our jurisdiction. The district superintendent up that way sent for Foster by name after reading the initial report. Neither he nor Sergeant Foster accept the scene as described. Ergo the constables who were first on the scene must have missed something, or somebody had trifled with the evidence before they got there.''

Longarm spotted carrion crows hovering a bit to the south of the way they'd been heading. He pointed with his chin and declared, ''Looks like something's dying or there's a garbage dump yonder. About the right distance for Lakota the Siksika were scouting without attacking yet. You were saying somebody got murdered at this trading post?''

Newton looked uncomfortable and said, ''The old Scotch-Cree who ran the place for the Hudson Bay Company was found dead under mysterious circumstances. We're still working on just how he died. It seems on the surface to be a case of spontaneous human combustion. Sergeant Foster says that's impossible.''

Longarm nodded and declared, ''He's right. I read that story Mr. Dickens wrote about a drunk combusting all by his fool self. I've read newspaper stories, likely inspired by Mr. Dickens, describing the same impossible fate. They generally read much the same. Some lonely soul living alone in a bitty cottage or furnished room bursts into flames and burns away to ashes and mayhaps some untidy leftovers, seated in a chair or lying in bed with no signs of a struggle and the rest of the place barely singed, if not pristine. It was a good story when Dickens wrote it. There's no way it could ever happen that way.''

Constable Newton nodded. ''Sergeant Foster says the average human body is seventy percent water.''

Longarm said, "I told you I agreed with him. I read a travel book by an Englishman who'd taken notes as he watched Hindu folks cremate their dead on the banks of the Ganges. I don't know why, but it was sort of interesting to a lawman. He said it took about a cord of wood soaked in butterfat. Like Foster says, you got all that water to boil out of the flesh. This interested tourist wrote that once you got the body sort of like well-done bacon, its own fat did commence to burn. He said the Hindu folks kept piling on more fuel because, out of doors at least, it's mighty tough to burn a human being to ashes. What a fire that hot would do to the inside of a room ain't at all hard to picture. In sum, you can burn folks up in a house and all. But there's no sensible way to leave them a pile of ashes in the middle of a charred rug!"

As they got closer to whatever those carrion crows were hovering above, they were no longer alone on the prairie. When Newton mentioned this in a desperately casual tone, Longarm said, "I see 'em. I make 'em to be *akicita*. The Cheyenne call 'em Dog Soldiers, but *lawmen* would be closer to the Lakota meaning. They know they're being scouted by Siksika. That's how come they're wearing paint. They want it known they ain't boys to be trifled with. Those coup marks on their ponies are more specific. The befeathered gent on the buckskin wants it known he's killed three men in hand-to-hand combat. You don't rate one of those red hands for just *shooting* a cuss. Those yellow horseshoes stand for stolen horses, and the black bars on his pony's rump denote his warrior lodge."

"Are you going to try that sign language on them?" asked the kid in as manly a voice as he could manage.

Longarm said, "Not yet. We're headed for their camp and they're not supposed to be at feud with us. If they challenge us I'll answer. If they don't, I won't. By rights a shirt wearer or village busybody is supposed to greet us as we ride in. It ain't polite to ask visitors what they want. You offer them hospitality. If they have any manners of their own they'll tell you why they rode in, after you've talked about the weather and such for a spell."

The Mountie said, "Well, we've agreed to let you do most of the talking. Were you, ah, rather tense the first time you ever rode into an Indian camp?"

To which Longarm could only reply, "I'm still tense every

163

time I do it. But don't worry. You don't look like you're scared either.''

The mounted perimeter guards sat their ponies impassively at a polite distance as the two white men topped a rise to see a ring of about two dozen tipis on the dusty flat beyond. Ponies milled and the dogs were barking up a storm, but the women, children, and most of the men in the camp hid out of sight as Longarm and the Mountie rode down the slope toward them.

A tall willowy figure in a deerskin dress fringed with sleigh bells and red ribbons strode forth to greet them, a turkey wing fan in one well-kept hand. The delegate's long braided hair was parted in the middle with the part painted red. As the two white men reined in, Newton asked, "Is that one of those . . . whiskey ones?"

Longarm murmured, "Looks like. Ain't sure whether we're supposed to feel honored or insulted."

He held up his free hand in the sign of friendship.

The effeminate but suspiciously tall Lakota called out in a fair English contralto, "I am called Tatokaga. My people are called the Miniconjou because, in our Shining Times, they planted the four good things beside standing waters. The shirt wearers have asked me to greet you because I speak Wasichu and because our leader, Hehaka Galeska, is out hunting for *pte*. Have you seen any *pte* in your ridings across all this empty range?"

Longarm replied, "Nary a one, Miss Southwind. When do you expect Spotted Elk and the others back? He's the one we've come all this way to visit with."

Tatokaga or Southwind blinked in surprise and tried some pure Lakota on him. When Longarm confessed he only knew a few words, Southwind said, "I think I know who you must be. I have heard the shirt wearers speak of a Wasichu *washtey* called *Ees ta hanska,* a good American called the one with long arms."

"*Hey miyey,*" Longarm was forced to admit, ears burning.

Southwind beamed up at the both of them as Longarm introduced the kid Mountie as a famous rider for the Grandmother Victoria with a heap of *wakan* of his own.

Southwind begged them to dismount and have something to eat for Wakan Tonka's sake. So they did, as some Indian kids materialized out of thin air to take charge of their ponies for them. Longarm casually drew his Winchester from its saddle boot as they did so. He was glad Newton took his Martini-Henry in hand just as casually. The helpful Lakota led both ponies away to be watered and fed as Southwind smiled wistfully and asked, "Did you really expect to be robbed after I had made you welcome?"

Longarm said soothingly, "No, ma'am. Regulations. You can look it up. These red sleeves are forbidden to eat or sleep apart from their guns, and as a visitor I feel obliged to follow the same *wakan*."

Southwind didn't look too convinced. Longarm and Newton had a tough time pretending to like the wood-ash-salted stew they were served out front of the main council lodge, with older shirt wearers seated gravely around but saying they'd already eaten that early evening. Constable Newton never asked what sort of meat they were eating. Longarm could only hope it might be rabbit, even though he knew better.

One of the shirt wearers waited until they'd finished and asked, through Southwind, what the lawmen from both sides of the border might want with Spotted Elk.

Hoping to cross that bridge once they got to it, Longarm explained the Grandmother Victoria had given them a personal message for their great chief alone. Then, to change the subject, he asked Southwind how come some folks seemed to call Spotted Elk by the name of Big Foot.

Southwind sighed and said, "You people have heard some of our own people being . . . Is the word sarcastic? When you call a woman skinny because she is so fat?"

Longarm allowed that was about the size of it.

So Southwind explained. "In the Shining Times, so they tell, a hero boy made friends with a ghost all the others were afraid of. The hero boy fed the lonely *wanigi* and they sang together, so they tell. Then the friendly spirit helped the hero boy capture many Pawnee medicine-dogs, or horses, and kill many *pte* until his people all had greasy chins, so they tell, and they called this hero boy Big Foot because he was wounded raiding the Pawnee and came back to them with his foot swollen twice as big as it had been, so they tell."

Longarm nodded gravely and said, "I get the joke. It *is* a sort of bitter one, ain't it?"

Constable Newton, who'd been following as best he could, piped up uncertainly to ask, "Didn't you tell me riding earlier that *tatanka* was the word for buffalo? Just what might *pte* mean, in that case?''

Longarm said, "Buffalo. Think bull and cow in connection with our word terms for *kine* or cattle. Indians shade meanings and contract as many words as we do. But let's not waste Miss Southwind's time on a lesson in Lakota."

Southwind said, "I *am* interested. We have trouble understanding why you Wasichu say some things so strangely. Some blue sleeves laughed at me one time when I asked them to let me watch their medicine-dogs fly. But isn't that what you Wasichu mean when you say you just saw a horse fly?''

Longarm had to laugh too. But he covered up quickly by explaining how an insect and a verb could sound the same in English. Southwind laughed too. You had to admire a good sport, and the prissy young *winkte* was damned near a dead ringer for a pretty gal, if you liked gals tall and sort of lanky-hipped.

Southwind's helpful but sort of disturbing company began to get more awkward as the sun went down. When they weren't holding a powwow, few Indians wasted fuel on outdoor fires after dark. So while some of the nearer tipis lit up like lanterns as night fires were lit inside, things got dark and sort of romantic out front of the council lodge as they were seated with Southwind so close on the same blanket.

One of the older shirt wearers rattled something off in Lakota. So Southwind said, "As you must know, Wasichu Washtey, my people rise and set with Father Wi, the great light in the sky. I have been asked to show the two of you to good sleeping places. *Hiyupo,* follow me.''

The two white men rose awkwardly to fall in on either side of the willowy Southwind. They hadn't gone far when the Lakota graciously opened the oval doorway of an empty tipi, a small fire lighting up Newton's saddle and bedding inside, and told him that this was his quarters for the night. The Mountie looked uncertain, shrugged, and muttered, "Everything but the farmer's daughter, eh, what?''

As he ducked inside, Southwind took Longarm by one elbow, never guessing how close Longarm had come to swinging without thinking, and purred, "We are putting you in another tipi near your friend. We have sent for someone to keep him company too.''

Longarm ducked inside, mostly to break free, and told the

alarmingly friendly Southwind, "I can't speak for another grown man as a rule, but I strongly advise against you fixing Constable Newton up with one of your friends, Miss Southwind!"

The dusky but young Lakota, downright alluring in that soft light, pouted a lower lip and demanded, "Why not? Are you afraid our colors will rub off on your frog-belly skins? Hear me, we don't think so much of your pale faces either. I was only trying to be nice to you in the best way to be nice to men. What makes you think you are too beautiful for us?"

Longarm sat down on a spare blanket by his saddle, staring into the small night fire instead of up at the Lakota as he groped for a nicer way to put it.

There wasn't any. He said, "I don't think I'm all that beautiful. I have to allow you're prettier and likely cleaner right now. I've been on the trail a spell."

Southwind sank down beside him, smiled at him in the soft red glow, and asked, "Is that why you seem so bashful? My husband used to come in from the hunt all covered with dust and sweat. I naturally washed him off all over before we made *tawiton* together."

As was generally the case with other tongues, a man learned all the dirty words first. So had Longarm, and there just wasn't any Lakota word dirtier, or at least more specific, than *tawiton*. Living closer to nature than Queen Victoria, the Lakota were inclined to be more specific than dirty. So *tawiton* translated as nothing more complicated than plain old *fuck,* and what was that other stuff about husbands?

He cautiously asked, "You say you're married up, Miss Southwind?"

The disturbingly attractive Indian nodded and said, "He was killed at the Custer fight. He took three of your blue sleeves with him. It was long ago and the cuts I made all over myself have healed. So other men have smiled at me and I have smiled back. But I have never met a man who could *tawiton* that nicely."

Leaning closer, smelling of sweet-grass smoke and musk, Southwind reassured him, "I am not looking for a Wasichu husband. I only want to make you feel welcome, and maybe count coup with my *shan.*"

Now, that was another dirty word Longarm had asked about a long time ago, and he'd been assured *shan* translated closer

167

to *pussy* than any other private part of the human body. But as the fool Indian reached for his shirt to unbutton it, Longarm drew back and protested. "Hold on, there, pard. Is it or isn't it true that the Lakota version of your name, Tatokaga, comes out *masculine* in form?"

Southwind looked blank, then smiled and replied, "I guess it does. As a *spirit* the wind is male. I'd never thought of that before. Do your women worry if somebody names them Mary Ander*son* or maybe Jane *Smith*?"

Longarm allowed he hadn't thought of that. But as Southwind made a more personal grab for some buttons, he blurted out, "Are you really a *Miss* Southwind or . . . somebody with unusual medicine?"

Southwind stared owl-eyed in confusion, then suddenly caught on and let fly with an embarrassingly loud cry of, "You thought I was a *winkte,* you poor *wasichu witko*?"

So he had to laugh too when she slipped her jingle-jangle deerskins off over her head to expose about five feet nine of willowy but surprisingly female flesh, hickory-nut brown and glowing with the sweet-grass-scented lard she'd rubbed all over her hide earlier.

So they sort of forgot about giving him a sponge bath before he was all over her, smelling of honest sweat and relieved as hell to discover he hadn't been that tempted by even a convincing imitation of the real thing. She liked it Indian-style despite her fine English. So they panted openmouthed like pups in one another's faces while he let her get on top, heels planted firmly to either side of his naked hips while she slid her genuine *shan* up and down his love-slicked organ-grinder until she came with a whoop he was sure they heard all round the tipi ring.

Later on, after they'd sponged off and shared a pipe she'd been thoughtful enough to have them leave beside the small night fire, Southwind said she could hardly wait to tell the other gals what a swell *tatoga* the famous Wasichu Washtey was. He knew better than to ask her not to. Modesty was a white man's notion. Sort of. Indians bragged downright obnoxiously next to most white men, until you got to details.

It was understood and allowed for that old Buffalo Bill got to say he'd fought a personal duel with a Cheyenne chief called Yellow Hand as long as he had witnesses to his picking off a brave with some blond scalps decorating his pony. The cuss *could* have been called Yellow Something, and old Cody had shot him from afar, but fair enough. But let an Indian who'd been *second* to touch a fallen enemy with his coup stick claim *first coup* and be found out, and the little kids would wave their dicks at him and call him a liar for the rest of his days. When an Indian bragged on doing wonders and eating cucumbers, he crossed every T and dotted every I. So Longarm could only hope it paid to advertise when Southwind declared he was hung like a medicine-dog and that she'd feel obliged to slash her face if her own young men had to kill him on her.

She said she had no idea how Spotted Elk was likely to take Constable Newton's eviction notice. Gall, Rain in the Face, and Jumping Bull had all advised against risking trouble with the Canadian tribes. Sitting Bull was hunting, buffalo or trouble, south of the line along the Upper Milk. Southwind said a lot depended on whether her own kinsmen *found* any buffalo to the forbidden west.

Snuggled atop a fuzzy robe with Longarm, she confided, "If there are no *pte* to fight over, there should be no fight."

He said, "The Siksika are so sore about the poor hunting this year that they're going to blame Spotted Elk whether he gets any *pte* or not. We're going to have to talk him into moving back to rejoin the other Lakota around Wood Mountain, honey."

She shrugged a bare shoulder against his chest, liked the way that felt, and arched her spine to thrust her bare rump deeper in his lap as she demurely replied, "*You* talk to him. He speaks Wasichu and he can be very contrary when he does not like what he is hearing."

Longarm took a hip in each hand to guide his renewed interest up between her tawny buttocks as he asked if Spotted Elk was a paid-up member of the Contrary Lodge or just a muley old bastard.

She said, "He's not a sworn *heyoka,* but he hates to agree with anyone younger than he is, and he is getting old. Could you move it just a little faster that way?"

He could. So a good time was had by all, and they even got a little sleep before Wi came back up and all hell broke loose outside.

Southwind got dressed and slipped outside. She came back to tell Longarm the hunting party had returned empty-handed. The disgusted Spotted Elk didn't want to talk to anyone before he'd had a stiff drink of medicine water and a few hours sleep.

Southwind wanted to get laid one more time. Longarm was soon up to the chore, and later, as she was serving a corn mush breakfast to both Longarm and Constable Newton out front, Southwind acted as demure as all get-out.

So Constable Newton never thought to ask, but confessed as soon as he had the chance, "One of those queer whiskey chaps crept into my tipi late last night. I thought I'd have to fight for my virtue for a time, but fortunately, the whiskey was a good sport and left, giggling like a girl, as soon as I made it evident I just wasn't interested and... What's so funny, Yank?"

To which Longarm could only reply, wiping the grin off his face, "Nothing. I'm sure Crown Sergeant Foster would have approved."

Chapter 14

Longarm would have waited longer, maybe holding hands with old Southwind, to allow a trail-sore and mortified chief to cool down.

But as soon as Constable Newton heard Spotted Elk was awake and pissing about the red sleeves not bringing any presents, he sent word he wanted that powwow now. Now being well into the afternoon.

Longarm and Southwind had to go along. Left to his own devices a whole morning, the young Mountie had set his white helmet aside for a pillbox garrison cap, instantly earning the named of "Drum on Head" from the bemused Indians. But he'd had the sense to hang onto his Martini-Henry as well as his Webley revolver as Southwind led them as far as the council lodge and then, being a woman, hunkered down to wait for them outside.

Spotted Elk was seated with a hangover, facing the entry hole, a dozen other shirt wearers seated around him. They'd spread a mostly white Hudson Bay blanket in the middle of the lodge, its four corners carefully oriented to the four cardinal directions. A stern-looking cuss wearing a buffalo-horn headdress told them to sit at the south corner and let Hehaka Galeska look at them. So they did.

They looked at old Spotted Elk in return. The erstwhile lieutenant of Crazy Horse and occasional follower of Sitting

Bull was a lean and hungry-looking older man who might have had some white blood and surely had consumption. He had that bright-eyed edgy look of that mean white lunger Doc Holliday south of the border. The consumptive Indian wore a battered U.S. Cavalry hat with a coup feather. Lest Wasichu miss that brag, he'd put on the blue tunic of an officer in the Seventh Cav. He let them wait a spell, as if he thought he was the dean of boys at some strict school, before he got right to the point. He suppressed a cough and demanded, "Why have you people up this way driven all the *pte* away? When we first came up here after the Custer fight there were *pte* to skin and grease our chins with! The Grandmother Victoria said we could hunt them. So we did. We sold the robes for the other good things to eat. But now they have all gone away. My young men and me have ridden all over in search of the herd and we can't find it. I think this is a very bad thing. I think somebody has been making *Wakan Shica* around here!"

Constable Newton said, "The buffalo are becoming scarce because too many people are hunting them. The Grandmother Victoria only gave you permission to stay on her blanket a little while and—"

Longarm pinched him viciously and growled. "Stop talking like a cigar-store Indian and let me try."

Then, in a louder tone, Longarm said, "My heart hangs heavy to hear a great chief speaking *ta-chesli*."

Spotted Elk gasped, coughed, and snapped, "You call my words bullshit? You dare?"

Longarm shrugged and answered easily, "Don't shit us and we won't shit you. You're a grandfather wise in the ways of the herds. You have killed more *pte* than you can remember, so they tell. You have greased the chins of captive Pawnee and Absaroka, so they tell, before you let the women kill them."

"I have always been generous, generous," Spotted Elk modestly admitted.

Longarm said, "We have all shot a heap of *pte*. For a long time there was good hunting. The herds always came back, no matter how many died. But now they are hard to find anywhere. I have spoken with the Siksika. They call *pte enueh,* but say they can't find any this moon either."

Spotted Elk almost sobbed, "I know this to be true! My young men and I have flushed Siksika riders to the west without finding so much as fresh *pte-chesli*. There is plenty water. The grass is greener up this way than down around the Paha Sapa where we used to hunt. What will become of us, of all the people who paint themselves, if there are no more *pte*?''

Longarm dryly remarked, ''For openers, there may *be* no more Minneconjou if they don't get off these Siksika hunting grounds. My red-sleeve brother here can tell you the Grandmother Victoria has just told her Siksika children they can't buy guns to attack you right now, but—''

''Let them come!'' Spotted Elk declared, more certain of his options now. ''I count coup as a *blota hunka* who wipes his ass on the scalps of Blackfoot! I have lifted hair at the Custer fight. I have raided Pawnee. This is harder, so they tell. Hear me, my band is not as big as it used to be. Some of my people have chosen other leaders. But my young men and me are not afraid to take on all the tame pets of the Grandmother Victoria! *All* of them! At one time! Without guns!''

Constable Newton said, ''If you start up with one band of our own Indians, you will have the North West Mounted Police to deal with.''

Longarm muttered, ''I wish you hadn't said that.''

But Newton had. So Spotted Elk choked back a cough, pointed at the Martini-Henry across the kid's lap, and sneered, ''You think we fear you red sleeves, armed with single-shot rifles?''

Before Newton could answer, Longarm smiled innocently and asked how come such a mighty hair lifter was hiding out north of the border from other Wasichu armed with single-shot Springfields.

Spotted Elk licked a spot of blood from his lower lip as he looked away and grumbled, ''That is not the same. Star Chief Terry has as many men as I have hairs on my head. The red sleeves with their single-shot carbines number no more than . . . *shi ami ni shoh tan?*''

''We'd say three hundred,'' Longarm replied. ''It would be a good fight for you at first. You ain't the only one who's noticed a handful of Mounties are policing a whole lot of prairie with single-shot saddle guns. They'd stand and fight. All real men have to follow their own *hanblechya wakan*. But you'd likely win, lift lots of hair, and swap that blue coat for a red one.''

Constable Newton murmured, "I say, which side are you on?"

Longarm said, "I ain't finished. My Lakota uncle here knows my words are true. If he has the wits of an *inyan,* which is a rock, he knows that before the last Mountie goes under, the Grandmother Victoria will have the British Army out this way with Gatling guns and four-pound howitzers. The Grandmother Victoria has ten times the troops to spare that Great Father Hayes has. So unless he can get the Grand Lama of Tibet to take him in, my Lakota uncle and his young men will get chased back home quick, where Star Chief Terry and the troopers of the Seventh Cav are waiting, waiting for another crack at the Sioux, so they tell."

Spotted Elk stared down at the blanket between them, muttering he was not afraid of anything or anybody.

Longarm told him not unkindly, "I never said you were as smart as the average rock. I know you're brave as you say. But hear me and remember my words if you ever get anywhere near the old Seventh Cav again. They've all promised Miss Libby Custer that if they ever get the slightest excuse, they mean to butcher you and your kith and kin like hogs. I ain't saying this to scare you. I'm warning you as a *kola* not to start up with any more Wasichu, in red sleeves or blue. You'll go under the way a brave *tatanka* standing its ground on the railroad tracks would go under, huffing and snorting and ground to stew meat before it could understand what was hitting it!"

The older man looked up, the fire burning less brightly in his feverish eyes now, as he quietly asked, "What do you think this person should do, Wasichu Washtey?"

Longarm told him gently, "Heading back to the Wood Mountain fort would make a fair start. Stick close to Gall's band and follow his lead. Gall gets along better with us than your average Lakota."

Spotted Elk grimaced and said, "Gall has lost his love of battle. He has learned to get good things from both the Grandmother and Great Father by speaking sweetly to them."

Longarm nodded. "I just said that. Red Cloud is eating well on the reservation these days, and Quanah Parker's been collecting grazing fees for his Comanche Reserve. You folks have to eat *something,* and the *pte* ain't there in numbers to feed you any more. Go on back to the Wood Mountain fort and

174

wait for the new Canadian commission to cut the cards fair with Uncle Sam for you."

The Indian grumbled, "We tried living quietly on the Grandmother Victoria's blanket. She is stingy, stingy! As bad as the Great Father treated us, our agents used to give us *some* rations if we stayed at those bare and dusty agencies. The red sleeves give us nothing, nothing, and take back any medicine-dogs our young men steal!"

Constable Newton started to say something else about law and order. Longarm pinched him again and told Spotted Elk, "There is going to be a big powwow between the Grandmother and Great Father this summer. Grandmother Victoria and her Canadian children don't want you up here anymore, so they tell. But she has not forgotten how everyone talked about her when she let others starve on another blanket they call Ireland. So she will make the Great Father promise he will treat you well when you return to *his* blanket."

Spotted Elk looked as if he was fixing to bust out bawling as he shook his head and protested, "They can't send us back to those bare reservations! There is nothing to *hunt* there anymore! My people don't like wheat flour or the Wasichu beef the BIA issues them!"

Longarm started to say something about the theft of that notorious Mormon cow leading up to the first Sioux War, but decided not to rake up old grudges. So he just said, "Mayhaps you can all take up that vegetarian diet some professors advocate for everybody. In the meantime, no *ta-chesli,* don't you reckon we'd all best get moving before you get into a pointless war over all them *pte* that used to be?"

The Indian looked undecided.

Longarm prodded him gently. "It would be a bad fight. Even if you won. Your folks would be on the run as well as hungry, and *then* what would they call you behind your back— Stone Boy or Corn Maiden?"

It worked. Spotted Elk alias Big Foot turned to the one with the horns to rattle a string of orders too rapid for Longarm to more than guess at.

But once he savvied they were jawing about tobacco, salt, sugar, and such, he turned to Constable Newton and murmured, "I suspect we've won. Or, since I ain't here officially, *you* get the feather in that odd little hat as soon as you all get back to that trading post near Wood Mountain. I got to haul ass after the Calgary Kid. So I'll be leaving now.''

But the Mountie followed him outside, protesting, "You
can't ride off and leave me on my own with a whole tribe of
Indians, damn it!"

Southwind, waiting just outside the doorway, leaped to her
feet and wailed, "You can't leave us! Not so soon! Why do
you hate me now? Didn't you enjoy our *tawiton* this morning?"

Then she ran off bawling as she held her deerskin skirts up
over her eyes, with everything from the waist down exposed.

Constable Newton blinked and exclaimed, "I say, that
doesn't seem to be one of those whiskey chaps after all!"

Longarm said, "She has a friend. We'll talk about that later.
Did you say Foster's headed directly northeast?"

Newton replied, "Not exactly. He'll be following the river
trail and the river is inclined to meander. Why do you ask?"

Longarm said, "If my mental map makes a lick of sense,
that Wood Mountain fort is due east. If I was to tag along
with you all that far, I'd be due south of that Hudson Bay
trading post, and provided I could talk these Lakota out of
some good trail stock, I could likely beeline due north and get
there not much later than Foster."

Newton smiled uncertainly and said, "I suppose so. Are you
an authority on spontaneous human combustion?"

Longarm growled, "Not hardly. But I'm after a cuss who's
already gunned one Indian trader for certain. I want to talk to
that French Canadian trader Legare, where this outfit's heading. If the Calgary Kid ain't shot *him* too, he may have something to tell me. In the meantime, I'd best make up with Miss
Southwind before Spotted Elk tells us all to start striking
camp."

Making up with a bawling sex maniac in a windowless tipi
wasn't all that tough, once she'd punched him with her fist
and been slapped more gently on her naked bottom. But after
he'd gotten her to climax twice, she rolled over on her perky
tits and sobbed, "Why does everybody hate us? Why? Why?
Why?"

He sat up and leaned a reassuring elbow on her firm buttocks as he quietly replied, "I can't speak for Miss Libby
Custer. But it's hardly fair to say that *everybody* hates you,
wichinchala."

She pouted, "You just call me your pretty little girl because you like to *tawiton* with anybody. I'll bet you would shove that thing in a *pte* if you could get it to hold still long enough!''

He chuckled and asked, ''Didn't Stone Boy fix his uncles up with a couple of buffalo wives, so they tell?''

She laughed despite herself, then sobbed, ''You understand us better than most of your people. You may not hate us as much, but *they* do!''

He stared about in vain for that damned pipe as he told the upset Lakota gal, ''Not all of 'em. I'll allow more than one of my kind has been mean as all hell to all sorts of folks for all sorts of reasons. Some folks, of any complexion or faith, are just afraid of anyone who looks different or prays different. Others are spiteful because they feel their own looks and ways make them too grand to have other kinds around. Then, of course, there'll always be sons of bitches like the late President Andrew Jackson who use any excuse to bully weaker folks out of anything worth taking from them.''

She turned half over and said, ''That was what those *maza* hunters did to us in the Paha Sapa! When they found yellow *maza* to dig up, they told the Great Father bad things about us and stole our Black Hills, all of them!''

He grimaced and said, ''Let's not get into who scalped whom first. You're right and you're wrong about the history of your own nation. Let's just say some of my kind are down on you and some of my kind are still sticking up for you.''

She smiled bitterly and demanded, ''Who has ever said or done one thing in our favor? No Wasichu has ever taken the side of any other kind of human being!''

He shook his head and insisted, ''That just ain't true, *winchinchala.* I just *agreed* there were white men, a heap of white men, who'd kill anyone the least bit different if they could get away with it. But they've never been able to get away with it entirely because there have always been enough decent folks to stop 'em.''

She sniffed and asked, ''Are you trying to tell me nice white people helped us when Star Chief Terry was hunting us down like rabbits?''

He nodded. ''That's exactly what I'm saying. Your boys had just wiped out a third of the Seventh Cav, and a bigger star chief we call Sheridan had already declared that the only good Indian was a dead Indian. The Great Father in Washington tries to do what most of my people want. If most of my people had wanted it, the colored people would still be picking cotton and all of your people would be dead. A heap of white folks, as you say, would like things to be that way. All it would take would be the *rest* of us looking the other way for a spell. So spare me that *ta-chesli* about all us mean white folks. If *half* of us were all that mean, you'd be in one hell of a fix!''

She sat up and grabbed his dong to see if she could calm him down. They came again, and even caught a few winks before some little girl stuck her head in to tell them in Lakota to quit fucking and take the damned tipi down.

They got dressed first. Longarm offered to help, but Southwind said taking down and putting up tipis was reserved for women. He knew better than to argue. It wasn't true that lazy Indian men made the women do all the work, when you studied on it. A band in a state of confusion, either striking a camp or setting one up, was vulnerable as hell to attack, and every member of a warrior society knew this. So men who'd grabbed their own share of hair and horses from enemy bands under those same conditions kept a sharp eye on their innocent surroundings while the women and children got the livestock and portable property ready to move out.

Indian men walked ahead of heavily laden women, their own hands free to strike back at anyone or anything out ahead, by the same long-established logic. It was only in a white settlement, or on a secured reservation, that Plains Indian manners began to seem less gallant.

They left before sundown, painted outriders alert to any Siksika scouts who might come whooping in through the gloaming. It was partly true that Plains Indians didn't like to attack in total darkness. But it was an old soldier's tale that they were afraid of the dark. Charging at full tilt in the dark was simply a stupid cavalry operation. Lakota raided a lot in the dark on foot. The Plains sign for Lakota was the hand motion of a throat being cut.

But possibly thanks to Sergeant Foster's attitude toward tribal funds, Longarm's Siksika pals never attacked his Lakota pals and they made good time across the well-watered and lush but empty prairie.

Longarm naturally took advantage of the six- or eight-hour trail breaks to make more pals among Spotted Elk's band. He had to get away from Southwind now and again.

But it was just as well she was tagging along, a couple of

days along the trail, when he stepped innocently up behind a younger Lakota headed toward the same pony string. Suddenly sensing Longarm behind him, the young *hokshila* whirled, Sharps rifle aimed right at the Winchester-toting white man, to stare owl-eyed and froth at the mouth in oddly distorted Lakota.

Southwind got between them, making rapid hand signs to the kid as she shouted in English at Longarm, "Don't hurt him! He is deaf, not a bad person! He has a hard time understanding the rest of us. That is why he acts so *witko*!"

The wild-eyed young Indian screamed, *"Mica Sapa hey mi-yey! How ke chewa?"*

That added up more politely than his expression and tone suggested. So Longarm made the friend sign and replied, *"Tran woo an."*

Southwind said, "He can't hear you. I am signing your answer and now you have exchanged greetings. He talks funny. But he wants you to call him Black Coyote. I have just told him who you are, and of course everyone has heard of Was-ichu Washtey."

Longarm tried shaking hands with the disturbed youth. Black Coyote just looked more disturbed. Longarm signed they had to be moving on and stepped around him, muttering, "Hear me, Southwind. If ever your band returns to the States, steer clear of that deaf kid whenever you get anywhere near *my* kind. It's plain he don't cotton to us, and it's easy to have mutual feelings when a young cuss waves a gun at you. That boy's going to get his fool self shot one of these days!"

Southwind locked elbows with Longarm to say lightly, "He is not a *wichasa* of any importance. Who would take him seriously enough to shoot him? Where are we going, my *wo-niya*?"

Longarm replied, "Wanted to see about borrowing a fresh mount. I'd say Black Coyote's best chance to get shot would be to put on that wild-eyed act around green nesters or army recruits. The way some of your boys carry on takes a little getting used to. Wasichu who've been around Lakota a spell understand it don't mean that much when one of you proves his maturity by screaming like a hysterical witch with the broom in the wrong place. Rightly or wrongly, Crazy Horse got himself bayonetted by staging such a tantrum down to Spotted Tail Agency back in '77. When a blue sleeve has the drop on you and tells you to hold still, it unsettles him when you go bug-eyed and commence a war dance whilst singing in a high soprano. If you ever notice Black Coyote acting that way around red or blue sleeves, *duck*!''

She insisted the deaf kid was harmless as they went on to the pony line, with her paying less attention to the wicked grins they attracted along the way. Village gossip was as popular in an Indian camp as anywhere else, although sometimes more imaginative. It wasn't true that the Lakota lingo didn't provide for double meanings, puns, or downright dirty jokes, but as was the case in Spanish, Lakota were less likely to say you fucked your mother than they were to mildly ask whether your mother, your sister, or your pony had the biggest twat.

Longarm was more concerned about Indian ponies than Indian humor at the moment. Simple geometry told him that since he and the Indians were headed due east whilst Sergeant Foster was diverging to the northeast at about forty-five degrees, Spotted Elk's band would reach the Wood Mountain fort before Foster could make it to that other one, which was almost due north.

But after that Longarm had one hell of a northbound beeline to ride. So he needed good riding stock. At least four horses if he wanted to trail spares at all times for himself and a pack saddle of supplies.

It was too early to approach any Indian owners about selling him some stock. Most every man and some of the women owned ponies galore. So they were sort of in the position of Georgia planters after old Sherman had marched past. They had nothing but property nobody else seemed anxious to buy. With neither buffalo nor government allotments to rely on, they were only rich in ponies, dogs, and kids. Everything else was in short supply, and some of the fresher kids were starting to call their chief Stone Boy, as if Big Foot wasn't sarcastic enough.

The original Big Foot had only been a great provider. Stone Boy went back to the Lakota creation myths, and it was as if they'd started calling a poor provider Santa Claus.

But the one good thing about the piss-poor hunting all around was that it kept the band moving, past the undisputed Cypress Hills and beyond, at better than thirty miles a day.

They were now downright desperate to get to Legare's trading post.

180

Southwind had cried the night before when she'd had to feed Longarm and Constable Newton *wishtonwish* and grass roots. Longarm had told Newton the prairie dog was something like rabbit. He'd had a time comforting Southwind later dog-style. She'd allowed they were out of buffalo jerky, and he'd already noticed the *chanshasha* they'd been smoking afterward had lots of dry grass in it.

But he knew he'd get a better deal on horseflesh if he waited until they got to Legare's, when the horse-poor Lakota would be anxious to make their own purchases. So he just strolled the pony line, with Southwind translating, as he jawed with proud owners about the points of their stock, and got them to offer him free rides on fresh ponies with his jaded but handsome roan as security.

The plan was to ride as many as possible before he made his real move. As any horse trader could tell you, a watered and curried mount trotted out for sale ain't the same as a horse you've ridden a dozen miles or more, and Indian ponies tended to look unpromising to begin with.

The Indian pony, like the Indian, seemed living proof of old Professor Darwin's new notions about evolution. Your average Indian tended to seem tougher and healthier than your average white man of the same age because weak and sickly Indians died younger than most white folks. The Indian pony was a tough, wiry example of what Darwin had explained. It got foaled and weaned without the service of a vet, or even the roof of a manger over it, with coyotes and worse testing its dam and its luck on many a raw windy night. Its bloodlines were said to be mostly Spanish barb. In point of fact it was hash of every breed of horse that had ever strayed or been stolen west of the Big Muddy, with unforgiving marginal range and even less-forgiving riders weeding out the stock that couldn't measure up to almost impossible standards.

The Horse Indian expected his mount to carry him where he wanted to go when he wanted to go there. He watered it less often than the U.S. Army Remount Service advised, and fed it nothing but such grass as might be there to graze. If the pony couldn't take such a hard life, its owner abandoned it, ate it, or tried to sell it to some asshole who didn't savvy *Shunka Wakan* (or *Tashunka* if they were talking about a stud).

It wasn't true the Plains Indians were the superior horsemen they and their Eastern admirers assured everyone they were, however. So a man who really savvied horseflesh could sometimes get a bargain.

For a society that moved by steam or horse and buggy, it was a caution how many folks Longarm had met believed those fairy tales about horses at least as smart as the average reader, or Stone-Age youths meeting up with the first horse and teaching it to do tricks no mere white man could ever get a horse to do.

Some Stone-Age *white* boy had caught and tamed that first horse. Then white folks had spent at least five thousand years on the subject before the first Indian had seen his first horse.

Longarm had it on sensible red as well as white authority that the first time Indians had seen Spanish riders, down Mexico way, they'd thought man and beast were one spooky critter. Ancient myths about centaurs and such in the old countries had likely started the same way.

Nadéné or Apache down Texas way were said to have rounded up or stolen the first Spanish horses, with a view, at first, to skinning them. It took a while to copy the riding habits of the Spaniards who kept chasing them. The Comanche, pushing down into Texas to drive the Apache off to the southwest, took up the new critters with more enthusiasm, even if they weren't sure what they were. All the Plains Indian names for horses described them as some odd species of oversized dogs. Buffalo-dogs, elk-dogs, medicine-dogs, spirit-dogs, or whatever. The Indians had used them as oversized dogs at first, then slowly picked up pointers from their Anglo or Hispanic foemen. It was no longer true that the "natural cavalrymen" rode bareback, bare-ass, on ponies trained to know more about battle tactics than J. E. B. Stuart. Indians who could buy or fashion them preferred saddles with stirrups for the same reason the Ancient Goths had invented stirrups to start with. It felt dumb to fall off a horse. Falling off one in a fight could get a fighting man killed. So while you had to be careful about mounting Indians ponies from the near side white-style, you rode them much the same and they'd give you what they had, like any horse. It was more important to know what a jug-headed runty Indian pony had than it was to admire its pretty forelock and big brown eyes.

With Southwind's help on that and other occasions, Longarm managed to ride more than two dozen good, bad, and indifferent ponies by the time they tottered in at last to Legare's trading post near the Wood Mountain fort of the NWMP.

Young Constable Newton naturally pipe-clayed his webbing and white helmet to ride on over to the Mountie fort and tell Inspector Walsh the good news about Spotted Elk's change of heart, or bad hunting.

Longarm wasn't supposed to be there. So he rode over to the trading post with his Lakota pals.

Jean Louis Legare was trading down by Willow Bunch with another band that afternoon. So Longarm had to talk to a friendly enough junior clerk while the Lakota fingered price tags and counted their few saved-up coins. Longarm felt sorry for them. Even though he had to allow General Sheridan's point about feeding Indians *on* the reservation and fighting them *off* it.

First things coming first, he questioned the young French Canadian in vain for word on the Calgary Kid. No white man of any description had stopped by for even a short visit. The clerk suggested, and Longarm agreed, that a fugitive white from the States might avoid an area overgrown with Quill Indians.

Longarm purchased a lot of supplies, commencing with three-for-a-nickel cheroots, and took a couple of Quill Indians outside on the veranda to talk about horseflesh in Plains sign. So a few minutes later they had more good things to take home to their families than they'd promised, and Longarm had a buckskin, a cordovan, and a stocky but deceptively frisky roan to go with the steady paint he'd been aiming to hang on to.

Southwind caught him saddling the roan and cordovan over at the pony line near sundown. She quietly asked, "Are you really too tired of me to spend one last night in my tipi?"

He kissed her white-style and gently said, "It ain't what I want. It's what I have to do. We've been over all that. I want to remember you smiling up at me, not weeping like a *hokshi.*"

She smiled weakly and murmured, "I shall not weep. *Heh-etchetu,* it is over. *Nunwey!* But I shall never forget you, and maybe someday we may meet again."

Longarm nodded soberly and said, "*Mitakuye oyasin.* Where do you reckon you and this band might wind up down south once this is all over, *winchinchala?*"

She said, "I don't know. I suppose we'll settle by the BIA Agency at Chankpe Opi Wakpala, a creek you would call Wounded Knee."

Chapter 15

Longarm pushed the four ponies hard through the crisp prairie night. He figured they'd covered close to forty miles by dawn, and if they hadn't, it sure felt that bad.

There were sullen red clouds in the west, but it didn't look like rain just yet. He hobbled the four ponies in a wooded draw, with standing water, juicy sedge, and plenty of browse to discourage them from straying far. He spread his bedding on the grassy south-facing slope beyond, with those thunderheads to the west in mind.

He consumed a can of tomato preserves, and lit a long-overdue real smoke before he spread a more important purchase from the trading post across his top tarp.

He couldn't find the HBC Campbell's Station on the famous survey map by David Thompson. But Constable Newton had said those other Mounties from Fort Carlton had ridden south, up the river, a good four days. Finding both Wood Mountain and Fort Carlton without any fuss, Longarm decided the place had to be somewhere near the junction of the South Saskatchewan and Qu'Appelle, a river in its own right winding west across the rolling prairies from the east. It was a good spot to trade with Indians, although pretty far south of those Métis settlements north of Fort Carlton.

Longarm figured he could make the hundred and more miles in three hard days in the saddle. Meanwhile, his saddle was airing and he had to catch some damned sleep.

So he did, out like a snuffed candle until somebody seemed to be pissing in his face and he sat up, spewing and cussing in the warm but heavy rain. When he heard old Wakinyan flapping his thunderous wings, Longarm struggled into his crunchy rain slicker, got a tarp over his saddle and loose possibles, and got down to the ponies to tether them before they were spooked by lightning.

Plains Indian ponies, like Plains Indians, had an unholy but not irrational fear of lightning. The Thunderbird didn't fool around with trees, tipi poles, or anything else much taller than grass if it could catch an Indian or a pony atop a rise, or even out on an open flat when there was nothing better to aim at.

Tethering the spooked ponies to shorter trees far enough apart to keep from losing more than one to a single bolt, Longarm left his tarp-covered possibles where they were for now. He'd seen an old boy catch a bolt from the blue while running uphill for something he'd forgot.

So a miserable noon was enjoyed by all as they waited for the storm to blow over. It soon did. But not before soaking Longarm to the knees with a gully-wash that might have chased a greener plainsman up on the more dangerous high ground.

Then the sun came out some more to steam everything alive like the clams wrapped in seaweed at a New England clambake. So Longarm got himself and the riding stock up in the wind and moving some more.

Ponies couldn't tell you how many winks they might have gotten as they browsed and dozed a night away. Solid sleep was a luxury only meat eaters could afford. Cattle, horses, and other critters used to getting eaten caught a few uneasy winks at a time, whether on their feet or sitting up.

Riding the frisky paint, with the buckskin packing and the two he'd started out on trailing behind on the one long lead, Longarm settled into a ball-busting but mile-eating trot across the rolling sea of grass. The Canadian extension of the North American High Plains was greener and the buffalo grass rose taller than you saw even as far north as Wyoming Territory. Why nations such as the Comanche, Kiowa, and Nadéné had worked their way all the way south to the brown plains of Texas was one of those mysteries you got when folks recorded no written history.

185

A lot of the Canadian prairie was really wooded bottom-lands. You got tanglewood in the deeper draws, where sudden flooding and spring thaws tended to pollard trees off at the roots. The wider flats where the floodwaters could stand more gently offered miles-wide strips of pure forest, mostly aspen, birch, soft maple, and willow. There were plenty of bogs, ponds, and even lakes that looked good for the whole summer. So there were all sorts of critters, but most tended to be small and shy this close to all those refugee Indians from the States.

Longarm hadn't met any, but Southwind had told him there were a mess of Assiniboin, Gros Ventre, and such hunting both sides of the border between Wood Mountain and those Cypress Hills the Siksika claimed. So even where you'd expect to see deer or even elk, the bigger meat had been shot or driven off.

But by his third day on the trackless beeline, Longarm began to flush deer, at least, crossing wooded draws. Up on the mostly high and open prairies between he spotted distant pronghorn, in all directions. It didn't seem too far for those refugee Indians to ride compared to their longer invasion of the Siksika hunting ground to the west. So the Lakota had been ordered or warned by the Mounties or a *Wakan wichasha* not to hunt up this way. He doubted a warning from the native Plains Cree would cut any ice with Lakota.

He didn't see any Indian sign as he navigated the sea of grass, resting his ponies on the hour, changing them often, but pushing them harder than livery nags or run-of-the-mill Indian ponies could have kept going. He'd told Southwind why he'd kept trying different mounts on their way to Wood Mountain.

So he knew he'd made damned good time when, along about ten one morning, he topped a rise, sitting the paint, to regard what had to be the east-west valley of the Qu'Appelle.

"Now ain't that grand?" he asked his mount, reining in to take in the view. You could tell the Qu'Appelle River itself had to be running through that winding corridor-forest in the middle of the wide but not quite flat valley. Scattered groves of old-growth maple stood on gently sloped hills that might have been glacial drumlins left over from far colder times. Whatever they were, they offered perfect sites for home spreads, high, dry, but surrounded by well-watered bottom-land. A nester could surely grow a lot of crops, or cattle, be-tween spring thaws up this way.

But the only sign of civilization this far west was a distant line of telegraph poles, following the river but not too closely.

Constable Newton had told Longarm there was a single-strand line running from Fort MacLeod to Wood Mountain, with other lines spiderwebbed across the prairies to other posts and even Denver, by way of the new settlements in Manitoba. But Western Union had to relay messages to the Canadian Post Office north of the border. For as was the case in England, the Canadian Post Office laid claim to public telegraph and even those new-fangled Bell Telephone lines.

As a rider who wasn't in Canada officially, Longarm had naturally felt no call to ask the NWMP telegrapher at Wood Mountain to put him in touch with his home office. But he'd been away a spell, and by now Billy Vail would no doubt be sort of curious. Also, Longarm was running low on pocket jingle. Indians sold horses cheap, but French Canadian trading posts expected a man to pay two bits for a can of pork and beans. So it was costing him over a dollar a day just to eat up this way. But he was sure the office would advance him some of his six-cents-a-mile travel allowance if only he could wire home for it.

He'd ask when he got to a Canadian cable office, as they called them, how you went about that in these parts.

He rested his stock on the rise, rode on to the telegraph line, and swung left to follow it. He saw a sort of service road, or at least an occasional wagon rut, leading the same way. Thompson's survey indicated they all had to be headed for the juncture of the Qu'Appelle and South Saskatchewan, and common sense told you Campbell's HBC station would be the logical spot for a telegraph relay. They had to run the wire through a battery of wet cells every now and then to keep current flowing up and down the line. With any luck there'd be a cable office there as well. Remote general stores and trading posts tended to double as rural post offices north and south of the border. That breed who'd apparently burst into flames so mysteriously had almost surely been the local postmaster, if not a part-time cable operator. The Hudson Bay Company had given up governing the North West Territories, but not doing business out this way for fun and profit.

Following the line where it led between two wooded drumlins, Longarm heard what he took at first for more thunder. But the sky above was cloudless and when he looked back he saw dust, one hell of a lot of dust, rolling his way like an incoming ocean wave.

So he yelled, "Stampede!" and heeled his roan up the nearest slope with the other three ponies trailing. But that frisky roan at the far end of the lead slipped its halter and broke free at one hell of an awkward time!

Longarm got the other two, along with his trail pack, as high up the slope as the trees. He half-hitched the lead line to a maple limb, and lit out at full gallop after the infernal roan. The paint carried him downslope faster than they should have been going in prairie dog country, but he still doubted they'd be able to catch up with a riderless horse that moved pretty good under a rider.

But they had to try. He needed all four ponies if he was to keep besting thirty miles a day. He spotted the hide of the runaway out ahead, running in fool circles as if it had gotten into loco weed somewhere.

That thundering to the east was louder now. So even as Longarm rode west toward the paint, he twisted in the saddle for a better look and groaned, "Oh, shit!" as he saw what was coming at him and his ponies.

It was buffalo, a whole damned herd of buffalo, coming heads down and tails up, as they darkened the sky behind them with the dust it took a whole lot of sharp pounding hooves to paw out of green sod!

It got worse when you looked the other way.

There seemed to *be* no other way. Freak winds, or clever hands, had piled dead brush and tree limbs up in saddle-high windrows leading on back to a westward-pointing V with no exit. That was why the roan was running in circles, and running in circles was no way to get out of the way of a stampeding buffalo herd!

His own skin coming before that of any fool horse, Longarm looked around for another way out. Then a hearty voice called, *"Ici, mon ami!"* and Longarm headed that way without trying to translate the words.

The roan followed after, like a scared pup, as Longarm rode through the narrow gap that had suddenly appeared in the high wall of sun-silvered deadwood. As he circled on the flat grass beyond to grab that fool roan by its mane and rein both ponies to a stop, he saw two gents on foot in those blue denim smocks French painters, or farm folks, favor for sweat-work. They were shoving the root end of a dead willow back in the gap they'd just opened for him. There were other French Canadians all along the outside of the buffalo barricade, looking the other way and mostly armed with single-shot but heavy-caliber rifles. As Longarm rode back to thank the ones who'd just saved his bacon, all hell broke loose and he couldn't talk to anyone until the roar of gunfire faded away.

A distant voice called out, *"C'est assez!"* and Longarm could hear the milling buffalo on the far side of the barricade heading the other way now. This outfit was only taking such hides as it could cope with. He'd been told by French folks that French folks prided themselves on being *practique,* or sensible.

It wasn't easy, but Longarm managed to fumble out some pigging string with one free hand as he held the reins of his paint between his teeth. As he was improvising a new halter for the runaway roan, one of the buffalo hunters who'd just saved their hides came over and remarked dryly, "You no get ground to sausage meat so long you stay out from under *sauve-qui-peut, Anglais*!"

Longarm went on knotting the new halter as he replied just as dryly, "If you're talking about stampedes, I can't argue. But I ain't no Englishman, and I had it on good authority that there weren't half so many buffalo left up this way."

The hunter on foot, whose freckled face and blue eyes went with a mighty high set of cheekbones and black braided hair, spat in disgust and agreed. "Those Sioux Américain have drive ze Cypress Hills herd south. Ze herd you almost get run over by are *buffles du bois* or what you call wood buffalo. Zey run in more *petite* herds and one must know where to hunt for zem. But we have talk enough for now, by gar. I must get back to work, *mon ami*!"

Longarm said he had his own chores. So leading the wayward paint at close quarters, he headed back for the other two ponies.

Riding through another gap in the now partly demolished barricade, Longarm saw that a dozen-odd Métis men and boys had joined the mounted stampeders inside the trap, where the grass was littered with about four score dead buffalo. The two ponies didn't cotton much to the smell of gunsmoke and blood all around. But men rode horses, instead of things being the other way around, because they had more willpower.

But once he'd ridden back to that wooded drumlin and put the whole outfit back together right, he decided on riding back outside the barricade. He knew there'd be even more blood in the air once those hide skinners got really serious about peeling buffalo.

Before heading on, Longarm changed his saddle and bridal to the cordovan, letting the roan carry the packsaddle to steady it some. Leading the paint and buckskin after them, he made his way around the deadwood barricade to where a dozen Red River carts were circled on their six-foot rawhide-rimmed wheels. A strung-out line of men and boys were already hauling fresh buffalo hides over to be salted and loaded up. They dragged them as far as the carts, one at a time, for green buffalo hides were thicker and heavier than cowhides, which were heavy enough.

Longarm reined in when an older man with European features and skin as dark as a gun stock hailed him from atop a pile of hides aboard a cart. "By gar, we would not have try to run buffalo over you if we had know you are not Anglais. Give us ze time to load zese carts and we make talk *avec café, non*?"

Longarm shook his head politely and replied, "I ain't got the time it will take you gents to skin out such a smart move. I'm headed for Campbell's Station on the big river. Am I right about yonder telegraph poles heading the same way?"

The older man said, "*Oui, mais* Jacques Campbell, he is dead, him."

Longarm nodded and replied, "I'd heard. Wouldn't the Hudson Bay Company have another agent in charge there by now?"

The Métis shrugged and said, "*Que sais?* Old Jacques, he was all right, him. *Mais* we no longer trade *avec* HBC. We are not, how you say, born yesterday in ze wigwam, and now that our Louis Riel has shown ze way, we sell our robes for real money, not zose tokens HBC doles out for furs and hides, *hein*?"

Longarm allowed that made sense, whether he understood or not, and said, "In other words, you-all won't be hauling these robes over to Campbell's Station, right?"

The Métis replied, "*Mais non.* We cart zem up to Batoche, beyond Fort Carlton, where our own traders now pay ze cash on barrelhead and raft them downstream *past* HBC Headquarters at Cumberland House. Ze Riel family has been in, how you say, competition weez Hudson Bay for lang time now. You did not know zis?''

Longarm sighed. ''I do now. A pretty lady I trusted had me convinced it was pure idealism. But then, they do say old George Washington made a handsome profit selling quarry stone for the Capitol Building, and I reckon he was mostly sincere.''

The older Métis looked as if he was having trouble following that. So Longarm thanked him again for not letting him get run down, and rode wide of the camp and on along the service road to the telegraph line. He followed the wire through most of the rest of the day as the Qu'Appelle dug its bed deeper and the valley walls drew closer together instead of the way you'd expect.

He saw why when they got to what had to be the South Saskatchewan. More water was running north past the junction between steeper banks. The main stream's valley had the fresh V profile of a new channel cut through soft soil. As he followed the telegraph line along it to the north, he saw by the late afternoon sun that the river ran like foaming hot chocolate, washing over boulders in some places and forming brown rapids in others. A few birch and willows grew on the slopes up from either bank. Now and again a tangle of uprooted timber would drift by to tell you why there weren't as many back up the Qu'Appelle.

Longarm was wondering how he'd ever ford such a torrent of spring runoff with four ponies when he rounded a bend to see a long stretch of calm slack water, where a low-slung complex of log buildings had been built on higher ground. There was no sign out front to proclaim the place much of anything. But he knew he'd come to the right place when he saw the familiar figure of Crown Sergeant Foster among the half dozen others who'd stepped out on the veranda to admire the sunset, or a strange rider coming in.

Foster seemed the Mountie in charge. The other two wore no stripes on their scarlet tunics. A sandy-headed woman with mighty high cheekbones stood beside Foster in a summer-weight dress of light green calico and a dark green tartan shawl. The other two seemed to be full-blood Indians. Plains Cree if they belonged in these parts.

As Longarm reined in and dismounted, Foster called out,

191

"Constable Newton wired us about those Sioux from Wood Mountain. Don't you agree he did a fine job on his first mission?"

Longarm handed the reins to a helpful grinning Indian station hand as he dryly replied, "All alone too. Will he be joining us?"

Foster shook his head and replied, "Inspector Ward wants him to stand by at Wood Mountain, seeing he has such a way with Indians. I take it you'll be headed back to Montana now?"

Longarm quietly allowed he might have a few chores to attend to up their way. Foster shot him a warning look and introduced him to the three white, or mostly white, people with him.

The two Mounties were down from Fort Carlton to assist in the investigation. The gal, in her twenties and sort of pretty, once you got used to blue eyes and sandy hair with classic Algonquin bone structure, turned out to be Una Campbell, the daughter of the late HBC trader, Jacques Campbell. She was the one who said supper was almost ready. So they all trooped inside, where the purebred help had set an extra place at the big table in the dining room without being told.

As they were working out who sat where, Longarm quietly asked just where the gal's father might be at the moment.

Foster muttered, "Later. At her insistence we buried the few parts left over. But we've preserved the scene of the crime, or whatever. I'll show you later."

So they all sat down to be served smoked venison along with what would have passed for boiled potatoes if Longarm hadn't recognized it as bread-root, a mighty fine prairie weed.

Longarm knew that despite the patronizing attitude some breeds and even educated full-bloods accused it of, the HBC did proud by its employees and customers when it came to trade goods, at least. Hudson Bay blankets were preferred by red and white bed-makers alike on both sides of the border, wherever the winter winds blew seriously. Hudson Bay traps were superior, and their trade rifles never blew up in a man's face just because he'd double-charged them by mistake. So it came as no surprise that the tea Miss Una poured was all the way from East India and as fine a brand as London ladies might serve guests.

Longarm liked even cow-camp coffee better, but he had to

allow tea tasted better when anyone from the British Isles, or even British Canada, made it. He suspected it had something to do with the way they poured what into what. But every English, Irish, or Scotch tea-maker he'd ever asked seemed to think everyone made tea the same natural way.

As they were having more tea with their Scotch shortbread dessert, they naturally got to talk more, and it developed that Miss Una had been away, attending college in Ottawa, until she'd headed home that spring to spend the summer at the trading post. By the time she'd arrived it had all been over, or leastways, her father's just-about-cremated remains were already being investigated by the NWMP.

She didn't seem to want to dwell on this. So Longarm didn't press her, and after supper, Sergeant Foster drew him aside and murmured, "I'll show you what we have and fill you in on the little we do know. But I'll be expecting you to ride on in the morning, and I do advise you to ride south. As I just wired your hysterical superior, Marshal Vail, nobody up this way has seen hide or hair of your goddamned Calgary Kid, and I assure you we've been looking!"

He led the bemused Longarm through the well-stocked showroom of the trading post and out a side door, pointing at a stoutly built log cabin a dozen yards on. "Telegraph junction and relay. Has to be a safe distance from the other buildings because of the danger of fire. Danger of *normal* fires, I mean."

Longarm glanced skyward as they crossed the yard in the soft light of the gloaming. He made out north-south and east-west lines against the salmon-colored sky. As if Longarm had asked, Foster said, "NWMP wire from Wood Mountain to Fort Carlton. Winnipeg-to-Edmonton public line east to west. Both belong to the Canadian Government, of course, so they feed off the same battery of wet cells here. Spare acid as well. You always add sulfuric acid a little at a time to water. Do it the other way round and you can have one hell of an explosion."

Longarm allowed he'd heard that before.

Foster opened the door cautiously and said, "Let me light a lamp before you follow me, and watch where you plant those big feet!"

So Longarm waited on the threshold as the Mountie lit an oil lamp on a worktable running along one wall, under shelves of jars bigger than fish bowls, each bathing metal plates in corrosive acid.

Two telegraph keys sat side by side under the battery, a handy pad of notepaper nearby. Foster pointed at the dirt floor in the middle of the small space. They'd set up a sort of bed frame of planks to keep drafts from drifting things. Foster had already told him they'd salvaged enough meat to bury. What appeared to be a pile of pipe-ash two feet across and two yards long still looked disturbingly close to what you'd find if you torched a human body till it just wouldn't burn anymore.

Foster said, "The two Indian servants found things this way when they got back from Fort Carlin. Campbell had sent them up to the NWMP with a canoe load of trade goods they wanted for their own Cree scouts. Before you ask if they could have done this before they set up such a perfect alibi, they couldn't. Whatever did this left Campbell's hands and feet intact, like the paws of a mouse left over by an untidy cat. By the time they returned, retraced their short voyage to Fort Carlton to report, and our own arrived on the scene, the hands and feet were naturally a bit flyblown and smelly, but we still fix the time of death as after his Indians left Campbell alone here. The daughter you just met was even farther from the scene when whatever happened . . . ah, happened."

Longarm hunkered down and struck a match as he quietly asked what Foster thought might have happened.

The Mountie waved a hand at the greasy-looking log walls as he let fly with an annoyed snort and replied, "Nothing that obeys the simple laws of nature. You can see everything but his hands and feet burned to finer ashes than you'd get with a cord of wood. You can see how the considerable amount of oily soot that resulted settled on the walls in such a confined space. But there's no sign of *charring,* even within yards of these ashes, and I have it on good authority that one does not leave open jars of sulfuric acid on the hearth in front of a merry fire. Yet the battery was operating and there was current on both lines when those Indians got back, got around to searching for their superior after not seeing him for half a day and a full night, and finally found him in here like this."

Longarm could make out what seemed to be human teeth and some fair-sized shreds of calcined bones, along with the steel rims of some heat-shattered reading glasses. So there went a couple of notions.

Rising back to his feet, Longarm said, "You don't fall asleep in bed with a smoke when you have on your specs and you ain't in bed to begin with. What if somebody burned the body out in the yard and then hauled this mess inside to mystify us?"

"To what purpose? We obviously have human remains here, and have you a better way to settle oily soot from a cremation all over this interior than by cremating the poor chap *in situ*?"

Longarm got out a cheroot and lit up, both to give himself time to think and to taste more appetizing smoke before he said, "All right. Say Campbell or somebody with similar hands and feet lays dead at our feet, by fair means or foul. How do we burn just him and never set the blamed little place on fire?"

Foster sighed and said, "You tell me and I'll give you that blank check you've been asking for! The literature is filled with reports on cases much like this one. On the other hand, there's supposed to be a man-eating tree on some island in the Indian Ocean, and let us not forget those eyewitness reports on zombies that keep coming out of Haiti."

Longarm smiled thinly and said, "I've always looked forward to meeting up with that bare-ass white goddess who rules an African valley filled with diamonds. But this apparent case of spontaneous human combustion ain't in some penny-dreadful magazine, Sarge. It's spread out on the floor at our damn feet!"

Foster muttered, "I wish you wouldn't say things like that. But I rather like your idea about burning the body out of doors and bringing the ashes in here to hide them, the more I think about it."

"Do you reckon that's what happened?" Longarm asked mildly.

Foster grimaced and said, "Of course not. But we have to say *some*thing and I'm absobloodylutely stuck!"

Longarm said, "Let's forget how they might have done it and think about *who* done it. You say his daughter and two hired hands were far away when he met his fate. Have you wondered how come he met it here in this telegraph shack?"

Foster said, "Of course. I contacted all the other operators, on both lines, when I arrived the day before yesterday. I don't know how often Jacques Campbell may have sent or received messages in the past. But none have been sent or received at this desk, on either line, for over a month.''

Longarm shrugged and said, ''Some Métis I met along the way told me they didn't trade here no more. I can't see *Indians* using the public telegraph too often. Let's say he just come out here to check the acid level in them jars. Then let's say . . . forget it. You might render a body down in sulfuric acid, in a big tub, which I don't see. But you wouldn't wind up with dry ash and leftover body parts, to say nothing about that nasty soot all about the premises. So we have him here, alone or with his killer. Then we have him spread out on the floor, on fire. That dirt floor could take the heat right under his flickerings, but I can't see it *giving off* enough heat to burn much.''

Foster said they were arguing in a circle.

Longarm nodded and said, ''When you're right you're right. I know how to use a telegraph key, if you're too tired. Do I have your permission to see if I can patch a message through to Western Union and then on to my boss down Denver way?''

Foster shook his head and stiffly replied, ''You do not. To begin with, you're not here. Meanwhile, I've assured Marshal Vail in a guarded way that you're alive, well, and still on a wild-goose chase.''

Longarm insisted, ''I'll be the judge of whether the Calgary Kid is up this way or not. Meanwhile, I'm running low on pocket jingle. So I want to see if I can get my boss to wire me some damned money.''

Foster shifted and said, ''He can't. Not here. Even if Campbell was still alive to manage things, no HBC trading post could cash a cabled money order for anyone.''

Longarm started to argue, thought, then nodded and said, ''Those Métis I met earlier said Hudson Bay uses some sort of play money in dealing with its mostly pure-blood trade. I'd need to have real money wired to me at some town where there's a real bank, right?''

Foster nodded, but said, ''I'm sorry. I just can't give you permission to ride on over to Edmonton. I've already risked my stripes for you as it is!''

Longarm asked innocently, ''Not even if I solve this here case of spontaneous human combustion?''

Foster stared soberly down at the white ash spread across the dark brown floor and replied, ''Give me something sensible to put down on paper for my official report and I'll advance you ten quid from my very own pocket!''

.Longarm said, ''Don't want your damn money. I want you to stand aside and let me do my own job, once we figure this case out.''

So Crown Sergeant Foster agreed and they shook on it.

Chapter 16

Back in the main house after sundown, a Cree hand showed Longarm to his quarters for the night. They'd already brought his saddle and possibles in there for him. But there was no call for him to unlash his bedroll. They'd spread fresh linens along with Hudson Bay blankets on the handsome feather bed. A reading lamp stood on the bed table. There was a corner washstand with a filled pitcher. There was even a braided rug on the split-log floor. The moment he was alone he tossed his hat aside, sat down on the soft bedding, and lit a last cheroot. He'd had a hard day and, early as it was, he was ready for a good night's sleep.

Then it came to him how risky smoking alone in bed could be. So he got back up and went out on the veranda to finish his smoke standing in the cool night air.

He discovered he wasn't alone out there. Miss Una Campbell was down in front of another doorway, and it looked as if she'd been bawling before he came out to surprise her and inspire her to get a grip on herself.

He strode on down to her, wishing he had his hat on to tip, as he quietly said, "Evening, ma'am. I was having a time getting sleepy my ownself."

She sniffed and said, "My mother was Ojibwa and Clan Chatten. She was descended from chiefs on both sides. My father's people were not to be despised. One of his French

198

great-grandfathers was born in a famous chateau. Another was a younger son of the Duke of Argyle. How can they slight me like this?''

Longarm smiled uncertainly and asked, "Who might be slighting you in what way, Miss Una?"

She said, "Cumberland House. The HBC is sending another agent to take my father's place at this station. I won't have it. I was born here. My mother and now parts of my father are buried just up the slope. I am an educated woman, even if I am a breed. I know the stock. I am known to all the full-bloods who trade here. I wired them that I was ready and willing to take charge. They wired back that they were sending someone else. Someone untainted by Indian blood, no doubt!''

Longarm took a thoughtful drag on his cheroot and leaned against a veranda post as he calmly pointed out, "Your father had as much Indian blood as yourself, Miss Una. I suspect it's your sex, not your race, as stands in your way. No offense, but this far west, ladies who have green eyes ain't considered Indians. Not Quill Indians leastways.''

She sniffed again and said, "The snobs running the HBC don't dwell out west. I saw how people looked at me back in Ottawa. I was going to tell my poor father I never wanted to go back to that fancy school with all those stuck-up girls. I never really understood Louis Riel and his rantings about a prairie republic before I'd been treated the same as one of his Métis back East. I'll never go back there again, never! But what's to become of me if I can't stay here and run this trading post?''

It was a tough question, deserving of practical answers.

Longarm blew a thoughtful smoke ring out into the darkness before he said, "Down Denver way I room west of Cherry Creek, where folks ain't as snooty as, say, up on Capitol Hill. These Arapaho full-bloods run a bakery just down the street. Given the choice of being reservation folks or self-supporting folks, they've chosen to live white, like your late mother and father.''

She sobbed, "Of course we've always lived like white people. Can you see me in a wigwam, chewing some brave's moccasins to make them soft again after a rain?''

He shook his head and replied, "I can't see the Plimmons sisters, who work at that family bakery I just mentioned, giving up the good things in life that they've come to expect. You're

199

going to have to marry up with some white boy, or at least a prosperous Métis, if you don't aim to get a job and support yourself white-style in some town out this way."

She said, "Edmonton! I'll go to Edmonton and become a dance hall girl, or maybe teach school. They say things are booming over that way and women of any complexion are still too scarce to be slighted!"

He said, "There you go. We'll talk about your future plans some more in the future—say, tomorrow after breakfast. I don't know about you, but I just rode all day and even outrode a buffalo herd. So I may make more sense in the morning."

He did, although Una Campbell still lay slugabed as Longarm popped out of bed at daybreak, wide awake and grinning like a cardplayer who'd just drawn four aces.

A good night's sleep could do that to a man mulling over a lot of things in his mind. He washed up, got dressed, took a crap out back, and got right to work. Crown Sergeant Foster, another early riser, caught up with him coming out of the telegraph shack with a cheese box full of clues.

Foster said, "I was just about to use the telegraph. What have you been up to, Yank?"

Longarm said, "Spontaneous human combustion. Mr. Charles Dickens coined the term. When he had Mr. Krook combust in his newspaper serial *Bleak House,* scores of folks wrote in, taking him to task for trying to sell them such superstitious shit, So Mr. Dickens published a whole list of such cases from real life. Allowing that a lot of such tales were just tales, he still came up with official police reports and some studies by your British Royal Society."

Foster said, "I've just read some. I told you I've been using that telegraph setup, and police libraries are meant to be consulted. Where are we going?"

"Smokehouse," Longarm replied. "What comes next may get smoky and stinky. A smokehouse is poorly ventilated on purpose. Reliable reports on folks being combusted entirely, not just running down the street with their pants on fire, seem to agree on the same tight conditions. The victim is often a heavy drinker or sickly soul, alone, indoors, and he or she *seems* to have just burnt to crisp parts and ashes, without setting the fool house on fire."

As they made their way to the low, partly dug-in smokehouse downwind of the other buildings, Foster said, "I told you I've been boning up. I know all about that famous case where a Dr. Le Cat got that French innkeeper off when his shrew of a wife was found burnt to a crisp in their kitchen. Le Cat persuaded the court that no matter how the late Mme. Millet might have died, there was no way her husband could have cremated his wife on the kitchen floor without setting the whole place on fire. He demonstrated how much heat it took to consume a small portion of fresh meat, and almost set the *courtroom* on fire."

Longarm opened the smokehouse door and struck a match as he stepped inside the dark reeking interior. He lit a wall sconce to illuminate an interesting collection of smoked critters, from Canada goose to pronghorn, on hooks overhead. A pit in the center of the dirt floor was filled with hardwood ash. Longarm pointed at it and remarked, "You don't want a blazing fire when you smoke meat. You want a slow smolder with poor ventilation, lasting for days."

Foster stepped in after him, snorting, "Please don't tell me how you smoke a ham. Jacques Campbell wasn't smoked. He was burnt away to fine ashes, damn it!"

Longarm set his cheese box on a chopping block and proceeded to spread things on the block as he replied, "I noticed. Last night it came back to me that there's combustion and combustion. You don't get a blaze of glory in a smokehouse, and a hotel mattress can smolder under a drunk for hours, smothering him in his sleep, before it bursts into flames, if at all."

Foster snorted, "Good Lord, are you about to suggest Campbell was smoking in bed in that telegraph shack?"

Longarm said, "Not hardly," as he got out two similar wads of rags and spread them on the chopping block. Then he took out his pocket knife and cut two healthy hunks of smoked meat from the same bear carcass as he continued. "Forget that part about the victims being heavy drinkers. Save for the fact that drinkers living alone tend to run to fat. Bear meat has about the same amount of fat in it as our own. But you'll have to admit smoked bear has to contain less water than your average human corpse. So pay attention."

He wrapped both hunks of meat in rags. He picked up a small bottle of brandy from the trading post stores and poured it all over one of the bundles. Foster said, "I say, there was no evidence that Campbell had been bathing in brandy either. Wouldn't that sting a bit?''

Longarm shrugged and said, ''Can't say for certain. I've never had the experience.'' Then he struck a match to light the brandy, and of course it blazed blue and merry for a time to consume the cloth and char the meat a bit blacker.

Before Foster could say anything, Longarm said, ''That's the way we tend to picture it. Open flames dancing over the combusted human. It would never do the job because, as you see, even smoked meat has too much water in it to just set on fire like kindling wood.''

He struck another match to apply it to the frayed edge of some blanket wool wrapped with linen around the other meat sample, saying, ''This is going to take a spell. You can step outside for some fresh air if you like.''

Foster said, ''I wouldn't miss this for the world. But what would I be missing if I did?''

Longarm said, ''A possible answer. I wouldn't be experimenting if I was sure. Some philosopher from your Royal Society has already come up with this notion, but I'd rather see it happen for myself.''

They both lit tobacco smokes in self-defense as the rags smoldered, foul-smelling but without any other effect, at least at first. Foster said, ''All right. I can picture Jacques Campbell falling down drunk or suffering a heart stroke in that other stuffy space. I can see him setting his pants on fire with a lit pipe or cigar. But . . .''

''He wasn't drunk. He wasn't sick.'' Longarm took the steel rims from the reading glasses, some copper buttons, and three dull gray blobs out of the cheese box. ''He was shot. Three times. I found what was left of the slugs amongst his ashes, about where his chest would have been as he lay there combusting.''

Foster picked up one of the melted bullets and hefted it, smiling crookedly as he observed, ''.45-caliber, I'd say. But lead only melts at nine hundred degrees!''

Longarm nodded. ''Twice the temperature of burning paper. A lawman has to study on things like melting lead, and that ain't so hot. They have a balance on the counter in the showroom. I'll tell you what caliber they were after I weigh the three of 'em.''

Foster wrinkled his nose as the smell got worse, and objected that they weren't coming close to nine hundred degrees on that chopping block at the moment.

Longarm couldn't deny this as he blew smoke out his nostrils and stared morosely down at the smoky mess he'd made. You could hear a faint sizzle, and the smoke rose greasier now, but the dotted line of sparky smoldering had climbed up to consume most of the rags without more than singeing the bear meat. When Foster pointed this out, Longarm could only reply, "Wait. I told you this was an experiment, and things have to be just right or we'd hear about way more spontaneous human combustion than we do. It ain't as if folks are as easy to set on fire as *trees,* you know. And they say it took a good while for man to learn how to build fires with *wood.*"

Foster dryly remarked, "It's a good thing they didn't start by rubbing their palms together. Meanwhile, your smelly rags seem to have just about charred away after no more than cooking that meat a bit more, eh, what?"

Then he blinked and added, "I say!" as a small flicker of no-shit flame curled out from under one end of the smoldering specimen.

Longarm felt more relief than he let on as he quietly explained, "Rendered fat. Cloth *under* the meat, where it can't burn half as good, is acting as a candlewick might now. Such heat as there was, pinpoint-local, boiled off the water and melted the fat in just that one dime-sized morsel. But now it ought to boil water off faster."

He was right, they saw, though it took a longer time than either had imagined. There was never more than the amount of flame you'd see in an oil lamp as the very smoky process proceeded, consuming the meat as it crisped and got more greasy along the small but now-steady flame-front.

Foster marveled, "I see it all now. It must have taken *hours* to cremate that fat man a few ounces at a time, but that explains how it could be possible to burn a human corpse to ashes without setting the rest of the place on fire!"

Longarm nodded and said, "Oil lamps burn all night without setting the drapes on fire, unless you set 'em too close. If you leave bacon unattended in the skillet, it sizzles and spits for a spell. Then, once all the water's boiled out, it burns like hell, but might not set the wooden cabinets across the kitchen on fire."

Foster beamed at him. "Yet you *would* wind up with a very

smoky kitchen and greasy soot all over those cabinets! I like it! Campbell was shot dead by a person or persons unknown while he had a lit pipe or cigarette in his mouth.''

"Close-range muzzle blast could have set his shirt on fire,'' the American lawman pointed out. "A greasy wool shirt works even better. What say we weigh these melted-down bullets?''

Foster nodded eagerly. So Longarm swept the smoldering meat into the ash pit, picked up the cheese box, and led the way back to the main building's showroom.

They had .45 rounds in stock. But to save breaking one open, Longarm started with one of his own .44-40 rounds. He pried out the soft lead and placed it on the brass balance, opposite a glob from the remains of the late Jacques Campbell. The lead from the telegraph shack turned out to be just a bit heavier.

Longarm nodded and remarked, "Wasn't expecting a .45 or even a .44. Could I have one of your .442 rounds, Sarge?''

Foster removed a bullet from his own pistol belt, even as he protested, "Surely you don't mean to suggest Campbell was murdered by a member of the NWMP!''

Longarm took the round and pried out the slug with his teeth before he replied, "Not hardly. I'll tell you what I suspect when we find out how these two samples balance.''

They balanced perfectly. Foster groaned, "Oh, no!''

But Longarm said, "Not one of your boys. The son of a bitch I keep telling you about. The Calgary Kid has shot folks on both sides of the border with his handy-dandy Webley .442 Bulldog. Are you still so certain he's never been up this way?''

Foster said, "Let's not get sickening about it. I'm sure Webley exports a good many .442s on more than one frame. But assuming for the sake of argument that your homicidal Calgary Kid passed this way, what motive could he have had for killing poor old Campbell?''

Longarm said, "To begin with, he's homicidal. Next, he gunned another trader down by Fort Peck who wouldn't, or couldn't, do him the favor he asked. So let's say he rode in to find Campbell all alone at this remote trading post. Then say he demanded something Campbell just wouldn't or couldn't deliver. I understand the Hudson Bay Company coins its own money?''

Foster said, "Trade tokens. Brass. Face value in beaver

skins the Indians understand, rather than English or Canadian cash they might not.''

Longarm shrugged and replied, ''Whatever. I've been told neither the Métis nor educated Cree cotton to being paid off in play money you can only spend at an HBC trading post. I doubt a white man on the run would have much use for such pocket jingle either, and the Calgary Kid is inclined to get moody and start shooting easy.''

Foster snubbed out the last of his cigar as he wondered out loud, ''Why would they have had it out in that telegraph battery shack instead of in here, where all the money on hand would have been?''

Longarm said, ''The easy answer would be that the Calgary Kid was anxious to send or receive a telegraph message. We know he has pals willing to bust him out of jail down Denver way. You're certain that never happened out yonder?''

Foster shook his head and insisted, ''I told you I questioned up and down both lines, by International Morse. Nobody, sane or insane, had sent or received a cable out here for at least a month. What if the killer *wanted* Campbell to cable somebody else, but Campbell just refused?''

''French letter?'' Longarm mused, putting out his smoked-down cheroot as well.

Foster said, ''I beg your pardon. Did you just say something about a French letter?''

Longarm nodded. ''It's one of those tales that go around, like stories about folks following a ghost gal into a cellar to bust down a brick wall and find her skeleton, which was entombed alive a hundred years before. Nobody knows who starts these yarns. The one about the French letter starts with an American or Englishman in Paris finding a letter written in French shoved under his door. Not reading French, he takes it down to the desk to have it translated. Only, the desk clerk cusses him out and tells him to get out of the hotel on the double. So he takes the fool letter over to the police station, explains the situation, and hands it to a detective, who promptly has him deported from France. It goes on like that, with the poor simp getting in more trouble every time he shows his French letter to anyone who can read it. Like I said, it's just a tale. What could a man in real life ask a telegrapher to send that would cause such a fuss?''

Foster thought and decided, ''I wish you hadn't told me

205

about the French letter. I'm surely going to wonder about that on many occasions to come, and of course there'd be no story if there was any sensible answer. I'm beginning to see why you feel the man you're after may be off his chump.''

Longarm quietly asked, "Then I have your permission to press on after the Calgary Kid?''

Foster looked uneasy and replied, "My permission and my blessings. But remember I'm only an NCO, and once I report this affair as a murder by someone who might well be that pestiferous Percival Harcourt we've all been badgered about ... well, suffice it to say we may pick him up first, and you're not to interfere.''

Longarm asked, "What if *I* catch up with him first. Can I rely on you Mounties not to interfere?''

Foster shook his head. "It's our country and our jurisdiction. When and if you capture the bloody sod, you're to turn him in at the nearest NWMP post to be tried and hanged by Canada, on pain of being arrested and tried, even hanged, yourself if you've used your guns unlawfully in our North West Territory.''

Longarm blinked, grimaced, and pointed out, "Damn it all, Sarge, the kid is a lunatic killer who ain't about to come quietly. How do you expect me to take him without shooting him at least a little?''

Foster smiled thinly and suggested, "Go home and let *us* take him *our* way. It's odd but true that we Mounties do get our man a good many times without having to fire a shot. Perhaps it has something to do with the respect for Her Majesty's justice that we seem to inspire, eh, what?''

Longarm growled, "Respect, my ass. It's a known fact to the lowlifes from London Town to the wild Australian shore that when one of you tall-helmeted constable cusses politely asks someone to come along with you, they can come along with you politely, or have soup for supper and sing soprano a mighty long time after they'd been clubbed in the teeth and kicked in the balls!''

Foster shrugged. "Whatever. We like to say we're firm but fair. You're not supposed to shoot your Calgary Kid, and I agree he sounds like a bit of a boo to capture with a butterfly net. But we did make a deal and I shan't go back on it. I won't try to stop you. I won't even ask where you're going now, and I do so hope you're not going to *tell* me!''

So Longarm never did. He carried his own load out to the stable and loaded up his four Indian ponies to move out before the others got up for breakfast. He didn't want anybody laughing at him as he tried to ford the Saskatchewan. The trading post had been built by quiet slack water with such notions in mind. So he found he could swim the four across in two trips, getting soaked to his own armpits in the process.

But the morning sun beamed down warm and bright from a clear blue sky, and the prairie breezes would soon dry his rinsed-out duds and hide. Riding the buckskin, he took advantage of the way all of them felt, still wet from the cold stream. They loped a good ways along a grassy ridge as Longarm, at least, enjoyed just being alive without any pressing worries on such a grand spring morning.

The survey map put Edmonton 350 miles to the west-northwest by crow. He figured it would take him a little over a week on horseback. Any lawman with a lick of sense could watch out for likely ambush sites on mostly wide-open range, and so far, the Calgary Kid had been more than a week ahead of him. So Longarm figured on relaxing his mind until he was at least halfways to Edmonton, where he figured the Calgary Kid might wire home himself and . . . Damn it, there he went again, and he wasn't more than two hours out of that trading post!

By mid-morning he felt fairly dry and mighty hungry. He reined in on a south-facing slope to rest and graze his riding sock while he broke his fast on some bully beef from the Wood Mountain post.

He'd finished the can and lit a cheroot by the time Una Campbell came over the rise to the east, looking far more Indian as she sat her dapple gray astride in a split skirt of fringed buckskin and a loose floppy checked shirt, her hair wildly whipping about her shoulders from under a Glengarry hat with a Scotch clan badge pinned to one side of it.

He saw her British cavalry saddle had a hefty bedroll and a seven-shot Spencer rifle lashed to it. But as she reined in close to him to firmly declare her intentions of going with him, he had to ask, "How? I don't know where you're headed, but I got at least eight days on the trail ahead of me."

She said, "I know. Sergeant Foster told me when I asked him where you'd gone. He told me not to ride after you. That's why I didn't take time to stock up in the showroom. HBC might have considered it stealing and with three Mounties watching . . .''

"Never mind," Longarm said. "Get down and rest that poor gray. I reckon I can always eat prairie dog if my canned meat gives out this side of civilization. But after I feed you, I want you to go on back to the trading post, Miss Una.''

She dismounted and, to her credit, unsaddled her brute to let it graze while Longarm got out another can. Then she told him not to open it because she'd only noticed he was missing over her own breakfast. As he put the can away again, she sank to her knees in the grass beside him, saying, "We both agreed I should go to Edmonton to seek my fortune, remember?''

He said, "I remember. Me and my big mouth. How come you have a silver boar's head on your hat, Miss Una?''

She replied rather smugly, "It's the totem of Clan Campbell. I'm a turtle on the Ojibwa side. I'm a good hunter. I can do better than prairie dog on hunting grounds I grew up on. I won't be any trouble for you along the trail, and when we get close to Edmonton we can split up if you're ashamed to be seen riding with a breed.''

He reached out to take one of her hands as they reclined side by side on the slope. He smiled gently and said, "The first thing we have to do, if you mean to live white, is to get rid of that chip on your shoulder, Miss Una. I've had this discussion before with folks from other tribes, such as Swedish. Folks who feel certain everybody hates them because of who or what they are can beat themselves with what you call a self-fulfilling wager. Nobody likes to be called a bigot or a snob, even when they are.''

She squeezed his hand hard as she sobbed, "You should have heard those prissy white girls in Ottawa. You can't tell me they didn't know they were hurting me with those ever-so-polite questions about beadwork and basket weaving!''

He said, "Mayhaps they were curious, or stuck with something to say to a gal they'd just met. Let me try something on you that I one time suggested to a morose cuss of the Mex persuasion. Let's say some one-hundred-percent Anglo-Saxon Protestant from a quality family with no criminal record was to show up at a tea party, scowling, to insist everyone there was down on him for being a one-hundred-percent Anglo-Saxon Protestant.''

The pretty breed smiled at the mental picture, and asked if the others at the tea party were, say, Mormons or Papists.

He shook his head and said, "Nope. They're Anglo-Saxon Protestants from the same town who went to the same schools and have about the same amounts of money in the bank. But this one bird keeps on saying he can tell they're down on him, and when the hostess asks if he'd like more tea, he tells her she's just offering to hide the fact she thinks she's better than him."

Una shook her head in confusion and said, "That's silly. What's the point of such a silly story?"

He said, "I'd like you to consider how long it would take our hero to get unpopular as all get-out insisting he was so unpopular."

She did, laughed, and said, "I see what you mean by self-fulfilling. But it wasn't like that with those white girls and me back East. Some of them were really mean."

He nodded and said, "I'll buy that. Some folks are going to be mean to their own brothers and sisters. But remember, you just now said *some*, not *all* those Canadian gals back East. And that was you coming at 'em with a chip on your shoulder. When we get up to Edmonton I want you to try just acting natural, as if everyone there was some breed of human being instead of a member of some rival clan. You reckon you can do that?"

She allowed she was willing to try, if he was willing to carry her on to Edmonton. He said, "Well, you ain't that heavy. So I reckon we can work things out, with two ponies as spares as we wend our weary way west. But I warn you, the outlaw I'm after already has a greater lead on me than I like. So there'll be some rough riding for more than a week, on short rations unless we meet up with meat or bread-roots no more than a few yards out of our way."

He nodded at the grazing ponies down the slope to add, "We'll let the critters rest here a little longer. That gray you just lathered ain't ready to move on even riderless. I reckon I'll put your saddle on the stocky roan, seeing you're both so spunky and willful."

He let go of her hand and leaned back on both elbows without inviting her to follow his lead. But she did, rolling half on top of him and kissing him French-style till they were both flat in the grass with her on top, squirming.

When she let him come up for air, Longarm protested, "Hold on, Miss Una. The day's barely begun and we have many a mile to travel. I'd be proud to wrestle like this with you later this evening, but I hope you don't think I'm one of those brutes who expect a gal to return any favors by, ah, favoring 'em."

She kissed him again and sobbed, "Don't patronize me! If you find a girl who's part Indian distasteful, just say so!"

He laughed despite himself and assured her, "Lord have mercy. I've done my share of distasteful things inside a tipi in my time!"

She began to grope at his gunbelt buckle as she declared, "I'm glad. My mother's people say *wigwam* instead of *tipi,* but I was broken in at a sorority party under a hotel roof in Ottawa. I'll kill you if you let me go that far with you, then sneak me out a side door lest your white friends see you with a squaw!"

He said, "I ain't ashamed. I'm in a *hurry,* Miss Una!"

Then she'd somehow gotten his old organ-grinder out of his pants, and managed to impale her fool self on it, split skirts and all. So with one thing and another they never rode on for a good two hours. There was a lot to be said for green-eyed squaws, once you stripped them all the way down so you could watch yourself parting their sandy hair down yonder in broad-ass daylight.

But later that night, after a long day in their saddles and a fine supper of pork and beans with bread-root dug nearby, there was a lot to be said for bare tits in the moonlight too.

Chapter 17

So while some of the long trip to Edmonton was mighty hard, it wasn't half as tedious as Longarm had feared. Healthy young humans could push themselves harder than critters were willing. So they had to take lots of trail breaks, and sometimes when they did so by ponds of standing water, a good time was had by all as the ponies drank to their hearts' content while Longarm and the lusty young breed took a naked swim in the privacy of all that wide-open space.

Riding across rolling prairie was safer by daylight when you knew you were safe from Indians, and Una allowed they were. They both knew sign, and she claimed to be fluent in any of the related Algonquian dialects from Siksika to Woodland Cree. She explained it was something like an English speaker switching from, say, Dixie to broad Scotch. Some of the words and a lot of the twangs were different, but you could change from one accent to the other with a little effort. He said he was glad she could. He'd never been able to get past baby talk in any Indian lingo. It wasn't so much the sounds as the different rules of grammar. She said Indian grammar was nothing next to Highland Erse or Gaelic. She said that had stumped her completely when she'd tried to study it back East. He said he'd been assured by other Scots that learning Gaelic was a lot like learning the bagpipe. Both were a lot of work and when you got good at either, nobody else cared to listen to you all that much.

Una shot a pronghorn their third day out. There seemed to be no end to the pretty little thing's talents. She said her Cree playmates had taught her how to lure a pronghorn within rifle range by flashing a white kerchief at it from behind some rabbit bush. They could only take the choice cuts, of course. It made Longarm feel a mite wasteful. It wasn't true Indians or part-Indians only shot game when they meant to eat it balls and all.

They averaged twelve hours a day on the go, with a lot of time out along the way to average better than the standard thirty miles a day of cavalry on the move. That still left plenty of time for eating, sleeping, and sex, with Una enthusiastic about learning new positions. He never asked where she'd learned the many she already seemed to know. He shut her up every time their second-wind conversations strayed to her college days and how she'd tried in vain to be popular with white students, although he suspected she'd been more popular than she might have felt.

When she calmly told him, while doing it dog-style, that she was thinking of a new career as a fancy gal in Edmonton, he warned her she might not be cut out to become a full-time whore. When she arched her back and asked why, he shoved it in deep and told her, "You like this too much. Those young squirts who prey on old rich women are mostly interested in one another, whilst most really prospering whores are frigid. Folks who really give a hang about physical pleasure don't have the detachment it takes to demand the highest price for the sale of it. You'd be better off as a saleslady or schoolmarm with an . . . ah, active social life. I know this gal who's in charge of a whole orphanage down Colorado way. She makes good money herding orphans all day, and then screws like a mink in her spare time. She'd starve as a whore, though. She'd never be able to hold out for more money."

Una moaned, "Deeper and faster. Do you pound *her* this deep, you brute?"

"Of course not," Longarm lied, to be polite. Then they were too busy to chat for a spell, but later, cuddled close to him under the open sky without a stitch between them and the stars, Una agreed she might be too warm-natured to work at anything more exciting than, say, slinging hash or selling hats.

212

They had to be a bit more cautious about when and where they paused to rest their ponies and screw once they met up with the emigrant trail from the eastern provinces. They had to follow it because the telegraph line did, and you'd get lost on such a sea of grass if you didn't follow *something*.

They passed spaced-out wagon trains in the next few days. None overtook them, of course, moving slow and creaky behind oxen or at best slow-driven mules. He and Una naturally had to stop and visit with each emigrant party they met up with. But nobody expected a young couple honeymooning west to Edmonton to poke along at a walk with them. They never once told anyone they were honeymooning. But there was something about a man with a maid he'd been screwing a lot that made everyone accuse them of being married up.

The folks they met up with came from all walks of life, although most were land-hungry farm folks a lot like the ones headed west south of the border. Though its provisions were slightly different, Canada had its own answer to the American Homestead Act. Both were meant to get some damned taxpayers out to the wide open spaces. Because of the Métis and Indian tensions closer to the border, the westward tides of settlement veered further north than they might have, up toward the more peaceable prairies between the northern branch of the Y-shaped Saskatchewan and the sleepier Peace River.

Una Campbell began to blossom as they rode west together, meeting all sorts of folks who seemed to accept her as a plain old Canadian gal. Longarm figured a lot of recent arrivals from the Old World never considered that a gal with green eyes might be part Indian. It was safe to assume the native Canucks, some of whom had their own high cheekbones, simply didn't give a shit. Una began to believe what he'd told her about some spoiled white gals being snobbish to everybody, not just classmates from different backgrounds. By the time they rode into Edmonton after nearly two weeks on the trail, she'd broken out her Campbell tartan shawl to go with her clan hat, and you'd think from the way she was starting to talk that she'd just arrived on the North American continent after serving a hitch in some female Highland regiment.

Longarm didn't laugh at her. He'd met others so downhearted by the hand fate had dealt them that they had to brag about who their great-great-grandparents might have been before the family had sunk to working for a living.

The settlement at Edmonton was far older than it looked. It looked a lot like Dodge had looked when it was still in the buffalo trade. But the Hudson Bay Company had built a fortified trading post by the North Saskatchewan shortly after the American Revolution. The HBC hadn't been interested in *those* troubles in the south. It had had enough of a problem with the Siksika, who'd burned the whole post down in 1807.

But the HBC had ways of making peace with Indians. So once the survivors were dependent on sugar, salt, and gunpowder, the company had rebuilt the outpost around 1819. After the Canadian Government took control of law and order in the North West Territory, the NWMP had built a more serious base just east of town and dubbed it Fort Saskatchewan, leaving the civilian settlement of Edmonton to grow like Topsy, shipping furs and hides down the river by raft instead of rail. Folks working and living there had to eat. So truck farms and even some fair-sized cattle spreads had sprung up all around as Edmonton promised to become a capital like Denver some day.

But that day hadn't dawned, and the wayside inn Longarm got a room in with Una Campbell was two stories high and all log. Edmonton had too damp a climate for 'dobe, and it was cheaper to skid logs down from the Rockies to the west than haul milled lumber all the way up the Saskatchewan from Manitoba, where it was already expensive as hell.

After he'd calmed the delighted Una down by testing the bed with her, Longarm explained he'd be busy a spell, and left her in bed with some ladies' fashion magazines and a box of chocolates to await his return.

He made sure their five ponies were being cared for right out back, then trudged on over to the post office, where you sent or received those high-toned cables instead of telegrams.

They told him not to be silly when he inquired about night-letter rates, and said his message to Billy Vail was going to run him six cents a word, which came out out about fair at the current rate of exchange.

He had a hell of a lot to report. On the other hand, old Foster had warned him he wasn't supposed to be acting as a lawman up Canada way, and old Billy would understand. So he phrased his long-enough cable with care, hoping Billy would be able to grasp that he was up Edmonton way because he had reason to suspect anyone trying to sidestep the tension

214

and heavy NWMP presence to the south would be up this way. There was no need to spell out how Edmonton sat at the center of its web of trails, wagon traces, and good river rafting. Before signing anything, Longarm asked the cable clerk behind the counter how one went about sending money from the States by wire.

The clerk, a snooty-looking older man who turned out friendly when approached politely, told him to just have his home office wire a Western Union money order and let them worry about it. He said they had a money transfer agreement worked out. So assuming Longarm could get Billy Vail to go for that advance on his travel expenses, he'd be able to pick it up here as a Canadian postal money order.

Longarm asked if he'd have to carry it to that bank down the way, or whether they could cash it for him there in the cable office. The clerk said they could cash anything up to a hundred Canadian, which seemed likely to be more than Billy Vail was ever going to burden them with.

Seeing that he had the older Canadian in a conversational mood, Longarm casually asked if any other Americans had wired home for money from Edmonton recently.

The cable clerk stiffened, and primly replied he was not at liberty to divulge such information. So Longarm figured somebody had.

This didn't mean the clerk had to be covering up for any Calgary Kid. Lots of Americans had been drifting up this way, with or without cows, to get in on the opening up of the Peace River range to the north, or hunt such buffalo as might be left at higher latitudes.

He'd been on the range long enough to really need a haircut, and small-town barbershops were good places to hear gossip about mean drunks with rat teeth and miscolored eyes.

But all he got out of that notion was a shave and a haircut and some worried talk about that crazy Louis Riel and his fucking halfbreeds to the east, fixing to cut them all off from the rest of Canada with his infernal Prairie Republic.

Longarm went back to his hired quarters smelling of bay rum and figuring there were worse ways to while away an afternoon while he waited for money from home. He knew that unless he got some damned money from home soon, poor Una was going to have to start paying for their room and board.

215

When he got there, there was no Una to be seen. But that sounded fair. Edmonton was likely a big city to a gal who'd grown up around a trading post in Cree country. She was likely out shopping. He hoped she wouldn't spend all her money, however much she might have.

He went back downstairs, circled around to the stable, and found out that Una had asked them to saddle that dapple gray before she'd ridden off somewhere.

It was no concern of Longarm's. But he couldn't see reading a mess of fashion magazines, and there were other places to gossip in a frontier town. So he tried the Peacepipe Ordinary across the way.

It looked like a regular saloon inside. Canadians were inclined to talk more British than Americans and more American than other British folks. Longarm bellied up to the bar and ordered draft beer. Out west, at least, Canadians brewed their beer American-style, which was to say Dutch. But when he asked the Canadian barkeep to needle the schooner for him, he got a shot of that smoky Scotch whiskey instead of bourbon or rye. Lager beer needled with Scotch tasted sort of odd. But Longarm never let on. A man had to live with his own mistakes.

He was nursing the odd mixture at the bar—that wasn't tough—when a gent dressed oddly bellied up to the fake mahogany beside him. Observing his fellow drinker discreetly in the mirror of the back-bar, Longarm saw the lean and hungry-looking Mountie wore his revolver over his balls Mountie-style, but he'd swapped his white helmet for one of those small pillbox hats. It made him look like an armed and dangerous bellboy from some fancy hotel back East. But there was a little red and gold crown above the three inverted gold stripes on one sleeve. So he couldn't be a bellboy after all.

The cadaverous Mountie ordered porter, and waited until he'd been served before he quietly informed Longarm, "I'm off duty. So I'm not here and we're not having this conversation, Deputy Long."

Longarm stared into the mirror as he quietly replied, "That sounds fair. I take it you'd be a pal of Sergeant Foster?"

The matching crown sergeant suggested, "Let's just say one hand washes the other and never mind who I might be. The man you're looking for is not in this area. We do keep tabs on everyone drifting in, and it's not as if a tall rat-toothed

216

Yank with a brown spot in a blue eye would be hard to notice even in a *larger* community. If it's any comfort to you, the NWMP have just put out a want on Percival Harcourt alias the Calgary Kid in connection with the murder and cremation of one Jacques Campbell. The Hudson Bay Company has been informed, and they are not only not happy, but have their own ways of hunting beasts of prey. So you may rest assured that should your lunatic killer make it up into caribou country, he'll surely be spotted by HBC Indians and dealt with the way they usually deal with wolverines along a trapline.''

Longarm sipped some weird beer and replied, ''I doubt even a madman would be headed for the North Pole, like Doctor Frankenstein in that wild yarn about running desperately from the fruits of one's own labors. I figure he'd have wanted to work north of all the Indian and Métis troubles so's he could ease quietly down to the Inland Passage to the west. A man on the run with some pocket jingle could bribe his way aboard a boat, right?''

The NWMP sergeant shrugged his scarlet shoulders and replied, ''He could. Mayhaps he has. My point is that he's nowhere around *here* and you're frankly making us nervous. You can guess why I'd hate to have to arrest you, but . . .''

''On what charge?'' Longarm said, turning to face the lofty cuss with a polite but undaunted smile.

The Mountie sighed and said, ''Foster warned us you could be like that. I know it would be a bother to prove you never crossed into Canada lawfully further east where the present ban doesn't apply. But we could if we really had to. So don't push your luck, Longarm. I'll give you seventy-two hours here in Edmonton to satisfy yourself that the Calgary Kid is not in town. After that I want you *out* of town. As the Indian chief said, I have spoken.''

It would have been dumb to defy a man who'd given him three days before the three days were up. So Longarm said, ''I've wired my home office for some travel-jingle. I ought be richer and better informed by your generous deadline, Sarge. I tend to agree with you on spotting or not spotting odd-looking jaspers in a town this size.''

Then he shoved his beer schooner away and reached inside his jacket as he added, ''Like you say. One hand washes the other, and I have a photograph of the son of a bitch if you'd care to look at the same.''

The crown sergeant did. Staring soberly down at the small sepia-tone Longarm handed him, the Mountie mused, "So that's what he looks like in the flesh, eh? I was expecting something a bit more wild and woolly. Could I borrow this long enough to have our own negative run off?"

Longarm said, "Sure. But how long are we talking about? I have to take a pal to supper in four hours or less."

The Mountie said, "I'll be back before then. I mean to take this to a photographer just up the street."

So they parted friendly and Longarm finished his beer. There was a card game going on in a far corner, and Longarm figured the cuss in the pearl-gray Stetson and undertaker's coat for a tinhorn. But you didn't want to get started at draw poker unless you had plenty of time to draw with. So Longarm just ordered a refill of straight draft, paid at the bar, and drifted over to lean against the window jamb and watch.

The tinhorn was good. He was dealing to a couple of cowhands and a more prosperous-looking gent with a Swedish way of talking. Longarm figured the rich Swede was the mark the tinhorn was out to sting. But the game was young, and everyone seemed to be breaking about even. You never got a mark to bet high stakes before you let him prove he could win now and again.

As Longarm lounged there, sipping and smoking, another beer nurser joined him, murmuring, "I'd be Stu Murray. Used to ride for the Pinks. On my own now. He's not in town, but I suspect I know where he went from here. You want to go fifty-fifty on the bounty?"

Longarm turned slowly to regard the self-confessed bounty hunter more closely. Stu Murray, if that was his real name, was almost as tall but a bit softer-looking than Longarm. They were both dressed as rough and ready for riding. Murray packed his .45 Schofield side-draw, with the holster strings firm around his denim-clad right leg. Aside from a weak chin, Murray looked clean-cut enough to get hired by most outfits. But he'd just now said he was after bounty money.

Longarm indicated a nearby table, and they both moved over to sit and talk a spell. When Murray said he hadn't caught Longarm's name, the lawman cocked a brow to ask, "How come you figured I was after someone if you didn't know who I was?"

Murray smiled boyishly and glanced toward the bar, saying,

"Crown Sergeant Payson. He and I had very much the same conversation just the other day. So *my* seventy-two hours are half shot. I know who you have to be after because the Calgary Kid is the only outlaw up this way with a price on his head."

"Who put all this money on it and how did you know he was here in Edmonton?" Longarm asked, cheroot gripped between unsmiling teeth.

Murray replied easily, "The bounty's been posted by the Collier clan of Morgan County down home. There's naturally all those murder warrants out on the crazy cuss, but the Colliers have a personal hard-on for him. They stand ready to pay five thousand dollars to anyone who brings him in, dead or alive. That would be twenty-five hundred for each of us if you'd like to throw in with me. How did you figure he was up this way?"

Longarm sipped some suds and quietly replied, "I'm still waiting to hear my own questions answered."

Murray shrugged and said, "No mystery. As I said, I used to ride for Allan Pinkerton, the cheap Scotch bastard. I still enjoy the same contacts I cultivated working cheaper. A whorehouse madam I'd as soon keep in my own little black book replied to one of many wires I sent far and wide. It seems that just a few nights ago our Calgary Kid was playing three-in-a-bed, dirty as hell, until they threw him out for abusing the furniture too. You were saying?"

Longarm hesitated, then said, "Call me West Virginia for now. I do recall others saying Harcourt liked to hide out in houses of ill repute. He shoots folks too. I traced him part of the way by weighing bullets he left in yet another Indian trader. I was only guessing he'd run for more crowded parts of a mighty open country. The NWMP are already on the prod for even innocent strangers to the south of here. You say you know where Harcourt headed after they threw him out of yet another whorehouse?"

Murray leaned forward to confide, "Dunvegan. Smaller settlement up on the Peace River. The end of civilization, as I hear it. My own true loves in the Edmonton pussy trade tell me there's a couple of Indian whores up yonder, and we know he likes to hire them two at a time. So how's about it? I know where to look and to tell the pure truth, I'd as soon have another gunhand backing my play. The kid may be crazy, but he's fast as spit on a hot stove."

Longarm thought before he asked, "What if he ain't there?"

To which Murray replied, "We ride after him, of course. There's nothing but fir trees and Slave Indians further north. The two of us ought to be more than a match for him in open country, and like I said, we don't have to worry about bringing him back alive."

Longarm asked, "How do you figure on getting him south past all them Mounties to begin with?"

Murray sounded as if he meant it when he calmly replied, "Saddlebag. Just his head. No need to drag *all* of him back to show the pissed-off Colliers. They say they'll pay as soon as they can be sure the son of a bitch who wiped out so many of them is dead. You can't get much deader than decapitated, can you?"

Longarm replied, "Reckon not. I can't leave for this Dunvegan town just yet, though. Got some loose ends to tie up here in Edmonton. How much time did you say that Mountie gave you?"

Murray said, "Seventy-two hours. I just told you that was a couple of days ago. I have to ride on by morning. Want to get an early start in any case. Dunvegan is almost a week's ride north, and we know how the Calgary Kid can be about wearing out his welcome!"

Longarm smiled wearily and replied, "I do, and a week in the saddle seems a hard ride for a short romp with a limited supply of whores. I can't see why in blue blazes even a lunatic would want to ride all the way up yonder!"

Murray shrugged and said, "Neither can I. But he asked the gals here what was up Dunvegan way, and he sure as hell left town for *some* damned place. Like I said, if he ain't there we'll ride after him. If we cut no trail, we can always turn back. I don't know how many wanted men *you've* trailed, but I've learned to live with the simple fact that you can't win every time."

Then Murray was suddenly on his feet, saying something about riding on alone in the morning unless he spied Longarm ready to ride with him out front.

Crown Sergeant Payson came in, waving the sepia-tone Longarm had given him. So Longarm figured that was what had inspired Murray to light out. Murray's hastily vacated chair faced that window. As the Mountie gave him back his own print, Longarm didn't mention the other American to the

Canadian lawman. He didn't even let on he knew Payson's name. That was the way such games were played.

Payson politely refused Longarm's invitation to have a drink on him. The Mountie said he had to get back out to his post. So he had been on duty after all, whether his superiors knew what he'd been doing in the Queen's high name or not.

As Payson left, Longarm put the sepia-tone print away, finished his beer, and got up to leave. As he did so he saw the pot was growing as that friendly game in the corner continued. He didn't warn the Swede as he passed. It wasn't his job or even his *country*, and if a man wanted to play cards for high stakes, it was up to him to learn how the game was played.

He went back to the inn to find Una's gray back in its stall and Una upstairs in bed, bare-ass but not able to meet his eye for some reason.

He said, "I was fixing to take you to supper first. We got all night, and I don't know about you but I'm hungry."

She almost sobbed, "Please make love to me, Custis."

So he sat down to shuck his boots, got rid of the rest of his duds, and proceeded to do so, as most men would have. For the late-afternoon sun through the lace curtains made her tawny skin and sandy thatch mighty interesting to contemplate as she tossed the covers off to show she'd been waiting for him with a pillow thrust under her firm but well-rounded behind.

So he left his socks on and thrust into her with a full erection as she sobbed, "Oh, yesss!" and spread her shapely thighs wide with her knees up in line with his rib cage. He didn't know why in blue blazes she was crying. But he kept thrusting when she begged him not to stop. She dug her nails into his back and bit his lips almost painfully as they kissed and came together fast. Then she wrapped her legs around him tightly and demanded, "More!"

He stayed in her, but let it soak a mite as he drew his lips from hers enough to ask, "What's got into you, Una? Aside from my cock, I mean? You're acting like the world is about to end at sunset and this is the last chance we'll ever have to screw!"

That really inspired some waterworks. She was bawling like a baby and he couldn't get her to stop, even though she moved her hips in time with his as they went at it some more hammer and tongs. She was still bawling when she shoved him off and

221

rolled over to shove her ample behind up to him, sobbing, "Shove it anywhere you want and *hurt* me, Custis!"

He said he liked it in her pussy just fine, and tried to get her to tell him what was eating her as he screwed her dog-style. But all he could get out of her were silly noises and scandalous suggestions.

So they wound up doing things they'd never done in all the time they'd known one another over hill and dale. It was as if she were some desperately needy whore who'd been paid a bonus she'd have to give back if she failed to pleasure a man in every way.

Longarm didn't mind that part. A gal busting a gut to please a man could be pleasing as all get-out. But it puzzled him, and even spoiled the fun a mite, when she kept bursting into tears after he'd just said something nice to her.

The sun was low, but still shining golden in the west, when she took her lips from his sated shaft and murmured, "Oh, Custis, I wish we could make this last forever!"

He sighed and said, "Me too, but nothing lasts forever outside of fairy tales, honey. So could we get dressed and go to supper now? No offense, but I couldn't get it up again with a block and tackle, and even if I could, I'm hungry as a bear after a winter in a den!"

She rolled out of the way so he could sit up. But she then commenced to cry some more as he moved over to the wash-stand to tidy up.

He wiped off his privates with soap and water, dried them, and came back to the bed, gathering scattered duds along the way. He sat down beside her and softly ordered her to just calm down and tell him what in blue blazes he'd done to deserve all this weeping and wailing.

She said, "Oh, darling, it isn't you. It's me!"

He said, "All right. What have you done to deserve all this weeping?"

She said that, just as he'd suspected, she'd been out riding on her dapple gray that afternoon. She'd gone to look up another gal she'd known in school back East. The gal was now married up with a shopkeeper here in Edmonton, and Longarm had been right about not all of her schoolmates looking down at her for being part Indian. She said her old school chum had never mentioned that. But when Una had told them about having to leave her dad's trading post because her dad was dead, she'd been offered a job on the spot as a saleslady in one of the finest female notions shops in town. So she didn't think she ought to go out to supper with . . . anyone else.

Longarm said he understood her position. She covered her face with her hands and told him it made her feel worse to have him so understanding. But when he suggested she just wash up, get dressed, and take her fancier friends up on that invitation to supper, she didn't take nearly as long as one might have expected.

But what the hell, he thought, as she kissed him on the cheek and scampered out of their room before he could get his pants on. He barely had enough left to have bought her a good supper in any case.

Chapter 18

Longarm dined on the last of his canned goods. The ponies would be getting grain and water until it came time to pay up. It was way too early for any reply to his appeal to Billy Vail. So he drifted back to the Peacepipe with the last of his drinking money.

It was more crowded, and that friendly card game in the corner was getting serious. The tinhorn and his shill, the prosperous dumb Swede, were still at the table. But the other players were new and there were more of them. The game had been switched from draw poker, a game of some skill, to red dog, a game for suckers and faster than twenty-one for the bank, if the bank got to hold on to the deal.

Longarm watched at some distance, nursing a draft, and saw that the tinhorn was sure enough dealing every hand. It seemed incredible but true that the four other gents he and the Swede had roped in never protested. But then, gents who knew shit about cards seldom played red dog.

Any number up to ten could play red dog, and more made for the merrier pots. Each player was dealt five cards, aces high and deuces low. The cards left over from the deal, called the stock, were placed facedown in front of the dealer, who neither bet nor collected when he was dealing, which showed how honest and unselfish the tinhorn had to be. If he kept the deal as banker, that meant the dumb Swede's luck was sure to change before this night was over.

They were playing with chips, sold to them at the bar, to avoid any crap from Queen Victoria about public gambling for cash. So the management was in on it too. Nobody smart enough to tend a bar was about to take red dog for wholesome entertainment.

Before each deal each player anted one chip, and the more players the bigger the pot. Betting circled the table from the dealer's left. If a player didn't care for his hand he could pass, but had to add another chip to the pot. The first player willing to bet could raise the ante by matching what was on the table, forcing each of his fellow players to toss in one more chip. He was betting he held one card of the same suit and a higher face value than the unseen top card in the stock.

When the dealer turned that card over, the bettor raked in the pot if he'd won or forfeited his bet to the growing pot. The pot could grow some as such a simple game continued fast. The slickers running this one were playing it safe but sure. They let a buffalo hunter win a modest pot, then built it some as player after player somehow failed to get the face card or ace it took to beat those eights and up in the stock. Then—what a surprise—that dumb Swede suddenly produced a jack and carried on comically as he apparently won for the first time in his life.

Longarm set his schooner on the counter, told the barkeep he was only going out back for a leak, but went down the street instead to a tobacco shop that naturally sold playing cards as well. The idea was to have the same brand so the backs would match up.

Returning to the scene of the ongoing crime, Longarm nursed his beer till that buffalo hunter decided to quit before he'd lost *all* his winnings back. As the Canadian rose from his seat at the table, the tall American stepped forward to ask how many chips a man might be able to buy for five bucks. The tinhorn said Longarm had to see the barkeep about that, since *he* was only playing for fun.

So Longarm followed the buffalo hunter, who was grinning like a greenhorn, and waited politely until the Canadian had swapped his chips for cash. Once he had, Longarm was told chips sold for two bits each. Longarm said that sounded fair, and wound up with twenty chips, or five dollars' worth.

When he got back to the table, another Canuck had taken the buffalo hunter's place. But the friendly tinhorn smiled up at Longarm and told him they could always fit another player in. So Longarm hauled a chair over from another table and straddled it, innocently asking if this game was anything like piquet.

There came a round of derisive laughter, and a bearded cattle man demanded, "Do we look like them frog-eaters from Montreal? Red dog ain't nothing like piquet!"

Longarm had already known that. But he listened wide-eyed as the dealer explained the simple larceny he had in mind. So Longarm said he understood and the game continued. Longarm wasn't too surprised when he was dealt a mighty low hand. He bet like a sport, but didn't up the ante. So he was only out one chip when, surprise, the top card in the stock turned out to be the queen of clubs.

The next two players lost as well. The dumb Swede passed. So the rascals weren't ready to claim the pot yet. They let it grow till the round was over with nobody having won. Then, with the already handsome pot still on the table, the tinhorn asked everybody to ante so he could deal some more.

Longarm counted the loose chips in the pot. As best he could tally, there was now about a week's salary there for the next winner. Longarm wasn't greedy. But he saw that if that dumb Swede was, he'd never get to bet before the dumb Swede raked in every damned chip.

But, surprise, the round went the same, with some players losing by no more than one pip and nobody losing enough, each time around, to get sore. That was why tinhorns liked red dog. Their profit was in volume, and fewer gents got shot dealing red dog than, say, faro or twenty-one.

Longarm wasn't nearly as greedy. So the next time it came his turn, with over a hundred dollars worth of chips on the table, he smiled like a farmer at his hand and raised fifteen chips. The tinhorn told him he could only raise by six, there being six other bettors there to add one chip each. So Longarm took back the offending extra chips with a sheepish grin and said, "Well, I still reckon I can top that top card in the stock."

The dealer, who knew very well what he'd dealt him, only smiled and turned over the jack of hearts.

His tolerant smile turned sickly as they all watched Longarm place the ace of hearts on the table.

"How did you do that?" demanded the dumb Swede, with no accent at all, as Longarm raked in the whole fat pot.

Longarm innocently replied, "Do what? Win? As I understand this game, you win when you draw a higher card in the same suit, and any fool can see the ace of hearts beats the jack of hearts. I could have won with a queen or king, for that matter."

"If you'd been *dealt* a king or queen!" snapped the dumb Swede, and Longarm decided he had to be the real boss.

The other players were mighty quiet as Longarm softly replied, with a nod at the stone-faced dealer, "Yonder is the man who was dealing the cards just now. Are you saying him and me are in cahoots?"

The dumb Swede sputtered, "Of course not. But it just so happens I have the ace of hearts myself!"

It got *really* quiet. Gents at other tables stopped talking. Longarm just kept smiling as he almost purred, "Do tell? It's too bad I got to bet my high card ahead of your own. How did you manage to draw the ace of hearts, seeing there's only supposed to be one in the deck?"

"Are you accusing *me*?" the sincerely baffled card shark demanded.

Longarm placed his .44-40 on the table, turned his hat over beside it, and proceeded to fill it with chips as he calmly pointed out he'd just come in. He added, "You two gents have been playing cards here all day. Likely the day before. Do we really want to wind up over at the police station with some Mountie desk sergeant taking down all our little secrets?"

The dealer quietly suggested, "Let it go, Lars. I don't feel up to explaining sudden accidents to the Mounties!"

So nobody tried to stop Longarm when he sniffed he'd had enough of their sore losing and carried his chips over to the bar. The barkeep had been paying close attention to the tense conversation and that .44-40, now back in its cross-draw holster. So he was a sport about exchanging the chips for more money than Longarm had seen since leaving Denver.

He was hoping that was the end of it. But as he headed back for his hotel, he was suddenly confronted on the dark street by both the dealer and the Swede.

Longarm nodded soberly and said, "Howdy. I thought you said you meant to let it go."

The dealer purred, "That was in there. This is out here

227

without as many witnesses. I know what you did. You palmed the cards I dealt you and switched them for five of your own. By holding all the aces you knew you had every other card in the deck beat. They call that cheating where I come from. So we'd like our money back now."

Longarm said, "You can't have it. I beat you as fair and square as you were dealing. Where *I* come from, it ain't considered cheating to cheat a cheater."

The one called Lars blustered, "Are you out of your mind? You've out and out admitted you diddled us out of our own money, and you surely see it's two against one here!"

Then another voice chimed in from the darkness. "Correction. It's two against two and I've already got the drop on you."

Longarm nodded and said, "Evening, pard," as Stu Murray stepped out of the shadows with his Schofield drawn but politely down at his side.

The threatening Lars looked sicker to his stomach than the tinhorn as that gent said, "For Chrissake, we're only talking about a hundred and fifty dollars!"

Murray said, "I don't have much use for shits who'd rob at gunpoint for a lousy hundred and fifty dollars. So I'll tell you what I'm going to do. Did I mention both West Virginia here and I are bounty hunters? I don't know about *him*. But *I'm* going to ask around by wire, and if either of you birds are wanted anywhere, he'd better not be in town when I find out!"

They turned and walked away without answering. Murray chuckled and said, "I doubt there's any real money out on such assholes, but they surely have records. So we've likely seen the last of them. Are you ready to ride up to Dunvegan with me, West Virginia?"

Longarm said, "Nope, and it breaks my heart because I owe you. I just improved my finances, but I'm still waiting on a wire from home. I can't leave here before I get it."

Murray said, "I *have* to leave town. What did Sergeant Payson tell you about me, by the way?"

Longarm said, "Nothing. I had no call to ask about a man I'd never met yet, and I get the feeling Payson plays his cards close to the vest."

Murray sighed and said, "You know it," as he put his six-gun away. "I'm certain he's keeping an eye on me. Mayhaps both of us. He's supposed to be the sergeant major out at their

228

fort. But he's been working the desk at their police station here in town."

Longarm shrugged and said, "I heard they were spread thin by all that trouble to the south. They have a heap of territory to cover. Down our way, there'd be town and county law to handle a heap of shit. But those three hundred Mounties are all the law there *is* out here. All criminal law is federal here in Canada."

"They can't have the Calgary Kid," Murray grumbled, pointing at another drinking establishment across the way. "What say we go wet our whistles whilst we plan our ride up to Dunvegan?"

Longarm shook his head and said, "You go in if you want to. I've had a harder day than you might think, and Dunvegan sounds like one hell of a long ride. If I'm ready to go there in the morning, I'll be right about here with four ponies and fresh trail supplies. If you don't see me, it'll mean I'm still waiting on that wire from home."

Murray repeated he was leaving for Dunvegan in the morning come hell or high water. So they shook on that and parted friendly.

The newly prosperous Longarm stopped for a bedtime snack of elk steak, fried potatoes, and mince pie at a beanery he found open near his hired quarters. The waitress was sort of fat, but pure white and almost pretty. But when she coyly informed her lone good-looking customer she'd be closing soon, he resisted the temptation. He knew he was going to regret it some lonely night in the near future, but he'd meant what he'd said to the sex-mad Una Campbell earlier that same evening, and it would hurt like fire to have a plain dumpy waitress laughing at him when, not if, he just couldn't rise to the occasion.

Back in his musky-smelling bed at the inn, he began to have second thoughts about that waitress as he lay there naked in the dark, considering how long he might be on the trail with another man, and the way the lamplight at the beanery had shone on that fat gal's tight brown bodice.

But he fell asleep before he could get up again, and when he woke up with a piss hard-on, he decided not to waste it on a fat gal who'd likely cry when a man rode off after one quick roll in the feathers.

It was sad but true that a man who really liked women could never be a real Don Juan. For old Don Juan had been forced to treat women like shit while he ran up such a score.

After a crap, shave, and shower, Longarm got dressed and strode back to that post office to see if Billy Vail had wired back.

He was glad he'd met up with the card sharks when he saw Billy Vail had wired ten dollars and orders to head back to Denver. Vail said he'd had those photographs from Helena blown up and distributed far and wide to no avail. So the Calgary Kid didn't seem to be anywhere important to the Denver District Court, and it was Canada's own chore if the rascal was headed for the North Pole after killing that breed at Campbell's Station.

Meanwhile, the last two members of that train-robbing gang were in jail in Texas and singing sweetly after trying to cash one of those stolen postal money orders in San Antone. So old Billy wanted to wrap it all up and get on with more important business.

Longarm put the wired cash in his wallet and filed the rest in a handy wastebasket. Then he went back to the wayside inn, paid them off, and led the four Indian ponies to the nearest general store.

He stocked up on tobacco and trail grub. Then he forked himself up on the paint, with the cordovan packing, and trained over to where Stu Murray had said they'd meet when and if they rode on to the north together.

There was nobody there. Both the sun and his pocket watch agreed it was way past sunrise. As he dismounted, an old-timer came up to ask if he might be called West Virginia. When Longarm allowed he was, the old-timer said his pal with the tied-down Schofield had asked him to say he couldn't hang around any longer. So Longarm thanked him and got back in the saddle to ride after the bounty hunter. He figured his tough trail-tested Indian ponies would catch him up to Murray if he pushed them a mite. Murray would have less reason to lather his own stock, and he seemed to know the damned way to Dunvegan.

The wagon trace Longarm followed north from Edmonton looked much like the one he and good old Una had come in on from the southeast a good many orgasms ago. Folks farming within an easy buckboard haul of any fair-sized prairie

230

settlement tended to keep milch cows and raise the same pigs and chickens, along with garden truck. He saw no windmills. They got more rain or snow up this way, and the water table was high enough for bucket wells. When he came upon a nester cultivating cabbage, he reined in to ask if he was on the right wagon trace and whether Stu Murray had passed by.

The man with the hoe came over to assure him those twin ruts would surely take him to Dunvegan on the Peace River, if only he kept track of them. He added that he'd been choring closer to those buildings a furlong away until just recently. If Longarm's pal had left at daybreak or even earlier, he'd gotten past them there.

Longarm thanked him and rode on. The spring morning was just right for riding at a mile-eating trot. So Longarm did, standing in the stirrups to preserve his balls as, with not another soul in sight, he felt free to sing out:

> The one old maid,
> She up and said,
> My hole's as big as the ground,
> The trains roll in, the trains roll out,
> They even turn around!

Then he caught a scarecrow staring at him from the rise ahead, and reined in to a walk to light a smoke, muttering to himself as he wondered why in tarnation he kept singing that nasty kid song about those old maids from Canada.

"I'm up Canada way," he told the scarecrow as he and his four ponies passed. The row crops sprouting from the dark soil around the scarecrow looked like those giant Swedish turnips they grew to feed milch cows. So the crows perched on either shoulder had only paused for a harmless rest there. Longarm patted the stock of his saddle gun to see whether Canadian crows acted differently.

They didn't. Crows always knew when a human being meant business. You couldn't spook them unless you were really out for them. Cats were said to read minds too. But crows were better at it.

Longarm rode on to another rise, the prairie being fertile but a bit bumpy this close to the Canadian Rockies, and stood tall as he could in the stirrups to see whether he could spot that other rider out ahead of him.

He couldn't. Murray had to have left early and ridden hard. But the day was still young, so what the hell. Then Longarm looked around. How come there weren't any telegraph poles along this main wagon trace?

Gripping the cheroot in his bared teeth, Longarm decided, "There'd be no call to string wires that far to such an out-of-the-way place. Dunvegan is the last outpost of civilization to the north, remember?"

He remembered, then swung the paint around, and they all retraced their steps to that friendly nester at a trot.

The gent was still out in his cabbage patch with his hoe. Longarm asked if he'd hold on to the packsaddle and three extra ponies for a dollar a day.

When the nester said they had a deal, Longarm handed him the lead rope along with the dollar, and lit out for town on the paint at a lope.

He chose another path into town, but rode the paint to the same stable, where he knew the help.

A young Irish hostler greeted him with, "Sure and I thought it was up to the Peace River you'd be after riding."

Longarm dismounted gracefully but quickly, saying, "I don't want it known that I'm back. I'll settle with you later for watering, feeding, and rubbing down this paint."

The Irish kid agreed, and Longarm was off at a fast walk on his long legs and low-heeled cavalry stovepipes. By now he knew the layout of the town well enough to circle the post office by way of side streets, coming around the far corner and, seeing he was either too early or too late, pausing by another watering trough to thumbnail a match-head aflame and light a fresh cheroot.

A million years and half a smoke went by before the man who'd introduced himself as Stu Murray came out on the walk, still reading the pale blue cablegram he'd been there to pick up.

He broke stride and froze when he saw Longarm standing there. He smiled uncertainly and said, "Morning. You ready to rid up to Dunvegan with me now?"

To which Longarm replied just as casually, "Not hardly. Have you ever flushed a plover bird and had it flop away from you across the grass, trying to get you to chase after it by dragging one floppy wing?"

The plover bird he'd been chasing let go of the cablegram and went for his gun.

Longarm had suspected he might, and the sudden movement of the blue paper at chest height gave Longarm enough warning to get his own gun out just in time. It was still close. The man called Murray splashed the water high when he got one shot off at that trough.

By that time Longarm's barely earlier first round had punched the two-face in the chest and bounced him off the post office wall and out into the dusty street, where he flopped like a fresh-caught trout as Longarm kicked his Schofield a good ways off and bent over to pick up that cablegram.

Then he hunkered down by the man he'd just shot to say, "Our gunplay is sure to bring you such medical attention as you might be able to profit from. This wire from your Aunt Martha in Denver says they sure miss you and want to know how soon you can get back to them. I see they sent you a money order to pay your way home too. I'd be proud to tell them what just happened to you if you'd care to give me their real return address."

The dying killer smiled up at him in a surprisingly sporting way, but sounded sort of tangle-tongued as he said, "They told me you were good. But that was black magic! I watched you ride out of town and waited until I was sure you were gone. And you had no right to beat me cross-draw. How did you do that?"

Longarm said, "Practice. The jig's up, Hamish, Detective James, or whoever you might be. I regret to say I'm going to have to give you to Canada for the killing of Jacques Campbell, among others. But you could do me a lot of good, at no further harm to yourself, if you'd like to go over some loose ends with me."

"Don't you like guessing games?" the man sprawled before him asked in a good-natured tone, considering. Then he coughed, choked on his own blood, and went into convulsions that soon faded to the snake-tail twitching of one booted foot.

Then there were no signs of life at all. Longarm felt the side of the still figure's throat, flicked open an eye with the back of a fingernail, and got back to his feet as others came out of the post office and from up and down the street.

One of them was an NWMP constable. So Longarm

233

holstered his .44-40 and called out, "I can explain all this, Constable."

The Mountie said, "I'm sure you can, sir. But you might as well explain to my sergeant major. So I must ask you to come along with me, and you'd better hand me your gun. The derringer too, Deputy Long."

Longarm handed over both weapons as someone in the crowd around them murmured, "Now the Yank's for it! Must have thought he was in Dodge City and all that!"

The NWMP substation wasn't far. Crown Sergeant Payson was in the doorway waiting for them as they arrived. He looked really pissed as he told Longarm, "I warned you what would happen if you shot that Calgary Kid on my watch, Yank."

As Longarm followed the disgruntled Mountie inside he protested, "Don't get your bowels in an uproar. In the first place, it wasn't the Calgary Kid exactly. And second, it was self-defense. I caught him in a little fib and he slapped leather on me."

Payson moved around to the far side of an imposing desk, leaving Longarm standing with two constables guarding him. Payson sat down and said, "I've sent word to my inspector. Once he gets here it's out of my hands. Meanwhile, I'm listening."

So Longarm told him all he knew, from the beginning, dirty parts and all. By the time he'd finished, another Mountie had come in with a pair of saddlebags. He whispered something to the crown sergeant as he placed them on the desk. Payson dumped the contents out. He picked up the Webley .442 Bulldog and quietly observed, "These saddlebags went with the man you just shot. He told people here in town to call him Stuart Murray, as Scotch a name as Hamish. I never heard of him before you shot him, as I said, on my watch."

Longarm pointed at the .442 with his chin and said, "He lied about you too. That's the plover's wing you're holding. Pretending to be me, he got the Calgary Kid out of jail in Fort Morgan. Then him and his little darling split up. I'm still working on where Harcourt lit out to. Hamish or whoever held on to Harcourt's unusual six-gun. He was packing that Schofield for public view, but he used the smaller Bulldog to wipe out the Collier family. I was wondering how a wiped-out family could place a bounty on anybody's head, but I didn't see the

234

light until I almost followed his bum steer to Dunvegan just now.''

Payson demanded, ''Why did he murder those relations of the Collier boy? What had they ever done to him?''

Longarm grimaced and said, ''They knew him on sight. Knew Percival Harcourt, that is. It must have been simple for a perfect stranger to ride in and kill them all as they were fixing to coffee and cake him.''

Payson asked, ''What about that Indian trader near Fort Peck?''

Longarm replied, ''Poor old Debrun had never had any dealings with either of the skunks. But they knew we knew Debrun was a smuggler, and they wanted me to follow that plover bird further north. Putting a .442 slug in him after loudly demanding passage to Canada worked as well as a blazed trail might have. We added two and two and arrived at six or eight. I got sidetracked up your way, like they wanted me to. You got a mighty big country here, and I had no notion where to look for somebody else entirely!''

Payson asked, ''Is that why he shot Jacques Campbell, to draw you deeper into Canada with his nesting-plover act?''

Longarm shook his head. ''Not exactly. But he couldn't pass up the opportunity to use the Bulldog on another man with a Scotch name, especially when Campbell refused to do something for him.''

Payson wanted to know what Campbell had refused to do for a strange rider at a remote trading post.

Longarm said, ''Wire home for money. The reason there was no record of any such transaction is simple. Campbell must have explained why he couldn't cash any wired money order unless Hamish wanted to take HBC trade tokens. Hamish didn't. But he'd told the trader he was from Denver and had someone there who'd send him money. So he shot Jacques Campbell before he rode on, lest Campbell wire something about such an odd visitor to someone else.''

Payson asked about that mysterious combustion in the late Jacques Campbell's telegraph shack.

Longarm said, ''I thought Sergeant Foster explained all that to you. The killer never did anything mysterious. He gunned an old fat man and rode on. A smoke in Campbell's mouth, or mayhaps a muzzle blast, set his duds to smolder in a poorly ventilated place. The body was consumed a slice of bacon at a time until things looked spookier than they really were. This undertaking gal I met up with down by our other border told me some tales about the odd things that can happen to a corpse. Spontaneous human combustion ain't much worse than having them bursting at their funerals.''

Payson sniffed and said, "I'm familiar with postmortem chemistry. How did you trace the killer here to Edmonton?"

Longarm modestly replied, "I never did. I wanted to use the telegraph connections over here for the same reasons he did. He must have shit when he spied me jawing with you in the Peacepipe yesterday. But he was a cool son of a bitch, and he knew I'd never gotten a good look at him when he helped those two gals handcuff me in a cellar down Denver way. So he pretended not to know me while he tricked me into telling him I wasn't really on to him. He pretended to be a bounty hunter I might be slick enough to use as a tool to get at the rascal I thought I was after. He knew Harcourt was no more in Dunvegan than he was here in Edmonton. He wanted me to tear ass up yonder so he could wire home for money, the way he'd been wanting to since before he'd killed Jacques Campbell. But on my way to the Peace River it came to me that your telegraph lines were the only reason anyone might have for riding all this way, no offense. So I doubled back, and the rest you know."

Crown Sergeant Payson picked up Longarm's gun rig and derringer as he rose and murmured, "I do indeed. Come along with me, Longarm."

Longarm did, seeing he had so little choice. But when they got back by the prison cells, occupied mostly by bleary-eyed drunks left over from the night before, Payson led Longarm on by and out a back door.

Then he handed back the guns, large and small, saying, "I told you our inspector is on his way. You'd better not be in town when he gets here. If you're stopped by anyone else this side of the line, we never had this conversation."

Longarm strapped on his .44-40, saying, "I follow your drift. But how are you going to explain that nameless plover bird I just had to shoot?"

The Mountie asked innocently, "You mean the illegal immigrant we wanted for murdering a British subject over at Campbell's Station? You let the NWMP worry about that, Yank."

So Longarm allowed he'd heard the Mounties always got their man, and they shook on that and parted friendly.

Chapter 19

Longarm had been back on the trail long enough to need another haircut when he reined in on a rise and told the cordovan he was riding, "That must be Calgary down yonder, and wasn't that a swell site to put an outpost?"

The palisaded NWMP stronghold, surrounded by a tipi town and some sizable canvas tents, reminded Longarm of the way Denver had started out as a prairie gold camp where Cherry Creek ran into the South Platte in view of snowcapped mountains to the west. They hadn't struck gold at Calgary. They'd chosen the site with strategy in mind. But you could see how a fair-sized town was certain to grow up at that junction of the Bow and Elbow. Some slick thinker had already turned cattle loose to graze by the year-round water. Stock would be safe from Indians this close to a Mountie company.

Longarm dismounted, explaining to his ponies, "We don't want to ride in until after dark, lest some nosy soul in scarlet spot us at a distance and . . . aw, shit!"

For a white-helmeted and red-coated rider was already headed their way, sitting his chestnut mount like he was glued to the saddle with his spine welded solid.

Longarm glanced over at the telegraph line he'd been keeping company with for some time, and got out a cheroot to light as he let his pals graze. The Canadian High Plains never went quite as brown as they got by July around Denver. But the short grass up this way had about topped off for the summer, and its stems were starting to make a grazer chaw.

As the Mountie rode closer, Longarm saw he was older than Constable Newton, with a neatly trimmed brown beard. He trotted his chestnut up the rise, reined in near Longarm, and dismounted gracefully to remove a white gauntlet and hold out a bare hand, saying, "Senior Constable Wilcox here. Your man's not down there in that shanty town, and even if he was, our inspector can be a bit of a prick."

As they shook, Longarm quietly said, "We had officers like that when I was in uniform. They thought they were running the outfit. It's nice to know Her Majesty has her own NCO club tending to her beeswax here in Canada. Who wired you I was coming, Foster or Payson?"

Wilcox replied, "Let's move these horses back down the north slope a bit. I tell officers what they want to hear, so what they know for certain can fit. I believe I'm questioning a cowboy over this way in connection with some unbranded stock he'd better see about. There's no need for you to know who vouched for you and explained your mission. One hand washes the other, but there are limits to how much informal help we can offer a man with no damned jurisdiction up this way. I can tell you nobody anywhere has spotted your rat-toothed killer with the mismatched eyes."

As they got all five mounts to grazing on the greener north slope of the rise, Longarm asked if they'd found out anything about that cuss the NWMP had caught up with in Edmonton. The one who'd killed Trader Campbell.

The Mountie got out a little black book to consult as he nodded and said, "They said to tell you the murdered man's daughter, a Miss Una Campbell, seems quite happy with her new position at some fancy shop near our Edmonton station. They failed to say what connection this might have with the Calgary Kid."

Longarm smiled wistfully and replied, "It hasn't hardly any. That other rascal covering for the Calgary Kid killed her daddy, and I was so sure nobody was watching when we parted friends in Edmonton."

Wilcox said, "The killer would be one James Morrison, age thirty-seven, U.S. citizen, who once worked for your Pinkerton Detective Agency as an armed guard. Fired for pilfering two years ago. Reputed to be acting as a one-man unchartered de-

238

tective agency based in Denver, Colorado, since then.''

Longarm whistled softly and said, ''Foster told me you gents have your own telegraph lines, and it must be a comfort to have public lines a crook might use the property of the same government.''

Wilcox shrugged and said, ''Western Union in Denver says the return address on the money order from a worried relative was that of a junkyard where they'd never heard of any Stuart Murray.''

Longarm said, ''That don't surprise me. The nest that plover bird was trying to lead me away from has been somewhere in or near Denver all the time. But they've naturally been coy about real names and return addresses. I don't suppose there'd be any way you could get the NWMP to sort of sit on the news that one birdie from their nest just got his fool self killed up Edmonton way?''

The Mountie looked pained. ''Please don't tell a man how to wipe his arse. Of *course* we're hoping Dear Old Aunt Martha will be trying to cable her far-away nephew again. But do you really expect her to use her right name and address?''

Longarm said, ''Nope. But it's good to hear great minds run in the same channels. When you see a plover bird dragging its wing all over, you can chase after it, like I just did, or you can turn around and see if you can spy the damned nest all those dramatics were meant to distract you from. I knew as early as Fort Morgan that somebody had been wiring money regular to that loco self-styled Calgary Kid. Yet I let them sucker me into chasing after a confederate hired to throw me off, which he surely did, and I feel dumb as hell!''

Wilcox asked where he thought the man he was really after might be. Longarm shrugged and said, ''Most anywhere on this old earth. It ain't as if he has to support himself and his nasty habits. A man who can pay can get drunk and screw three-in-a-bed from here to Timbuktu. The only way we'll hear he's there will be when, not if, he kills somebody else. You might say the Calgary Kid has the disposition of a murderous spoiled brat. Ain't Murray and Morrison both Scotch names, by the way?''

Wilcox said, ''They can be, and Calgary is the name of a village in Scotland. But Harcourt is an English home county name, and if the late James Morrison was only hired by . . . Who are we talking about?''

Longarm said, "Somebody evil but sane who's been backing the play of our man's self-indulgent mean streak. Percival Harcourt sounds as if it was made up on the spur of the moment by a witty drunk. The Calgary Kid gets even more sardonic if he had a village in Scotland in mind."

"You think the Calgary Kid could be from Scotland?" asked Wilcox.

Longarm said, "He ain't from around here. Folks who've known that bastard better say he sounds like a lime-juicer. An upper-class Scot who'd been to school in England might talk the same way. And I've noticed along the way that a heap of folks feel more comfortable hiring their own kind. Swedes hire other Swedes, Irish hire other Irish, and us Anglo-Saxons are supposed to be real snobbish about giving the best jobs to our own kind. The late Jim Morrison was called Hamish, which is Scotch for James, by at least two other members of the Calgary Kid's gang, clan, or whatever. Wouldn't you say that makes 'em at least more familiar than most with Scotch names?"

Wilcox shrugged and declared he was ever so glad Longarm was looking for the whole bunch south of the border. He added that the earlier the American got started, the sooner he'd get there.

Longarm started gathering his ponies closer as he asked how far he had in the saddle to Fort MacLeod.

Wilcox shook his head and said firmly, "Do both Crown Sergeant Foster and yourself a favor and don't go anywhere near his post. I've stuck my own neck out bringing you up to date on all we know."

Longarm made ready to mount as he lightly replied, "No, you ain't. I mean to leave these ponies with some Indian pals nearer the border, and I'd like to be able to tell 'em what happened to their money, a lot of their money, should they ask."

Wilcox didn't sound like he was hiding anything when he smiled and said, "Oh, that's easy. Foster turned the money over to his superiors and it's been invested at three percent for the Blackfoot in British Consols."

Longarm took his foot out of the stirrup and asked the Mountie to run that past him again.

Wilcox explained. "Government securities. Consol is just short for Consolidated Annuity. To save paperwork and spread the risk, the Bank of England consolidated nine different government annuities back around 1800. They've been ever so popular with modest investors ever since. If three percent a year sounds modest, consider that nobody has ever lost a farthing on the famous—''

''*British Consulates* if you're an ignorant American repeating that carelessly to a dumb lawman who never heard of *British Consols* till just now!'' Longarm shook his head with a sheepish grin.

He didn't take the time to explain further, seeing he was in as big a hurry as the NWMP to get his ass back to the States. So they both got back in their saddles, shook on it, and rode their separate ways.

In a lot more time than it would take to tell, Longarm found good homes for his four good ponies, gave Rain Crow a good talking to on the topic of running guns to his Canadian kinsmen, and even managed a good haircut between trains on his way back to Denver.

He got in on a warm, bright Monday morning, and Billy Vail didn't raise a fuss for wasting all that time and distance. But he explained why they'd best not have Henry bill the taxpayers for more than half the distance, lest they have to try and explain that side trip east to Wood Mountain in pursuit of a white fugitive.

Seated with Longarm in his smoke-filled oak-paneled office, Vail said, ''It's just as well the Mounties are taking the case off our hands. I got better chores for you than tracking down mean drunks.''

Longarm shook out the match he'd just used to light up in self-defense and mildly but firmly pointed out, ''No, they ain't. It's now official that a renegade Pinkerton man named James Morrison gunned a British subject named Jacques Campbell, on Canadian soil, and fled to Edmonton where he was shot whilst resisting arrest by the North West Mounted Police. They don't want the Calgary Kid as a free gift. Canada has no charges against him. We do. It's a simple fact that the crazy bastard owes us for one federal deputy, amongst others.''

Vail looked uncomfortable, shrugged, and replied, ''If he's still alive. He's gone to ground mighty slick for a wayward youth with no self-control. Or, as your pal Sergeant Nolan suggests, those naughty gals who were working with him and Morrison may have killed him to get rid of a loose cannon.

Nobody but the Calgary Kid ever acted as mad-dog vicious, you know.''

Longarm blew a thoughtful smoke ring and decided, "Nobody ever went to that much trouble for anyone they were fixing to bury in the cellar either. I suspect that once Morrison got Harcourt out of jail pretending to be me, the crazy one who'd be easier to spot ran for cover, whilst his hired savior went on that killing spree with his .442 Webley Bulldog, playing plover bird with us. I suspect that means their nest has to be somewhere closer than Canada because plover birds don't drag their wings towards their nests when you're watching.''

Vail chewed his soggy stogie like a bone and growled, "Let's not keep rehashing that dead private detective. We've distributed enlarged copies of those photo prints you sent from Montana. We've gotten Western Union to go along with us more than they ever wanted to, and none of those return addresses on money orders sent to either Harcourt or Morrison, as Murray, panned out. No telegraph clerk can recall what Aunt Martha might have looked like. A man signing himself that way might have been remembered better. Whoever the *woman* was, she was slick enough to come in when the office was busy, lay down the cash, pick up her receipt, and git. She ain't sent money to her nephew up Fort Morgan way since he got his fool self arrested. She ain't sent any wires to Edmonton for some time. They must have agreed that when the nephew didn't wire back, he was likely caught.''

Longarm nodded, but pointed out, "That still leaves Aunt Martha in this neck of the woods.''

Vail said, "She ain't been making any use of Western Union whether she is or ain't. They agreed to at least tell us if any customer wired Percival Harcourt anywhere in the country, which nobody has.''

Longarm sighed and said, "Billy, nobody was ever really sprinkled Percival Harcourt. It sounds like a made-up name from some romantic English novel. If he ain't hiding out here in Denver, he has to be off some other place, getting his regular allowance under some other name.''

Vail made a wry face and grumbled, "I wish I'd been born into such luxury. I also wish you hadn't suggested that. If he's more than a day's ride out of Denver, getting his usual allowance . . .''

"Couldn't we ask Western Union to tip us off on anyone

wiring the same amounts regularly from anywhere closer?''

To which Vail replied in a weary tone, ''We could. I did. They told me the notion ain't practical. They handle hundreds of money orders a day from any state capital. All Aunt Martha would have to do would be to sign different names at different offices betwixt, say, Golden and Aurora, either suburb an easy carriage ride from wherever the hell she really lives.''

Longarm started to suggest something dumb. Then he sighed, blew smoke out his nostrils, and said, ''The Calgary Kid could pick up and cash 'em under as many names. I see what Western Union means. We have to track down Aunt Martha some other way.''

Vail asked bluntly, ''Why? We've agreed that hired gun you gunned up in Canada must have been the one who gunned U.S. Deputy Marshal Braxton on us. Nobody had seen the Calgary Kid around Helena, Montana, because the nasty drunk never went anywhere *near* Montana! The killer was Jim Morrison, the man you got, who killed up the Colliers and killed that old lady behind that hotel counter. So mean as he may be, the self-styled Calgary Kid ain't much more than a mean drunk who killed some train robbers.''

Longarm said, ''I thought you didn't want to rehash him. He *is* a *killer* and his Aunt Marthas, both of them, owe me for an abduction and helping their pal, Hamish or James Morrison, impersonate an officer of the law!''

Vail sniffed and said, ''Picky, picky, picky. No harm was done to you in the end, and if their mean nephew is still alive and if he's still killing folks, he's sure to get picked up again and let's hope they try him and hang him *local*. We've wasted enough time hunting for the asshole. These enlarged photo prints are going to be as tough to explain to the paymaster as your apparently fruitless trip to Canada.''

Longarm absently asked to see how the enlargements had turned out. Vail rummaged in his desk, found a set, and handed them across it to Longarm, who leafed through them twice before he said, ''Hold on. I sent you more than one close-up of the Calgary Kid posing alone. He looks about like everyone else, even enlarged, posing as part of a group like this. Where's the damned close-ups?''

Vail said, ''That's all you sent, old son. Are you sure you meant to send others?''

Longarm growled, ''I didn't *mean* to send others. I stuck

243

'em in the envelope with these and . . . Oh, shit, won't I ever learn?''

Vail naturally asked what they were talking about. So Longarm had to confess to picking up the warm and friendly Aura Taylor along the way and staying in that hotel with her the night Aunt Nelly, the old hotel lady, had her poor throat cut by someone she'd let walk right up to her.

Vail said, "I follow your drift. But what proof do you have that your mysterious Aura Taylor was the killer?"

Longarm felt sort of sick to his stomach as he numbly replied, "She was the only person on earth, after me and Aunt Nelly, who knew I'd left those photo-prints in a hotel envelope to go out in the next morning's mail! She screwed me sleepy, or may have even slipped some more dope to me, then got up to pee in the wee small hours, went down to the lobby to kill the old lady easy, and just opened that first hotel envelope and removed the really helpful pictures before sending the rest on in a fresh envelope."

Vail thought, nodded soberly, and said, "She must have been great at coming up with new positions. Had she simply destroyed every one of these prints, we'd have noticed sooner!"

Longarm said, "I'd have noticed right off. The sealed envelope I thought I'd left with that poor old lady was one of the first things I checked. Since it was still there, I just sent it on, at a loss for her killer's reasons. Sweet Aura knew how easy it would have been for me to have more prints made, there in the town they were printed, if she'd removed every one."

He flicked some ash on the rug for the carpet mites and swallowed the green taste in his mouth before he added, "She *was* as imaginative in bed as you suggested. Both times."

"*Both* times?" asked Vail with a puzzled frown.

Longarm smiled sheepishly and said, "She must have been the siren called Ginger in the cellar of Glover's Warehouse. The one who wanted to be called Candy had these three moles on her belly, which I never felt on either Ginger or Aura."

Vail gasped. "Jesus H. Christ, are you saying you laid the same gal twice and never noticed it was the same gal?"

Longarm nodded wearily, and said, "I told you she was imaginative in bed. Aside from screwing different, I was slickered by the heavy paint job she wore as Ginger and, well, it

244

wasn't as if I was in bed with Candy and then Aura with nobody else in between.''

Vail laughed despite himself and warned, ''One of these days you're really going to get in trouble with that frisky dong of yours. Do you reckon you could recognize the frisky gal on the streets of Denver, seeing you've know her so well without all that heavy makeup?''

Longarm shook his head and said, ''Not from more than a few yards away, given a total change of duds and mayhaps hair color. It's sad but true that a woman can change her appearance a lot easier than a man. We ain't allowed to fandango ourselves with even light makeup. If those two gals were smart enough to tart themselves up in that cellar the way they'd never appear at a family gathering, we have to figure Aura Taylor and whoever she really is don't look too much alike. I'm sure I'd know her in bed a third time, but a change in dress and hair color could make her a bitch to recognize at the opera house.''

Vail shrugged and said, ''Like I said. The trail's gone cold as a well-digger's socks, and that killing in that hotel, mean as it might have been, wasn't federal. So as for your next assignment . . .''

''I'm still on this one, or you can take this badge and shove it!'' Longarm declared. ''Aunt Nelly was a nice old lady, Billy. That ruthless cunt slit her throat from ear to ear, and then doubtless went back to tell the one with the moles how she'd made a total sap of me a second time!''

Vail started to object. Then he relented. ''All right, we can give her to Montana and let *them* hang her. But where in blue blazes are you figuring on finding her? We've tried in vain to connect any two of all those fake addresses together. This ain't such a small town, and you just admitted you might not recognize her across the street!''

Longarm rose to his feet with a glance at the banjo clock on the wall, saying, ''Banking hours are a pain in the ass. So I'd best get cracking.''

''You think she works in a *bank*?'' asked Vail in a confused tone.

Longarm didn't answer. He was already out the door and he didn't have much time. He legged it over to Seventeenth Street faster than most men could run, and even so, a snooty-looking guard tried to shut the glass door in his face, but relented at the sight of Longarm's federal badge.

Inside the stuffy branch of the biggest London bank Longarm knew of, he asked his way to the manager's office. But when he got there a stuffy bird with distinguished gray temples and one of those fancy monocles stuck in one eye said he'd be only too happy to cooperate with the United States Government if he didn't have another pressing engagement. When Longarm allowed it was important, the dude rang a bell on his desk and a mousy little secretary gal came in, staring at them through her more practical glasses.

The manager introduced her to Longarm as his Miss Shrimpton, and said he was sure she could accommodate Longarm in every way. For some reason this made her blush and look away. But if her boss noticed, he didn't care. He lit out as if the bank was on fire, leaving Longarm and the mouse to smile at one another awkwardly.

He explained he was looking into one or more crooks who seemed to be dealing in those British Consols put out by the British Government. She agreed you had to purchase them in England or through an English bank such as her own. She said, "They're not as popular here in your American West, with railroad stocks paying six percent and mining shares paying even more. But a conservative investor holding a few thousand in British Consols can rest assured of that three percent a year, rain or shine, in peace and war."

"I ain't out to invest in any annuities, ma'am," he replied. "I've reason to suspect some wanted criminals are living off such a block of British Consols as you describe."

She led him into her own office, sat him down beside her on a leather chesterfield, and said she was all ears. So he told her the whole story, leaving out some dirty parts, and had her owl-eyed and doubtless hungry by the time he'd finished. For by then it was *really* after regular banking hours and folks outside were heading home.

She'd told him along the way to call her Mavis if she was supposed to call him Custis. She said she found American manners refreshing for a girl who'd been brought up stricter in London Town. Then she spoiled it all by saying, "I'd love to help, Custis. But I don't see how they'd ever let me spend that much of the bank's time on a purely American matter. I agree that somewhere amid an absolute blizzard of filed paper there may be some indications as to where in this city a single individual may be holding the amount of Consols you suggest, but . . . How did you come up with your estimate, Custis?''

Longarm read off his notes again as he said, ''It's been my sad experience that dealers in stolen money rake off at least two thirds for themselves. They'd doubtless rake off more if it didn't cause clients with guns so much anguish. Until things went really hard on him, that self-styled Calgary Kid was drawing forty-two dollars a week in play money. That means whoever was doling it out to him had to be raking off at least eighty-four. Meaning at least a hundred and twenty-six a week, or five thousand and fifty-two a year, as mere *interest* on the British Consols they have to be holding in *somebody's* name. They were holding a war the year I should have been graduating from school. So I ain't such a whizz at arithmetic. But drawing only three cents on the dollar a year, wouldn't you need a fair-sized pile?''

Mavis made a little O with her lips and said, ''We're talking about the capital some belted earl might settle on the backstairs offspring he'd banished to the colonies!''

Longarm said, ''I told you he acted like a spoiled rich kid. Ain't it safe to say anybody in these parts with such a big block of those Consols in his or her name would tend to stand out a mite?''

She sighed and said, ''I suppose they would. I can go through our ledgers and tell you if anyone's been cashing such large interest checks with us on a regular basis, if you'd care to come back in a few days. I'll have to look through the ledgers when I have the spare time.''

''Hold on,'' Longarm said. ''Are you saying the birdies in the nest I'm looking for would be getting their money from England in the form of dividend checks?''

She allowed that was about the size of it, and added that such paper from the Bank of England could be cashed most anywhere.

He said, ''I can see that. They'd be too slick to cash 'em anywhere all that regular. I have to track their filthy lucre back to its source. Could you cable the right money changers in London Town for me, Miss Mavis?''

She blanched and said, ''Not bloody likely! It would be worth my job to muck with my betters without orders from on high! You'll have to ask Mr. Chalmers, the bloke you spoke to earlier. He's off for Colorado Springs with someone I'd

247

better not discuss with you. But he should be back by Wednesday next, and to be honest with you, I haven't had my supper yet.''

He rose with her, asking if she liked Italian noodles.

When she confessed she'd never eaten any, he said he'd take no excuses and insisted on springing for supper for two at Romero's.

He saw it had been a wise choice when the little drab's eyes first took in the checked tablecloths and candles stuck in wine bottles. He ordered some of their dry red wine to go with their exotic grub. It was easy to feed a working-class gal from London Town exotic grub. He had it on good authority that gals like Mavis were raised mostly on boiled potatoes, jam, and bread. She had a lot of fun learning to eat spaghetti with a fork, and since he had to wipe her chin for her a lot, he got her used to being touched by him. So it only seemed natural, riding her home in a hansom cab after coffee and dessert, to help her out of her glasses and kiss her when she gushed about what a lovely evening it had been.

She kissed back, with more pucker than one might expect just looking at her. But when he murmured that the evening was hardly over, she protested, ''I can't invite you in when we get to my boardinghouse! Whatever would the others think?''

He said, ''My landlady is a fuss too. But we could always go to the Tremont House and you could wait across the lobby whilst I signed us in.''

She drew back wide-eyed and gasped, ''Are you suggesting I'm the sort who'd go to a hotel with a strange man?''

He held her closer and put his spare hand in her lap to comfort her as he replied, ''Aw, I ain't so strange, and nobody else we know would ever know, right?''

She insisted it was wrong, all the way to the Tremont House near Broadway and Colfax, and then, after he'd gotten her up to their hired room, she said she couldn't, and wouldn't, because it made her feel so low. Then he trimmed the one lamp and lowered her to the mattress across the room, kissing her to smother her protests and feeling her up to change them to moans of desire. There was nicer stuff to feel than he'd expected when he'd made up his mind to grit his teeth and sacrifice himself. She was the one who allowed it was so *working class* to go any further with one's *duds* on. So he undressed

248

them both in the dark, and had her gushing with passion by the time he slid it in where she said she wanted it, although few if any men could have gone as deep as she seemed to desire.

He cupped a palm under the curvy little thing's perky behind, and they really got to be good friends for a while as she tried to stick her toes in his ears for some reason.

He believed her when she moaned she was "so pleased," and after he'd come too, he was pleasantly surprised when he struck a match to light a cheroot for them and noticed how pretty she looked, smiling up at him half-blind without her glasses and not nearly as prim-looking with her mouse-brown hair unpinned and down around her naked shoulders.

Her tits were even prettier. But he let her think he meant her face when he told her how swell she looked.

She said, "Thank you. You do have such a loverly cock."

He laughed, lit the cheroot, and shook out the match as she sighed and added, "I suppose I'll never know whether you just made love to me because you really thought I was pretty or because you want me to cable London about those perishing Consols for you."

She was right. Longarm wasn't dumb enough to tell her the truth. But it was only half a lie when he held her closer, placed the tip of the cheroot between her lips, and said, "Men can't get it up when they really *hate* a gal. You don't have to do another thing for me but this if you don't want to, pretty lady."

She took a sensuous drag, let it out, and sighed. "We'll have to be discreet. Nobody at the bank or anywhere else must know we're more than casual acquaintances. It may take me some time. I rather *hope* it takes me some time, but after I get the names of all the heavy investors in Consols here in Colorado, we'd better not make a habit of this."

He said that he could agree to those conditions, wistful as it made him feel already.

So she laughed, enjoying her feeling of power for the moment, and suggested he put out that bloody cheroot so she could get on top and see if she couldn't screw him bloody tired of her while they still had to work together in the cause of truth and justice.

Chapter 20

Mavis Shrimpton tracked on paper as good as she screwed in bed. So by the end of the month Longarm was holding a bright and early tactical meeting with Armenian George Mandalian from their Helena District Court and Matrons Boyle and Caplin from the Women's House of Detention. Matron Boyle was hefty and earthy. Matron Caplin was a petite brunette it wasn't smart to mess with. Billy Vail had told Longarm it was his play, so after introducing the two tough matrons to the rugged deputy from Montana, Longarm said, "We're moving in on an address atop Capitol Hill. I know that stretch along Sherman well because I once busted up a robbery at the Tabor mansion at one end of the same block a . . . pal of mine lives on. Marshal Vail here lives a couple of blocks north."

Vail growled, "I know where I live and the sun's climbing higher by the minute. Get to the point, damn it!"

Longarm said, "I like my sidekicks to know what we're trying to do before we try to do it. The point is that we figured out the crazy Calgary Kid was being aided and abetted by someone here in Denver who holds a block of tricky English annuities we don't have to delve into any more in depth. I've run up a telegraph bill we could all have a grand time on, and suffice to say, this banker pal and me narrowed it down to less than a score of Colorado investors content with a safe but modest speculation with all those mines in the mountains to the west offering higher dividends. The slippery eels we've been hunting tried to slither and slicker us by cashing their regular checks from London Town hither and yonder. They never guessed what a paper trail they were leaving by not leaving the same trail as everyone *else* cashing the same Consol dividends at their regular banks.''

Armenian George started to ask a question, nodded in satisfaction, and said, ''I follow your drift. An annuity holder with nothing dirty to hide would cash it, over and over, at the most handy bank, store, or whatever.''

Longarm nodded and went on. ''A Bank of England check can be cashed most anywhere. But cashiers do remember cashing a monthy check made out for two hundred dollars and change. After that, said endorsed and cashed checks do go back to the Bank of England in London Town. But the real sore thumb was the endorsements. You can change the way you look. You can cash a check where nobody knows you. But you still have to endorse the check on the back with the name on the front. So it was dumb for a Mrs. Anne Shannon to make herself the only one on the list who didn't seem to cash her checks where she banked.''

Matron Boyle brightened and asked, ''This dreadful woman would be Irish then?''

Longarm shook his head and said, ''Scotch. I was surprised by that too. You wouldn't expect Myers, Rose, or Taylor could be Scotch, but they can be, and let's get back to Widow Shannon. I heard she was a widow because, like I said, I know folks who live nearby and I'd heard tell of a widow from Baltimore buying a brownstone down the way. We're going up there now with a search warrant signed by Judge Dickerson down the hall. I want you two ladies to handle any hysterical females as we search the premises for the Calgary Kid or his sign. I won't be positive before we get there, but I suspect Deputy Mandalian here may be taking at least one of the bunch back to Montana to stand trial for murder.''

The two matrons exchanged wide-eyed glances. Their eyes got even wider when Billy Vail had young Henry issue each gal her own holstered six-gun. Nobody asked if the federal matrons were qualified to handle guns. They knew both gals had to be.

Longarm, Mandalian, and the two gals trooped outside, where a closed carriage was waiting at the curb with another deputy holding the whip and reins. Sherman Street was a short haul from the Federal Building to drive, but a tedious uphill walk.

As they were moving up Colfax Avenue with Longarm and Matron Boyle riding backward, facing Deputy Mandalian and Matron Caplin, the Irish girl nudged Longarm and slyly inquired, "Why would you be after humming that dorty song, you forward man?"

Longarm blinked in surprise, smiled sheepishly, and said, "Shame on you too. 'Old Maids from Canada' has been going through my head for weeks. It must keep springing from cobwebs in the back of my fool head. I'd heard of two newcomers from *Baltimore* down the way from . . . a pal of mine. They must have heard some about me in the same manner. I knew I was after someone fairly rich who knew me on sight. But Lord only knows how I might have suspected these gals where we're headed before I'd had occasion to really go over their odd finances."

Across the carriage, Mandalian said, "I've been told about those hunches you get, Longarm. Which of these two old maids from Baltimore killed poor old Aunt Nelly up our way?"

Longarm looked away, ears warm, as he replied, "I hope to tell you when we get there. These ladies with us may have to help by undressing at least one. It's a long story, and we'll cross that bridge later. The two of 'em claim to be widow women instead of old maids, by the way."

Their driver swung them around the State House, and drove south to the imposing brownstone mansion of Silver Dollar Tabor, the mining magnate, a long block beyond. He swung the corner and reined in by the entrance to the alley running the length of the block behind all the grand homes. Longarm and Mandalian helped the gals down and told the driver to sit tight. Then the four of them strode down the alley abreast in the bright but slanty sunlight from the east.

It just happened to be a Monday, and so another widow woman with light brown hair piled high and her summer dress all hiked up was hanging laundry out back with her colored maid when she caught sight of the formidable quartet and ran over to her back fence to demand, "Custis Long! What on earth are you up to now?"

Longarm told her, "Can't stop to talk. But I promise I'll drop by and tell you all about it later."

She opened her back gate. Longarm said, "Don't. We're on our way to search some premises and mayhaps make some arrests. So no offense, you'd best tend to your laundry this morning."

She didn't argue. She admired masterful men. Longarm led Mandalian and the other two gals to another backyard gate, closer to the far end, and paused to tell them, "I have some pals on the Denver police out front. We get along with them just like Armenian George here gets along with the local Helena law. I asked Denver not to horn in if nobody runs out the front as we go in the back. So let's go in the back. You ladies stay here till I wave you in. Would you cover me as I cross the yard, Armenian George?"

Mandalian drew his six-gun and said he would. So Longarm drew his own, took a deep breath, and ran like hell across the backyard and up the back steps to hit the kitchen door with all his speed and weight.

It crashed open, whether it had been locked or not. Longarm knew all the houses along this stretch of Sherman were built much alike. So he tore through the kitchen, out into the central hall, and threw down on the man running for the front door half dressed, calling out, "Freeze where you are and get them hands high! You won't hear such an offer twice!"

The total stranger whirled to face him, with a Harrington & Richardson .32 whore pistol in hand. They both fired at the same time.

Something plucked at the tail of Longarm's frock coat. His .44-40 slug punched the stranger in the chest and crashed him against that front door, which opened to spill his limp form out on the porch.

Then Longarm was tearing up the stairs, two at a time, smoking gun in hand as he readied to fire it again.

But when he burst into the bedroom at the top of the stairs, he only saw two naked ladies with gray hair cowering in a far corner on the far side of a rumpled four-poster.

He said, "Morning, Miss Ginger, Miss Candy. Is there anyone else up here or do you ladies still like to go three-in-a-bed?"

"Bastard!" shrilled the one with no moles on her belly.

253

"What have you done to poor Jock and who turned us in to you?"

He lowered his gun muzzle politely and moved to the nearby window as he said, "We'll get to your questions after we answer some of mine."

He signaled from the window. Mandalian and the two matrons dashed across the backyard. Mandalian had to pause down below to explain a body on the front porch to the Denver police as best he could. He sent the two gals up to join Longarm and the other women.

Longarm told them, "These young ladies with deliberate gray hair would be Miss Anne Shannon and Miss Iona MacInnis. We're still working on which is which and other minor details. Matron Boyle, would you be good enough to get *that* old maid from Baltimore dressed, down the hall, whilst Matron Caplin and me help this other find something?"

As the burly Matron Boyle took the one Longarm knew as Ginger or Aura Taylor by one naked arm, the prisoner warned the younger one with three moles on her naked tummy, "Stick to the story we agreed on! They don't have anything on us! They're trying to divide and conquer!"

As soon as he and Matron Caplin were alone with the scared, skinny Candy, or Iona MacInnis as it turned out, Longarm smiled fondly at her and said, "She was right. You're fixing to turn state's evidence. But first we'd best let you throw something on. Don't you even have a kimono or something in here?"

Matron Caplin found a bathrobe crumpled in another corner. As she handed it to their prisoner, Longarm explained, "You don't want to bluster and pout before I deal all your cards out to you face-up on the table. To begin with, I ain't about to press charges against you for that prank you played on me in the cellar of Glover's Warehouse."

Candy-Iona slipped on her robe, blushing, as she murmured, "I should hope not, honey donger. You know I was just having a little fun with you."

"Honey donger?" marveled Matron Caplin.

Longarm said, "I just now said it was all in fun, as far as Judge Dickerson or any other judge and jury have to know. So now let's get to murder in the first, a hanging offense in Montana Territory."

"I never murdered anybody!" wailed the fake old maid who

254

could screw so fine, her eyes filled with tears and terror.

Longarm let her cry a bit before he put a gentle hand on her trembling shoulder and quietly told her, "Ginger, Aura, or Anne did. She cut a nice old lady's throat from ear to ear, and folks up Helena way are mighty sore about that. From the endorsements on many a check we've traced, your meaner sister in sin was in charge of this confusion too. So I could put it down in my report that you were no more than her used and abused maid-of-all-work, forced against her will to be a mite naughty now and again."

Their prisoner sat down on the bed and covered her face with her hands as Matron Caplin muttered, "Honey donger?" again.

Longarm hushed her with a warning look and got out his notebook, saying, "Never mind anything I don't want you signing to as a witness. Miss Candy-Iona is fixing to give us a full statement now, starting with where they mean to wire the next money order to their nephew or whatever, the Calgary Kid."

She did. The tangled web they'd woven called for him to cut in and back her up now and again, and before she'd agree to sign as a federal witness, Matron Caplin asked, "What on earth is a remittance man?"

Longarm said, "Black sheep from a rich aristocratic family, paid off to stay the hell away from their kith and kin lest they disgrace them with a tavern brawl, a chambermaid, or whatever. I thought they had some more sensible reason than three-in-a-bed to keep helping out such an unreasonable cuss."

He moved to the door and called the others back. As Matron Boyle led the smarter but meaner one in, now wearing a shantung kimono, the one on the bed sobbed, "I had to, Anne! You never should have killed that lady up in Montana! I don't want to hang for what you did! They give mighty short rides on this merry-go-round to begin with, and I'm just not ready to get off!"

"You little fool!" shrilled the one called Anne. "I told you and told you he'd never be allowed to appear against us in court. I told you his superiors would never let him once we told them what we had on him! Why do you think we went to all that trouble to get him in bed with us before Hamish borrowed his clothes and badge?"

Iona looked up through her fingers at Longarm, giggled, and said she'd sort of liked it.

Matron Caplin nudged Matron Boyle and murmured, "Remind me to tell you about honey dong later."

Feeling foolish, whether he showed it or not, Longarm pointed his chin at Deputy Mandalian as he told the two prisoners, "I hate to bust bubbles. But I won't have to testify in a local Montana court. Armenian George will only be taking the one of you back with him, along with this deposition, typed up more formally and signed by Miss Iona, Matron Caplin, and yours truly. You might get off with life at hard if you'd plead guilty like a sport and save them the expense of a tedious trial. They have you cold without the testimony you doubtless had no fear of hearing from this child. I never saw you cut Aunt Nelly ear to ear. But you did register in her hotel under the false name of Aura Taylor, who never owned any shares in that local mine or a swell house on Logan Street in Denver. So lots of luck with that Montana jury, and Miss Iona here can help me catch Mister Ivor C. Balfionna, as we now know the Calgary Kid."

"You stupid treacherous sow!" wailed Anne Shannon.

Longarm didn't see how she could be talking to him. So he told the matrons to get the prisoners dressed while he went down to explain that second hired gun to the Denver police.

He did. It had been obvious for some time that the Detective James who'd pestered Morgana Floyd about him in Denver could not be the James Morrison leaving a false trail across Canada.

Longarm got everyone over to the Federal Building, ran for the Union Station, and had time to consult his new notes and send a wire to the new alias of the Calgary Kid, explaining how his new Aunt Rhoda was having a problem at the British consulate, but hoped to wire him better news the following day.

Then Longarm caught the train to Leadville. The ride was winding and seemed to take forever, but starting so early in the day got him there just before sundown.

He knew what the Calgary Kid looked like. Ivor Balfionna, alias the Calgary Kid, had only seen his three-piece suit and gun rig, worn by another man entirely, in the different surroundings of Fort Morgan.

Had Longarm wanted to play it safe and mean, he could

256

have simply hung around the Western Union in Leadville until a rat-toothed cuss with a brown spot in one blue eye showed up, then slapped leather on him and ended the sad saga there. But he didn't want to.

He began his evening in Leadville with the usual courtesy call on the town law, explaining he'd come up from Denver to pick up a federal want he didn't need any local assistance with, as long as nobody shot him by mistake when and if he had to get noisy.

Then he strolled down to the Western Union through the brimstone aroma of the recently renamed mining community. Leadville had started out as Slabtown, which had struck some as less than elegant. It was now named for rich lead-silver carbonite seams in the slopes all around, but things smelled much the same, thanks to the big Meyer & Harrison smelter on one side of the valley the town got to share.

He saw the Comique Theatre was featuring *Who Shot Keyser's Dog?* that evening, with *The Female Bathers* promised for next week. It was too bad he'd told Billy Vail he'd be back sooner. He'd heard that was a mighty spicy show, even for Leadville.

At the Western Union he casually asked if his pal, Rob Baxter, had been by to pick up any messages. The clerk glanced through the yellow telegrams under his counter, found the one Longarm had sent hours earlier from Denver, and allowed he'd have to sign for it if he meant to deliver it to his pal. Longarm said he'd just tell old Rob there was a wire waiting for him and let him pick it up himself.

Then he went outside, took his frock coat off as he crossed the street, and sat down on the edge of the plank walk in his shirt and vest to whittle scrapwood he found handy.

He could have carved a wooden chain or a Pennsylvania Dutch courting spoon in the time he spent there, had he really been whittling. The sun went down, but there was a street lamp handy to the lit-up doorway of the Western Union across the way. Longarm put his coat back on, since it was darker where he sat and a man in shirt sleeves after dark at this altitude stood out worse. There was no call to whittle if nobody could see just what he was doing. So he put his pocketknife away and lit yet another cheroot.

At the rate he was waiting, he was going to have to buy

more tobacco before that son-of-a-bitching Calgary Kid ever showed.

Then, just as Longarm had convinced himself the man was drunk and lying three-in-a-bed in some shanty on Smelter Row, he saw the son of a bitch he'd been chasing all over creation. There was no mistaking the Calgary Kid, even at that distance in this light. Longarm had been worried he might not recognize him. But he'd been studying those old photo prints, distant as well as close-up, until the overall shape of the elusive cuss had sunk in good. So even though he rose to his own feet, Longarm stayed put across the street, lounging against an awning post and smoking, while the Calgary Kid went into the Western Union, stayed there a million years, and came out cussing to stomp up the plank walk the way he'd come.

Longarm followed by walking almost abreast on the far side of the street. As he'd expected, the Calgary Kid looked behind himself just before he whipped around the corner. Longarm didn't run after him. He'd caught others tailing *him* that way. He just kept walking on toward the brighter lights ahead. He paused in front of a shut-down shop to go through the motions of lighting up. He saw the Calgary Kid's reflection in the dark shop window. Longarm had thought he'd be headed for the night life along State Street. It was good to know the spendthrift bastard was likely running low on pocket jingle. Iona MacInnis had tearfully confided they'd been planning to send him a money order. He'd just wired his new address to their other gunslick, Jock Purvis. Longarm had been right about even Scotch-American gals from Baltimore feeling they could trust a crook with a Scotch name better than, say, an Armenian or Swede. He hadn't put down what the sobbing Iona had confessed about screwing and inciting the gunslick. Longarm had promised her she'd go free in time, and old Jock had lost in the end, so what the hell.

As he tagged along after the Calgary Kid, he saw the cuss turn into the Gaiety, which was a so-called "wine theater." The show was free as long as you patronized the bar a lot. Longarm had figured his man didn't have anough left for another night of three-in-a-bed. So he was likely out to inspire a jerk-off, the poor bastard, with that evening's presentation of *A Shot in the Eye,* featuring Miss Erba Robeson sort of spilling out of her bodice.

Longarm drifted in after the Calgary Kid, located him at the long bar where standees could watch the stage over the heads of the bigger spenders served at their tables, and bellied up beside the Calgary Kid to order Maryland Rye, by brand, without looking at him.

Anyone who'd ever bellied up to a bar could tell you only suckers ordered by brand name. Longarm knew he'd be overcharged, and he was.

But he just turned with his shot glass in hand to watch the show on the gaslit stage with his elbows hooked on the bar behind him. He let the cheap rotgut they'd sold him as Maryland Rye dribble down to the sawdust on his far side, clapped loudly when Miss Erba made a bawdy aside to the audience, and turned to order another as the Calgary Kid nursed his false-bottomed schooner of beer.

On the third try, the Calgary Kid couldn't stay out of it. When Longarm paid up and turned back to the show, the leaner but nearly as tall remittance man murmured, "I say, this may be none of my business, but you're being taken for a fucking chump!"

"How so?" Longarm asked innocently.

He noticed that, as he'd suspected, Ivor Balfionna of the castle-keeping Balfionnas of the Great Glen spoke in a more Oxford than Braugh Bricht way as he confided, "They wouldn't know real whiskey if they were bloody drowning in it. You're paying brand-name price for burnt sugar dissolved in grain spirits!"

"Do tell?" replied Longarm with a suspicious look at his half-filled shot glass. "I thought it tasted bland for Maryland. So how does a man get the real thing in this joint?"

The Calgary Kid sniffed and said, "He doesn't. He orders a needled beer and enjoys the show. They say that actress lets you see her nipples during the last act of the second show. But I can't recommend their bloody booze!"

Longarm chuckled and asked if his mentor would let him buy them both needled beers. It came as no great shock that the Calgary Kid would. As they clonked schooners, the killer not having drunk enough to get mean yet, Longarm said, "I've heard it said her nipples ain't all the notorious Erba has been known to show a man, for a price."

The Calgary Kid shrugged and said, "A man with the price can get anything. I'm not sure I'd want to pay what most actresses seem to feel they're worth, though. Having men applaud them while they still have their clothes on seems to give them delusions of loveliness.''

Longarm said, "I follow your drift. I'll stick with a couple of less stuck-up gals I'll be meeting later.''

The self-indulgent cuss brightened to ask, "You know a couple of girls around here who put out at a reasonable price?''

Longarm said, "Hell, they don't charge if they *like* you. Leastways, they never charged *me*.''

Longarm drained his schooner, slammed it back on the bar with a clumsiness he was only faking, and decided, "By damn, I'm glad I run into you, stranger. You've just shown me the error of my ways, and I reckon I'll go see them friendly gals right now instead of drinking expensive shit and hoping to get a peek at an actress gal's old tit!''

As he lurched away from the bar, the Calgary Kid came right along as he'd hoped, asking plaintively if Longarm thought they'd let him in without any flowers, books, or candy.

So it was simple to lure the Calgary Kid down near the depot, knock him out cold on the dark street, handcuff him, pay no mind to all his cussing when he finally woke up, and hustle him aboard a night train to Denver to bring him back alive.

Later the next day, after a certain widow woman on Capitol Hill had dismissed her maid for the day and led Longarm upstairs to see if she forgave him, he waited until she'd drawn her lace curtains and begun to undress for him before he asked her what he'd done to need forgiving.

She said, "You left me hanging in midair all this time, after promising over twenty-four hours ago you'd come right back and tell me what all of you were up to out back!''

Longarm heaved a sigh of relief, knowing she wasn't talking about all that time going over bank transactions with Miss Mavis Shrimpton.

As he hung up his hat and gun rig, she continued. "I had to read about it in the *Rocky Mountain News* this morning. About you arresting one of those old maids down the block for Montana Territory yesterday, then whipping up to Leadville to bring that terrible Calgary Kid back alive!''

As she slid between her fresh linen sheets, naked as a jay but a hell of a lot more curvaceous, Longarm sat down beside her to take his boots off, saying, "It's a mighty long story, starting back in London Town, when this one kid from a famous family owning all sorts of estates in Scotland, Ireland, India, and such just couldn't be made to behave. He busted all his toys, tipped over suits of armor, and waved his little wiener at his governess when he was six years old.''

The widow purred, ''Take off your damned clothes and wave your own wiener at *me,* damn it! You've been away so long and I've missed you so much!''

So he let his duds fall wherever they had a mind to and got under the covers with her.

The covers were soon cast off, and he suspected she'd missed his old wiener at least as much as she'd missed the rest of him, judging by the way she moved her junoesque hips as he parted her light brown hair with it.

But then, being a woman, she wanted him to tell her the reason he'd been away all that time. So he rolled half off to let it sort of soak in her throbbing flesh as he began again. ''This mean little kid got even meaner when he grew up to swill redeye and study how us gents are built concave whilst you ladies are built convex. We're talking about a worthless polecat whose only interests in life were pampering his own appetites and dominating others, with his pecker or his shooting iron.''

She wrapped her shapely legs around his waist and purred, ''Dominate me some more. But first tell me the whole story, darling.''

So Longarm continued. ''His real name was Ivor Balfionna. His dad was the laird of this big Scotch estate, but they lived in London to avoid drafts. He never finished school. When he wasn't setting fires in the cloakroom, he kept running away. You don't really need to be all that educated when your dear old dad owns factories and such. But that didn't work out after he'd raped a secretary atop that manager's desk they'd bought him. They'd just hushed *that* up when he shot one of the servants back home for serving too slow.''

The widow woman opined, ''He sounds crazy. I don't just mean crazy mean. I'm talking about certifiable lunacy!''

Longarm got more comfortable in her open lap and told her, ''Their family doctor thought so too. But fancy folks who sit next to the fat Prince of Wales at the Ascot races don't like to send loose cannons to the lunatic asylum. So they sent him

261

to the colonies. The ones they'd lost. I reckon they figured it would serve us right.''

"How do those mean girls and hired guns fit in?'' she asked.

Longarm explained. "Anne Shannon and the weaker Iona MacInnis who told me all this were sort of distant kin, as some Scotch folks total up their *clans*. Their grandfolks had been evicted to make room for sheep. But when they were asked to serve their clan chief by watching a blacker kind of sheep, for fun and profit, they said it would be an honor. So the current Laird Balfionna settled a tolerable income on the whole bunch, with Miss Anne in charge. But a spoiled brat grown to lunatic manhood wasn't easy to manage. He liked to play Western bad man under assumed names, for one thing. If the ladies refused to play along he'd run away, and if his dear old dad heard he was missing, or if there was a breath of scandal, all bets would be off. They were only getting the interest on those annuities. The Consol certificates never left the family lawyer's safe in London Town. So they backed Ivor's Wild West adventures with money orders that came out in odd numbers to us because of the rates of exchange.''

"How did you learn so much about British banking?'' she asked with a languid thrust of her warm and friendly hips.

Longarm reached for another pillow to slide under them as he casually replied, "I've had some help from a British banker. When Ivor's two indulgent keepers heard he'd gotten in a lethal shootout over an underaged gal up Fort Morgan way, they got together with those two shady private detectives and hatched a plot to bust him out of jail and convince everyone a mythical Calgary Kid was headed for the North Pole. That Scotch poet Mr. Burns warned what a tangled web you can weave acting sneaky, but by the time they knew Ivor was likely to beat any manslaughter or cradle-robbing charges, it was too late. They'd already spattered more blood, trying to cover up for him, than he might have managed on his own. Crazy Ivor was only crazy. Anne Shannon and that one hired gun, Jim Morrison, were just plain vicious!''

She began to move her hips with more enthusiasm as she purred up at him, "Now I see why you went to so much trouble to take the poor loon alive. You were considering his poor family, right?''

To which Longarm replied with a deeper thrust and a

wicked smile, "I surely was. The stuck-up snobs got a whole mess of other folks hurt just to hide a family secret. So it ain't going to *be* a secret no more. Their black sheep is being held for observation in the loco ward over to Denver General. Once they certify him as insane and lock him away for keeps, I aim to cable the *London Times*. This British banking pal I just mentioned feels sure they'll be proud to publish every word of my official final report on the Calgary Kid."

Watch for
the following books in the bold LONGARM
series

LONGARM AND THE BRANDED BEAUTY

233rd adventure in the LONGARM series
from Jove

Available now!

LONGARM AND THE RENEGADE ASSASSINS

234th novel in the exciting LONGARM series
from Jove

Coming in June!

LONGARM

Explore the exciting Old West with
one of the men who made it wild!

_LONGARM AND THE INDIAN WAR #220	0-515-12050-2/$4.99
_LONGARM AND THE BACKWOODS BARONESS #222	0-515-12080-4/$4.99
_LONGARM AND THE DOUBLE-BARREL BLOWOUT #223	0-515-12104-5/$4.99
_LONGARM AND THE MAIDEN MEDUSA #224	0-515-12132-0/$4.99
_LONGARM AND THE DEAD MAN'S PLAY #225	0-515-12144-4/$4.99
_LONGARM AND THE LADY FAIRE #226	0-515-12162-2/$4.99
_LONGARM AND THE REBEL EXECUTIONER #227	0-515-12178-9/$4.99
_LONGARM AND THE VOODOO QUEEN #228	0-515-12191-6/$4.99
_LONGARM AND THE BORDER WILDCAT #229	0-515-12209-2/$4.99
_LONGARM AND THE WYOMING WILDWOMEN #230	0-515-12230-0/$4.99
_LONGARM AND THE DURANGO DOUBLE-CROSS #231	0-515-12244-0/$4.99
_LONGARM AND THE WHISKEY CREEK WIDOW #232	0-515-12265-3/$4.99
_LONGARM AND THE BRANDED BEAUTY #233	0-515-12278-5/$4.99
_LONGARM AND THE RENEGADE ASSASSINS #234 (6/98)	0-515-12292-0/$4.99

Payable in U.S. funds. No cash accepted. Postage & handling: $1.75 for one book, 75¢ for each additional. Maximum postage $5.50. Prices, postage and handling charges may change without notice. Visa, Amex, MasterCard call 1-800-788-6262, ext. 1, or fax 1-201-933-2316; refer to ad #201g

Or, check above books and send this order form to: **The Berkley Publishing Group** P.O. Box 12289, Dept. B Newark, NJ 07101-5289 Please allow 4-6 weeks for delivery. Foreign and Canadian delivery 8-12 weeks.	Bill my: ☐ Visa ☐ MasterCard ☐ Amex _____(expires) Card#_____ ($10 minimum) Daytime Phone #_____ Signature_____ Or enclosed is my: ☐ check ☐ money order

Ship to:

Name_____	Book Total	$____
Address_____	Applicable Sales Tax (NY, NJ, PA, CA, GST Can.)	$____
City_____	Postage & Handling	$____
State/ZIP_____	Total Amount Due	$____

Bill to: Name_____

Address_____City_____

State/ZIP_____